Charlotte Lamb (Mrs Sheila Holland) has written more than 150 novels – from romance to thrillers, from historical sagas to tales of the occult – in a writing career spanning more than a quarter of a century. Her worldwide sales are well in excess of 100 million copies. Born in Dagenham, she comes from a long line of Cockneys, but now lives with her husband and eldest daughter (herself a novelist) in a house overlooking the sea in the Isle of Man.

In the Still of the Night

Charlotte Lamb

CORONET BOOKS

Hodder & Stoughton

First published in in 1995 by Signet
A division of the Penguin Group
This edition published in 1999 by Hodder and Stoughton
A division of Hodder Headline PLC
A Coronet Paperback

A CIP catalogue record for this title is available
from the British Library

ISBN 0 340 72867 1

Printed and bound in Great Britain by
Clays Ltd, St Ives PLC, Bungay, Suffolk

Hodder and Stoughton
A division of Hodder Headline PLC
338 Euston Road
London NW1 3BH

THE SICK ROSE

O rose, thou art sick!
The invisible worm
That flies in the night,
In the howling storm,

Has found out thy bed
Of crimson joy,
And his dark secret love
Does thy life destroy.

1

Annie Lang stood in the wings waiting for her name to be called and trying to hide the fact that she was trembling and sweating, even though the stage-school theatre was unheated and draughty. She was the last in the long line of hopefuls who had queued there today. She had almost been too late.

'Weren't you told nine o'clock prompt?' the man on the door had grumbled, ticking her name off a long list without actually looking at her.

'Sorry, I . . .' She was so nervous she started pulling a wisp of her pale blonde hair down to her mouth and chewing it: a childish habit that had always earnt her a slap from her mother.

The stage-door keeper was in a bad temper; it was nearly opening time at the local pub and he needed a drink. 'Never mind the excuses. You were told nine and I shouldn't send you in there.' She made an anguished noise; he gave her a quick look then grunted at her. 'Oh, alright, alright. But you're the last. Tell them that. Down the corridor, turn right, then left, and join the queue.'

Pale and feeling sick, she followed his directions. She didn't know this part of London. She lived on the other side of the city; London was a web of little villages whose inhabitants stayed on their own patch most of their lives. She had got lost within minutes of leaving the Underground station. She'd asked someone the way and been misdirected; panic-stricken, she had run round corners, asked in shops, had finally found the street by accident, turning into it, seeing the name on a sign on a wall, and feeling her body sag with sick relief.

Now she was here and she wished she hadn't come. There were a dozen people still waiting; she'd seen all the heads turn, had felt their eyes strip her, hard with rivalry and fear. One look and they had all smiled triumphantly, turning away again. She was no threat. Annie had almost turned and run then, seeing herself with their eyes. She had always hated looking in mirrors.

She was wearing black leggings and a black T-shirt – so were several other girls, she noticed. Black made Annie look paler than ever, a thin, gawky girl with very big, very blue eyes – her one claim to attention. She wore no make-up because she had had eczema most of her life and any sort of cosmetics could trigger an attack. Her hair was long and straight, almost colourless, it was so blonde. She would have liked to have it all cut off, but her mother got hysterical if she so much as talked about it.

What on earth had ever made her think she could ever make it in the theatre? Her dream was crazy; she didn't even believe in it herself. She would never have had the nerve to apply, but her mother had stood over her while she filled in the application forms – had even her mother really believed she would get as far as an interview, though?

'Is that the last one?' she suddenly heard from the dark auditorium and realised the girl who had been in front of her had finished and gone.

Annie hurried out on to the lit stage and almost stumbled over her own feet. 'No, there's me . . . please . . . Annie Lang . . . I'm the last.'

A silence, and she peered out into shadows, could see nothing, then a small pencil light was switched on over a desk, and a man's face came out of nowhere, gleaming eyes, a widow's peak of hair, a full, moist red mouth.

'Annie Lang? How old are you, Annie? You don't look old enough to . . . were you on our list? Ah, here you are, got you. Still at school, Annie, right? Seventeen?'

She nodded, dry-mouthed. His eyes were worse than those she had met in the queue. She felt his stare like ants under her skin.

'Looks about twelve!' she heard, from someone else – a woman's voice.

The man ignored that. 'Tell us something about yourself, Annie. Have you done any acting at school?'

'Yes,' she whispered.

'For instance?'

For a second her mind went blank, she struggled to remember, hoping she didn't look as stupid as she felt, then blurted out, 'I . . . was J-Joan of . . .'

There was faint, quickly smothered laughter somewhere in the seats around him, and she flinched.

Her eyes, accustomed to the dark by then, picked out two other faces, both women, one who wore dangling, glittery earrings, the other wearing pearly lipstick which gave her the look of a phosphorescent marine creature, a decomposing brilliance.

'Anything else?' the man asked her.

'The Diary of Anne Frank.' She shouldn't be here; she shouldn't have come, she hated being laughed at.

'You played . . .?'

'Anne.' She wished she was dead. Why . . . why . . . had she come?

3

'How did you feel about the play?'

'It . . .'

'Did you enjoy it?'

She gulped, then blurted out the truth. 'I got so wound up, doing it, it gave me nightmares.'

She felt their attention. A moment, then the man said, 'Which of the Shakespeare pieces we suggested did you prepare?'

'Ophelia.'

The two women smiled again.

'Why did you choose that?' asked the man.

She fought not to stammer, her hands screwed into balls. 'It's very d-dramatic.' She could never get what she felt into words. How did you say: madness is terrifying, losing yourself is being sucked into a nightmare? She knew something about it. She had loved her mother's cousin Edie, who'd often looked after her when Annie was small; now the old lady was senile, didn't know who she was or even where she was. Annie had only visited her a couple of times. She couldn't bear to go again after that.

Her class was studying Hamlet that year; its disturbing echoes of madness made her stomach clench. What if her mother . . . what if it was hereditary? What if she, herself, one day began to forget? How did it feel to be Auntie Edie? Did you know what was happening to you?

'Begin, please,' said the voice beyond the footlights, and she jumped back to the present, confused.

She wasn't going to remember the words. Her mind was a blank. She stared at the back of the theatre, where a little red light lit the Exit sign, trying to concentrate – and at last the first line came up out of the well of memory and then another and another.

4

When she had finished there was a silence. It seemed a long time before the man said, 'Thank you. What modern piece did you prepare?'

'Look Back in Anger,' she stammered. 'The scene where . . .'

'Fine, off you go,' he interrupted, and she flushed with humiliation, realising he knew exactly which scene she would have picked, who she would be playing.

But she couldn't get out of it, she was there, standing in a blue light, on the bare stage, her knees knocking, feeling hopeless, feeling sick. What was the point of going on when she was bound to fail?

It would be too humiliating to run away, though. She took a deep breath, and after a few words forgot herself in the pain of the woman she was pretending to be.

Coming out of it, she was dazed for a second. The dark dazzled her. She heard breathing, then the light on the desk was switched off, and she heard seats banging back as the three people below stood up. They hadn't said a word.

She'd known she wasn't going to get in. She wasn't good enough. Why had she thought she could act?

Turning away, shaking, icy cold, she stumbled off the stage to go back along the corridor to the stage door.

'Where are you going?'

They met her in the wings, three of them, the man the tallest, between two women, one of them with a very familiar face, an actress she had often seen on the stage of the National Theatre. The women smiled at her.

'Well done. Enjoyed that. Must rush, Roger will talk to you. Bye.' They looked at the man and said,

'Bye, Roger,' in voices that seemed teasing, or mocking, then they walked off.

Annie began to follow them, muttering, 'Well . . . thanks . . .'

The man caught her arm. 'I haven't finished with you yet. One or two more questions. Come to my office.' He urged her round the back of the stage. Annie dragged her feet, wanting now just to get away. It was so cold back here, cold and dusty. She found herself going through a door, into a corridor that led to an office with a name plate on the door.

She read it as he waved her inside. Roger Keats, Senior Tutor.

Her favourite poet was John Keats. She had a picture of him pinned up on the wall over her bed: a thin, pale, willowy young man with golden hair. Nothing like this man, with his fleshy mouth and those eyes that kept staring at her in a way that made her very uncomfortable.

She looked away. He'd called this his office, but although it held a desk and filing cabinet, it looked too cosy to be an office. Lined with shelves of books, the walls hung with faded old prints of famous paintings, the room was dominated by a red velvet Victorian chaise-longue piled with cushions of many colours.

Roger Keats shut the door and strolled forward. 'We'll let you know, in a week or so.' He threw his clipboard, rustling with papers, on the desk, and lounged there, his hands gripping the edge of the desk, his stare wandering over her in that odd, smiling way. 'I see from your application form that you sing, you're in the school choir, and have had ballet lessons since you were four.'

'Yes.' She wasn't good enough at either to think of making a career as a singer or a dancer, though.

'Your posture is terrible. Hasn't your ballet teacher tried to correct it?' He took a leather-bound book off the shelves and put it on top of her head. It wobbled and was heavy. She grabbed for it before it fell.

Mr Keats slapped her hand away. 'Leave it. It should balance there if your posture is correct. Come on, head up, shoulders back. Don't slouch. Let me see you walk towards that wall.'

Annie walked, trying not to shake. Reaching the other side of the room, she turned to go back, but he blocked her way. Grabbing her shoulders, he pushed her up against the wall; the book fell to the floor with a crash and she jumped, eyes wide.

He stared down into them. 'Always be aware of your body, Annie,' he softly said. 'I am. Think about it now. Your head. Your neck, balancing your head on top of it, feel it, concentrate on it,' he ran a hand up her nape and the little hairs on the back of her neck prickled unpleasantly. He pressed her backwards until she felt the wall forced into her spine. 'I don't ever want to see you stooping and hanging your head down again. Walk like a queen – and keep your stomach in . . .' His hands released her shoulders and slithered downwards, making her nerves jump, making her stiffen, with a little gasp. His fleshy mouth smiled wider. 'What sort of bra do you wear? Do you wear one?' He squeezed as he asked. 'Doesn't feel as if you do, your breasts are small but soft. These little tiny buds are breasts, aren't they? How old did you say you were? You have the breasts of a little girl.'

He looked into her frightened eyes; his mouth was moist and very red. He smiled as if he enjoyed her fear. 'Never mind, I like little girls. I like them very much.' His fingers smoothed, pressed, dug into her.

Frozen in panic like a rabbit in headlights she didn't try to get away, just trembled.

'There is a lot of competition to get in here, Annie, and we expect our students to work hard and do as they're told. It's up to you, Annie. We've seen fifty girls, all of them talented. To get in, a student has to have something special. I make the final decision – so, do you want a place here, or don't you?'

Annie lived in one of the older suburbs of London, South Park, on the wrong side of Regent's Park. Her street was shady in summer with plane trees whose dappled bark gave a sleepy country air to the white and green Edwardian houses with their gables and pink roofs, and on warm evenings there was a heady scent of privet from every garden as you walked past. On very hot days flying ants swarmed from the sand below the paving stones and dive-bombed you as you walked over them, terrifying her when she was a child. Even today she panicked if an insect flew at her.

The house had been left to Annie's mother by her first husband, whose parents had bought it while it was still half-built in 1907, and had lived in it until they died.

In those days this had been a very middle-class area, with servants sleeping in the attic and a horse and carriage stabled at the back of the house in a cobbled mews. Today there were no horses in the mews, although the cobbles remained; they gave class to the tiny, pastel-painted cottages where trendy, highly paid secretaries and city executives lived.

By the time Annie was born the road had become

shabby. Some of the houses were sub-divided into flats; the gardens were wildernesses. The sixties were in full swing and living was easy, except for women like her mother. Sometimes Annie felt her mother had been born middle-aged, always worrying, always working. From her first husband she had inherited a green-grocer's shop just round the corner, as well as the house, but they had had no children. Annie suspected that that first marriage had not been happy, but her mother never talked about it. She only talked about Annie's father, long since dead. Her mother still ran the greengrocer's shop; it was their only source of income now and Annie was expected to help whenever she wasn't at school or doing schoolwork.

Her mother was back from the shop when she got home. The table in the long, shabbily furnished lounge was laid with a blue glass bowl of salad, a dish of cold meat and some cheese. The kettle was boiling as she walked into the kitchen. Her mother looked round eagerly. 'Well?'

'They said they'll write in about a week.' Annie couldn't look at her mother. If she told her . . . but she couldn't tell. If she did, she would never get that place at drama school, she would never be an actress. Who would believe her? He was an important man there; the senior tutor – he'd just say she was making it all up, it would be her word against his, and who was she, after all? Just another stage-struck kid.

'But how did it go? Did you think they liked you?'

'I don't know,' Annie mumbled. 'I must go and wash.' She rushed upstairs to the bathroom and was sick; her stomach was still churning as she splashed her face with cold water. She avoided seeing herself in the little mirror over the washbasin.

'Did they like you?' her mother had asked.

'Be a good little girl and I'll be pleased with you,' he had said.

Her stomach heaved again. 'Do you want to be an actress?' he had asked, his hands wandering up inside her top, his fingers hot on her cold skin. 'Do you want a place at the school? How much do you want it? There are lots of others who would jump at the chance, Annie.'

She closed her eyes and leaned on the wall. No, she could never tell. She hated the memory of what happened; it would be impossible to tell anyone about it, especially her mother.

The letter came a week later. Her mother stood over her while she opened it. Annie's hands trembled. She couldn't see the words.

'Well?' Trudie Lang was too agitated to wait, she tried to read the letter over Annie's shoulder. 'Don't just stand there reading it over and over – what does it say?'

Saying nothing, Annie gave her the letter. What should she do? All those hopes and dreams of being an actress – she couldn't give them up now. When she first applied, she hadn't dared hope she would be accepted. Now she wasn't sure she could go through with it. People always said, 'You get nothing for nothing!', but how could she bear to pay the price tag on her dream?

Her mother's hand was shaking as she held the letter and read it. Trudie Lang had never been beautiful; now she was nearly sixty, grey-haired and lined after years of hard work, and she had the worn brightness of old silver, her strong nature showing through her bony face. She had had a tough life, worked hard from her childhood up, been married twice, often been hurt and lonely, only had one child, Annie, born when she was nearly forty.

Annie watched her, knowing that her dream had been Trudie's dream first. From when she was very small, her mother had encouraged her to perform: she had paid for private music lessons, dancing lessons, elocution lessons, paid money they could ill afford, and all to see Annie get up in front of an audience and shine.

'You got in!' Trudie burst out. 'Annie! You'll get your chance, that was all I wanted, for you to get the chance I never had. I'd have given my eye-teeth to be an actress, but of course there was no chance of that, not with my family. They'd rather have seen me dead.'

Annie knew all this, had heard it a hundred times before. She didn't listen now.

'But this makes up for it,' her mother said. 'One day you'll be famous, I'll sit in the front stalls and listen to them applauding on your first nights.'

Desperately, Annie broke out, 'Mum, I . . .' But her voice died away. She couldn't kill the joy she saw in her mother's eyes.

Trudie wasn't listening, anyway. She was too excited. 'This is the chance of a lifetime, Annie. Don't waste it.'

Her heart sank. She was trapped – how could she explain wanting to turn it down? Except by telling her mother . . . and she couldn't, she couldn't. Oh, maybe he had only been kidding when he told her what he would expect from her if he awarded her a place? She'd never been pretty: she was too thin, flat as a pancake. None of the boys at school had ever given her a second look.

Even her best friend, Megan, had given up trying to do something about the way Annie looked. Megan had left school now and worked in an office; she lived for Friday and Saturday and spent all her wages on clothes. She had curly hair and big breasts, wore tight skirts and sheer stockings, giggled a lot and made out in the backs of cars; the boys all liked her. Annie didn't see much of her any more. If Roger Keats had made a pass at Megan she'd have giggled and probably let him do whatever he liked. Megan hadn't been a virgin since she was fourteen. Annie was. And she hated the thought of Roger Keats touching her.

'But, Mum, the grant I'll get is only for the tuition, but I'll need lots of books, and they've sent me a list of clothes I'll need – you'll have to keep me while I'm there. Can we afford it?'

Her mother turned away as the kettle boiled. Over her shoulder as she filled the kettle she said, 'I've been thinking about that. You're right, equipping you will cost a lot, but I've thought of a way to make some more money. I'm going to let out that spare room. I should have thought of it before. I'll put a card in the shop window. I'll only let it to a woman. I don't want any men here, especially when I'm out at work so much and you're here on your own.'

On a humid morning in late July, a gangling boy in jeans walked into the shop while Annie was piling potatoes into an old woman's basket.

'There's a card in the window,' he said to Trudie, who looked sharply at him. 'A room to let? Has it gone yet?'

Annie's customer held out some coins; Annie took

12

them and turned to the till to ring up the amount, listening to her mother talking behind her.

'What's your name?'

'Johnny. Johnny Tyrone.'

'How old are you?' Trudie bluntly asked, and he went a bit pink.

'Twenty. I'll be twenty-one in October.'

Trudie Lang studied him with wary eyes. 'Got a job?'

'I've just started working on the local paper.'

'Where d'you work before that?'

'I've been at college, this is my first job.' His voice was excited; Annie looked over her shoulder at him. His eyes shone, dark blue and thick with long black lashes. Longer than hers. She'd never seen eyes like them before, on a boy, anyway. He's beautiful, she thought. It sounded odd to say that about a boy, but no other word applied.

'Why aren't you living with your family? Don't you come from around here?' Trudie Lang was staring at him, too, her face uncertain, but Annie could tell she liked him; her voice was softening.

His face changed slightly, Annie thought she saw sadness in his eyes. 'I only have a grandmother. She lives too far from here for me to go home every day.'

Trudie hesitated. Annie crossed her fingers behind her back. Let her say yes, let her say yes. Her heart was beating so hard it shook her chest.

'The house is just around the corner. I'll walk round with you and show you the room. It isn't very big, and there's no cooking facilities, and you'll have to share the bathroom with us. I'll throw in breakfast every day, and if you like you can eat with us in the evenings, but I'll have to charge extra for that.' Trudie took off

13

her apron and hung it up behind the door. 'Annie, mind the shop. This is my daughter, by the way, Annie.'

She went to get her coat from the room behind the shop. Johnny Tyrone watched Annie, who was automatically polishing apples; her mother disapproved of idle hands and liked to see her keeping busy when there were no customers in the shop.

'Hi.'

'Hello,' she shyly whispered, turning to face him. He had a wonderful smile; his face was so open and friendly when he smiled. His good looks didn't seem to have spoilt his character – at school Annie had often noticed that the best-looking boys were often the most unkind, the vain ones, the ones who made fun of other people. Of her. She was often a target for their idea of a joke. Could Johnny Tyrone be an exception to the rule? Or was he clever enough to hide his real nature? Was she having the wool pulled over her eyes?

'How much for one of those?' He pulled a handful of coins out of his jeans pocket. 'I'm starving. One slice of toast for breakfast and I won't get anything else until I get back to Grandma's tonight. Those apples look awfully good to me. I could eat a horse.'

Annie speechlessly held out two apples.

'I can only afford one,' he said. 'How much?'

She pushed the coins away, then heard her mother coming back and just had time to whisper, 'Don't tell her!'

He caught on at once. Pushing both apples into the pocket of his blue denim jacket, he gave Annie a slow, warm smile, his eyes searching her face as if he liked what he saw.

'Thanks. See you again soon,' Johnny said, following Trudie Lang out of the shop.

Annie stared after him, trembling with happiness.

That evening at supper, her mother told her what she had found out about him. 'Irish family, I knew it the minute I heard that name. Tyrone; Irish name. He looks Irish, too. His parents are dead. He's been living with his grandmother for a couple of years, but she lives in Epping; he wouldn't be able to travel here and back every day. He got the job from an ad in a trade paper; he says it's tough getting a reporter's job, too many people chasing every job, so he had to take this one, even though it means leaving his grandma alone.'

'He's very fond of her, then?' Annie was so interested she wasn't eating; her mother looked at her untouched plate, clicking her tongue impatiently.

'Don't waste good food, girl!'

Annie hurriedly forced some potato into her mouth while her mother watched her. Only then did Trudie go on, 'I liked the way he talked about his grandma; most kids his age don't care about old people, but he said he would be going back to her house most weekends, doesn't want her to feel he's gone for good. He said he would be out a lot. He will have to work late some nights – they work them hard on those little local papers. Sounds as if he really wouldn't be any trouble.'

Eagerly, Annie asked, 'So are you going to let him have the room?'

'I can always tell him to leave if it doesn't work out,' Trudie thought aloud.

'Yes,' Annie said, breathlessly, fighting to hide her joy.

He moved in a week later. He only had one suitcase;

it seemed heavy as he dragged it upstairs. 'Books, mostly books he brought,' her mother told her next day, shaking her head. 'Not much money there; all he has to wear is jeans and sweatshirts and one cheap suit. That's what he wears to work every day. I suppose journalists have to wear suits, to impress people.' She had inspected his wardrobe while he was out at work, to Annie's shame. She only hoped Johnny Tyrone hadn't realised his room had been searched.

Annie didn't see much of him at first, because as the latest newcomer on the newspaper he was landed with all the boring jobs nobody wanted to do, he explained. Church fêtes, flower shows, funerals, making a daily tour of the police station, the churches, to check up on any possible story. The court cases were covered by one of the senior reporters and any big news story went to them, too. Johnny was just the dogsbody, learning his trade, even though he had studied journalism at college.

Annie didn't even see him at breakfast because Mrs Lang always sent her off to open up the shop, so she had her tea and toast and left the house long before Johnny came downstairs.

She heard a lot of him, though; his room was next to hers. At night she heard him get home late, often after midnight, creep upstairs, the creak of the bathroom door, the discreet flushing, the running of water as he washed, then his tiptoeing across the landing, the give of springs as he sat down on the bed to take off his shoes, his movements as he undressed, and then the long sigh of relief with which he finally got between the sheets.

He was always sleepy in the mornings. He spent his

16

long day running from job to job, and never had enough sleep, even at weekends.

His room was a narrow, oblong box, holding just a bed, a small chest of drawers, a wardrobe and a chair. A mirror hung on one wall. The window looked out over the garden; the curtains matched the coverlet on the bed, light green cotton. The walls were painted cream; there was something springlike in the colours. Annie had chosen them, had helped her mother do the painting, had made the curtains too.

When he was out and her mother was busy at the shop, Annie sometimes crept into the room. She liked to imagine him in there. She made his bed and tidied up, looked at the titles of the books he had put out on top of the chest of drawers. Some stood up, their spines showing, propped there by a little pile of other books on either side.

She listened to him breathing in the night sometimes, knew when he was asleep and when he was awake and reading. She even heard him turn the page, a light fluttering sound. He read a lot. He liked poetry, he had a lot of poetry books. Annie liked it, too; she was thrilled to see he liked the same poets.

One day when her mother was out shopping Annie lay down on his bed, her long blonde hair brushed down over her shoulders, and read Tennyson aloud.

She was so engrossed that she didn't hear him let himself into the house or come quietly upstairs.

When he pushed open the door of his room she almost fainted. She dropped the book and jumped off the bed, her face dark red, trembling violently.

'Don't stop,' he said, staring at her. 'You read beautifully. You're going to be an actress, aren't you? Your mother told me. You've got a wonderful voice. Do you

17

like Tennyson? He's my favourite poet and that's one of my favourite poems.' He murmured some of the words she had just read aloud. 'O, for the touch of a vanished hand and the sound of a voice that is still.'

His voice was so sad Annie's eyes stung with tears. Had he been in love with someone who died? He sounded as if he really meant the words.

He sat down on the bed, patted the place next to him. 'Read me some more. Please.'

That was how it began.

She started at drama school mid-September, a windy, bright, chilly day with leaves chasing down the gutters and wet cobwebs glittering like diamond windows in the hedges as she walked to the station.

She was tense and shaking as she joined the little crowd of other students pushing in through the open doors of the school. All the time, Annie was looking out for Roger Keats, but he wasn't in sight. She checked her name on the lists hanging in the hall, and went off to the room indicated. That first morning was spent in having the daily routine explained, being shown which rooms to go to for fencing, dancing, singing lessons, after which they went to see the well-equipped gymnasium, the music rehearsal rooms, which were full of pianos and other musical instruments, and had padded doors with goldfish-bowl windows in them, double-glazing, and sound-proofing in the walls.

The new students soon began to recognise each other's faces, got to know some of their tutors, and saw a lot of their year tutor, a short, ferocious man with a droopy moustache.

It was a long morning. Everyone was starving by the

time they broke for lunch in the gloomy, narrow dining-room. It was self-service. They queued up with their plates to get salad and cold meat.

'And I hoped I'd got away from school dinners!' a girl behind Annie said glumly as they sat down again at one of the long, scratched tables. She had introduced herself earlier; Scott Western was her name, she claimed, but Annie suspected she'd made it up. A redhead, sylphlike and blue-eyed, she had already got a lot of attention from the tutor and every other male who had so far set eyes on her. She wore what Annie wore, jeans and a black top, but Scott wore it with a difference – on her it looked expensive. Maybe it was? She talked as if she came from a moneyed background.

Annie felt a jolt of shock as Roger Keats walked into the room. A gleam of autumn sunlight lit up his high forehead, the dark brown widow's peak of his hair brushed back from his face, that very red mouth.

'The vampire has arrived,' Scott said in a sepulchral voice, and Annie almost choked on her salad. It fitted him exactly.

She wished she could laugh at him. She wished she had Scott's laid-back assurance.

'That's the guy who auditioned me,' Scott said.

Had he propositioned her, too? She was so lovely – surely he must have been interested in Scott?

Scott didn't seem bothered, if he had. Annie was so on edge, she couldn't swallow; she kept chewing one piece of ham over and over. Her throat seemed to have closed up.

He was prowling from table to table, pausing to talk to people.

Finally, he arrived at theirs. 'Ah,' he said, his moist lips curling upwards and his eyes glinting on Annie.

'My Alice in Wonderland. I hadn't forgotten you – but I'm rather busy just at present. I'll see you soon.'

He walked away and Scott gave her a curious, sidelong look. 'What was all that about?'

Annie swallowed the ham at last and almost choked. 'No idea.' She knew Scott didn't believe her.

On her way to fencing class a week later Annie caught sight of Roger Keats again and tensed, but luckily he was too busy talking to a small, dark girl to notice her.

'Dirty old man,' muttered a boy behind her.

'Is she his latest?' someone else asked.

'Yeah, silly bitch. I don't know why they let him get away with it. But there's a new one every term. I wouldn't mind his job with perks like that.'

Annie took a look at them; she'd seen them in the dining-room, second-year students who thought they knew it all.

One of them grinned at her. 'Hi. I saw you this morning, you were with a set of first-years who came into ballet class on a tour of the school.'

'Oh, you're a dancer?' Annie smiled back shyly, wishing she dared ask him questions about Roger Keats, but afraid of the questions he might in turn ask her.

'No, I was playing the piano for the dancers. Mrs Gundy, the usual accompanist, is off sick, so they asked me to stand in for her.'

Annie hadn't noticed him, but she remembered the music she had heard and looked at him, very impressed. 'You play very well – did you ever think of doing music rather than drama?'

The boy with Rob said maliciously, 'He thought of it, but his father isn't a governor of a music college.'

Rob gave him a lazy punch on the arm. 'Shut your face.'

'Just a joke, Rob!'

Annie stared at them both blankly. 'I don't get it, sorry.'

'My father's a governor,' Rob said, offhandedly.

'So how about a date?' his friend teased, and Rob punched him again.

'Shut up, Jeff.'

'Whoops, sorry, I forgot you're gay!'

Seeing Annie's bewildered face, Rob said cheerfully, 'Take no notice of him, he's a fathead with a crazy idea that he's a comedian. How do you like it here so far?'

'I love it,' Annie said breathlessly, and both boys laughed, as if they felt the same.

Time flashed by that first term at the drama school. She could hardly believe it when they reached half-term and were given a week off. It was November, cold and rainy, raw winds blowing the last leaves off the trees.

On the Sunday, Johnny had breakfast with her while her mother was at the shop, stock-taking. She had told Annie to stay in bed another hour.

The phone rang as they drank coffee and ate toast and egg and bacon which Johnny had insisted on cooking for them both.

He answered the phone and came back looking white and shaken. 'I've got to go. Sorry.'

'What's wrong?'

'My gran. She's been taken ill. That was a neighbour. It sounds bad.'

He looked scared, suddenly younger. She knew by

now how much his grandmother meant to him, the only family he had.

Uncertainly, Annie offered, 'Would you like me to come with you?'

'Would you?' His face brightened, he gave her a grateful look. 'Please. I'd like that; I'm scared of being alone.'

The words rang in her ears as they drove there on his old motorbike. If his grandmother died, Johnny would be left totally alone, with no family at all. How would I feel if Mum died? wondered Annie, and shivered.

He made Annie put on his helmet; he didn't have a spare. She belted her old school raincoat round her waist. The wind drove into their faces and soaked them both to the skin. It took nearly an hour to get there, although he drove as fast as he dared. There was a lot of traffic until they got to the other side of London, the forest outskirts beyond the dormitory suburbs on the east. There the roads were less crowded. The trees on either side darkened the winter sky.

They arrived to find Mrs East, his grandmother's neighbour, waiting in the house with the news that she had been taken to the local hospital in an ambulance. Johnny and Annie drove on there at once. The old lady was in intensive care in a small ward. The ward sister saw them and gave them a searching look, her face critical, as if she blamed Johnny for his grandmother's illness.

'You don't live with her? A pity. If she hadn't been alone she might not be so poorly.'

Johnny's face grew even more haggard and the woman's voice softened a little.

'You see, she had a heart attack during the night and must have fallen out of bed, lain there for hours, getting colder all the time. Lucky her neighbour had a key and let herself in when she didn't get an answer at the front door. Otherwise your granny would have died. As it is, the hypothermia complicates the heart problem. She isn't very well at all.'

'Do you mean she's going to die?' Johnny hoarsely asked.

'We'll do our best for her. But she is frail and very old, and she hasn't been eating properly, for a long time, I'd say.'

'Can I see her?'

'For one minute, then you must leave. You can come back tomorrow.'

He saw his grandmother alone. Annie waited, staring out at the driving rain and grey skies. The hospital was a short drive from the forest, surrounded by trees, all leafless now, black wet branches shining.

'Not a day to die on,' Johnny said behind her, and he sounded angry.

She looked round at him and wanted to put her arms round him. His face was drawn, pale, lost. He looked like a frightened little boy.

'Was she conscious?'

He nodded. 'Just about. She looks terrible, but she was able to ask me to take care of her cat.' His voice broke. 'Typical of her. She may be dying – but all that's on her mind is that damn cat. I'll have to go to her house before I take you home, Annie, to catch the cat. Do you think your mother would let me bring it back to your house?'

'Oh, yes, she doesn't mind cats.'

They drove back to his grandmother's house in

pouring rain. Buried in Epping Forest, one of London's playgrounds, an ancient forest where English kings had once hunted, Trafalgar House was Victorian, built in 1830 on classic lines, and later ornamented with a battlement along the edge of the roof and a new Gothic wing with a tower. Ramshackle and eccentric in design now, it stood alone, at least ten minutes' walk from any other house, on a back road through the forest, half-hidden among ancient trees which creaked and wailed in the wind as Johnny pushed open the gate.

Annie was shivering, her clothes saturated. The next-door neighbour had gone now, but she had lit a big fire in the long drawing-room which dominated the ground floor of the house. The trees crowding in on it made the rooms dark and full of shadows.

'You're cold. Take off that wet coat, and come and sit by the fire,' Johnny said, trying the switch of the central light. 'Damn, the chandelier bulbs have all gone, I'd forgotten. Grandma can't get up there to change them. She just uses a lamp in here.' He walked off and turned on a standard lamp, which gave the room a soft pinkish glow.

Johnny turned and took Annie's coat from her, draped it over a chair, which he stood to one side of the fire, where it soon began to steam.

Annie sank into a deep armchair on the other side of the hearth, stretching her hands out to the flames.

'You need a hot drink,' said Johnny. 'I'll make us some coffee while I look for the cat. It can't have gone far.'

'I'll make the coffee.' Annie tried to get up but he pushed her down gently.

'No, you stay in front of the fire. I'll look out one of my old sweaters for you.'

She watched him go out, her nerves prickling at being left alone in this shadowy room. With Johnny gone she could hear noises. Stiffening, she listened; somebody was creeping up behind her.

She jumped out of the chair, whirled round, but there was nobody there. Her sudden movement dislodged the old lace antimacassar on the arm of the chair; it slithered to the ground, and that made her jump, too.

Everything in the room seemed to be draped with one of these filmy bits of lace – the arms and backs of chairs, the centres of tables. Annie picked up the lace which had fallen and smoothed it back over the arm.

She had never seen anything like this place. It was like a museum. Her eyes searched the corners of the room, which was crowded with objects: mirrors on the walls, paintings, prints, ornaments, mostly dusty and very old. Heavy red brocade curtains, torn and shabby, hung at the windows, and between them fell ancient lace curtains weighted at the hems with little blue beads to make them hang straight; they were moving in the wind, knocking on the glass.

There was a dark red Axminster carpet on the floor, but on top of that lay smaller rugs, spread here and there, on which stood sofas and chairs, none of which matched.

Something shrieked near the window outside. Annie gasped, her heart in her mouth, staring. The long-drawn-out screech came again, and she realised it was a branch scraping along the side of the glass.

Knees sagging, she looked away towards a a litter of photographs in wooden or silver frames on the mantelshelf. Johnny's face leapt out at her from one of them; she leaned forward to look at it.

There was a woman in the picture; she looked just like Johnny, the same eyes, mouth, hair.

'My mother.'

Annie turned to look at him as he walked towards her with a sweater over one arm and a tray in his free hand.

He put the tray of coffee down on a table and handed her the sweater. 'It'll be miles too big but it will keep you warm.'

She pulled it over her head; it dropped almost to her knees, old and baggy, but warmth enveloped her with it.

'I guessed it was your mother in the photo – you're just like her.'

Johnny's smile lit the whole room. 'I wish you'd known her. She would have loved you. In a funny sort of way you're rather like her, not so much your colouring as the shape of your face, and your eyes.' Then his smile died. 'Mum died while I was still at school. It was lucky I had Gran. If I lose Gran, there won't be anyone left.'

Annie shyly curled her fingers into his hand. 'Poor Johnny,' she whispered.

Tears came into his eyes, horrifying her. He dropped to his knees beside her chair and put his head down on her lap. She stroked his hair, bent down to kiss his cheek.

They stayed like that for a long time before they collected the cat and bundled it inside Annie's raincoat for the drive back to her home.

As they were leaving, Mrs East met them at the gate of the house, waving. Johnny hit the brakes and the motorbike stopped.

'Hello, Johnny – how is she? I keep ringing the hospital but they never tell you much.'

26

'I don't really know any more than you do, Mrs East. They let me see her, and she looked terrible, but they said she might still pull through. They'll let me know at once if she gets worse.' He broke off, swallowing audibly, and Annie felt his body shiver against her. 'I'm going back tomorrow morning. I hope I'll see her again then.'

'Well, give her my love.'

'I will, and thank you, Mrs East. They told me in the hospital that if you hadn't found her she would have died.'

'I'm glad I went in when I did; I was thinking of going shopping first. I see you've got Tibs.' Her sharp eyes fixed on the cat's head poking out of Annie's coat.

'Gran asked me to look after her.' Johnny started his engine again. 'Sorry, we have to get back, Mrs East. I'll keep in touch.'

'I hope your gran pulls through,' the other woman called after them, and Annie tightened her arms around him, feeling the tremor running through his thin body.

Her mother was not too pleased by the cat's arrival. Their own cat immediately took umbrage at the sight of it and started a fight, but Trudie Lang was sorry for Johnny, so she let the animal stay and it settled down gradually.

His grandmother died a week later and the house was shut up by the executors; it would have to be sold. Johnny inherited everything, but there was no money and he could not afford to keep the house.

'I'd love to live there, I've always been so happy in that house,' he said unhappily. 'But I shall have to sell. They say I have to wait for probate before I can put it on the market.'

'But surely that won't take long? I mean, there is a will and you were her only relative.'

'Lawyers take forever to do anything. In a way, I'm not sorry. At least I can visit it now and then. Once it's sold it's gone forever.'

That winter, whenever they were both free, they drove over on Johnny's motorbike and spent hours there, pretended they were married, and the house was their home, like children playing house. They brought food with them, chops or steaks, which they cooked in a battered frying-pan on the old range in the spidery kitchen; potatoes they baked in the ashes sifting down through the old iron grating. Annie tossed salads to go with the meal and they ate fruit afterwards. The food was ambrosial: neither of them had ever tasted anything so marvellous.

Those days were dreamlike. They were both so happy Annie was scared. It couldn't last, but while it did they both breathed the air, promise-crammed.

Annie had very little free time towards the end of term, because she had been given the part of Ophelia in a production of Hamlet which her year were putting on in the drama school's little theatre. They had rehearsals five times a week after school hours during the last fortnight before the first night; you were expected to forget about a private life while you were in a production.

The play was on for four days; both Johnny and her mother came. Annie hadn't wanted her mother there; she had been too nervous, too afraid she might forget her lines, dry up, drop something. Having her mother in the theatre was the last straw on a night which she knew already promised to be an ordeal.

The theatre was going to be packed with parents

and friends of the cast, as well as some very important names in theatre who had once been students here and were always invited to any major production the school gave – famous actors and directors whose presence in the audience would attract the attention of agents, theatre proprietors, and, most importantly of all, critics from national newspapers.

The night went well; afterwards Annie couldn't actually remember a thing about the actual performance. She seemed to wake up when the cast assembled on stage and there was a sudden roar of clapping. Dazed, she stared out into the auditorium and saw faces. Clutching the hands of those on either side of her, she bowed as they did for several curtain calls, not daring to look at the seats where Johnny and her mother sat.

Roger Keats came on stage with a cellophane-wrapped bouquet of roses. Annie almost dropped them when he gave them to her. Dumbfounded, she stared up at him and Roger Keats leaned forward and kissed her, his mouth wet and hot, his tongue tip sliding in and out between her lips like a snake going into a hole.

It was over in a flash, then he was holding her hand, pulling her towards the audience, who applauded again. He kissed her hand, bowing, then gestured to the boy playing Hamlet and stood between him and Annie while the audience clapped, before bringing forward several others from the cast to take special bows.

Afterwards Annie stumbled off stage into her dressing-room and threw up in the lavatory.

Scott patted her on the back. 'I was sick before we went on! Now I feel great. Stage fright's a funny old game.'

Annie wished she dared confide in Scott, but she was too afraid.

A second later, everyone else crowded in, laughing and talking, glasses in their hands. Someone forced a glass on to her. A party had begun on stage for all the important members of the audience. Annie didn't want to go to it, but was dragged there once she had changed out of her costume.

Her mother found her way back-stage; she was over the moon, hugging Annie and half-crying.

'It was wonderful. Wonderful.'

Before Annie had a chance to ask her where Johnny was, Roger Keats grabbed her. She looked up at him, starting to shake again.

'Don't hide away, little Alice,' he said in that soft voice which was a veiled threat. 'Important people want to meet you.'

Her mother shifted, and he glanced at her, his shrewd eyes narrowing. 'Ah. Is this your mother?' Immediately he oozed charm, pressed her hand, said, 'Yes, I can see the likeness. You've got a talented daughter, Mrs Lang.' He had his arm round Annie's waist, wouldn't let her wriggle away. She could feel his fingertips brushing the underside of her breast. 'I'm looking forward to exploring the extent of her talent, and I'm sure I'm going to be well rewarded. I have a lot of ideas for her. So long as she is ready to learn, it will be a pleasure to teach her everything I know.'

Trudie glowed.

'Now, will you excuse me for a moment while I take Annie to meet some people?'

Annie felt as if she was hallucinating. The bright lights, the familiar, starry faces, dazzled her but it was all unreal.

'And this is Derek Fenn – one of the great Hamlets of our time.'

Annie had heard of the man, but not as a stage actor – wasn't he in TV? She managed a smile and stood there while the man said something polite, then Roger wafted her on to someone else. To her relief a few minutes afterwards the important guests began to leave and Roger darted off to say goodbye to them.

Annie hurried to find her mother. 'Why didn't Johnny come to the party?'

'He wasn't allowed back-stage. Mr Keats said it was parents only.'

Swallowing, Annie said, 'Let's go, Mother. I'm so tired.'

She couldn't wait to hear what Johnny had thought of her performance, but although he was waiting when they got home, her mother pushed her straight upstairs to bed, and Johnny only managed to whisper, 'You made me cry.'

Next day he said a great deal more, but none of it meant as much to her as that first husky whisper.

After the play she had three days off, and she and Johnny spent most of it together at his grandmother's house. They were still just kissing, holding each other, touching each other with exploring hands without undressing, but the heat between them kept growing. She knew it would end in making love and she wasn't scared, the way she was when Roger Keats looked at her; with Johnny she burned to be touched.

One bright, cold day in December, Johnny pushed up her T-shirt and buried his face in her warm breasts, groaning, 'I need you, Annie, I need you . . . you're all I've got in the world now. I love you.'

She held his head, feeling her insides cave in, a strange satisfied sensation as if he was a baby at her breast, his mouth sucking at her, taking life from her. 'Darling. Darling,' she whispered, rocking him on her body.

He pushed her knees apart and slid down between them, moving on top of her, gasping as their bodies rubbed together.

Hands trembling, they undressed each other. He was pale and tense, she was so shy she couldn't look at him, and afraid this was going to hurt. It did; when his hard flesh pushed at her she arched in pain, crying out, and Johnny stopped at once, looked anxiously at her.

'Did I hurt you?'

She looked into his beautiful, worried eyes and loved him so desperately she would have died for him. She tightened her arms around him and pushed him down again, opening her thighs wider, lifting her buttocks off the carpet to make it easier for him. 'Go on, darling, go on.'

As he finally forced himself inside her the pain was intense but she didn't cry out this time. She let the waves of pain wash through her with each thrust until pain became pleasure, she was gasping and arching to meet it.

Afterwards Johnny lay on top of her, breathing thickly, almost sobbing.

'We belong to each other now,' he said. 'Forever. Don't we?'

She went on holding him, her cheek pushed against his. 'Forever,' she echoed.

After that they made love every time they went to the house, slowly undressed each other, caressing, exploring each other's bodies with curiosity and pleasure, before making love by firelight, their pale, naked bodies dappled with moving shadow, while the old trees scraped and scratched at the windows as if wanting to get at them.

The house already smelt damp and upstairs on the landing mould was growing on the wallpaper, but they were in love and wildly happy with that out-of-all-proportion passion that marks first love.

They could lie naked together in total silence for an hour at a time, just staring into each other's eyes, not even touching, just breathing and absorbing each other.

And then Roger Keats told Annie to meet him in his office after classes one Friday night.

Her first reaction was to decide to tell him to go to hell, but what if she did? What might he do to her? He had enormous power at the school, he could blight her life.

The work she was doing, the reactions of her tutors, watching other students perform, had convinced her she did have a chance of making it in the theatre, if she got the right break. She wanted to be an actress more now than she had before she began to train.

Annie spent that day thinking desperately. She couldn't just refuse to go; she had heard enough gossip about him at the school to know that he would take his revenge. He meant what he said. He could ruin her career. Get her kicked out of the school. Make sure she got none of the offers which came in every so often for students. Make sure she didn't get big roles in school productions which were a shop window for agents and producers looking for new talent. Her performance in Hamlet had been noticed, but it was only a first-year production – she had to follow it with better work.

She couldn't confide in anyone. Least of all Johnny. She knew he would go crazy if she told him what had happened at that first interview, what Roger Keats had done to her, made her do with him. Her stomach heaved at the memory: his hand on the back of her neck, forcing her down on her knees.

She had tried to blank out the memory. She couldn't bear to remember.

She certainly couldn't tell Johnny. It would hurt him too much, because he loved her and Johnny was romantic, an innocent. If she told him what she had been made to do she knew he would never look at her without remembering and being sickened.

Roger had got her backed into a corner. There was no escape that she could see.

During lunch she saw Lee Kirk, the little dark girl Roger had been seen with a lot that term. She was picking at a tiny salad. Annie went over to sit next to her.

'Can I talk to you?'

Lee gave her a brief, unfriendly glance. 'What about? This is my last day here. I'm leaving I've got a place in a touring company, we fly to Australia next week.'

'Did Roger Keats get you the job?'

After the last class, when the school was almost empty, Annie slowly made her way to Roger Keats's office.

She walked into the room she remembered so well from her first visit there, and Roger was sitting on the cushion-piled chaise-longue, drinking a glass of red wine.

'Shut the door, lock it and come here,' he said, looking her over with bright, greedy eyes.

She stayed there, without moving, as if paralysed. 'Mr Keats, I don't want to do this.'

Act, act, she thought. She gave him a pleading look.

His red mouth smiled in enjoyment. 'Roger, call me Roger, and don't waste my time. You wouldn't be here if you weren't ready to keep our bargain.'

'Bargain?'

'We made a deal, remember? You got a place at the school, and in return you were going to be nice to me, so start being nice. Lock the door, little Alice, and come over here. We'll have a run-through of what you did for me before, to start with – you were good at that.'

She didn't have to act her sickened revulsion; she almost threw up at the memory he'd conjured up, that hot, stiff flesh in her mouth, his grunting enjoyment, the way he stared down, watched her.

'No.' She looked at him with hatred, not moving. 'I won't, I'll never do . . . that . . . again. You can't make me!'

'But that's what I like about you, Alice – I can make you do anything. Sweet little Alice with your long blonde hair and big, frightened eyes. You didn't say no last time, you were very obedient.'

'I hated it!'

'I know you did. That was half the pleasure, to know you hated doing it to me, but to have you do it all the same.' He ran his tongue-tip over his fleshy lips. 'If you'd enjoyed it, it wouldn't have been so much fun. This time we'll try something new, something even more enjoyable.'

'No!'

His voice hardened. 'Yes. I can do so much for you, remember. I've just been asked to recommend a girl for a small part in a children's TV drama. Remember Derek Fenn, who judged the end-of-term competition? He's looking for someone to play a fifteen-year-old in his school series. You won't even have to act. It's type-casting.' He laughed, taking another sip of the red wine; she watched it stain his tongue, and shuddered. 'Only a few weeks' work,' he drawled. 'But the pay's OK, it's good experience, and nothing gets your face known quicker than TV.'

Her voice rising she said, 'You mean, if I sleep with you, I get this part? And if I refuse, I don't?'

'Do you have to have everything spelt out for you? Stupid girls don't go far, little Alice. Of course that's what I mean!'

'Do you think Lee Kirk will go far?' she shouted. 'You got her a job in return for sleeping with you, didn't you?'

He laughed, unworried by the accusation. 'Jealous? No need to be. Lee was hot stuff in bed but I couldn't teach her a thing, she knew it all already. I'm going to have more fun with you, sweet, innocent little Alice. And remember, I always keep my word, darling. Give me what I want, and I'll make sure you get what you want. So come over here and start by taking your clothes off.'

Annie just stood there. Waiting.

It seemed to her an eternity before the door behind her was pulled wide open and two of the school governors walked in. One of them was Rob's father, a broad, bald-headed man who was a leading film director.

Roger jerked upright, spilling red wine. He had turned grey; he suddenly looked old.

'We've heard enough,' Rob's father said. 'You can go now, Miss Lang, but we may need you to give evidence to the police if Keats isn't sensible.'

Roger's eyes turned on her; she flinched at the look in them. His voice hoarse, he muttered, 'You little bitch.' He came off the chaise-longue in an angry lunge, dropped the glass, which shattered into fragments in a glittering shower, splashing wine like blood on the floor, on the chairs, on Roger's trousers.

'I'll kill you,' he grunted as his hands reached for her. 'You set me up! I'll kill you, you little bitch.'

She was paralysed by fear. Roger's hands closed round her neck, squeezing inwards, her breath choked in her throat. Her eyes rolled upwards; she was half-blind, dark blood flooding her face.

'Let go of her, you bastard!' she heard somebody say, then the two other men tore Roger away from her. He fell backwards, crashed into the wall and tumbled over, arms and legs sprawling.

'Are you OK?' Rob's father asked, putting an arm round her.

Her throat hurt, she was gasping for painful breath, and she was shaking violently.

Annie nodded, then had to get away from there. She turned and ran out, her stomach churning.

She never remembered afterwards how she got home – the whole journey was a blank. She was in shock.

Her mother was still at work when she walked into the house. Johnny was there alone, sitting at the table, working on a piece of copy for that week's paper, his brow creased as he checked a word in a dictionary.

'You're late, darling, I was beginning to get worried,' he said, absently, glancing up and smiling.

Annie was shivering. It was February the thirteenth,

the day before St Valentine's day, and there was snow whirling in the cold wind, snow piling up in gutters, against garden walls, on bushes and trees. She was wearing a thick woollen jacket, but she was bitterly cold. She stood in front of the fire, holding out her frozen hands to the blaze.

'Annie? What's wrong? What is it?'

Johnny came towards her but she held her hands out, palms towards him, stopping him.

'No! Don't come any closer, Johnny.' She felt dirty. She didn't want him to touch her. Not until she had told him. She hadn't meant to tell him, but now she saw she had to, or what had happened would poison her life. Telling Johnny would be like lancing a boil, letting the sickness and corruption ooze away.

She started talking before she could change her mind, her voice disjointed, sobbing; the words poured out of her, tears running down her face without her noticing.

Johnny went white as he listened. His eyes turned wild. Crazy. She didn't know his face any more.

She saw his mouth moving and barely heard his groaning. 'Christ, Christ.'

'He made me do it to him,' she sobbed. 'I hated what he made me do.'

She wanted him to hold her and tell her he loved her and he would never let any man hurt her, never again, she was safe now and Johnny would protect her – but he didn't. He turned and almost ran out of the room suddenly without a word.

'Johnny, where are you going? Johnny!' For a moment she was too shocked to move, then she ran out after him and was just in time to see him roaring away on his motorbike, in his black leather jacket but not wearing his helmet.

He was driving too fast. If he crashed without a helmet he'd be killed.

'Johnny!' she screamed after him but he didn't look back.

She stood there on the path, waiting for him to turn round. He spun round the corner so fast, his bike leaned over, almost touching the ground. She heard the sound of the engine fading. Then silence. Still she stood there, minute after minute, like a statue, only her eyes alive. Johnny would come back to her. He was upset. He would come back when he got over the first shock.

Then the phone began to ring. Annie ran to answer it, her face lighting up, but it wasn't Johnny.

'Don't think you're going to get away with what you've done to me,' Roger Keats said thickly. 'I'll get you, if it takes the rest of my life. I'll have you, one way or another. You're going to pay, you little bitch. I'm going to make your life hell.'

She dropped the phone blindly.

Her mother came home a minute or two later and found the front door open, snow blowing in across the carpet, and Annie lying on the hall floor in a dead faint.

Trudie Lang acted the way she always did, quickly and with commonsense. First, she shut the front door, then she called their doctor, and only after he had said he would come at once did she deal with Annie, help her to her feet, make her lie down on a sofa, got her a glass of water.

The doctor only lived two streets away. He arrived before Trudie had had a chance to talk to Annie.

He examined Annie, asked her questions; and that was when Trudie Lang discovered that her daughter was pregnant.

Annie had suspected it for a couple of months, but had kept hoping it wasn't true, that her periods would start again. It was the way she always dealt with problems, she knew that and she kept meaning to change, but she didn't. She went on hoping that by ignoring a problem she could make it go away. That was why she had ignored Roger Keats until he forced her to do something about him. Now she was being forced to admit that she was going to have a baby.

'Ring and make an appointment for your first check up at the antenatal clinic,' the doctor told her, writing out a prescription. 'And get these – they'll calm you down a little.'

Trudie Lang had just stood there without making a comment while the doctor was there. She had grown up in the school that didn't wash the family's dirty linen in public. She waited until the doctor had gone before she let her rage show. Coming back into the room where Annie still lay on the sofa, she came over and slapped Annie violently round the face.

'You stupid little bitch. And don't look at me with those big eyes. I'm not a man to be taken in by them. You're not so dumb you don't know what you've done. That's the end of acting for you. That's your whole career down the drain. And for what?' She shook Annie until it felt as if her head would come off.

'Don't, Mum!'

Hoarsely, Trudie threw at her, 'It's Johnny Tyrone's baby, isn't it? Oh, don't lie. I can see it in your face. I knew you were seeing a lot of him when I wasn't here, but I thought you had more sense than to. . .Christ,

Annie, if you had to sleep with him, why in hell didn't you go on the Pill?'

Helplessly, Annie shrugged. 'The first time, it just happened, there was no time to think, and after that it didn't seem to matter.'

Her mother looked at her as if she hated her. 'How could you be so bloody stupid? After all I've sacrificed for you, the years of scrimping and saving to pay for your lessons, all the hours I've spent taking you to ballet class and piano lessons.'

'I didn't ask you to! It was all your idea in the beginning, you wanted me to be an actress, you pushed me . . .'

'You little bitch!' Trudie shouted. 'I did it all for you – and you've started to get somewhere, I saw all the fuss they made of you when you were in Hamlet, you could be famous and rich – but you've chucked your chances away by letting some boy talk you into his bed. Well, he'll have to marry you, he isn't getting out of it. It takes two. He can take responsibility for what he's done. I'm not keeping you and your bastard.'

Tears ran down Annie's white face. 'I'm sorry, Mum. Don't be angry, I'm so sorry.'

'Too late for that, isn't it?' Trudie bitterly said. 'You had your big chance and you blew it. I'll never forgive you.' But the black rage had died out in her eyes as she watched her daughter's tears. 'He's working tonight, is he? Did he say when he'd be back? I'll wait up for him. I want to speak my mind before I get some sleep tonight. Butter wouldn't melt in his mouth. I should have known, but I trusted him, I trusted the pair of you. More fool me. Wait till I see him! You'd better get to bed, you look half-dead.'

Annie was afraid to let her talk to Johnny alone. 'I'll wait, too,' she insisted, and wouldn't let her mother bully her into going to bed.

They waited until the early hours but Johnny didn't come back. Disturbed and anxious, Annie went to bed at last, but didn't sleep. Next day, her mother got in touch with his newspaper, but he wasn't at work.

The editor had no idea where he might have gone. He said he had just been about to ring them to ask if Johnny was ill.

After hanging up, her mother turned on her, her mouth bitter, 'He knew about the baby, didn't he? You told him, and he's bolted.'

'No, I didn't tell him!' Annie was frantic with worry and unhappiness. Where could he have gone? Why had he run out like that? Had he been so appalled by her story that he never wanted to see her again?

'Well, he owns that house, he can't leave that behind. His lawyers will know where he is. I'll get the truth out of them.'

Trudie rang Johnny's solicitors later that morning, but they claimed they had not heard from him either.

'I didn't believe a word of it,' Trudie said furiously. 'But I'm not giving up on Master Johnny. He isn't getting out of this. He had his fun, now he's going to pay for it.'

Annie put her hands over her ears, screaming. 'Don't say that, don't say that.'

She ran upstairs and locked herself in her bedroom. She got under the bedcovers, pulled them up over her head. She felt as if she was falling to pieces, her mind made scratchy, disconnected noises, like the sound of a fingernail down a window, every time she remembered yesterday, those moments with Roger Keats, the hatred in his eyes when he leapt to grab her by the throat.

'I'll kill you, you little bitch, you set me up . . .'

And the bone-white tension of Johnny's face as she told him, the way he had rushed out, her last glimpse of him on his motorbike driving away through the snow, much too fast when the roads were so icy. Motorbikes were dangerous enough at the best of times, but when black ice coated the roads it would be so easy to crash.

She sat up in bed. That was it. An accident, he must have had an accident. Why hadn't she thought of it before?

A second later, she was running barefoot down the stairs in her nightdress. Her mother was in the kitchen; Annie could hear the kettle whistling. Her hand trembling, she looked up the local police station number and rang them, but they had no reports of any accident involving a motorbike in the past twenty-four hours.

'He's your lodger and he's gone off without a word? Paid his rent, has he?' said the police sergeant she spoke to, and when she hesitated, said drily, 'Ah, run off without paying, then? Happens every day. Chalk it down to experience, miss.'

She rang the local hospital next, but there had been no motorbike rider brought in after an accident. No Johnny Tyrone was a patient on any of the wards.

She tried to think what other avenue she could explore, but her mind had gone blank. Her brief spurt of energy all gone, she went back to bed.

Johnny might have gone to ground in his grandmother's house, of course. Maybe he would be back once he had got over the shock of what she had told him? If he didn't come tomorrow she would make her way there; it was a long, roundabout route on buses or Underground, and then a long walk along the little-used back road through the forest. She didn't feel up to the journey today. She would go tomorrow.

Next day, however, she was running a temperature so high that the doctor was afraid it might turn into pleurisy. Her mother shut the shop for the day to stay with her; Annie was almost hallucinating, flushed and breathing thickly, tossing and turning in the bed. It was a week before she recovered enough to get up and come downstairs in the afternoon.

There had still been no sign of Johnny; she was beginning to think he was never coming back.

That evening she and her mother had a visit from Derek Fenn, the TV actor-producer who had been at the first night of the school production of Hamlet, and who Roger Keats had claimed wanted her to appear in his children's series.

Derek Fenn was in his late thirties, a slight, distinguished-looking man with rather mournful dark eyes. She had asked around about him after meeting him at the first-night party for Hamlet. Everyone else seemed to know all about him. He had once been a Shakespearian star at Stratford, but his star had set when he started hitting the bottle, forgetting his lines and even falling over on stage.

'Went to pieces, couldn't cut it any more,' Scott had told her. 'He drifted into TV, an easier option for a drunk. He only has to remember a few words at a time and if he bangs into the furniture they sober him up with black coffee and start again. Easy-peasy lemon-squeezy.'

'How sad,' Annie had said, remembering his melancholy eyes.

'Drunks aren't sad, they're pathetic,' Scott had said scornfully. 'He's lucky – he's still a big name. TV makes you more famous than Shakespeare.'

Her mother was certainly impressed by him, but she wouldn't leave Annie alone with the man; she was afraid of what Annie might tell him. Derek Fenn seemed to find that amusing; he was flattered, imagining that it was his reputation with women that was making Trudie Lang so edgy.

'You know why I'm here?' he smoothly asked Trudie, accepting the small glass of sherry she had offered him.

Trudie smiled hopefully. 'You tell me.'

He gave her one of his practised smiles. 'I saw Annie do Ophelia – a very moving experience, such a little, lost girl. I've never seen it played quite so young before, but it worked, I was very impressed. I think she would be perfect for a very interesting part in my new series.'

'I can't. I'm pregnant,' Annie bleakly said, not caring.

Trudie almost hit the roof.

'Oh, that's right! Ruin the last chance you're likely to get! Why did you have to open your mouth? You stupid little bitch.'

Derek Fenn stared at Annie, frowning. 'How many weeks? Are you going to have it?'

'Well, that's it,' Trudie said. 'The boyfriend has dumped her and God knows what she's going to do.'

Tears came into Annie's eyes. They still hadn't heard from Johnny; she was afraid he had gone for good. She missed him badly, she had never been so unhappy in her life. She had believed he loved her as much as she loved him. Why had he gone away? Did he blame her for what Roger Keats had made her do? Oh, God, surely, surely, he hadn't thought she enjoyed doing it? Didn't he know her better than that?

'Go to bed, Annie. I'll talk to Mr Fenn,' her mother ordered, and Annie listlessly got up. She didn't care about losing the TV job. All she thought about was Johnny, and her mother would never let her leave the house; she wasn't left alone all that week. Trudie had closed the shop, hung a sign on the door, Closed Through Illness.

All Annie's decisions had always been made by her mother. Trudie made them now and Annie didn't have the strength to argue. She no longer cared what happened to her. Sadness consumed her; she just did what she was told, unquestioning, indifferent, even to signing a letter to the drama school which her mother wrote for her, resigning her place.

She got a phone call from her friend Scott a week later. Annie was helping her mother cook lunch when the phone began to ring out in the wide hall passage.

Trudie hurried out to answer it. Annie checked on the potatoes simmering on the stove, then looked out of the kitchen window at the grey wintry day, hearing her mother say sharply, 'Yes, who is it?'

Annie went on staring out at the garden, bare trees, a few snowdrops under them, a robin on a black branch chattering angrily.

Trudie came back into the kitchen, her face uncertain. 'It's that friend of yours from drama school – Scott. Do you want to talk to her? I could tell her you're ill, but she said she might come round and we don't want that, do we?'

Annie shook her head obediently. No, they did not want visitors. She was too weary and listless to want

46

anything. She went out into the hall with its odour of polish and chrysanthemums, the chill February wind whistling under the sill of the front door.

'I just heard you were leaving,' Scott said. 'Why? Annie, you're good – don't give up! You're a born actress!'

Annie told her about Derek Fenn's offer and Scott said, with scorn, 'TV? A children's programme? You could do much better than that – you should be in the theatre, not on TV!'

Annie changed the subject. 'How is everyone?'

Scott was distracted by gossip. She talked about the latest play being put on at school, love affairs among their friends, then said, 'And of course we've lost Roger Keats. We've got a new senior tutor, quite dishy. Everyone's talking about Roger – nobody knows for sure what happened, but there are all sorts of rumours flying about.'

Annie was silent, her stomach cramped with sickness. Had it all got out? Did everyone at the school know? Did Scott?

'I've got to go, Scott, sorry.' Annie hung up, turned slowly, and found her mother watching her, frowning.

'What's wrong? What did she say?'

Annie was trembling, she couldn't meet her mother's eyes. 'She was just talking about school.'

Trudie gruffly said, 'Forget about school. You don't need them any more. You're a professional now.' She put an arm round Annie and hugged her. 'It will be OK, you'll see. We're doing the right thing. The future is what matters.'

After talking to Scott, Annie was so scared of Roger Keats that she wouldn't go out of the house, wouldn't

47

open the door if anyone knocked until she had checked through a window, never answered the telephone.

But week after week went by and there was still no sign of him. Or of Johnny. She began to believe she would never see either of them again, until a year later, on another cold, raw, February day, she opened a Valentine's card. The message was printed in capital letters.

'Did you think I'd forgotten you? I haven't, so don't forget me, because I'll be back.'

2

Seven years later, on a mild, rainy January morning, a man sitting in a dentist's waiting-room saw a photo of Annie in an old magazine among those littering a low coffee-table in the middle of the room between the chairs lining the walls, and felt his body jerk as if he had touched an electric wire.

The article on the TV series in which she was starring was very short and told him nothing he did not know. He had seen every episode and read every article on the series that he could get his hands on. But he obsessively read every word, and then his gaze returned to the photo.

She never seemed to change, except that she'd cut her hair; it was short now, and he didn't like that, it made her look like a boy and he had loved it the way it was, all that long, straight, silky hair, pale and shining, especially when she wore a blue headband to keep it back from her face, like Alice in Wonderland.

He remembered touching it, remembered her face, looking up at him. Those eyes . . .

His body burned. He shut his eyes, remembering, breathing fast.

One day. One day, he promised himself, then opened his eyes to look at the photo again. God, it never ceased to amaze him – eight years and she still had that wide-eyed, shining innocence, the shy, nervous mouth.

The years had done almost nothing to her. They had crucified him.

He deliberately dropped the magazine and knelt down to pick it up, his body hiding what he was doing from the three other men in the room. Soundlessly, deftly, he tore out the page and slid it into his pocket, then stood up, holding the magazine, and sat down again.

Another one for his collection. He had dozens of pictures of Annie pinned up in his room on every available piece of wall; he lay on his back, staring at them for hours.

'Next,' the dentist's nurse said, looking at him, and he dropped the magazine back on the table and followed her into the room which smelt of disinfectant and fear and years of polish on the woodblock floor.

The dentist was a middle-aged man who reminded him of his father; something about the mouth, the cruel lines around the eyes. As he leaned back in the worn, old leather chair he stared at the man with hostility. He had hated his father.

'Which tooth hurts? Upper right molar? What . . . here?' grunted the dentist, probing mercilessly. 'Oh, don't be such a coward, man. It can't hurt that much. Just a little spot of decay. Have to be cleaned out and refilled. Relax, this won't hurt. Much.'

It did, of course. He gave a gasp of pain as the needle went in, then slowly his mouth began to go numb; he closed his eyes to try to ignore the buzz of the dentist's drill. At least he wasn't in pain any more. He had been in agony with it all night, not that anybody cared.

There was nobody in the world who cared about him. He had lost everything. He had had to leave everything he knew, it was years since he had been back, and all because of Annie.

He knew there was no man in her life. From time to time the press had talked about some actor she was seeing; there had been a few photos of her at first nights or arriving at a party, or having dinner with someone, but it had never lasted. He had watched feverishly each time until the stories faded away.

So far she was still alone. And women alone were vulnerable: helpless, fragile, easy to hurt. He tightened with memory, remembering another woman. The whispered pleading, the fear in the voice, and then the moans of pain, before the screaming began.

'Please don't, please, oh, no, please don't . . . Oh, God help me . . .' She had been so terrified. So helpless.

'There you are, all done, rinse out now,' said the dentist, stepping away.

He was almost dazed as he leant over to rinse his mouth in the pink disinfectant fountaining in the white china bowl.

Pink turned red with his blood as he spat the liquid out again. He stared at it, eyes fixed. Blood. Blood got everywhere; it took forever to clean it all away and you had to make sure you got rid of every trace of it or it might betray you. Luckily, it hadn't mattered the first time.

Well, after all, it had been an accident, that first time, hadn't it? That was what he'd told the police, and it was true, in a way, because he hadn't meant to do it. He had been scared into it, he'd acted in self-defence. And they'd believed him, they hadn't guessed the truth.

'Send the next one in,' the dentist said.

He stumbled out of the chair and walked unsteadily towards the door.

'Make sure you brush your gums properly in future,' the dentist said.

'I will,' he promised and smiled, thinking: go to hell, you sadistic bastard, you enjoy your job, don't you?

Hurting people could be addictive. He was no sadist, but he couldn't deny he'd enjoyed killing that first time. He enjoyed remembering it.

The face surprised, not believing what was happening; the open eyes, staring up at him. The mouth open, crying out, soundlessly, going backwards, going backwards, very slowly, so that it felt like watching a slow-motion film, the body going backwards, backwards endlessly, with the hands flung out, trying to grasp, to grab, to hang on, but meeting only empty air.

Usually that was all he remembered, but sometimes his mind ran on like a video and the noises came through – the crashing, the sickening thuds, the screaming.

He didn't want to remember that.

He preferred to remember afterwards – the silence, the body lying very still and silent, not hurting any more, at the foot of the stairs. Over. Finished.

He stood at the top, staring down, transfixed. Then he realised what had happened, saw what it meant. All safe now. All quiet.

The second time he hadn't acted on impulse; he had planned it all, worked out how and where and what to do with the body afterwards. And it had all gone exactly as he planned, except for one, stupid unforeseen accident.

Life wouldn't let you get away with making plans. It always tried to trip you up if it could.

Leaving the dentist's surgery, he walked neatly and quietly back home.

Safely in his room, he put up the picture of Annie among the others, and stared at it for a long time, then he got out the new Valentine's card. He had had it for weeks: he liked to have them with him for as long as possible before he sent them, to enjoy imagining her opening the envelope, looking at the card, reading his message. He'd give anything to be a fly on the wall, able to see her face, watch her reaction.

This year he had chosen an old-fashioned Victorian-style card, all dark red roses and white lace.

The outside carried the words 'Forever mine' in shimmering red foil. He traced the words with one finger, smiling. How would she look when she read that? And she would be his . . . soon. He couldn't wait.

The following month, Annie was thinking about Valentine's cards, too, as she sat in a chair in make-up, with other actors yawning all round her in the location caravan as the make-up girls attended to their faces.

It was the thirteenth of February again.

An unlucky day for her, she thought, shivering.

'Working on a Sunday!' one of the other actors moaned. 'And in weather like this! I wouldn't be surprised if it snowed!'

'Not cold enough,' someone else said. 'And overtime, Paul – remember that. Overtime for working a Sunday.'

'I'd still rather be in bed!'

So would I, thought Annie, staring at her reflection in the mirror in front of which she sat. She was having a cut built up on her cheek; it had to match identically with the cut she had had there on Friday. Deirdre, the girl working on it, paused, her brush in her hand, to look down at a colour polaroid she had taken of the cut after she finished building it up the first time. Annie had only been in the chair for twenty minutes and it could sometimes take hours to create a make-up. It was six o'clock and outside it was still dark. She wanted desperately to go back to sleep but instead she mentally ran through her words again. She had a big scene coming up; they had only rehearsed sketchily, and the moves would be much harder to remember than the words, so it helped to know your part before you began, then you could concentrate on getting the moves right.

Outside she could hear the stentorian roar of the unit producer, Frank Goodwin, a big man with a beer gut and a grin wider than a house.

'Shift those bloody vans! We need room for the dolly to go through there. And don't take all day over it! The market will be waking up any minute now and we need to be ready before the first stalls arrive. God, it is perishing. Whose brilliant idea was it to shoot at this hour of the bloody morning? And will somebody get those braziers working?'

They were shooting in Middlesex Street, one of London's oldest and most famous street markets, popularly known as Petticoat Lane because it had once sold largely clothes.

Working in a real location was always tough. People resented you getting in the way, you had to combat exterior noise, voices, traffic, planes overhead, and the public tended to stand about and stare, and even shout out comments, or laugh, which made things difficult for the soundman and cameraman.

Despite the difficulties, real locations was one of the secrets of the success of their TV series.

The Force was a police series that went out twice weekly, using the City of London as their living backcloth. Where you had crowds, you always had crime, their police adviser had told them, which was why they were here, in the busiest weekend market in London.

'I missed you in wardrobe – can I just check you?'

Annie blinked at the continuity girl and smiled at her. 'Oh, hi, Joan. Yes, sure.'

Joan looked down at the clipboard she held and muttered under her breath. 'Grey suit, white shirt, black stockings, black shoes . . . are those the same shoes you wore on Friday?'

Annie nodded.

'Don't move the head!' Deirdre moaned, jumping back with her brush held up in front of her.

'Sorry.' Annie gave her an apologetic grin in the mirror, making sure not to move her head again.

'Not ready yet?' another voice said from the door of the caravan, and in the mirror Annie saw Harriet, the series producer, frowning at her.

'I'm going as fast as I can!' Deirdre muttered. 'It isn't my fault we keep getting interrupted.' She glared at the continuity girl, who glared back.

'We've all got our job to do! And it isn't easy out on location!'

'Don't be so ratty, the pair of you!' said Harriet cheerfully. She wore a thick workman's jacket over jeans, a thin cotton top, a thin sweater and then another sweater, because it was freezing out in the street at this hour of the morning and the more layers of clothes you wore the better. Her knee-high black leather boots lined with fur kept her feet warm however long she had to stand around.

The clothes suited Harriet, who was as slim as a boy, wore her dark brown hair cut very short, tucked behind her ears, and had the calm, smooth face of a nun, a face which hid her true nature: her driving energy, her ambition, her sense of humour and her toughness.

'Looking good, darling, for six o'clock in the morning!' she said now, grinning at Annie in the mirror.

'Well, I feel like death. I could do with another couple of hours in bed,' groaned Annie.

'Who couldn't? That's the business. Know your lines, I hope?'

Annie gave her a thumbs-up.

'Good for you.' Harriet patted her on the shoulder. 'I hope to Christ Mike does. He isn't even here yet. He was out with that new ASM last night – the little redhead straight from training school.'

Annie rolled her eyes in mock disgust and Harriet laughed.

'Right. We all knew he'd make a play for her the minute we set eyes on her, didn't we? Just up Mike's street, another rabbit for him to bowl over. Well, I suppose it's all experience.'

'Do we shoot round him?' asked Annie as the make-up girl stepped back to admire her finished handiwork. Staring at her own reflection, Annie said, 'That's great, Dee. I feel quite sorry for myself with a nasty cut like that.'

'Suits you!'

'Oh, thanks!'

Deirdre grinned at her and moved off to deal with another actress.

'We might leave Scene 5 until later,' Harriet murmured. 'Don't worry, I'll sort something out. I'm getting used to re-jigging Mike's shooting schedule.'

'I warned you what he was like, you can't say I didn't.'

'Oh, but he's so damned good, he's worth all the trouble he causes.'

Was Harriet in love with Mike Waterford? Annie had a suspicion she might be and was worried. Harriet might be tough and capable but she was also warm-hearted and emotional. That was why everyone on the crew adored her. She always noticed if someone was upset, and did something about it; Annie had grown very fond of her, and would hate her to get badly mauled by someone like Mike. Watching her in the mirror, she tried to read Harriet's eyes, but they gave nothing away. Annie's stare moved on to her own reflection, her mouth twisting.

She gave nothing away, herself, did she? Well, she hoped not. Anyone from the press who interviewed her always asked about her love life and tried to surprise some telltale reaction out of her. They never got one, because she didn't have a love life. Oh, she had dates, now and then, but she hadn't been in love since . . . oh, who knows when?

You know, she thought, staring at herself in the mirror. – Stop pretending you don't remember his name. Johnny. You've never been in love with anyone else.

Just saying his name brought it all back, those hours in the old house, making love in front of the fire, the laughter and the poetry, and then the black plunge into misery and grief.

She had never seen him again. He had vanished off

the face of the earth and she still didn't know why, not for sure. She had been too ill to think straight at the time, and for a long time afterwards she had been in a state of numbed trauma, but later she had tried looking at it from Johnny's point of view. He must have been so appalled by what she told him that he never wanted to see her again. Johnny had been a romantic, an idealist; his image of her would have been tarnished forever when she confessed what Roger Keats had made her do – she shouldn't have told him.

She had kept thinking he would come back when he got over his first horror, but he hadn't, so eventually, many months later, she had gone to see his lawyers, but got nothing out of them.

'I need to see him,' she had pleaded, and the partner who had agreed to see her had looked faintly curious, but had shaken his head.

'I'm sorry, I'm afraid I can't help you.'

'But you do know where he is?'

'I'm sorry, I can tell you nothing at all about him.'

'But he is still your client?'

She had tried to read the man's smooth, bland face and got nowhere. He looked, she thought, like a spoon with a suit on: a bald head, narrow shoulders, a thin body and long legs, and that empty face.

He had paused to decide how to answer her question, then murmured, 'We do look after his affairs, yes.'

There had been something evasive in the answer – what was he holding back?

'His house . . . in Epping forest . . . has it been sold?'

'I'm sorry, but I am not at liberty to discuss a client's private affairs. I am very busy this morning, and I really cannot tell you anything else. Good morning, Miss Lang.'

She had stood up, hesitated. 'If . . . if he gets in touch with you, will you tell him that I'd like to hear from him?'

She had learnt to drive by then, and had come there in her small red secondhand Ford. She had driven away from the office trying to assess what she had learnt – only to wonder if she had learnt anything at all.

Was Johnny even alive? Why hadn't that house been sold? Why wouldn't his solicitor tell her anything about him? There had been something furtive in his face when he talked about the Epping house. He hadn't wanted to talk about it at all. Why?

A blinding light struck her. What if Johnny was living there? Why else wouldn't the house have been sold?

She had been on her way home but she had turned the car round and driven back to Epping there and then, her heart beating painfully inside her breast. All the way through the winding forest roads, she had felt feverish, possessed, imagining walking up that path, knocking on that door. She refused to think any further than that.

If he came to the door she didn't even know what she was going to say, what she could ask.

'Why, Johnny? Why? Why did you go away and never let me know where you were?'

That was what she had to ask, but how could she bear it if he looked at her blankly and just answered, 'I stopped loving you. When I heard what you had done with that man I didn't ever want to see you again.'

Could she blame him? She hated the memory, too, didn't she?

She had had no problem finding the house, although it was almost hidden on a rarely used road through the forest. She had stopped her car just short of the house and stared at it through the crowding trees.

It was spring and new leaves were unfolding on the branches, vivid green spirals of life exploding into air. The first time she saw it, it had been winter, the forest shadowy and quiet; now there were birds all around the house, busy and important as they built their nests, pausing breathlessly on a post or a tree to flute a few phrases before they got on with their work. The air was sharp with hope and anticipation.

Annie had got out of her car and walked to the gate, stood there, staring, her heart plummeting. The house was empty.

Nobody could live in a house that looked like that. It had deteriorated since she last saw it, the windows dusty, thickly cobwebbed, the garden a wilderness of scrubby bushes and trees and weeds, choked with nettles and rough grass among which the daffodils shone, golden as sunlight, dozens of them in clumps, their frilly trumpets blaring at the blue spring sky.

Nobody had lived here for ages, you could feel it. It was a house abandoned, forgotten, except by jackdaws nesting on the battlements who cawed angrily at her appearance, making her jump. The Gothic tower rose against the blue spring sky, shutters banged in the wind beside the high, arched windows.

She had peered through the dirty glass into the drawing-room. The room hadn't changed an inch; the hearth where they had built up great fires of logs had been swept clean, although a sprinkling of soot had fallen since then and was sprayed across the shabby old carpet, the furniture was all covered in sheets, everything was tidy, so someone had been here, to clean the place, but there was an air of desolation.

The house was haunted, by memories, by ghosts, and a multitude of spiders. Spiders spun great grey swags of webs from every corner, sunlight glinted on the delicate fibres of a web across the window, they had swung silk ladders from light-fittings and picture rails. Flies which had somehow got into the house had bred there and buzzed hopelessly against the window, trying to escape into the light. There was an earwigs' nest on the windowsill, and wood lice, which an actress from Lancashire she knew called parson's pigs, clicked along the floorboards in their grey, primeval armour, like tiny armadillos.

She had gone back to look at the drawing-room, had closed her eyes and seen it as it had been all those wintry days when they drew the curtains to shut out the world, turning the room into their own private universe, lit a fire in that cold hearth and lay in front of it, naked, making love.

'I'll love you for the rest of our lives,' he had whispered, his cheek against her warm breast, and she had echoed what he said.

'I'll love you forever.'

Three months later he had walked out of her house, out of her life.

But she hadn't stopped loving him or thinking about him. All those years, while she was building her career, working in TV or on the stage, she had tried to forget Johnny, but she couldn't. No other man she met had ever matched up to her memory of him.

Well, at least she had more confidence now, she controlled her own life instead of letting her mother do it, not that Trudie could, any more. Trudie couldn't even look after herself. Annie increasingly found herself taking on the role of adult to her mother's child.

She knew that getting this part had helped her grow up a lot. The series was set around the City of London police force; her character was an detective inspector in CID for which she was grateful, as it meant she did not have to wear a serge police uniform, which would have been hell under the lights. Actors who had to wear them were always complaining.

Slightly built, her breasts still small, although her hips had a more rounded curve now, Annie knew she looked younger than her actual age. The bone structure she'd inherited from her mother made her face striking rather than pretty; she was lucky it was so expressive, reflecting every thought, every emotion for the camera to pick up. She found it easy to act on the small screen – the less you did, the better. She just let a thought fill her head, and it would show on her face without her trying.

Her skin had cleared up, she no longer had a tendency to eczema, and she had cut her long blonde hair. These days she wore it very short and straight, the part she played demanded that. Women police officers generally did wear their hair short, for good reasons, Harriet had explained when she asked Annie to have hers cut. Long hair was too easy to pull, if you were attacked, for one thing, and for another, short hair was a police tradition, and easier to keep tidy. Looking neat and capable also disguised the fact that you were a woman, and, in a male-dominated world, that helped.

Annie still saw herself as plain, for all the attention she got, but she'd discovered with surprise that a lot of other actors were just as shy and uncertain. Acting was one way of dealing with shyness. You hid inside the shell of someone else. When she was in a part, she could feel beautiful, brilliant, exciting, and make her audience see her that way.

When she took off her make-up, her real self-image took over again and her confidence crumbled. Her slow but steady rise in her profession hadn't made any difference to the underlying uncertainty about herself.

She looked into her eyes and saw the nervous glitter in them; she was always keyed-up before she started work, afraid that this time the magic wouldn't work, she would fail, make a fool of herself.

'CID card, put it in your inside jacket pocket,' said the girl who looked after props. 'Handbag, check the contents with me?'

Annie pulled herself together to go through the neat black handbag item by item while they were ticked off to make sure continuity was preserved for that day's filming.

She had to open the bag in the first scene; the contents would be visible and there was always an eagle-eyed viewer who would spot any discrepancy.

'Valentine's card,' Props said and Annie's head jerked up, her face turned white.

'What?' She looked at the stiff white envelope in the bag then, not touching it, suddenly sick. Oh, my God. How had he got it in there?

Then she heard the giggles and realised. She took a deep breath, forced a smile, reached for the card, willing her hand not to shake, opened the envelope and read the scrawled words.

'Love from all of us!'

In the mirror, she saw them all crowding into the doorway, grinning at her and looking a little sheepish: all the technical people, cameramen, electricians, soundmen, Frank Goodwin towering behind them.

'A day early,' Frank said, 'But you won't be working with us tomorrow, and we wanted to give it to you, not send it.'

'Thanks, guys! It's gorgeous,' she said, putting a hand to her lips and blowing them a kiss.

'That's enough fun and games from you lot, get back to work,' Harriet said, but she was grinning too. She had been in on the joke.

Annie relaxed again but she was trembling faintly now, a thin film of perspiration on her forehead.

Automatically, she took her house keys and car key, from her own handbag, and her wallet, containing her credit cards and money, then her chequebook, and dropped them into the bag she would use on the set. She had nothing else of any value in her handbag; she could leave it locked in the caravan she used as a dressing-room.

Of course the Valentine couldn't have been from him! Roger always sent them to her home. For seven years now, every Valentine's Day, a card had arrived, printed in the now-familiar capitals. The message was always the same, too.

She hated the month of February. The minute it began she was on edge, waiting for the fourteenth and what it always brought. Other people yearned to get a Valentine. Annie dreaded them. One day, she knew, he wouldn't just send a card – he would come himself. At first she had hoped he would stop, would forget about her – but he hadn't, and gradually she began to understand that the waiting was part of the punishment. He wanted her to sweat. He was biding his time somewhere out there, playing cat-and-mouse with her, making her wait until he was ready to pounce.

It wasn't bluff, or an empty threat; the waiting was part of the pleasure for him. He was in no hurry to end her agony; he was enjoying it. Sadists got their deepest pleasure out of the slow twist of a knife in a wound, and Roger Keats was a sadist, a man who loved to humiliate and terrify.

Eight years was a long time to wait for revenge – but Roger hadn't forgotten or forgiven. She had once expected him any minute, any day – but gradually she realised he wasn't in a hurry. She had come to see that he wanted a long-drawn-out revenge, the slower the better, and the irony of sending her a Valentine's card would appeal to his tortuous nature.

Where was he living? The postmarks on the Valentine's cards gave her no clues – they were posted in a different place each time, as if he was always moving about. What was he doing? Working in a theatre? Repertory? A touring company? Or had he got a job in another field altogether? Maybe he was a travelling saleman? That was a job that would suit him, with a new woman in every town.

Would she even recognise him now? Eight years can change someone. Look at the way it had changed her. She had been a nervous teenager; now she was a woman used to giving out an aura of self-assurance, even if, on the inside, she was still prone to nerves and uncertainty.

But she couldn't disappear the way he had. Fame made it impossible for her to hide. Since The Force took off up the ratings, her face was recognised everywhere; millions of TV screens took her into every home in the country.

She was a tethered goat waiting for a tiger to leap out of the jungle, hearing it move around, out of sight, in the darkness of the thick green leaves, hearing it breathe, feeling the gleaming eyes fixed on her.

Of course, she could have changed her address, moved to a new house, but her mother wouldn't leave their home in the London streets among which she had lived for so long, and Annie couldn't leave her mother.

She couldn't even explain to Trudie why she wanted to move, because Trudie no longer had a grasp of reality. Annie loved her mother, and it frightened her that Trudie was becoming so forgetful, always having little accidents, unexplained breakages happening if you took your eye off her. Annie wouldn't do anything that upset her mother because Trudie was scared enough as it was; she knew she was losing her mind and she went in dread of getting worse.

It was all too much like Auntie Edie, who had died without ever remembering who she was, let alone who anybody else was. How long before Trudie's memory lapses grew longer, her moments of lucidity fewer?

Annie paid someone to come in and look after her mother while she was at the studio, but Trudie could be amazingly cunning. She kept getting out of the house alone, to go shopping and buy things she didn't need, pointless, inexplicable things.

Once she bought hundreds of light bulbs. Another time it was bolts of material for curtains she could no longer make, or she ordered carpets and furniture. Annie had a problem cancelling some of these purchases.

Other times her mother went out and was missing for hours because she had forgotten the way home, or forgotten her name and address. Sometimes she began to cook and then wandered off, leaving a saucepan on the hob to burn and set light to the kitchen – the fire brigade had to be called.

She'll have to go into a home, Annie kept being told, but she hadn't the heart to take the medical advice. She would miss her mother too much. She would hate living alone and, anyway, Trudie would be so frightened and unhappy if she was taken away to a strange place among strange people with nothing familiar around her. Whatever the doctors might say, Annie was convinced that nothing would more surely hasten her mother's collapse.

Annie stretched with a yawn, and went out into the market, where Harriet was in conference with Frank Goodwin and the cameraman, Pete, over where the cameras should be sited. The three of them kept peering into the camera, checking out what would be in shot, moving the camera again, trying a new angle.

Trudie Lang sat in front of the TV set, staring into the blank screen and seeing herself reflected. She was knitting, making a scarf for Annie, a long, long bright red scarf which was trailing down to the floor already.

'You haven't turned it on,' said the woman who was supposed to look after her, and went across to flick the switch. Bright, smiling, unreal faces zoomed up out of nowhere.

'I don't want to watch it,' Trudie said, but Jerri, her minder, ignored that.

'And now the weather, Janice,' said a voice from the TV.

'I'm not Janice,' said Trudie, hunting for the zapper down the side of her chair.

'I'm going to make your breakfast, Trudie,' Jerri said. 'You sit here and watch the programme. There's an interview with Annie later; you remember, she recorded it on Friday? You know you said you wanted to see it.'

Trudie's face lit up. 'Annie?'

'That's right, you see, you do remember. You'll enjoy that,' Jerri said. 'OK, sit there, like a good girl, and wait for it. I'll cook your bacon and egg now.'

Trudie stared eagerly at the TV screen. Jerri went out and a moment later Trudie heard deafening pop music from the kitchen. She glared at the open door. What a racket. She got up stiffly and shuffled to the door to close it, but the grandfather clock in the hall began to chime as she got there so she slowly walked along towards it, counting. Four. Five. Six. Seven.

She got up early because she couldn't sleep any more. Her eyes wouldn't stay shut. They flew open every five minutes. She was afraid of sleep in case she died before morning. At one time she had prowled around the house all night until Annie started locking her bedroom door until morning.

She stood in front of the clock, staring at the cracked, yellowing face of it. Seven o'clock. Was it morning or evening? She opened the front door to look up at the grey sky.

The sun was a pale wraith like the moon; she wasn't sure if it was getting dark or the sun was coming up. The trees growing all along the street were bare. Winter, she thought, shivering.

A car slowed down opposite the house; the driver turned his head to stare at her. Trudie felt a jab of alarm. What was he looking at her like that for? He drove on a little way and parked. She saw him getting out of the car. Was he coming back here?

Trudie had a feeling she knew him and didn't like him. Was he one of the neighbours? Once she had known them all, everyone who lived in the street, but over the years one by one they had died, moved out, sold up, and now she knew hardly anyone.

He began to walk back towards her. I'm not talking to him, thought Trudie. She closed the door behind her and hurried away, down the road.

The air was chilly; she shivered. Have I got my shopping bag? No, she'd forgotten it. She felt in her pocket and hadn't got her door keys, either, so she couldn't go back; she would have to buy a plastic bag. What had she come out to buy, though? Oh, well, it would come back to her. Trudie set out down the road in her slippered feet, an old woman with thinning grey hair, walking along in a nightdress and dressing-gown which blew around her in the winter wind.

She had turned the corner long before Jerri came out, in a panic, to look for her. The quiet, suburban street was empty.

Derek Fenn, who played the wise old desk sergeant in the series, was smoking his first cigarette of the day and coughing, hunched in his blue serge uniform.

'That cough is getting worse. Why don't you stop smoking before it kills you?' Annie asked and got one of his morose looks.

'It isn't smoking that will kill me. It's getting up at this hour and having to stand about in weather like this.'

He was beginning to look old, his face thinner than

ever, lined and wrinkled like a monkey's from his long holidays in sunnier places, his flesh fallen in on the elegant bones, leaving him haggard, gaunt, so that only his melancholy eyes still reminded you that he had once been the best-looking actor of his generation. Now he was grateful for a small but regular part in The Force. He had been out of work for months before he joined the cast.

Annie had worked with him in his own children's series for a year before moving on to a part in a new play which toured the provinces before going into London and doing quite well. After that she had done a year with the Royal Shakespeare Company at Stratford-upon-Avon; she knew she needed to improve her technical grasp of acting. She had played small parts and learnt a lot; she didn't become a star overnight. Her career had been a slow and steady rise. But she knew she owed the start of it to Derek. So did he.

Hearing from a mutual acquaintance that Annie had got the lead in a new police series, Derek had rung her and asked, 'Would there be a part for me? Anything, darling. I need a break. I'd do it for you, you know that.'

She had heard the unspoken reminder that he had given her the first job she ever had. He wasn't the first to ring her, pleading for a job, but she owed Derek, and she knew that the part of the sergeant hadn't been cast yet. It was a key role, although it wasn't a lead.

'I'll see what I can do,' she promised. 'It wouldn't be a big part, though, they're all cast. And I don't have enough clout to get them to change their minds at this stage!'

'Anything, darling,' he repeated. 'So long as I'm

working.' Then he laughed. 'And getting paid, of course.'

'The money won't be wonderful.'

'It's got to pay better than social security!'

Harriet hadn't been keen to give Derek a chance because he had a name as a drunk, and hadn't done any work for months, had been written off as finished, far too high a risk even on TV.

'I haven't seen him in anything for a couple of years. He's not reliable, Annie. Drunks never are.'

Annie had pleaded. 'I'll see he keeps off the booze! And he is good, Harriet. He's a pro. Put him in front of a camera and he doesn't even need to act; he's so damned natural. He's got that special quality – you watch him, whenever he's on screen – know what I mean?'

Harriet had nodded. 'I do remember that, you're right.' Then she had given Annie a shrewd look. 'Why are you so keen for him to have the part?'

Annie had known what she was asking – had she had an affair with Derek? Theirs was a world of sudden emotions, brief romances, passionate affairs which faded just as fast – Harriet wouldn't have been surprised to hear she had had a fling with Derek.

She'd met Harriet's eyes. 'I owe him. He gave me my first job, and he needs a break.'

Then Harriet had given her that comradely grin and patted her on her shoulder, a response Annie was going to find very familiar in the months to come. Harriet's little pats covered a multitude of comments: sympathy, encouragement, congratulation, coaxing. That time it had been a pat which respected Annie's loyalty.

Harriet herself was always loyal to anyone who

71

worked with her and she was pleased when she got the same loyalty back. For her teamwork was a way of life. You had to trust the people you worked with; a chain was only as strong as the weakest link and Harriet liked to be sure of every tiny link in their chain.

'Ok, we'll risk it,' she'd told Annie. 'But if he lets us down you get the blame!'

Annie had talked a blue streak to Derek, made him swear to stay off drink if he was working next day, and always be on time.

He had promised faithfully, and he had kept his word. No doubt he still drank, but he never let it interfere with his work – and he had been perfect for that role. In fact, he'd discovered a new celebrity since the series began. He was one of the most popular characters.

It was a different sort of stardom for Derek; he wasn't a sex symbol these days, he was a father figure who got a lot of fan mail from older women and teenagers who could have a safe crush from a distance. But at least he was in the public eye again, his face showing up in magazine and newspaper articles, people recognising him wherever he went.

Annie was glad she had got him the part. She looked at him now, and, dropping his cigarette end he trod on it, hunching himself against the chilly wind. 'Annie, I'm sorry to ask you again, but . . .'

She knew what was coming at once and frowned. 'Not another loan, Derek! I told you last time I wasn't lending you any more money. You owe me hundreds already – and we both know you'll never pay it back!'

Head bent, he muttered, 'I'm going to, one day, I just never seem to have the spare money to do it, but I will, Annie.' He barely even bothered to make the lie convincing, and she angrily said, 'No, Derek! You know you won't because whenever you get any money you gamble it away! I'm not going to help you dig yourself a deeper hole. I won't lend you any more. Why are you such a fool?'

'Born one, darling,' he said, trying one of his charming, faintly sad now, smiles on her. It had once made women faint. Now it made his haggard face briefly almost young again. But with Annie it didn't work; it never had. He had once made a pass at her during the year she worked on his TV series; Annie had gone white and staggered away to throw up in her dressing-room. Derek couldn't fail to hear her. When she came out of the lavatory he had vanished, and he had never tried to lay a hand on her again.

She looked at him levelly now. 'It isn't funny! You promised never to gamble again.'

'I kept away from the clubs for months, for God's sake,' he said, becoming petulant. 'Then last Wednesday it was my birthday, and I suddenly realised I was forty-nine. Annie, I'm going to be fifty next year.' He shuddered. 'Fifty! Christ, I might as well be dead.'

She looked at him then with wry sympathy. Fifty seemed a long, long way off to her, but she was already dreading reaching thirty.

He saw her expression and eagerly said, 'You see what I mean? Fifty. I couldn't bear thinking about it, I had to have a few drinks, and then . . . somehow I ended up in a club and even the bloody cards were against me.'

'How much did you lose?' she asked in a softer tone.

'Three hundred,' he quickly said, and she groaned.

'Oh, Derek! Another three hundred! Do you think I'm made of money?'

73

Harriet was a hundred yards away, she couldn't have heard from that distance, surely – yet at that instant she abruptly swivelled to stare at them, frowning.

Derek caught her glance, too, and hissed out of the corner of his mouth, 'For God's sake, keep your voice down! Especially when Harriet's around – she's got ears like a bat. And I don't want the whole bloody world to know.'

Annie turned her back on Harriet discreetly, got her chequebook out of her bag, scribbled down the amount, signed the cheque, held it out without another word.

'Thanks,' Derek said, reading the figures before pushing it hurriedly inside his jacket pocket with a little sigh of relief. 'I won't ask again. Promise.'

'I meant what I said, Derek,' she warned him. 'Try again, and you'll regret it.'

'No need to be nasty, darling,' he said, buoyant again now he had the money, and walked off.

'How about that angle?' Frank asked Harriet, who turned back towards him and looked into the camera.

'Hmm . . . better . . .' she said, face hidden by a fall of sleek, straight brown hair. 'I'd like to keep the corner of that street in shot, all those Indian stalls. What do you think, Pete?'

'Lots of colour,' agreed Pete.

Harriet stepped back, nodding. Well, it wasn't perfect, but it would have to do. 'Yes, we'll have the camera here for this first scene.'

Pete looked up at the sky. 'Hope it isn't going to rain; where's that umbrella?'

'I've got it ready,' his assistant assured him. If it

began to rain they would hurriedly protect the camera without even thinking about themselves; they gave it the loving care a mother gave a delicate child.

A sound man wandered past eating hot, newly cooked doughnuts, crunchy with sugar.

'Breakfast, Adam?' teased Harriet and he grinned, winking.

'They're brilliant – I watched her cook them. Want one?' He held out a paper bag with several other doughnuts in it, rustling invitingly.

'Have to watch my diet,' Harriet absently said.

'You?' he scoffed. 'Thin as a twig.'

She always had been, but not because she dieted so much as because she burned up every calorie she ate. From the minute she opened her eyes at crack of dawn until the second she finally fell asleep again well after midnight, Harriet never stopped. She needed all that energy, too; she was the powerhouse of the series.

'Which scene are we starting with if Mike doesn't get here?' Annie asked, joining her. She hated the long gaps between actual filming – it sometimes took hours to get two minutes of film in the can.

Harriet looked into her face, trying to read it, but Annie gave nothing away. Whatever had been going on between her and Derek was well and truly hidden. They'd known each other for many years, of course, if there had been an affair neither of them had ever talked about it, and clearly it was long over, but Harriet did not believe in platonic friendships between a man like Derek and a woman as attractive as Annie.

She wasn't pretty, thought Harriet, staring at her, especially first thing in the morning, when her face was pale from lack of sleep, her eyes smudged in with bluish shadows. She was much smaller than you imagined on screen, she could look almost childlike in some clothes, especially if she wasn't wearing make-up. Harriet hadn't missed the way men reacted to her – there was something about her that made them feel she needed protection. She could look frail and helpless, a bit like a lost kid.

What exactly was going on between her and Derek, though? If any media hound sniffed it out it could hurt the series. Harriet glanced over at Derek again and Annie's gaze followed.

'Who's that with Derek?' she asked Harriet who shrugged.

'She started in wardrobe this week. Good references, she's been working at the National.'

Annie pulled a face. 'Oh, the theatagh . . .' she said in a superior drawl. 'Come slumming, has she? What made her switch to TV?'

Harriet grinned at her. 'We pay better.' They were both touchy on the subject of television's image, resenting the attention paid to theatre by the critics who mocked their own drama simply because it counted its audience in millions instead of hundreds.

'Her hair is unbelievable,' Annie said.

It exploded in a wild confusion of orange curls above a heavily made-up face. The woman wouldn't see forty again; might be over fifty, thought Harriet. Small and skinny; she wore purple jeans and a blood-red sweater, and the hands waving about as she talked excitedly to Derek had blood-red talons at the end of the fingers.

'Yes, Marty's quite a sight, isn't she?' agreed Harriet.

At that moment the other woman looked over towards them, as if picking up on the fact that they were talking about her, and gave Annie a poisonous look, her eyes like little black stones.

Annie was taken aback. Why that look? 'Marty?' she repeated, frowning. 'Marty what?'

'Keats,' Harriet said, and Annie did a double-take, turning pale.

'Keats?'

Harriet laughed. 'No relation to John – I asked! She didn't laugh, so I guess everyone does!'

Keats? thought Annie. It had to be a coincidence; Keats was not an uncommon name.

A black Porsche shot round the corner at the far end of Middlesex Street and was waved down at once by a policeman there to control the traffic and make sure the TV company didn't cause any problems.

'Here's Sean now!' Harriet said with satisfaction. 'That didn't take him long, I only rang him half an hour ago, and he was still in bed. He's such a pro. He'll probably have to rewrite if Mike doesn't show up at all, or we'd have to abandon this morning's shoot.'

'I wish he'd rewrite to leave him out of the series!' spat Annie, but Harriet merely laughed, watching Sean leap out of his Porsche.

He was big and muscular, with cold grey eyes, straight, short-cut blond hair and an aggressive chin. Harriet found his combination of threat and good looks irresistible. She did not like pretty men, or weak ones. She liked her men to be a challenge, and Sean Halifax had been that, from their first meeting.

Most of the TV companies had their own police series – it wasn't easy to come up with something different, but Harriet had managed it when she was a guest lecturer at a weekend conference on working in

TV, and met up with Sean, then a very young detective inspector with a drawer full of scripts about the City of London police force, in which he had been working for twelve years.

She had been instantly attracted, had let him take her out to dinner, had agreed to look at one of his scripts, not expecting much, but wanting to see more of him alone. As she read that first one, though, she had got more and more excited. Harriet had a passion for her job which was deeper than any passion she had ever felt for a man. She had had a couple of relationships but her job had always wrecked them; both the men she had been in love with had resented her obsession with work, had wanted her to be more interested in them, but no man she met had ever driven the job from her head. That was what set her adrenalin going every morning, the job and her desire to be the best at doing it.

Sean's script was crisp, well-written, fast-moving, but most of all the ideas were original, and the writer really knew what he was writing about. Harriet had had an instant hunch that this could be a hit.

She had taken that first script to Billy Grenaby, who ran the TV production company, and read some of it to him. Billy never read scripts himself; it wasn't even known if he *could* read – you had to act scripts out for him, sketch characters, scenes, a storyline, in as few words as possible.

As soon as she had Billy's approval, Harriet had assembled a strong, solid cast of actors she trusted. She wanted ensemble playing; no stars, no big names, just teamwork among equals, and Billy liked that, too. No stars, no big salaries. Even for the lead role she wanted someone who wasn't too well known. She had her eye on Annie from the start; she'd seen her in several good TV productions. Annie had acquired a reputation as a good character actress already.

'This will make you famous, if it takes off,' Harriet had told her. 'And it will, believe me! This series is going to be terrific.'

She had been a hundred per cent right. Always am, she thought complacently. That's my great knack – knowing what will work, and what won't.

The pilot had been a huge hit and Sean had been asked to write six more scripts – he had resigned from the City police then, and had worked on the scripts with Harriet until they were the way she wanted them.

He had taken a big gamble, risking failure, but he wasn't married and had only himself to worry about. Sean liked his freedom too much to want to commit to anyone, Harriet suspected, and he was fiercely ambitious. She understood that, because so was she, and Sean was also extraordinarily talented; so far Harriet was convinced he hadn't even begun to stretch himself, but he knew people inside out, and created immediately recognisable characters every week. He had an original mind, hard, cool, logical, and yet with a lot of instinctive understanding of human nature.

The viewers took to the series from the first episode. Every episode ran at least two subplots; they were busy scripts, never a dull moment.

Normally when a series was up and running the original scriptwriter who had come up with the idea moved on, and less expensive, less well-known people took over, but Sean had insisted on continuing to write the series. He didn't want to hand his brain child over to anyone else. No doubt he would one day, thought Harriet, when he felt he'd worked out the mine of storylines he had, but so far there was no sign of him tiring of the series.

But he had soon learnt to value his services, and had rapidly developed a good grasp of negotiating with a cheeseparing company. Billy hated parting with money unless you had a knife to his throat.

Other TV companies were beginning to approach Sean's agent to ask if Sean would work for them. Harriet was terrified that he would take one of these offers and she would lose him for good, both from the series and from her life. They were friends, nothing more, she was afraid they never would be more, but she would miss him if he moved on, and even though The Force was well established and other writers could carry on, the series would never be the same without him.

The actors would do a good job with their characters, but the originality wouldn't be there any more, that sharp, funny, sad spark of life wouldn't survive. It would turn into just another series, like all the rest.

Not that she showed how she felt as he joined her and Annie. 'Thanks for getting here so quickly.' She gave him one of her comradely pats on the shoulders and he grinned.

'He's not here yet, then?'

Sean had once had a run-in with a drunk holding a broken bottle; his face had a faint white scar down the edge of his left cheek which showed livid in daylight and gave him a faintly piratical air.

'No sign of him.'

'You've rung him?'

'Well, what do you think?' Harriet drily asked, and Sean grimaced.

'OK, give me a quiet corner, a copy of today's

shooting script, and ten minutes.' He had his laptop computer in one hand, his portable phone in the other, a battery of pens in the top pocket of his denim jacket.

He hadn't shaved yet, Harriet noticed, his chin bristled with fair stubble. Under the blue jacket he wore a black shirt, open at the neck and tie-less; his jeans were well-worn and faded. He looked more like a villain than a cop.

'Ah, here's your bit of rough,' Mike Waterford had said the other day, having somehow picked up on her feelings for Sean, and although Mike had meant it unpleasantly there was some truth in it. Harriet didn't like her men to be too smooth, and Sean certainly wasn't. He fitted in here, in the market – he could be one of the men busy setting up their stalls all around them. That tough, aggressive look was the last thing you expected from a writer.

'You can use my dressing-room,' Annie offered.

He gave her a brief glance, nodding. 'OK, thanks.'

She opened her handbag to get out the key; the caravan was kept locked while Annie wasn't inside it to guard against petty theft. When they were shooting on location things were always disappearing, which was why, even though she locked her caravan, she kept anything really valuable with her all day.

Annie held out the key to Sean. Behind them a motorbike engine revved noisily, but neither of them noticed.

As Sean took the key from her the bike roared past them. The rider leaned over and snatched Annie's bag out of her hand, at the same time giving her a push sideways.

Annie fell, face down, almost knocking over the

camera. For a minute she was too dazed to realise what had happened.

The motorbike swerved away, picking up speed, through the market, the gathering crowds of people scattering in front of it like the parting of the Red Sea as the children of Israel went through.

Harriet hurried to help Annie to her feet. 'Are you OK?' she asked anxiously.

Annie leaned on her, breathing raggedly for a minute. 'I've got a couple of bruises and my knee's grazed, that's all,' she said when she had got her breath back. 'My tights are ruined! I'll have to change them. And he got my bag!'

Sean had dropped all his equipment and was already running after the bike, shouting, 'Stop him!' to some of the crew, who were standing around a street-café van, eating hot dogs and drinking steaming mugs of tea.

The rider looked over his shoulder. Annie couldn't see his face – he was wearing a black helmet, his face invisible behind the visor.

'He's got a nerve! With all these policemen around! Even if most of them aren't real policemen,' said Derek, joining them. He seemed almost admiring of the thief's daring. Some of the cast in their uniforms were in hot pursuit, and some real policemen joined in the hunt, but the motorbike had disappeared up a narrow alley behind a tight collection of market stalls.

'They've lost him!' Annie groaned.

Sean and the others were a long way behind, but they all piled into the alley after him.

The crowd in the market had thickened; they stood there, faces oddly all the same, flushed with winter cold, eyes bright, staring at the chase, grinning and talking to each other – did they think it was part of the filming?

For heaven's sake, can't they tell it's for real? thought Annie. Yet how should they know? Increasingly people weren't sure what was real and what was acting.

How can they tell the difference between real blood and something out of a plastic bottle, when all they see is the image? Pictures, nothing but moving pictures. How can they distinguish between acting, and genuine naked terror? If the guy on the bike had killed me, would they have applauded? she wondered, shivering. Maybe they would. Christ, what sort of business are we in?

'Did you have much in your bag?' Derek asked her.

White and shaken, she muttered, 'My wallet, with all my money and credit cards.'

'Oh, Annie, how could you be so stupid?' Harriet took off the thick jacket she wore and wrapped it round her shoulders. 'You need some hot, sweet tea; you're in shock.' She looked at one of her trainees, who ran off at once like a well-trained dog to fetch what his mistress wanted.

'A couple of handbags got stolen from the caravans last year – remember?' said Annie. 'That's why I always keep anything valuable with me now.'

Harriet grimaced. 'Well, you'd better ring and cancel your cards at once, before he gets a chance to use them.' She held out her mobile phone. 'You know the number to ring?'

'It's in my diary,' Annie ruefully said.

Seeing her expression, 'Don't tell me!' groaned Harriet. 'The diary's in your handbag! You idiot.' Then she stopped, staring across the market. Sean was walking back towards them. 'Well, I'm damned. What a guy. He's got it back.'

Breathing audibly, his face flushed, Sean reached them and held out the bag. 'We almost got him . . .' He leaned against a wall, his chest heaving. 'God, I must be out of condition. I thought we'd lost him, there was no sign of him in the alley, then suddenly he came back towards us – it was a dead end, he was trapped. I was out in front of the others. When he saw I might catch up he threw the bag at me, put his foot down, swerved and took off again like a bat out of hell.'

'Is your wallet still in the bag?' Harriet asked.

Annie was already looking through the contents – car keys, diary, house keys, wallet, chequebook, credit cards and money all intact. Nothing was missing. She gave a sigh of relief.

'It's all here.' Looking up she smiled at Sean. 'Thank heavens for that. I owe you one, Sean. You were marvellous. As for being out of condition. . .I don't know anyone else who could run fast enough to catch up with a guy on a motorbike.'

'Buy me a drink after work,' he coolly said.

She sensed a leap of tension close to her, felt Harriet staring and looked quickly at her, but Harriet's face was calm and blank.

'Of course; thanks,' Annie slowly said, wondering if Harriet would mind. Some of the crew believed she and Sean had got something going, but they were very discreet about it. 'Actually, I wanted to talk to you, anyway,' she added.

His brows lifted. 'Complaints about my script?'

'Not complaints, of course not. Your scripts are always brilliant.'

His mouth twisted; he had a sardonic cast of face which reflected his instinctive cynicism. 'But . . .?'

Years in the fraud squad of the City of London police had taught Sean to distrust human beings and be wary of them. Annie had learnt to distrust people, too – all the same, she didn't like the hardness in Sean Halifax, he was not an easy man to deal with. He didn't suffer fools gladly; he made her feel uncomfortable, on edge.

'I just wondered how far you're going to go with the love story subplot,' she said with a mixture of defensiveness and aggression. 'I know the script committee decided to feed one in, but it's taking up more time every week, eating into the real meat of the storylines, it's changing the whole feel of my character.'

Sean looked at Harriet, his pale grey eyes ironic. 'Don't tell me, tell Harriet.'

'Look, it works,' Harriet said in a placatory tone. 'The ratings are the only things the board of directors understands or cares about, and they keep going up. You may not be happy, either of you, but our chairman is! Billy is a simple soul.'

Annie snapped, 'He doesn't have to work with Mike Waterford! How would Billy like to have Mike pawing him and trying to get his hand up his skirt?'

Harriet burst out laughing. 'What a picture! Billy doesn't wear a skirt! But if he did, and it would put the ratings up, he'd let Mike Waterford put his hand anywhere he liked!'

Everyone within earshot was listening; they all knew Annie hated working with Mike Waterford. She hadn't hidden her dislike and contempt for the man, and whenever they worked together he set about getting his own back: sabotaging her work: the usual cheap tricks, moving behind her during her big scenes, reacting to lines in a way that threw her off balance. He couldn't do that with Harriet's eagle eye on him, of course – if she spotted any tricks like that, she'd take him apart, but when she wasn't directing he took every chance he got to needle Annie.

He murmured jokes about her just out of earshot, mocked her slyly, gossiped about her, picked on any little mistake she made, made friends with anyone who didn't like her, and on any production there were always people who were jealous or hostile to the star. If she had disliked the man once, she detested him now.

But she had to admit that Harriet had a genius for what made good TV and attracted media attention.

Mike's performance had given a new bite to the series. He had an instinctive, arrogant masculinity with which Annie's character clashed. They were natural opposites, the two ends of a magnetic compass.

'Billy wants me to write in even more scenes of the two of you alone,' Sean told her. 'In fact, he wants me to go a lot further, and have some sex scenes, and I mean real sex, not just a kiss and a fade-out. He wants you both in bed!'

'Over my dead body!' Annie turned crimson with fury.

'The viewers would eat it up,' Harriet drily said.

'I am not getting into a bed with Mike Waterford, especially if I'm expected to take my clothes off first!'

'It's only acting,' Derek said gleefully, grinning ear to ear. 'You know how to act, don't you, darling?'

'Annie's a pro,' said Harriet soothingly. 'She's only making a point. She'll do whatever she has to do, when the time comes.'

Annie was torn between taking that as a compliment, and resenting it. She hoped she did her job professionally – but there were some things she was not prepared to do.

'You're wasting your time, Annie,' Sean said curtly. 'Give me that key. I'll get to work on the new scene.'

She handed him the key and he walked away.

'I'm sorry if you don't like the new storylines,' Harriet said. 'But the public loves them. We're selling the programme all over Europe and the States, Billy is happy, the whole board of the company are happy – their profits are up a fair bit because of the series, so the shareholders are happy, too. I'm afraid they wouldn't listen to any complaints from any of us.'

'You mean from me, don't you, Harriet? You're perfectly happy with Sean's new storylines.'

'Well, yes – they work, so I'm happy,' Harriet shrugged. She changed the subject, staring after Sean. 'He's really quite something, isn't he? Look at those long legs, and those shoulders. That's what I call sexy.'

'Yes,' Annie said absently, still brooding over Mike Waterford.

Harriet shot her a look. 'Been to bed with him, yet?'

Annie did a double-take, hardly believing her ears. 'What? No, I have not! What on earth makes you think I'd want to?'

'You're a woman, aren't you?' Harriet teased, but her eyes were sharp.

Is she jealous? wondered Annie. Is she in love with Sean – has she slept with him? She felt a queer little prickle in her chest at the thought. What's the matter with me? she thought. I'm not jealous over Sean; he annoys me. I hardly know the man outside work. Why should it bother me if he and Harriet have slept together?

'Have you?' she asked, and Harriet gave one of her Mona Lisa smiles.

'That would be telling.' She wasn't admitting to Annie that she had never got that far with Sean.

Annie might not be sleeping with Sean, but there was something between them, a charge of electricity in the air when they were together that Harriet picked up every time. She had built her entire career on her instincts, she was rarely wrong about people or situations, and she was sure there was some sort of situation between Annie and Sean, even if Annie was blind to it.

'I'll go and try to raise Mike again,' she added, changing the subject.

Annie noticed the deliberate evasion. 'You might as well try to raise the Titanic!' she crossly said.

Harriet walked away, laughing, and Derek Fenn growled, 'They ought to sack the bastard. He's past being a joke. Why should we all have to stand around freezing our balls off for him? Marty says he's sleeping with that new kid, the girl with no tits – he's welcome to her. I like a woman to look like a woman, not a boy with acne.'

Annie looked sharply at him. 'Marty?'

'Come off it, you know Marty.' Derek gave her a funny, sly smile. 'A redhead, working in wardrobe, I've known her for donkey's years. I have a lot of time for Marty, she's a fighter and she's had a tough life, bringing up those kids on her own.'

Annie felt a shiver run down her spine. 'I've never seen her before. What makes you think I know her?'

Derek's cynical eyes mocked her. 'She's Roger's wife, darling – don't pretend you don't remember him!

They sacked him from drama school because of you, remember?'

Remember? How could she ever forget? She had never talked about him to Derek – how much did Derek know about what happened?

'He couldn't get another job with that sort of reputation hanging round his neck, so he walked out on his family,' Derek told her. 'He ran off to Australia with some barmaid and Marty was left with three kids and no money coming in. She's pretty bitter about you.'

Angrily, Annie burst out, 'I'm sorry for her, but it isn't fair to blame me. It was Roger's fault, not mine. I wasn't the first girl he tried to blackmail into bed. If I hadn't blown the whistle on him he'd still be there, doing it to every promising newcomer he fancied.'

Derek shrugged his narrow shoulders, coughing. 'Oh, he was a bastard, you're right, but Marty's not very logical about the guy. She's still hung up on him, I think, although she did divorce him because her lawyer persuaded her it was the wisest thing to do, to establish ownership of their house.'

'And he didn't contest it?' Annie asked huskily, on edge to hear whether his wife was in touch with Roger Keats.

'They couldn't trace him. She had to wait years before she could divorce him in his absence – she only did it a couple of years ago. Funnily enough, a few weeks after the divorce came through she says she met someone who had seen him in Devon, working for a rep company touring the West Country.'

Annie was icy cold. She looked around the market – he could be here, now, watching them.

There were all these men working on the series – he could be one of them. Extras playing policemen, anonymous in their uniforms, wearing helmets which half-hid their faces; actors in one of the bit parts as market traders or criminals; the various craftsmen, electricians, sound men, carpenters who put together mock façades to change the look of shops and houses. There were a dozen different trades working on any programme and they were often switched around, apart from the top men who Harriet liked to have working with her.

Roger could have changed his appearance out of all recognition in eight years. She might be seeing him every day without knowing him.

Trudie Lang was lost; she had been walking for ages and she didn't recognise any of the streets. She had a feeling she had lost something. Had she been alone, or had Annie been with her? Her heart skipped a beat. She turned to go back home and stopped, confused. Which was the way home?

'I've lost my little girl,' she said to a man walking just behind her. 'Have you seen her? She's so high . . .' She held her hand knee high. 'With long blonde hair and blue eyes.'

The man was wearing jeans and a thick denim jacket with a black sweater under it. I've seen him before somewhere, Trudie thought.

'Do I know you?' she asked uncertainly, and then remembered the car that had stopped, the face staring at her. That had been him, hadn't it? He'd followed her!

'Do you?' he softly said.

Why had he followed her?

'Who are you?' Her voice quavered. She knew him, she was sure she knew him. A long time ago, she had done something terrible to him; she couldn't remember what she had done but she was sure he didn't like her, and she was frightened.

'Let me take you home. Come along.'

He smiled, but she wasn't taken in. She backed, staring. He was older than she remembered. What was his name? She tried to remember but it slipped away. That happened more and more often these days. She looked fixedly at his high forehead, the way his hair sprang back, thick and wiry, his eyes and mouth. Panic surged through her.

No, she knew now – she'd got it wrong. She hadn't done anything terrible to him. It was the other way round. He had done something terrible to Annie. He had hurt her Annie.

Rage flared inside her. She ran at him, began hitting him with screwed up fists, punching him in the chest, the face.

'You bastard ... bastard ... bastard ... stay away from my Annie! Don't you go near her, ever again.'

His face was livid. She saw rage, hatred, in his eyes, he reached towards her, she felt a blow in her chest, went flying backwards, off the pavement, just as a bus came towards them.

There was a grinding of brakes, the bus skidded sideways across the road, missing her by inches.

Trudie couldn't remember what had happened for a moment. The bus had stopped; the driver got out and began shouting at her, passengers stared out of the windows, passers-by stood on the pavement staring, too. Trudie limped hurriedly across the road to the other side, ignoring them all, began shuffling along beside iron railings, a green hedge behind them.

She looked through gaps in the hedge and saw green

turf, trees. A park, she thought – of course, that was where Annie must be!

Annie loved to play in the park, on the swings, chasing a ball across grass.

When she got through the gates, though, she couldn't see Annie anywhere. Maybe she had gone home? There were children running about everywhere, but Annie wasn't with them.

Trudie had to sit down. Under a bare, chestnut tree stood a green-painted wooden bench. She staggered along the path to it, a hand to her heaving chest, and sank down with a groan.

She watched people walking their dogs and children going down the slide or swinging. Annie always loved to swing.

People stared back but nobody spoke to her.

'Nosy parkers,' she shouted at two women who were giving her a wide berth as they walked past, eyes like saucers. 'What're you staring at? Haven't you got anything better to do?'

A policeman came through the iron gates of the park and headed towards her.

Trudie got up and began to run. The path was wet and slippery. She skidded and fell heavily.

Sean was back within twenty minutes, having rewritten the shooting script to cut Mike out of one scene; they began work at once, under the fascinated gaze of the crowds gathering in the market. It was a slow process with many stops and starts, and intensely boring for much of the time. People got bored with watching them after a while and wandered away, but there was always someone with time to kill.

Mike Waterford finally arrived at ten-fifteen. He

was clearly hung-over, pale and with red rims to his dark eyes, his auburn hair only roughly combed. Before going off to make-up, he came over to Harriet.

'Sorry I'm late, darling, I slept through my alarm. Touch of flu, I expect.'

'Too much whisky, more likely,' Annie muttered.

He ignored her, giving Harriet a coaxing smile. 'Can you leave my scenes until I've had some black coffee? I've got a pig of a headache.'

'There is some justice, then,' Annie said and he turned on her, baring his very white teeth.

'What's your problem, sweetie? Time of the month – or haven't you got it off lately?'

'I'm just sick of you swanning in here four hours late when the rest of us have been here since crack of dawn!'

'It shows, too,' he sneered. 'Or do you always look like death warmed up? Oh, yes, you do, don't you?'

Harriet grabbed his arm and steered him away before Annie could hit him, took him off to wardrobe and sent someone to get him black coffee, and lots of it.

'One day I'll kill that bastard!' Annie told her when she came back.

'It was your idea to have him in the series!' Harriet teased her, and her teeth met.

Unfortunately it was true, although the last thing Annie would have wanted was to put such an idea into Harriet's head.

When they first began working together Annie had complained to Harriet that she couldn't sleep late on a Saturday, although she usually had the day off, because at ten o'clock every Saturday morning the courier from the studio arrived on his motorbike with the script, which she had to go downstairs to accept in person.

'No excuses. Billy has a bee in his bonnet about it,' Harriet had said.

Billy Grenaby, the chairman of Midland TV, was approaching forty but looking much younger, a short man with wide shoulders and a deep chest, and dark hair turning grey in streaks. He had incredible amounts of sexual energy, which made him hyperactive; he couldn't keep still for a second, and kept his eye on every single nut and bolt in the organisation. His marriage had failed a year ago when his much younger wife took off with a tennis player she met in Florida on a long holiday. The shock to his ego had left Billy's temper on a short fuse, and he had become practically paranoid overnight.

The company offices came out in a rash of notices signed by Billy giving orders on everything from never, never going over budget down to remembering to turn off the light if you were the last to leave a room. He was unable to delegate, either because he didn't trust anybody after his wife's defection, or because he needed to know what everyone was doing.

'But why can't they just slip it through my letter-box?' Annie had asked indignantly. 'Why do I have to get up and sign for it?'

'That's what they used to do, but last year Mike Waterford turned up for a big day's taping on that nuclear series, Meltdown, not knowing his words. Claimed he'd never been sent a script. The couriers swore one had been posted through his letterbox, but they couldn't prove it. It was their word against Mike's.'

Knowing Mike Waterford, Annie had backed the

couriers. She had worked with Mike once or twice. Tall, with thick auburn hair and dark eyes, he was sexy and charismatic, with a multitude of fans, but his colleagues knew him better than the public did. He was lazy, a heavy drinker, a womaniser, and a selfish actor, always turning up late, going out of his way to upstage and out-act anyone even if it ruined a production. In Annie's book that was Mike's unforgivable sin.

'Billy should have sacked him,' she said vindictively, and Harriet laughed, giving her an amused, knowing look.

'What did he do to you? Personal, or professional?'

Annie had grimaced her distaste. 'It would never be personal, I wouldn't touch him with a barge-pole!' Mike Waterford reminded her too much of Roger Keats – they were the same type. Under all that phony charm there was cruelty, malice, a delight in humiliating and hurting women.

'He's big box-office, though,' Harriet had drawled, grinning. 'Billy couldn't sack him, much as he was tempted to – Mike *was* that series. No, they shot round him as much as they could, but it put the schedule back twenty-four hours and Billy went spare, you know how he hates delays. They cost money, and money is Billy's life blood.'

'Can I quote you?'

Harriet laughed wryly. 'No, I like my job too much. Anyway, since Mike screwed up, a courier has to deliver a script to the actor in person, and get a signature for it. So don't forget – you always have to be there on a Saturday morning to sign for the script.'

'I won't forget. At least Mike isn't working on this series,' Annie had muttered.

Harriet had done a double-take, her head whirling round as she stared with parted mouth and round eyes. Only six months later did Annie discover why – the day Mike Waterford's name appeared in the tabloids as the new chief constable and co-star of The Force. It infuriated Annie that she had put the idea of hiring him into Harriet's brain. Up till then, Annie had been the major name in the series: the rest of the cast were solid, well-known British character actors, trained in the theatre, highly professional, easy to work with, but none of them big names.

Annie herself hadn't been a big name when she began working on The Force, but Mike was, undeniably, a star, with an enormous following and a big salary. Billy hadn't wanted to pay anybody the sort of money a star would expect; the new police series had been intended to make money, not cost it.

Annie's career had been considerably enhanced by appearing in the series. It had been a plus that she really enjoyed the part. What she had liked, particularly, was the fact that her policewoman didn't have a man in the background.

Sean had created the central role of Inspector Ruth Granard as a very modern career woman, tough and ambitious, even abrasive in relation to the men she worked with, and so determined to get to the top that she had no time for a private life. She did not want to be distracted from her work.

There was an edge to playing the part that Annie enjoyed, and as Sean got to know Annie better he had given Inspector Granard more of Annie's real character, given a spin to the role which had not been there before.

Annie's very delicate, feminine looks made an ironic

counterpoint to the toughness of the policewoman she played, and Sean emphasised the contrast between the way the character looked and the job she did, and always listened to Annie's own views on the part.

They sometimes had lunch together, alone or with Harriet too, to talk over ideas for later scripts, and Annie liked the respect Sean gave her. Some writers got irritated if you tried to suggest ideas to them.

When they began work on a second series Harriet, though, had decided some changes were due. She'd felt the cast was unbalanced, and Billy Grenaby agreed with her.

He was a tough businessman, but he had a simple mind when it came to programme-planning; his ideas were old-fashioned, basic, always taking the obvious line, which was probably why he had been so successful. He backed Harriet up a hundred per cent when she took her latest idea to him.

Nobody had told any of the cast what was afoot when the company began talks with Mike Waterford.

'I don't believe it! Tell me it's not true!' Annie had yelled at Harriet, waving the newspaper which had broken the story.

Unbothered by her rage, Harriet had laughed. 'You gave me the idea yourself. Remember? When we talked about Mike and you said thank God he wasn't in the series. I had a flash of inspiration. Don't you see, this is what we need to turn a good series into a number-one hit? You two are going to make TV history. You loathe each other, and I'm going to make sure the media get to hear about it; they'll eat it up.'

She had been proved right; the press had become

obsessed for a long time with the famous 'feud' between the two stars of the series, and the torrent of publicity had pushed up the ratings week after week.

At eleven forty-five, with three brief scenes in the can, they broke for lunch from the mobile canteen. The food wasn't cordon bleu stuff, but it was adequate – smoking hot pea soup in a mug, which was very welcome on a cold February day after standing around for hours waiting for cues, followed by either a cheese salad or beef stew and dumplings.

'Stewed dog meat and cannon balls, you mean,' Mike Waterford said to the girl dishing out the food. 'Give me one of those cheese salads, darling.'

The girl gave him a fatuous smile. 'Here you are, Mr Waterford. Would you like a jacket potato too?'

Annie was stamping her feet and blowing on her frozen fingers. 'Get on with it, Waterford!' she told him and Mike gave her a look over his shoulder.

'What! my dear Lady Disdain, are you yet living?'

They had once appeared together at a charity benefit show in a scene from Shakespeare's Much Ado About Nothing, playing the quarrelling lovers, Benedick and Beatrice, and ever since Mike had enjoyed quoting from the scene. He liked everyone to know that he was what he called a 'serious' actor, had played in Shakespeare, was a star, unlike the workaday hacks of television soap opera.

'Oh, shut your face!' snarled Annie.

'Charming,' Mike drawled, strolling away.

The girl behind the counter gazed after him, sighing. 'He's so gorgeous, isn't he?'

'Pea soup and cheese salad, please,' Annie bit out.

The girl pulled herself together and handed over the

mug of soup and the salad, giving her a filthy look with them.

Annie took her lunch back to her caravan, where she ate in front of the warmth of an electric fire, reading over the lines of the next scene. The lunch break was short. At this time of year, the light went fast, and they would start again at twelve-thirty, hoping to shoot another couple of scenes by four o'clock, after which they could all go home.

The first of these scenes worked without needing any retakes; after that they got in some close-ups while anyone not involved drank black coffee and huddled in their coats in the caravans, gossiping and hoping it would soon be time to go home.

The final scene of the day involved Mike, Annie and a number of police vehicles. The logistics of the operation were eased by the fact that by then the market had wound down and most of the people had drifted off, clearing the street.

Annie was sitting in a canvas chair watching Mike getting in and out of a police car while other cars raced towards him. The timing had to be exact; the stunt manager kept stopping the action and conferring with his stunt drivers before he tried again.

Annie was very tired now, she had run out of energy and kept yawning. Harriet gave her a wry grin.

'Bored?'

'Tired.' Annie was never bored when she was working; she hoped to God she never would be.

'You and me both.' Harriet stretched, her face pale and exhausted by the strains of the long day.

One of Harriet's trainees came running out of the production caravan, looked around and hurried over to them. She bent over Harriet and began whispering urgently.

Harriet turned to look at Annie, and, seeing her expression, Annie felt a leap of alarm and got to her feet. 'Is something wrong? What is it? What's happened?'

Harriet came and put an arm round her, watching her with concern. 'There was a call from London Hospital – your mother's been taken there, she's had an accident.'

3

'I'll drive you there now.'

Annie was so distraught she didn't realise who was speaking for a moment or two, then she recognised Sean's deep voice and looked at him, her blue eyes wide and darkened with distress and anxiety.

'That's OK, I can get a taxi. Harriet will need you.'

Sean put a hand under her elbow, his face insistent. 'I've finished here for the day. Someone should go with you.'

'Yes, I agree, I'd come with you myself, but I can't leave until this last scene is safely in the can,' Harriet said. 'I hope it isn't anything serious, Annie. If you need time off, let me know — we can work round you or Sean can rewrite the script to leave you out of next week's schedules.'

Annie nodded, but she was too worried about her mother to think of anything else. She followed Sean over to the sleek black Porsche, stopped and looked down at her suit, said abstractedly, 'Oh, I should change into my own clothes. Wardrobe will want this back.'

'Never mind that now, don't worry about it.' Harriet kissed her cheek. 'Keep in touch. Ring me and let me know how your mother is.'

Sean started the engine and the Porsche shot away; Annie almost catapulted through the windscreen.

'Seatbelt!'

The bark of Sean's voice made her jump. She fumbled with the seatbelt, finally managing to slot it into place across her. What sort of accident had her mother had? It wasn't the first time Trudie had hurt herself — she was always doing it, she got cuts and bruises all the time, but she rarely hurt herself badly enough to be taken to hospital and Annie was frightened. This might be it, the moment when her mother was taken away from her for good.

Doctors had been warning her for a year past that Trudie was fast losing her grip on reality, but she kept hoping against hope that her mother would improve.

When they reached the hospital's grim Victorian grey walls, she stared up at them with foreboding.

'It looks like a prison, doesn't it? My mother hates coming here,' she muttered, shivering.

'She probably didn't see it if she was in an ambulance,' comforted Sean. 'My mother hates hospitals, too, but she never lets on what's really bugging her. She's too busy looking after everyone else.'

Annie looked at him in such obvious surprise that he laughed.

'What's the matter? Didn't you think I had a mother?'

She laughed too. 'Is she proud of you for becoming a famous writer?'

'She's a fan of yours, rather than mine,' he said, startling her again.

'I'm sure she isn't!' Annie got out of the car; so did Sean.

'Come home with me one day and meet her and find out.' He locked his Porsche and turned to join her. 'I'll come in with you.'

'I'll be OK, I'll get a taxi home,' Annie said, but he ignored her protest and followed her as she hurried towards the great glass doors of the hospital, which slid apart electronically.

She looked small and lost in the busy ant heap of the hospital reception lobby – like a child, in spite of the grey suit and police haircut. She didn't want him around, but he wasn't being shaken off. She might need someone around to lean on if she got bad news about her mother.

Annie asked at the reception desk where she could find her mother, and was directed to the right ward. 'On the first floor, keep turning left, follow the signs overhead, you can't miss it,' the receptionist told her, staring. She was a woman in her forties, plump, fresh-faced, with henna-dyed hair. 'You're . . . are you . . . Annie Lang? The actress? You're in that police thing, that soap . . . with Mike Waterford, aren't you?'

Annie nodded, desperate to get to her mother, turning away.

'I knew I knew you, the minute you walked in, I couldn't put my finger on it, but I recognised you.' The receptionist laughed excitedly, very flushed.

As Sean joined them the woman glanced eagerly at him, obviously hoping to recognise him, too. Her face fell when she realised she had never seen him before and she looked back at Annie.

'I never miss your series, it keeps you on the edge of your seat – and that Mike Waterford's so sexy. I love it when you and him have one of those fights. Mind you, in your shoes, I'd grab him before someone else does. Are we going to see you two get closer together? I did laugh this week, when he frisked that girl and she slapped his face! Tell him from me I'd let him frisk me any time.'

Annie managed a watery smile and escaped. Sean

laughed softly as they walked miles along narrow, shadowy corridors to find the ward.

'You see? The authentic voice of the great unwashed. She wants more of you and Mike – especially the fights, and she wants the two of you in bed. Billy's right, damn him. Sex is what sells.'

Annie wasn't listening to him, she would normally have snapped back angrily, but she couldn't care less at that moment. She was too anxious.

The ward sister, tall and willowy, in white and blue, came out to meet them and gave Annie an eager smile, recognising her.

'Oh, Miss Lang . . . it is you! You got our message, then? The TV people told us you might not get here for hours. You were quick.'

'How is she?'

The sister's face took on a more professional look. 'Well . . .' She glanced quickly at Sean and her expression changed, she seemed taken aback, even startled. 'Are you related to the patient, too?'

Annie kept forgetting he was there. She shook her head. 'A colleague.'

'I didn't feel she should come alone,' Sean said curtly. His eyes narrowed. 'Haven't we met before somewhere?'

'You're a policeman, aren't you? I met you a couple of times when you visited patients,' said the sister drily. 'In a professional capacity. And once when you came in to have stitches in that cut on your face – a bottle, wasn't it?'

He grinned suddenly. 'Of course – I remember you now, you weren't a sister then. Staff Nurse Collins, wasn't it?'

'What a memory! Typical policeman. Policemen and

elephants never forget.' Sister Collins was laughing, flattered.

'Was my mother badly injured?' Annie asked, and the sister sobered.

'Broken hip, I'm afraid; very painful and it will be a long time before she can get about again. She is sedated at the moment, but you can see her. She isn't making much sense, though – shock, of course. At her age any trauma can be serious. She doesn't have the reserves needed to recover quickly from an accident like that.'

'What exactly happened?'

'Apparently she was running away from a policeman,' the sister said, giving Sean a sideways look.

'A policeman?' His brows shot up.

'Was it you?'

'Running away?' Annie was bewildered. 'I don't understand. Why was she running away? Where did all this happen?'

'In Albert Park, just ten minutes from here. And your mother was in her nightie and dressing-gown!'

'What? But how could she have got out of the house like that? There should have been someone with her.'

'Well, she was alone.' The sister glanced at Sean. 'I'm sorry, you can't go in – just Miss Lang. This way, Miss Lang.'

She led Annie into the long, cream-painted ward closely packed with beds from which old, worried faces stared. Trudie was in a bed near the door. She looked frail, face lined with pain and age, bluish stains under her eyes, around her bloodless mouth. Annie picked up her clawlike hand and held it, her mother's skin like thin, crinkly tissue over the protruding bones.

Tenderness moved inside her chest. She stroked the

workworn roughness of her mother's palms, the bony knuckles, and thought of Trudie working in the green-grocer's shop all those years, up at first light, getting to bed late every day, looking after her when she was small, doing the shopping and cooking, running a home as well as running the shop. Trudie had had a hard life. It was ten minutes before Trudie sighed and opened her eyes, looked at her and pulled her hand free.

'Who're you?'

'It's me, it's Annie, Mum.' Annie wanted to burst into tears.

'Annie? You're not my little Annie.' Trudie looked around the ward wildly. 'Who are you? What do you want?'

Annie tried to take her hand again and Trudie slapped her away.

'No, let go of me! What are you after?'

'Mum. Oh, Mum. Don't. Look at me. It's Annie.'

The sob in her voice got through to her mother. Trudie peered at her, uncertainty clouding her eyes, then something leapt in her face and she reached out a trembling hand, clutched at her daughter. 'Annie?'

Wrenched with a sigh of relief, Annie smiled, hold-ing the thin old hand between both her own. 'Yes, it's me, Mum. How do you feel?'

Her voice tremulous, Trudie whispered, 'What's wrong with me? I keep forgetting . . . all confused, I forgot you'd grown up.'

'It's the drugs they're giving you,' lied Annie, hold-ing back the tears.

'I won't take drugs,' Trudie flared up, getting angry. 'Tell them not to give me drugs!'

'I will, Mum.'

The old woman sighed deeply and closed her eyes, but still held on to Annie's hand tightly.

Sean came through the swing doors and walked over to the bed to look down at her. 'How is she?' he asked Annie in a whisper.

'She's going to be OK,' Annie said, more because it was what she wanted to believe than because it was the truth. 'Didn't the sister say you shouldn't come in?'

'She's gone for a meal break and the nurse left on duty is busy in the kitchen,' Sean coolly said.

He leaned on the wall, half-hidden by the shabby green curtains that could be drawn around the bed when privacy was required. Around them old people coughed and shifted, sighed and snored. This was a geriatric ward; there were no young people here and there was an atmosphere of defeat in the air. Sean stared around at the other beds, the other old, tired, faces, absorbing the scene and memorising it for future use.

Trudie's eyes opened suddenly; she looked up with fear in her face. 'Annie . . . Annie, he tried to kill me.'

Sean stiffened, his eyes flicking back to her at once.

'Who did? What are you talking about, Mum?' Annie didn't take it seriously, her voice was soothing, placatory. Her mother never made much sense these days.

'I recognised him the minute I saw him, even after all these years. He'd changed, but I knew him all right and he knew me, he gave me such a look! Then he tried to push me under a bus.'

Annie inhaled sharply, convinced by the fear in her mother's voice. 'What? Where was this?'

'The bus almost hit me, it had to brake so hard it almost crashed. I ran into a park to get away – I was so scared. That's how I fell. I was in such a state I didn't know what I was doing.' Trudie's voice shook with terror, Annie tightened her hold on the cold hand she held.

'Ssh . . . Mum, it's OK, you're safe. Don't look so scared, I won't let anything hurt you.'

Sean moved and Trudie looked towards him, gasped, her pale mouth quivering. 'Who's that? Get him away . . . who is he?'

The ward sister appeared, frowning. 'I thought I told you to wait outside?' she crossly snapped at Sean. 'Please go out. Miss Lang, your mother seems upset. I'm sorry, I think you had better leave now.'

'Don't leave me, Annie,' pleaded Trudie. 'Don't let them give me drugs, I'm afraid of forgetting again. He might get in here while I'm asleep. He hates me. . .he blames us!'

Annie's eyes met Sean's. He read the fear and distress in her face and his brows jerked together.

The sister said, 'We'll make sure nobody gets in here, Mrs Lang, don't you worry. You mustn't get excited, it's bad for you. Say goodbye, Miss Lang.'

Annie obediently bent to kiss her mother, whispered soothingly, 'I'll talk to them, Mum. You have to have some drugs, to help you get better, but I'll tell them not to give you the ones that make you forget. Is there anything I can bring you? Your knitting? Some magazines?'

'Take me home, Annie. I want to go home.' Trudie tried to move and fell back with a cry of agony; the cloudy bewilderment came into her face again. 'What's wrong with me? I can't move. What am I doing here? Where is this place?'

'You'd really better go, we'll take care of her,' the ward sister said, steering Annie away from the bed.

Looking back at her mother, Annie saw a young nurse bending over her, talking calmly to her, giving her a drink of water.

'She told me someone tried to kill her,' Annie said uneasily. 'A man tried to push her under a bus, she said.'

The sister frowned. 'We were told by the police that she was sitting in a park and when she saw a policeman she started to run and fell over. There was no mention of anyone trying to kill her.'

'You think she imagined it?' Sean asked curtly.

The sister shrugged. 'Well, at her age, with her mental condition . . . that has to be a possibility, you know. They get these fantasies, I'm afraid; all sorts of ideas get jumbled up. When the mind is losing its grip on reality, people no longer always know the difference between real life and something they've seen on TV or read – they get confused, start imagining all sorts of things.'

'It happens even when they aren't suffering from senility,' Sean wryly said. 'A lot of our audience can't tell the difference between TV and real life at all.' He looked at Annie's white, troubled face. 'Come on, I'll take you home.'

'And don't worry too much,' said Sister Collins. 'We'll take good care of your mother.' She smiled suddenly. 'We're all big fans of your programme, Miss Lang. I shall watch it with even more interest now I've met you. It will make it more like real life.'

Annie went through the motions of responding, smiling, saying, 'Thank you, that's very kind,' before she began to move away, still smiling tightly, her jaw aching and her cheekbones locked in that mimicry of a smile.

Sean insisted on driving Annie back home. 'You're in no state to go alone,' he said, putting·her into his Porsche. 'You've had a bad shock.'

Annie didn't argue; she was too abstracted. Had Trudie imagined an attack on her? It had been horribly convincing, in spite of what Sean and the ward sister had said. But why on earth would anyone want to harm Trudie?

'I recognised him,' Trudie had said. 'He hates me . . . he blames us.'

Who on earth could she be talking about? Could it be Roger?

She frowned; she would start getting paranoid if she wasn't careful. Why on earth would he attack her mother? He had only met Trudie a couple of times, when she came to the school for public performances in which Annie had a part. He had spent some time talking to her after the first night of Hamlet, of course, and Trudie usually remembered faces – most shop-keepers had a good memory for faces. Trudie undoubt-edly remembered Roger.

Annie's stomach turned, remembering his kiss on stage when they were taking their curtain calls; she could even remember the smell of his skin, the after-shave he must have used, the odour of his sweat, could feel his tongue sliding in and out of her mouth like a wriggling snake.

Eight years and she hadn't forgotten a second of it. He had made sure of that. Or would she have been haunted by him even if he hadn't kept sending her Valentine's cards? Some nightmares keep recurring however hard you try to forget.

He had talked to her mother that night, during the stage party, while he had his arm around her waist, while his fingertips secretly fondled the underside of her breast, out of sight. Yes, he would remember her mother, and Trudie would certainly remember him because she had thought him charming, and because he had been important at the drama school.

But it had been Annie who blew the whistle on him and lost him his job. Trudie had had no part in that. But she was her mother, and Roger Keats would guess that if anything happened to Trudie because of her she would go mad.

When they got back to the white Edwardian house in South Park they found Jerri, her mother's companion, sitting in the lounge with her bags packed beside her, watching television while she waited for Annie to come home.

'What happened, Jerri?' Annie asked.

'I was cooking her breakfast and she got out, I didn't hear a thing, I'd left her in front of the TV and when I went back with her breakfast she'd vanished. I'm just not up to the job; she's a twenty-four-hour-a-day liability and I can't cope with her. If you'll just pay me what you owe me so far, I'll go.'

Annie didn't argue; she wrote out a cheque then asked, 'Nobody came to the house, did they? This morning?'

Blankly, Jerri shook her head. 'Were you expecting someone?'

'No, but my mother said there was a man hanging around outside, someone she recognised.'

'Well, nobody came to the house. It was probably one of the neighbours. After all, she knows nearly all of them. Look, Annie, she's out of it, she doesn't know tea from coffee any more. I don't know what she was on about but I do know nobody came to the house this morning. Sometimes Mrs Adams from Number 3 comes over to have a chat with her, or that old woman with the blue-rinsed hair calls in, but nobody came today. If anyone had rung the bell or knocked, I would have heard them. Can I ring for a taxi?'

Annie nodded. Sean wandered over to the window and was pushing aside the curtain to look out into the suburban street. It was dusk now, the street-lights had come on, making pools of yellow at intervals along the pavement, across which fell the shadows of the bare, pollarded plane trees which lined the street.

There was a taxi rank outside South Park Underground station; Jerri's taxi arrived five minutes later and Annie went to the front door with her while Sean wandered into the kitchen at the back of the house, made tea and carried the tea-tray through to the long, comfortably furnished sitting-room. The colours were faded, the furniture a muddle of periods. He suspected the room had looked this way for a long time; much of the furniture dated back to the nineteen-twenties but some of it was far more modern. Had Annie's family lived in this house for many years?

Annie shut the front door and came back, looking startled as she saw the tea.

'Did you make that?'

'I thought we could both do with some tea,' he half apologised. 'It's a habit you pick up in the police force.' He handed her a cup and she sat down, nursing it. Sean sat down too, his eyes intent. 'You took what your mother said about being attacked very seriously, didn't you? I think you knew what she was talking about. Are you and your mother in some sort of trouble?'

'I don't know. It's just . . . oh, something happened,

years ago, when I was at drama school.' Annie hesitated, she had never talked about it before, but Sean's steady eyes and air of never being surprised or shocked by anything somehow made it easy to talk to him. Was that, too, something he had picked up in the police force? Or had he been born with it?

She needed to talk to someone so she told him about Roger Keats, her eyes not meeting his.

'And ever since you've had a Valentine's card from him every year? Have you kept any of them?' Sean asked.

'All of them,' she said huskily, and his eyes narrowed.

'Although you hated him?'

Her lips trembled. 'Because I hated him,' she whispered. 'I was afraid to destroy them.'

'Could I see them?'

Annie shivered and knew she couldn't bear to show them to him. 'Not tonight. I'm so tired, would you mind going now? I'm very grateful, you've been very kind, but I've had enough for one day.'

'Has it occurred to you that tomorrow is Valentine's Day?'

'You don't really think I've forgotten that?' she snapped, at the end of her tether.

Sean gave her a quick look; it was rare for her to lose her temper, she was usually so quiet and cool. But then she was under a lot more pressure than he had realised when he went with her to the hospital. He had seen how upset she was, which was only natural, but now he knew Annie was disturbed about far more than her mother's accident, and her problems went back a long, long way.

'Alright, don't blow your top,' he said, pouring her

some more tea. 'I don't imagine either you or your mother are in any danger. If he has been sending you threats once a year all that time he isn't going to turn dangerous now.'

She had told herself that over and over again. She sipped her tea, staring at the electric fire he had switched on to warm the room up. Dusk had fallen; the glow of the fire was a reassurance.

'But if it was him . . . today . . . following my mother . . .' she stammered, glancing sideways at him with unconscious appeal, her blue eyes very wide and dilated.

'If it was,' agreed Sean, staring down into those eyes, with their huge, glazed black pupils, and thinking that they reminded him of the dark blue of gentians in the Swiss mountains in spring. What lay behind them, though? What went on inside Annie's head? 'But she isn't too strong on reality just now, is she? And why would he wait so long? It doesn't add up. He gets a turn-on from sending you those cards, that's all, getting his own back by making you jumpy. There's a pattern there; he's a type I've met before. They don't generally come out of the woodwork, just go on sniping from the dark. The sort who sends poison-pen letters – that's the category your old drama teacher fits in!'

She made a wryly amused face. 'You still think like a policeman!'

He shrugged. 'Can't help it. I did the job for too long – and it isn't a bad training for a writer, either. You see human nature in the raw, that's for sure.'

She looked at him curiously. 'Yes, your scripts are horribly realistic.'

He laughed shortly. 'Thanks – if it was a compliment! It didn't sound as if it was.'

Defensive, she insisted, 'I like the realism in the series, it gives it a far sharper edge.'

'Thank you,' he said, a faint flush creeping along his angular cheekbones, and she watched the faint, pale scar stand out because the flush did not show in it. Sean added roughly, 'Just don't fret over this guy turning up and threatening you – I think he's the wrong type to do that.'

She bit her lip. 'Maybe – it's just that . . . well, his wife showed up today, out of the blue.'

That shook Sean. 'His wife?' He almost spilt his own tea, put the cup down carefully. 'What do you mean – showed up?'

'She started working in wardrobe this week. While we were filming I saw her talking to Derek.' Annie swallowed hard. 'She . . . She looked at me as if she hated me.'

Sean was frowning again. 'Is she the woman who was wearing purple and bright red, and had orange hair?'

Annie did a double-take. 'You noticed her?'

His mouth had a hard amusement. 'She's not easy to miss, and she's the only newcomer in wardrobe, I knew all the other women. Policemen get used to watching faces all the time, even off duty. Look, why don't I have a casual word with her – find out if her husband is back in London?'

'Would you?' She looked up at him, eyes wide and dark with a mixture of hope and weariness. 'I'd be glad if you could.' She bit her lip. 'Be careful, though, he's a nasty piece of work.'

He touched her cheek with one long index finger. 'I'll be very careful.' He smiled down at her. 'Thanks for worrying.'

115

The gesture was comforting, she closed her eyes, sighing. 'He scares me rigid. He always did.'

Sean put his arms around her and held her gently, without pressure, his cheek against her hair. She leaned on him gratefully, tempted to ask him to stay all night. She was nervous about being left alone. All her life her mother had been there, she had never been alone in the house before, and it scared her to think of Roger Keats out there in London somewhere.

'If he comes near you again, let me know,' Sean quietly said. 'I'll sort him out, don't worry. I know how to handle men like that. So you can stop worrying about him, leave him to me.'

She was close to tears, looking up at him, trying to smile. 'You're very kind.' She was surprised to realise it was true – she had always thought of him as tough and determined; she hadn't suspected he could be gentle, too.

'Don't cry. Are you really scared? You know, I don't think you should be alone here.'

If she asked him to stay all night he would – that was what he was offering – but what if he expected to sleep with her? Her body quivered and grew hot.

She had found him attractive from the beginning, but she had thought he probably belonged to Harriet, and she wasn't into stealing men from other women. She still didn't know whether or not he was Harriet's lover – Harriet had never actually admitted it, she never talked about her private life, and Annie respected her for it. Everyone was entitled to some privacy. Sean had never given any clues, either. He was another one who kept his private life to himself. Interviews with him usually went into his police career, but she never remembered reading anything about his love life. Looking the way he did he probably scared most reporters rigid and stopped them asking the usual intrusive questions.

She never talked about her love life, either – but then she hadn't had a lover since Johnny vanished.

Sean said, 'You shouldn't really be alone, you know. I think I'd better stay, don't you?'

Contrarily, she at once shook her head, her eyes opening, her body cold again now that she had conjured Johnny up, as if the mere memory of him was enough to kill every other emotion. My once and future lover, she thought, wrenched by pain and loss. Will I ever get over him? Maybe I've never tried hard enough? Maybe if I went to bed with Sean I might finally break the spell?

But she couldn't, she straightened up, politely pushed Sean away. 'Thanks, but I'll be OK. I'll put the alarms on and lock the house up tighter than a drum. I'll be fine.'

His face changed, cooled. 'Well, up to you, of course,' he said offhandedly. 'But it might be wiser if you weren't alone tonight.'

She didn't meet his eyes. 'I'll be OK. I'll ring the police if I hear so much as a mouse. Goodnight, Sean, and thanks.'

His Porsche took off a moment later and she shut the front door, shivering in the cold February wind.

A small Ford was parked just down the road outside Annie's house. The driver leaned back in the shadows, watching the lights of the black Porsche disappear.

Sean Halifax had only stayed half an hour. He had begun to think Halifax might stay all night. He was the scriptwriter on the series – but maybe he was more than that. Maybe he was . . . a friend . . . of hers? Or something closer? Had she ever confided in him, talked about the past?

. The gloved hands tightened on the wheel. Halifax had been a copper, hadn't he? Nosy bastard. If he was too nosy, he might have to die too.

He had seen her talking to Halifax in Petticoat Lane that morning, for a long time. They'd been standing very close, talking softly to each other. Intimately. He had watched them, his eyes hard.

And he very nearly got me this morning, the bastard. I only just escaped.

Sliding a hand into his pocket, the driver pulled out a Yale door key and stared at it, smiling. It had been an easy job, after all, getting her bag, getting the key out and making a quick impression of it in a tin of wax.

And he had seen her again. In the flesh, not just on TV or in a magazine photo.

He kept seeing her face as it had looked this morning. He was angry because she had cut her lovely long blonde hair, and she wore make-up now, she never had before, she had been almost a child, in that marvellous halfway house, half-woman, half-child, seductive and innocent at the same time.

His mouth was dry, his body throbbed with heat. She wasn't like that any more, the bud had become a rose, the chrysalis had burst and the butterfly emerged, but she was still lovely and he still wanted her.

He breathed thickly. It excited him to know that she hadn't any idea how close he was, how easily he could get to her.

He saw a light go on upstairs in the big front bedroom. She was going to bed.

Taking off her clothes, shedding that horrible male

disguise, the grey suit, the shirt she wore for the TV series. He hated her in it.

He stared at the yellow square of window. The curtains were open, he could see some of the room – pale wallpaper, a gold-framed mirror in which shadows moved.

Annie, undressing, he suddenly realised, catching a glimpse of the bend of her slender body as she took off tights, the uplift of her arms as she slid a nightdress over her head.

She came to close the curtains and his breath caught. The silky white nightdress flowed down over her body but with the light behind her he could see right through it.

He moistened his lips, staring fiercely. The curtains closed, but he could still see her in his mind: slender, delicate, that smooth, creamy, soft, soft skin.

His mouth hungered to bury itself between her breasts, between her thighs, taste her, hear her whimpering. She would be terrified at first. When she saw him she would scream.

He would walk in there softly in a minute, go up the stairs and into her bedroom, and . . .

He closed his eyes, imagining it, as he had imagined it for eight years, with a deep, fierce pleasure.

He had grabbed her bag earlier on the off-chance that he would find her keys inside, but first he had done a quick check of the area and found a yard at the end of a narrow alley. After the snatch he'd ridden back there, taken off one of his heavy biker's gloves and got out the wax from his pocket; made a careful impression of her keys, his motorbike idling between his legs. It was hard to move fast in biker's gear, but he had needed to be as quick as possible because he knew the bloody Keystone Cops were after him, he could hear their heavy boots thudding through the brick arch which led from the market into the alley.

He had barely escaped capture. It had been a risk, but it would be worth it once he got inside her house. He pulled the key out of his pocket and held it in his palm. So long as he was right in guessing which number she would use for her burglar alarm, he could go in there any time he liked, and he would. Tonight.

The house seemed very empty. Annie was too tired to eat much; she had a boiled egg and a slice of toast, and went to bed with next week's scripts. At least she wouldn't have to go to work next day, she could sleep late.

She put the light out at nine and was half asleep when the phone rang. She stared at it as if it was a snake which might bite her if she put out her hand to it, but it might be a call from the hospital with bad news. She finally snatched it up.

'Yes?'

'Annie? How was your mother?'

She recognised the voice at once and sighed. 'Hello, Harriet. Not very good, I'm afraid. When she fell, she broke her hip.'

Harriet sounded shocked. 'Oh, no! That's serious, at her age, isn't it?'

'I'm afraid so. She's in a lot of pain, they've sedated her and she isn't making much sense.'

'Do you want some time off? Sean says he'll rewrite to leave you out of the next episode altogether, no problem.'

Was he there with her? wondered Annie, feeling that curious prickling in the chest again. Were they sleeping together?

'No, I'd rather work,' she said. 'I'll be able to see her on my way home every day, and if there's an emergency the hospital can always reach me at the studio. Most of next week is being shot on the set, isn't it?'

'Yes, no location work for you at all. OK, you're probably wise. Work will keep your mind off your worries. Well, that's a relief – Sean and I were just trying to figure out a way of rejigging next week's scripts. You're off tomorrow, aren't you? Back on Tuesday.'

'Yes.' So he *was* with Harriet? Annie frowned, her eyes dark. What had he said to Harriet about her? Had he repeated everything Annie had told him?

About Roger and the Valentine's cards . . . the threats . . . Annie shivered, resenting the possibility. She would never have told him if she had thought he might tell anyone else.

He must have driven straight to Harriet after leaving her. Were they lovers? Maybe he often spent the night there – for all she knew, he and Harriet could be living together. They were both highly discreet and far too clever to get caught out by dropping any clues.

Thank God I didn't let him stay here for the night. Her imagination was in a fever; what if he had stayed, had made a pass . . . what if she had been at such a low ebb that she let him share her bed? She felt sick. Betrayed.

She had wanted him for a minute, wanted him to hold her, to come to bed with her, make love to her, comfort her with the pleasure she had only ever felt with Johnny and sometimes dreamt about but had never taken with anybody else. She had suddenly needed it, wanted Sean, thought of sleeping in the bed with him, his arms around her all night, keeping her safe.

It was a tiny comfort that she hadn't.

Harriet said cheerfully, 'Well, have a good rest tomorrow. Don't spend all day at the hospital, try to get some fresh air and exercise.'

'I had enough of that today!' Annie muttered, and Harriet laughed; she was in a very good mood. Looking forward to getting to bed with Sean, no doubt.

'Freezing, wasn't it?' Harriet said. 'Never mind, back in the studio on Tuesday. Oh, and don't forget – Friday you haven't got any scenes, so publicity has fixed you a couple of interviews. A woman from The Sun and some guy from a real-life crime magazine. There will be a photo session, too, of course. Now, you get some sleep. Goodnight.'

Annie put the phone down and lay back against her pillows. She looked at the clock. Nearly ten. Had Harriet rung her from home? Or from Sean's place?

She switched off the light, turned over and thumped the pillows. She must get some sleep.

He let himself into the house an hour later. Before he moved an inch he studied the glowing panel of the burglar alarm. Yes, he knew this type. Taking a deep breath, he tapped in Annie's birthday. If he was wrong, all hell would break loose in a second.

He was poised, ready to run, if it did.

It didn't. The alarm print-out changed to STATUS DAY. It was off. He breathed again.

After closing the door silently he stood listening. No sound from above, every light out. Sitting down on the bottom stair, he slid socks over his trainers; it was a difficult job for his gloved fingers but he was in no hurry. The socks made his movements almost noiseless as he crept up the stairs later.

He stood on the landing, trying to work out in the dark which room could be hers. Only one door was closed. He crept from one open door to the next, checking each; they were all empty.

Hers must be the closed door. For a second sweat broke out on his brow as it suddenly occurred to him that the door could be locked or bolted. He put out a gloved hand to the door-handle. When it turned and the door clicked open he caught back an instinctive sigh of relief.

Then he froze, listening, in case she had heard the little sound. For half a minute he stood in the doorway, listening intently to the unbroken rhythm of her breathing.

The room was too dark for him to see her. He crept forward to the bed; by the time he stood beside it his eyes were accustomed to the darkness. They focused on her hungrily.

Her bedclothes had fallen back a little. He first saw the white curve of her naked shoulder and her face.

Her body curled up in the foetal position, facing him, her blonde hair ruffled, partly hiding her face. She looked like a child, a little girl. One hand was flung out, palm upwards. Such a small hand, a child's hand.

Christ, she's lovely, he thought, mouth parted, breathing thickly. And she looked so innocent.

She couldn't be, not any more. That wide-eyed childish innocence must be gone after years in show business, there were too many temptations in that world – but you would never know it from her face.

Anger stirred in him. What he'd been through because of her! His life ruined, everything taken away from him, including his future . . . all because of her.

He reached out and carefully lifted the bedclothes further back so that he could see more of her; angry eyes wandered up and down the soft, fallen body, breathing in and out with such innocent abandon; the nightdress had risen, leaving her legs bare to the thigh. Lace lay over her breasts, showing him soft white flesh, hard, pink nipples. His body tightened with desire.

Eight years he had waited. Eight years of waiting for this moment, living with the dream of getting her alone, where nobody could see or hear them and he could finally live his darkest fantasies.

He could do that now. He could fall on her there and then, while she was asleep, not even knowing he was there, so that she would wake up from her dreams to find him on her, in her, her body at his mercy.

His erection was hard and hot; he was breathing raggedly.

Yes. Why wait any longer? Why not end it now? But he hadn't planned it that way, and he hesitated. He didn't like changing his plans, he had taught himself to wait, to plan, to be patient. Impulses were danger-ous. If you gave in to them, you usually ended up paying for it. He'd learnt to plan; then when the moment was ripe you had the intense satisfaction of doing what you had promised yourself you would.

No, he would go on with the game as he had planned it. He would have her soon.

He bent to put what he held on her pillow, and stayed still, breathing in – he could smell her, the warm smell of a woman's body in sleep, in bed, as instantly evocative as the smell of new bread, and mingled with that her own personal fragrance, a light, flowery perfume from her skin, and the shampoo she must have used.

He bent closer, dying to put his tongue out and taste her. He could see the pores of her skin, a dusting of golden hairs on it as if she had a bodily halo. Bending even closer as if he was going to kiss her, he felt her warm breath on his cheek.

He was sweating, breathing much too fast, tempting himself beyond endurance, the torture sweet. One more inch and he would be touching her.

And then her lashes flickered. Was she waking up? He stiffened. She would see him, start screaming, and then he'd have to . . .

His fingers tightened on the rose he held and he started as one of the thorns on the long stem ran into him.

Damn! A drop of red blood oozed out, on his finger, and before he could stop it, fell, on to the pillow, right beside her head.

He stared at it rigidly; he hated the sight of blood, hated it and was fascinated by it.

There had been so much blood last time; it had taken him forever to wash it off himself, he had had to get rid of his clothes, burn them in the garden hurriedly before anyone saw them. For months afterwards he had kept smelling it on his hands, on his clothes . . .

Next time, there would be no blood.

Annie was dreaming.

She was back in the forest house with Johnny, lying together in front of the fire; he was taking off her clothes, his hands stroking, sliding over her warm skin. Filled with languorous pleasure, she watched him, heard his breathing, hurrying, quickening, heard the flames licking up the chimney, saw a spark of red as a log cracked open, and then Johnny's body was arching over her, strong, naked, dappled with fire-light.

She wanted him so much. She reached up to put both arms around him and pull him down to her, and suddenly she saw his face, and it wasn't Johnny, it was Roger Keats.

She cried out in horror and he laughed down at her, his red mouth open, coming down to clamp itself over hers, his tongue flickering out, as it had that night after Hamlet, when he deliberately kissed her in front of the whole audience, his tongue sliding in and out of her mouth like a snake.

She felt his hands, his naked body on her, heard his panting enjoyment and screamed, bucking and fighting to get rid of him. He dug his nails into her bare shoulder.

Her eyes flew open. For a second she didn't know where she was; then she took in her familiar room, full of grey light; it was morning. Weak with relief, she realised she had been having a nightmare.

But the pain had been real. She sat up, clutching her shoulder, and saw a long-stemmed red rose caught in the lacy neckline of her nightdress.

Where on earth had that come from?

Gingerly, avoiding contact with the spiny thorns in the stem, she freed it and dropped it on the floor. Had she brought it up to bed with her last night? She was still half asleep and couldn't remember.

She was always being given flowers, of course; people sent them all the time, fans of the show, men who wanted to date her – the house was usually full of expensive, extravagant displays, hothouse blooms without scent, so unreal they could be artificial.

She didn't like flowers in her bedroom, though, they sometimes made her sneeze in the closed atmosphere. Maybe her cleaner, Tracy, had forgotten that?

But why hadn't she noticed it last night when she got into bed? Her mind was blank for a few seconds, then she remembered her mother's accident. Of course! She had been upset last night, her mind occupied with other things. Still, it was hard to believe that she wouldn't have noticed a rose on her bed. Not that it was important.

She must ring the hospital and find out how her mother was this morning, check what time she could go in there to visit Trudie.

What time was it? She looked on her bedside table and froze. There was a Valentine's card propped in front of the clock.

For a second she thought she was imagining it, she had been on tenterhooks, dreading its arrival for days, maybe she had started seeing things!

All her colour went. She shut her eyes. You're going crazy! she thought. He was really getting to her. She was starting to see Valentine's cards everywhere.

But when she opened her eyes again it was still there. There was no envelope, just the card: wildly romantic, a huge red satin heart, trailing white lace ribbons which fluttered against her fingers as she shakily, reluctantly, reached for it.

There was a message above the heart in red, glittering foil. FOREVER MINE.

She shrank back from it, and that was when she saw the little spots of blood on her white pillow. She looked at the rose – when it ran into her shoulder, had she bled? Was that her blood? Or . . . his?

The blood and the card seemed to mock her – love and horror linked in her mind, inextricable, unavoidable, as in her dream – Johnny and Roger Keats, pleasure and pain . . . red roses, an agony like dying.

Annie's heart began to beat so hard it hurt. She couldn't breathe. She opened it, the stiff card rustling.

The printing was the same, but this time, for the first time, the words were different.

'BE SEEING YOU SOON, ANNIE. NOT LONG NOW. I TOLD YOU I'D BE BACK TO GET YOU, DIDN'T I?'

Panic surged through her. How had it got there? He must have got in while she was asleep. Oh, God, he must still be here. Where? Where is he?

She threw a terrified look around the room, half fell out of bed, stood there, tense and shaking, listening to the echoing silence in the house, then ran barefoot to the door and opened it, listened again. Not a sound.

Then it hit her. Her mother wasn't here, Jerri wasn't here. There was nobody but her in the house.

Her and him . . . wherever he was.

She closed the door and bolted it, then bit her lip. What if he was hiding in here? What if she had just locked herself in here with him? There were plenty of places to hide. Under the bed, in the wall-to-wall closet, in the bathroom . . . he could be anywhere. Her terrified eyes flicked round the room. Nothing moved. Not a sound.

She ran to her bedside table and unlocked one of the drawers in it, slid out the one thing it held. A handgun she had kept there ever since she had some police training on firearms – one of Sean's ex-colleagues, a retired police superintendent, had given her the gun when she had some rather nasty threats against her from a fan who was caught later trying to get into her house.

He turned out to be a schizophrenic who had stopped taking his medication and was in a manic phase. He had been returned to a mental hospital, but Annie had kept the gun. She had got a licence for it, but she had never for an instant imagined she might ever use it.

She almost dropped it, her fingers were shaking so much. It made her feel a lot safer and yet at the same time it scared her, it made the situation seem too real.

Holding it too tightly, she went down on one knee to look under the bed, pushing aside the frilled valance. No, nobody there.

She tiptoed over to the bathroom door, it was ajar and she could see the whole room reflected in the mirror on one wall. Empty. He wasn't in there.

Annie turned then and stared at the wardrobe. That was the most likely place, wasn't it?

She crept over there, hesitated, stiffened the hand that held the gun, pointing it, then slid back the first door, nerves stretched in case he leapt out at her. In the crazy way the mind worked, she thought of a jack-in-the-box; she had always hated them when she was small.

She hated anything that made her nerves jump. She could feel the blood beating in her ears, deafening her. Her fingers tightening round the trigger, she breathed fast, shallowly, as she opened each compartment.

Nothing happened; the clothes just hung there, moving faintly on their hangers. Taking an audible breath, she put out the hand that didn't hold the gun and pushed clothes aside, fingers trembling. Nothing.

Annie looked round the room – there was nowhere else in here for him to hide. Was he somewhere in the house? Downstairs?

She sank down on the edge of her bed, her knees giving, put down the gun on her bedside table, jerking at the little click the metal made on the wood. Her hands were shaking and damp with sweat. Thank God she hadn't had to use the gun – she had had a week's training, she was quite a good shot. But to fire at a human being . . . no, she could not imagine doing that.

She reached for the phone. What if he had cut the wires? But the phone purred obediently, so she hurriedly punched in the number of the emergency services.

'Emergency – which service do you require?' The female voice was indifferent.

'Police.'

'What is your name?'

'Annie Lang. Please . . .'

'Is that Miss or . . .'

'Miss,' she said, frantic to get help. 'Look . . .'

'And your telephone number and address, Miss Lang?'

Annie gave them impatiently. 'Hurry up, get me the police, I think there's a man in the house . . . a burglar . . . any minute now he might . . .'

'I'm connecting you now, Miss Lang. Hold the line.'

Another voice, male and matter of fact, spoke a few seconds later. She told him about the red rose, the card.

His voice changed then, took on a note of amusement. 'I see. So, miss, you found a red rose on your pillow this morning? And a Valentine's card on your bedside table?'

'Yes, he must have put them there while I was asleep. How could he have got in? My house is fitted with the most sophisticated alarms, I set them last night myself. The house should be as tight as a drum, nobody·should have got in!'

'It is Valentine's Day today, Miss Lang,' the man at the other end of the line said, a smile in his voice. 'Can't you think of anyone who might have let himself in and . . .'

'No! There are four sets of keys – I have one, my cleaner has another, my mother has a set, but she's in hospital, and her keys are still here, in her handbag, in the house.'

'And the fourth set?'

'I have that, too, now. My mother had a companion/ nurse, but she has left now, and I got the keys back. Look, will you please send a police car round here at once? For all I know he could still be here. I haven't dared look round the house yet. I'm in my bedroom, I've locked the door.'

'You said you had an alarm – is it still working?'

She hadn't thought of that. Panic had stampeded her too much. She turned to look hurriedly at the computerised panel beside her bed. It showed a glimmering green with the words STATUS ALARM standing out on the screen. That meant it was still set, the alarms all switched on so that if a mouse ran through one of the control beams it would set off a noise like Armegeddon in the house and down at the police station, with which the alarm was linked. Once or twice in the past it had gone off at night, through computer malfunction, and the police had been here within minutes. She had had to apologise profusely for the error and make them all coffee before they went back to work.

'Is it working, Miss Lang?' asked the policeman.

'Yes,' she said, biting her lip, almost ready to believe she had imagined all this. 'But . . .'

The policeman was fatherly, indulgent, patronising; his tone made her teeth meet. 'Well, then, no stranger can have let himself in there, can he? Or it would have gone off and woken you up. As I said, he must have a key – and knows the control number of your alarm so that he could turn it off when he came in, and on again before he left!'

'But . . .'

'Now, I suggest you have a little think, Miss Lang, and see if you can't remember anyone who has a key, knows the combination of your alarm – and might want to bring you red roses and a Valentine.'

By then she was so confused and bewildered she was half ready to believe him.

He waited a moment, then said with a smile in his voice, 'I love the show, by the way, Miss Lang. We all do, you have a lot of fans in the station. If ever you need any advice or suggestions for unusual cases give us a ring, we'd be happy to give you some ideas.'

'Thank you,' she said, remembering to sound grateful but wondering how they would explain it if, after having asked for their help and been turned down, she was found with her throat cut? 'I'll remember that.'

'Any further problems, give us a ring, of course, and I'll send a car round. But I think you'll realise you know someone who might have played a practical joke on you. But if I were you, I'd get that key back from him, unless, of course, you want him to come and go as he pleases!'

He laughed. She hung up, seething. As if she wouldn't remember giving her key to someone! Tracy, her cleaner, couldn't have brought the rose and the card – even as a joke. A single mother with two kids under five, their father long gone and untraceable, Tracy was disillusioned, down to earth and bleakly honest. She had been working for Annie for two years. When Trudie Lang began to forget things and started having her little accidents, Annie had asked Tracy to take care of her, but Tracy couldn't work full-time because of her children. She was quite happy to look after Trudie while she was there, but she could only work while her children were at nursery school in the afternoons.

Annie liked and trusted Tracy. They didn't meet very often because Tracy usually arrived long after Annie had left for the studio, and left before she got home, but when Annie was between series she liked to take a real rest, get up late, laze around in a dressing-gown, watching TV and reading novels as well as scripts her agent sent along.

Those times, Tracy would make coffee for her and sometimes sit and drink a cup too, while they talked; they had got to know each other pretty well. No, Tracy couldn't be involved in this, and there was absolutely nobody who had another key, despite what that desk sergeant had assumed.

Well, she had better search the house, anyway. She picked up her gun again, unlocked the door, and began a slow, thorough search from room to room.

But the house was totally empty, not a sign of

anyone having been there since last night, except the rose and the Valentine's card.

Frowning, Annie went back to her bedroom, locked herself in again, showered and got dressed in a pair of jeans and a warm sweater. She put her gun back into the drawer, locked it, and was about to go downstairs to have breakfast, when her eye fell on the Valentine's card still lying on her bedside table. A cold qualm hit her.

Nobody else had a key – yet there was no getting away from the fact that somebody had by-passed the alarm system, got into the house, into this room, while she slept. Icy cold and trembling, Annie stared at the card's red satin rose and ribbons – the thought of him, in here, standing by her bed, watching her, while she was so unaware of him . . . Oh, God, he could have raped her, even killed her.

Why hadn't he done anything except leave the card and the rose? He had been threatening her for years – why had he got in here last night and then gone away again without even waking her? Was this the final phase in the long-drawn-out game he had been playing with her for years – did he want her to know that he could get in and out of her home just as he pleased whenever he chose and there was nothing she could do to stop him?

Roger Keats had been sending her Valentines for seven years. Every year he had simply posted a card – now he had broken into her home. His campaign of terror was stepping up. What next? Was he going to show up any minute now?

But why *now*? After seven years? Why had he waited so long, and why was he coming *now*? Was it because his wife was close to her at work and could spy for him? Marty Keats could have told him that Annie was alone the house. She looked at the message again, biting her lip. See you soon, he said, and the threat raised the hair on the back of her neck.

Just when her career was really taking off – when the series was doing brilliantly, the ratings the highest they had ever been. In the late autumn she'd been voted the best actress in British TV – Roger was bound to have noticed that. Had Roger been waiting for her to reach real fame before he made his move? It would be just like him. She had ended his career eight years ago. She could be sure he would love to end hers.

4

She spent a lot of the day curled up on the sofa, wearing jeans and a sweater, answering fan mail, which piled up faster than she could ever reply to it, and most of which was dealt with by the studio if it fell into certain categories. Any letters asking for a signed photo, unpleasant or threatening letters, letters asking questions the studio could answer – none of those were passed on to her, but some letters were considered more personal and Annie answered those, dictating her replies into a tape machine for a typist at the studio to type out later, and, when they ran short of signed photos, signing more of them, to be sent out with the letters.

By lunchtime she had had enough of her correspondence, and wandered out into the kitchen to make herself a light lunch, a green salad, tossed in a vinaigrette she made up from a freshly squeezed lemon, a dash of olive oil and a little English mustard powder, served with a fillet of sole she grilled.

Sean rang her at three o'clock that afternoon. 'How's your mother?'

'A little better today.' Annie had rung the hospital twice; they were very reassuring.

'You don't sound too cheerful,' said Sean. 'Did you get another Valentine?'

She wished she hadn't told him about Roger, but now that she had she knew she wouldn't shake him off the scent easily, so she reluctantly told him how she had woken up to find it next to her bed.

Sean's voice deepened, roughened. 'He's got into the house? This is getting serious, Annie. Was that all he did, leave a rose and the card? Was anything moved or taken?'

She told him no and he asked, 'You didn't wake up at all? Had you taken a sleeping pill?'

She admitted she had, saying that she preferred not to take sleeping pills, but sometimes it was essential if she had to get to the studio very early and had trouble getting to sleep.

'Have you called the police?' asked Sean.

'Yes, and got laughed at for my pains.' Annie repeated what the policeman had said to her, and Sean sighed.

'Well, sorry they weren't more helpful, but they're probably up to their necks in burglaries in your area; it's a local hobby. Look, I'll come over and dust the place for fingerprints, take a look around.'

'No, don't bother. Even if you found any fingerprints, what good would that do? He isn't a criminal with a police record.'

'Well, you will have your locks changed, won't you?'

'Yes, I rang someone, first thing, and a locksmith is coming round this afternoon. I've got to go out, but my cleaner is here.' She could hear the buzz of Tracy's vacuum cleaner upstairs; they had had a cup of tea and a biscuit together half an hour ago. She frowned. 'I wish I knew how he got in without my alarms going off.'

'God knows. He must have found out the number you're using. What was it?' He gave a curt laugh as she told him. 'Your birthday? Well, that was clever, wasn't it? The first number he'd try. You must change that, too, at once. A good idea is to write down numbers from 1 to 9 on pieces of paper, throw them up in the air and then pick up four at random. And don't forget to memorise them before you key them in – you don't want to forget the number and have to get the alarm people round to let you in to your own house.'

'But I still can't understand how he got into the house – I keep my keys in my bag, and I always have my bag with me.'

A silence, then Sean said drily, 'Except for a few minutes yesterday, when your bag was stolen, remember? That motorbike was out of sight of all of us for a couple of minutes. Quite long enough for him to get an impression of your key.'

Annie turned pale. 'So the man on the bike could have been . . .'

'Roger Keats, yes, exactly.'

'It never even entered my head!' She was appalled by the idea that Roger Keats had been so close without her even guessing. She tried to remember what the man on the bike had looked like, but in black leathers, with a helmet visor over his face, he had made no impression on her at all. How many other times had Roger Keats been around without her knowing it?

How had he known where to find them out on location?

'His wife,' Sean said, as if reading her mind, and Annie started in shock.

'What?'

'His wife knew you would be on location in Petticoat Lane Market on Sunday morning. I'll have a word with Harriet, we'll have to get rid of her.'

'No, don't!' Annie protested urgently. 'If Harriet had her moved and she complained to her union, it would cause a lot of trouble – what possible excuse could I give? It would look as if I was being vindictive. After all, she hasn't done anything. She'll just tell them I was responsible for her husband losing his job, now I'm trying to get her fired – what do you think her union is going to say? We don't want a strike hitting the production.'

Sean argued with her, but had to admit she was right. Then he tried to talk her into having someone move into the house with her while her mother was in hospital.

'I'll think about it,' she said, not wishing to admit she had no relatives except her mother, and very few close friends. As a child she had had friends at school, but her mother was so protective that she would never allow Annie to play out in the street, or go to anybody's home. Trudie had insisted that Annie should come straight home after school and she was rarely allowed to take anyone home with her. She had begun to make friends at drama school – but then she had been forced to leave, and for some years after that she had been so traumatised she hadn't wanted to talk to anyone unless she had to. When you worked in the theatre your world shrank to a small circle; you went to bed late and got up late, you worked all evening, you couldn't go out to dinner or the theatre, so you saw very few people except on a Sunday. Your only friends were often the others in the cast, for the run of that play, and, however close the friendship, it always faded once the play ended. You might stay friendly, but you simply didn't see each other very often any more.

Television was different only in that you worked hard all day and went home in the evening, but you were usually so tired that you didn't want to go anywhere after dinner, except off to bed, to get up at crack of dawn next day.

Sean said, 'Harriet lives alone, too. Why don't you have her to stay for a few days? I'll talk to her.'

Annie noted his calm assumption of being able to talk Harriet into anything. He was probably right, Harriet always took anything he said very seriously; Annie had several times watched Sean talk Harriet into changing her mind. Just how close were they? And why did it bother her so much to think about that?

'I'd better get back to her,' he said, 'We're working on the location schedule for six months ahead. The location manager is still negotiating with the police and a couple of big banks over two locations in Cheapside – if we agree to all their demands we'll go over budget, and Billy will go bananas.'

'I hate working on location in winter,' Annie said, remembering the raw and bitter weather in Petticoat Lane on Sunday.

'Everyone does, but it really makes the series,' Sean said drily. 'I hope your mother is better today. Bye, Annie.'

Trudie seemed to be in less pain, but she was very vague; Annie was worried that the drugs they were giving her were making her memory lapses worse. She remembered who Annie was but she kept forgetting where she was, and why. When she did remember, she pleaded, 'I want to come home. Take me home, Annie.'

Annie wished to God she could. The ward was so crowded. She hated the mingled smells of floor polish, antiseptic and tired flowers, and it was depressing to see all these frightened, sick old people crammed together like sardines.

She looked unhappily at her mother. 'I can't, Mum – you can't walk, you know that. As soon as you're well enough to travel, though, I'll take you home, I promise.'

Trudie closed her eyes and drifted off to sleep. She didn't mention anyone trying to kill her this time. Annie left after a while; the sister said her mother wouldn't wake up for ages.

'She seems to be drugged up to the eyeballs,' accused Annie.

'We have to keep her sedated because the pain is pretty bad, and she's in no state to stand it. Don't worry, Miss Lang, we do know what we're doing.'

'I'm sure you do,' Annie hurriedly soothed, hearing the touchiness in the other's voice.

The ward sister hesitated, then said, 'You know, you are going to have to face it, your mother is very confused and she's getting worse. She needs a secure environment where she can be watched twenty-four hours a day. You should be planning for the future.'

Annie left, heavy-hearted. When she got home Tracy was still there, waiting for her, so that she could let Annie into the house and give her the new set of keys.

'Can't stop, my sister's got the kids. There were a couple of phone messages, I left them on the pad.'

'I'll find them. Thanks for staying late.'

'That's OK.' Tracy's hazel eyes were concerned. 'Look, if you get nervous during the night, give me a ring. I'll have to bring the kids, but I'll come over if you need me. I don't like to think of you being here alone at night if there's some crazy guy trying to break in! You ought to get someone to stay with you until your mother comes back. Not that . . .' She stopped and gave Annie an uncertain look, flushing.

'Not that my mother would be much help in an emergency,' Annie finished for her, grimacing. 'No, poor love, she wouldn't, but I still feel better having her in the house!'

Alone again, Annie went round the house, checking that every door and window was locked, then she settled down to go over her words for tomorrow's filming. They had rehearsed last week, but that seemed a very long time ago.

She went to bed early, afraid to go to sleep and yet knowing she had to – she was tempted to ring Harriet, but she had to face being alone sooner or later, so she took a sleeping pill to make sure she got some sleep or she wouldn't be fit to work tomorrow.

She had set her alarm as usual; when it went off she woke with a violent start and then sat up, in pitch darkness, fumbled with her bedside lamp, and as it came on looking hurriedly around the room. This morning there was nothing out of place. She gave a long sigh of relief and slid out of bed. She had to hurry; the car from the studio would be here in fifteen minutes.

Before she left, she rang the hospital; the night sister was still on duty and was irritable when she first answered the phone, but as soon as she heard who was calling her voice changed.

'Oh, hello! Your mother has had a good night, Miss Lang. Now don't you worry, we're taking the best of care of her.'

'Was she still in a lot of pain during the night?'

'No, she's coming along nicely, for someone her age.'

Annie sighed. 'Sorry to call you so early in the morning, but I won't get another chance later.'

'Off to the studio, I suppose?' The night sister's

voice was fascinated. 'You do get up early. Practically a night worker, like me, but your life is much more glamorous and exciting.'

'Don't you believe it,' Annie said wryly.

'Well, I'd change places with you any day,' the sister said. 'I bet you got hundreds of Valentines – I only got one! But that's the one that matters!'

She couldn't get away from reminders of Valentine's Day, thought Annie later, as she was driven past shop windows still covered in a rash of red hearts and romantic cards, shiny heart-shaped balloons bobbing against the glass. It was an icy grey morning; she couldn't stop shivering.

'Why do we have Valentine's Day at such a dead time of year?' she thought aloud.

'Cheer us all up and keep us going until spring? And make money,' her driver said cheerfully, swearing as a boy on a motorbike swerved past them. 'Lunatic!' he yelled after the rider.

The boy looked back, saw Jason's black face and snarled, 'Get stuffed, nigger!' sticking two fingers in the air in an obscene gesture.

Jason didn't respond but his shoulders, under his black leather jacket, rose and fell in an involuntary, revealing shrug. Although she couldn't see his face, Annie felt his anger and his pain.

'How many Valentines did you get, Jason?' she asked, to comfort him.

His shoulders relaxed again, he shot her a grin in the mirror over his head. 'Six. One of them from Angela, my fiancée.'

He had been engaged to Angela ever since Annie met him. A backing singer with a group which was doing good business in the London pubs that year,

143

Angela had a figure that made men's heads turn and a voice like molasses. Annie had met her at a party thrown by Harriet for everyone associated with the series: technical people, actors, the catering staff, the drivers. Harriet had left nobody out, typically generous and thoughtful.

Angela seemed nice enough, but she was not, Jason said, favoured by his mother, who had very strict views on the sort of girl she wanted for her only son and thought Angela wasn't good enough for her boy. Neither of the engaged couple seemed in a hurry to get married, however. Annie suspected that marriage was not actually on Angela's mind at all. She enjoyed her life as a single girl too much.

'Who were the others from?'

'I got my ideas,' Jason said, laughing.

Annie knew that quite a few girls who worked at the television studios fancied him, including one of the make-up girls who always asked after him when she was doing Annie's face and hair. With his warm black skin, Jason was sinewy and lithe, had a lazy, sexy way of walking and a grin as wide as Texas.

'How about you?' he asked. 'A couple of sackfuls, right?'

She managed a smile, nodding.

'I love getting them, don't you? Especially when they're not signed and you have to guess who sent them . . . and you can send them yourself without feeling stoopid. You can write something really lush . . . yours forever . . . be mine forever . . . without being afraid of getting laughed at. I love it, I'm a romantic. Yeah, that's me!'

Annie wished he would stop talking about it. She couldn't bear it. 'How's your mum?' she asked him.

'She's fine,' he said, beaming because she had asked, and watching her in the mirror, making a mental note of what she was wearing this morning, so that he could tell his mum that night, when he got home. Proud as punch, his mum was, that he drove Annie every day.

She never missed an episode of The Force, and the first thing she would say when Jason got in that night was, what did she wear today? Mind you, it was usually the same thing in the mornings; old blue jeans, a warm jacket in winter, a shirt in summer, a sweater, soft leather moccasins. She never wore make-up either, not that she needed it, with that clear, pale skin, and those great big blue eyes.

Jason's mum wanted to hear about the designer label gear. Mum couldn't afford stuff like that, of course, but she spent every spare penny she had on clothes, she loved them, and she was still a good-looking woman, although she was big, with rich, smooth skin and lots of it – a cushiony woman, with big breasts and swinging hips.

She loved to get dressed and go out dancing, and she knew what suited her, she had a good colour sense. That was important to Jason, too. Colours changed his moods – red put him into fight mode, orange made him happy, green was better than a tranquilliser. Angela wore a lot of black; black was sexy on a woman, especially when she wasn't wearing much at all, a black lace bra and panties, or a black slip with nothing underneath – that really turned him on, seeing all that smooth coffee-coloured skin through black silk and lace.

'Did you go anywhere hot on your night off?' he asked Annie, who was being very quiet.

She started as if she had been miles away, then

blinked, shook her head. What could she tell him? That she had been half out of her mind? He didn't want to know that, and she couldn't talk about it. Who could she talk to about what was eating her up inside?

'You wasting yourself, girl,' Jason said and she laughed, her mouth crooked with irony.

'Am I?'

'Sure are – wasting your opportunities.' That was what his mum always said when he told her Annie wasn't the party type.

'She prefers to go home and take a hot bath and relax, she isn't one for ritzy occasions, no first-night parties for her,' he always told his mum.

'If I was her!' his mum would sigh. 'What a waste!'

'If you was Annie, mum, you'd set the town on fire!' he agreed, and his mum always began to laugh with her deep old-whisky laugh, not that she drank whisky, not mum. She liked a drop of rum in her coffee now and then, but she was no heavy drinker. Her voice just naturally came out with that smoky, husky sound because she had spent so many years singing her tonsils out, first in church, where their gospel choir was famous, and then in the clubs.

'I should have gone on singing when I was a girl instead of marrying your father. I'd have been another Bessie Smith,' she said. And she would have been, he'd bet his life on it. She had tried to get him to sing when he was a little kid, but he hadn't inherited her voice, nor did he want a showbiz life. He loved cars, that was all he ever wanted to do, drive cars, own cars, maybe one day have his own garage.

'You a big disappointment to me, Jason, honey,' his mother would say, shaking her head. 'With your looks you could have been a star, if you'd only had a voice and some temperament. You got no temperament, boy. That's your problem.'

'Mum, my problem is you,' he would say, and she would start to laugh again.

'No, boy – you wrong. Your problem is trashy girls with no class.' You could never win an argument with his mum.

Jason slowed as they reached the studio gates, where they had to be checked by the uniformed man in his glass cubicle.

There were usually a few people hanging around the-gates to celebrity-spot, even at this hour in freezing Febuary. The old faithfuls knew what time the actors arrived; they peered into the windows of the car, recognised Annie in the tight blue jeans and white sweater, her slicked back, very short blonde hair under a midnight-blue and silver Chanel scarf.

'Annie!

'It's Annie Lang!'

Some of them rapped on the car windows to get her attention, leaned on the side of the car. That always alarmed her.

'Loved the show on Tuesday!' one of them said, and hands waved in a flurry of pink palms and fingers.

'Did you get my Valentine's card?' yelled someone, and in a reflex action she swung her head to stare, but it was only a teenager, a boy with spots and long hair.

She managed a forced smile, gave him a wave, then the gates opened and they drove through into the studio complex. Purpose-built a few years ago the three black-glass towers were set well apart in grass lawns, bisected by wide roads along which studio traffic permanently moved; carrying costumes, props, furniture from place to place. The complex was often used as the background for sci-fi productions; filmed by night from the right angle it took on the slightly sinister air of a futuristic city, the black glass windows glowing like a string of black opals against the sky.

Filmed by day it looked pretty weird too, thought Annie, staring out of the car as they drove to the back of Tower Two, which housed the studio where the indoor scenes of her series were shot, and where the offices of the staff who produced the programme were housed. As well as shooting on location, in the City itself, in order to get convincing backgrounds they had a mock-up of a city street which had been built for them and which could be changed as required by the carpenters and scene designers.

Many offices were unlit, the staff hadn't yet arrived, but when they passed the bay of the mail department it was blazing with light. A post office van was unloading.

Jason pulled up beside the main entrance of Tower Two and Annie smiled at him as he came round to open her door and help her out.

'Thanks, Jason, see you.'

She hurried inside and walked up a flight of stairs to the wardrobe department, a huge open barn of a place filled to bursting with rails of clothes from every period, from futuristic plastic uniforms for space drama to fur tails for cavemen. There was a surreal feel to the place, but the women who worked there seemed unaware of the bizarre nature of their surroundings.

In her black case Annie had the clothes she had worn in Petticoat Lane; she checked them back in to the woman in charge this morning.

'Sorry, I had to rush off before I could change. I don't need anything else – I'm only in two scenes today, and I'm supposed to be off duty, so I'll be wearing what I've got on.'

Indifferently, the woman nodded, and Annie hurried away to make-up. When she got down to the studio, she found the rest of the cast already there, huddled on hard wooden chairs feverishly reading their scripts while lighting men swarmed around adjusting overhead arcs, trying not to trip over the snaking cables which littered the floor.

The director this morning was Henry Walpole, a short, bristly man with a lot of hair and a low boiling point.

'I wondered when you were going to get here!' he said, scowling at Annie.

'Sorry, am I late?' she asked, consulting her watch and seeing that she was five minutes late. 'Oh, come on, Henry – only just!'

'I don't like clock-watching! I wanted to talk the scene through with you and Derek before we had a run-through.'

They were working in one of the usual sets the series used, an interior shot in the City police station. Derek Fenn was already in position, leaning his elbows on the desk, in uniform, watching her take up her own position for this scene, which they had rehearsed midweek.

Harriet in a black leather jacket and black jeans, came along after a couple of takes. 'How are things going, Henry? OK?'

'Bloody awful, Derek keeps forgetting his words and Annie seems to have five thumbs on every hand this morning, she keeps dropping things,' he growled, his face resentful because he thought she was checking up on him.

Maybe she was? thought Annie. Harriet was getting just like Billy Grenaby – she had a hundred different jobs to do but she still checked up on everybody who worked for her and made sure they were doing their job properly. She couldn't delegate easily.

'I'm sure you'll get great performances out of them, Henry,' said Harriet soothingly, and went over to talk to the gaffer, Jack Wilkins, and his best boy, little Jim. They went into a huddle while Henry watched them sulkily.

'We're discussing next month's schedules,' Harriet reassured him as she came back. She handed him a printed sheet of schedules. 'It goes up on the board tomorrow, everyone!' she told the rest of the crew. Harriet was popular with the technical people; she always treated craftsmen with enormous respect – she took their advice before every scene, standing with them, studying every angle of the picture framed in the camera's eye, before they made up their minds where to position a camera, earnestly discussing noise levels with the sound man, frowning over cables with electricians, watching closely as the lighting people worked.

She's very ambitious, and she's going places, Annie thought, watching her and Jack, but she is so clever in the way she manages people.

Mike Waterford and Annie had a short scene later that morning. Mike was in a playful mood; the scene required him to bend over her while she was seated at a desk, so, while they waited for the lighting to be adjusted he curled his hand upwards to fondle her breast. She smacked his hand down, but a few seconds later it was back, squeezing her nipple.

'Keep your bloody hands to yourself!' she snapped at him.

He turned a wide-eyed look. 'Sorry? What did I do?'

She glared back. 'As if you didn't know!'

Henry interrupted with a bellow like an angry bull.

'Shut up, the pair of you! Mike, stop touching Annie up, for God's sake. Everyone, ten minutes for coffee, OK? And be back promptly.'

Annie drank black coffee, glaring at Mike's back as he chatted up one of the studio staff, a lithe little blonde in tight jeans. Mike's hand strolled softly up and down her back, over her smooth buttocks. She giggled.

Silly little bitch, Annie thought. Why do women fall for men like him? The very idea of his hands on her made her sick. She couldn't understand her own sex; they must be deaf, blind, dumb. Most of all dumb. Or so many women wouldn't climb into Mike Waterford's bed. He didn't even have to use bribery or blackmail, the way Roger Keats had done. Women fought to let him use them.

'OK, people, let's have you!' Henry yelled, and Annie put down her empty paper cup. Mike gave the little blonde a last, confident pat on the behind, and walked back on set. Annie followed, imitating his swagger.

There was a smothered chuckle from some of the lighting men. Mike swung round, gave her a narrow-eyed, suspicious look. She didn't meet his eyes, her face innocent, calm as a glass of milk.

'What are you up to?' Mike asked.

'What are you talking about?'

'Come on, come on,' Henry snarled. 'Stop brawling and do some fucking work, will you?'

Trudie Lang hated the night time on the ward. She had been there for days now; she couldn't remember how many but it seemed like a lifetime. They gave her a sleeping pill every night, with her cocoa, but sometimes she didn't take it, she just pretended to, holding it under her tongue until the nurse had left and then slipping it out and hiding it in her secret place, a hidden pocket in her plastic-lined toilet bag.

Who did they think they were? Hardly out of their teens, some of them, girls of eighteen or nineteen, ordering her about and treating her like a crazy person.

'Now then, Grandma, got to take your pill,' they said. 'Open your mouth and show me it's gone. I don't trust you.'

'D'you think I'm running a drugs racket in here? Selling sleeping pills to all the old loonies?' She stuck her tongue out at them, and then they switched off her light and went away.

Trudie was saving the pills up. If it got worse she would take them all and get away from here while she was still herself. One day she knew she wouldn't even remember who she was and then it would be too late. The pills were her safety exit to a kinder oblivion than the one waiting inexorably for her along the line.

It was a high price to pay, though, lying here in the dark, wide awake, listening to the other patients snoring, breathing, calling out in their sleep in quavering, old, frightened voices. It reminded her of her first husband's death. She had married Frank because nobody else had asked her and at least she would escape from her home, and her father's relentless pressure.

'Oh, I was weak, weak as water, I should have stuck to my guns,' Trudie said aloud.

That first marriage had been a disaster. She had been expected both to work in the greengrocer's shop and to run the house. There had been no love, and no children. Frank had said it was her; he was full of resentment, told her she was barren, kept wishing he had never married her. After a few years, they hadn't even slept together. He had ignored her around the house except to complain – until the illness started and then he'd become pathetic and taken to his bed. She had almost liked him once he was powerless and dependent on her. She treated him like a baby, fed him and changed him and kept him clean, and he was grateful, but it went on too long. The daily strain wore her down; she'd felt as if she was dying too, at times.

His death was a release for both of them. She had been thirty-five, young enough to marry again, and this time she had chosen the man. Her parents were dead by then, and Trudie had nobody to please but herself.

He had been a good man, too, had Bill Lang. A quiet man, a solicitor's clerk. She had met him when she went to the solicitor's office so that she could have Frank's will explained to her.

She was left the shop, but there was very little money; Bill had visited her a few days later, bringing her some papers to sign, and advised her to keep the shop going.

She made him tea and brought scones and home-made biscuits, and he had stayed a long time; they found it easy to talk to each other.

He had told her about his own first marriage – his young wife had died in childbirth, her baby had died with her, and he blamed himself.

'She was a little slip of a thing. I should have waited until she was older, we were both eighteen, it was selfish of me, but I loved her so much, and I killed her.'

'Oh, no, don't say that!' Trudie had protested, shocked.

'It's the truth, and that's why I couldn't face marrying again and having some other woman go through what my Jenny went through.'

She had told him then that she couldn't have babies, she had never been able to have one with Frank. She was afraid it would put Bill off, but he had asked her out to dinner the following weekend and again they talked easily, so relaxed together it was as if they had known each other for years.

After she had been widowed for six months Bill asked her to marry him. They were both conventional: they didn't want fingers to be pointed at them. The neighbours were openly critical of a recently widowed woman seeing so much of another man, so they waited another six months before they actually got married.

By then Bill had told her, 'I don't want kids, Trudie, I couldn't risk it, I couldn't bear to see you die the way my Jenny did. I'm not marrying you to have kids. I'm lonely, Trude, and I think you are, too. I think we can be happy together, don't you?'

She did; she hated living alone, she hated the silences, thick as centuries-old dust, the empty rooms, the feeling of dread she got at night when she was alone and afraid someone might break in and murder her in her bed.

So they had married, and six months later she was told by her doctor, smiling slyly at her ignorance, that the worrying symptoms she had noticed meant that she was pregnant.

'I can't be!' she gasped.

'You're married, aren't you?' he said, almost laughing out loud.

'But I thought I couldn't . . . I never had one with my first husband.'

'Then that couldn't have been your fault, because you are definitely pregnant now,' smiled the doctor.

'Oh, my God, what will Bill say? He doesn't want any kids. He'll be afraid I'll die.'

'Why on earth should you die? A healthy woman like you should have babies as easy as shelling peas.'

'His first wife died and her baby died with her.'

The doctor sat silent, gave a sigh. 'Ah, well, send him along to me, I'll reassure him. Now, don't you let him worry you. You aren't going to have any problems.'

Bill had burst into tears when she told him, and despite everything the doctor said to him he had watched over her like a mother all the months of her pregnancy, made her stay in bed, treated her like an invalid, but the doctor proved to be right. She had had the baby easily enough, although it was a first birth: a lovely little girl with dark, dark blue eyes and a skin that looked perfect even then.

'She's beautiful,' Bill had said, perspiring with relief the day she was born, holding her gingerly, as if she might break.

He adored her from the first, but he was determined

that Trudie should have no more babies, so he had had a vasectomy, and Annie had been their only child. They loved her the more for knowing there would be no others.

Bill had died of a heart-attack after running for a bus one hot summer day when Annie was eleven. He hadn't ever complained of his heart before. He had never had a day's ill health.

It had been a terrible shock for Trudie and Annie, coming out of the blue like that. Annie had loved her father almost as much as he had loved her, and Trudie had become very fond of him although her feelings had never been deep. She had married Bill because she felt comfortable with him and she was lonely, and she knew he had married her for the same reasons. Neither of them had been wildly romantic.

All her capacity for loving had been focused on Annie from the minute the baby was laid in her arms. She had responded instantly to the child's weakness and helplessness, to knowing it needed her, and with Annie still there, needing her, she was able to cope with Bill's death, although it came as a terrible shock.

'It always is,' she thought aloud, and jumped when someone answered her from the dark.

'What?'

'What?' she repeated, bewildered, blinking into the shadows.

'You said something always is . . .'

'Death,' she said, 'a shock . . . it's always a shock even if you know it's coming.'

'That's true, but it can be kind, too, can death – it can be your friend,' said the nurse, coming towards her bed, and she smiled, recognising the face.

'Oh, it's you, Cinders. I didn't think you were on tonight!'

'I wasn't, but Claire got a migraine and had to go off, she rang me and asked if I could take over, so I'm working a split shift. Feel like a cup of tea? I was just going to have one.'

'I'd love one,' Trudie said eagerly.

'Well, don't go anywhere. Wait here till I get back.'

'Chance would be a fine thing! God, if I could walk I'd be out of here like a shot!'

'If you could walk, we'd throw you out, don't worry!' Cinders grinned.

Trudie giggled like a little girl. 'I believe you!'

Cinders went to the door. 'OK, love, I'll be back soon, and we'll drink our tea together, have a nice chat.'

Those were the best nights, when Cinders was on; she always made sure of staying awake if Cinders was on duty. They often had a cup of tea or cocoa together. Trudie had begun calling the nurse Cinders because at night there were so many dirty, routine jobs left over from the day rota, like taking the soiled bandages to the boiler and disposing of all the garbage a busy ward managed to make during the day – and it was Cinders who seemed to be the one who got the worst tasks.

They were very understaffed in the ward; the nurses all got bad-tempered at times but Cinders never did, whatever the provocation. Trudie was always glad to see Cinders coming on duty.

'Did you see the show tonight?' Trudie asked when Cinders brought the tray of tea and Nice biscuits.

'Now, what do you think? Of course I did, never miss it, do I?' Cinders passed her a mug of tea and a couple of biscuits.

'Derek Fenn looks older every time I see him. Getting past it, losing his hair, and those teeth don't fit, do they? Ought to get some better teeth than that.'

'Derek Fenn?' repeated Cinders, not really listening.

'You know – the desk sergeant.'

'Oh, the father figure who patronises her every time he opens his mouth!'

Trudie giggled. 'Father figure! He wouldn't like it if he heard you call him that. Oh, quite the ladies' man, Derek Fenn, once upon a time, that is. He was after our Annie once, years ago, mind.'

Cinders sat up. 'But he's old enough to . . .'

'Be her father!' ended Trudie, chuckling. 'Well, that never stops them, does it?'

'She didn't . . .?'

'Didn't what?' Trudie couldn't remember what they had been talking about, and panic surged through her. 'What was I saying?' she whispered and Cinders gave her a soothing smile.

'Derek Fenn, love, remember? You were saying he chased Annie once – remember? How did Annie feel about him?'

Suspiciously, Trudie said, 'Why are you asking so many questions about my Annie?'

'I thought you liked talking about your Annie? If you don't, never mind, we'll talk about anything you like.'

Trudie subsided, her little flurry of temper gone. 'I just don't want you telling anyone what I say – reporters are always trying to get sleezy stories on stars. And Derek Fenn has plenty of sleeze in his life; he's a drunk, can't stay off the stuff. Why d'you think his career went down the drain? He was at the top once, now look at him . . . grateful to play a bit part for peanuts. My Annie would never have let him lay a hand on her, though, don't worry! But she never forgets he got her her first big chance.' Trudie leaned back, sighing, closing her tired eyes, remembering those days. 'She almost never made it in the business. She said to me, "It's over, Mum, I'll never be an actress now." It broke my heart.' She sighed heavily. 'I wanted to be an actress when I was a girl – my parents wouldn't hear of it. From the minute my little Annie was born I was determined she was going to get what I didn't. I knew she would make it, there was always something special about her – oh, she wasn't pretty, but I knew somehow, always knew, she could be a star.'

'She's that, alright!'

'I made sure of that. If I hadn't pushed her she'd never have taken that job with Derek Fenn. But nobody was standing between my Annie and her future, nobody! That bastard! If I could have got my hands on him I'd have killed him. She was all for giving up; I had to do something fast or it would all have been over. But my little nest egg had run out by then, I was short of money myself.'

'Why did Annie need money? Was this for drama school?'

The old woman opened her eyes then and gave the nurse a sharp, narrow, wary look.

'I didn't say she needed money.'

'Yes, you did, you said . . .'

'I never said any such thing. I was talking about the show. Good tonight, it was, although I hate that superintendent . . . what's that actor's name? Too pretty, teeth too white, smiles too much, over acts, but thinks he's the cat's whiskers.'

159

Cinders never made her feel she was going crazy just because she forgot things now and then. 'Mike Waterford.'

'Mike Waterford, that's right,' she said with satisfaction. 'Thinks he's God's gift, doesn't he? My Annie can't stand him.'

'So the press stories aren't true? She isn't having an affair with him?'

'With Mike Waterford! Never on a Sunday. No, she hates the man. My Annie hasn't got any time for men now. One man let her down badly. . . No, she doesn't want any men around her now. Pity, she's a lovely girl, but she's learnt you can't trust them.'

'Not even Derek Fenn?'

'He's different,' the old woman reluctantly admitted. 'He's a bit of a bastard, too, but he came along just at the right moment, I'll say that for him. He saw her act at drama school and came round to see us, and offer her this part in a TV series he was doing – I'd prayed and dreamed about a chance like that for her, and I had to tell him the silly little bitch had got herself knocked up.'

'What?'

The startled voice made Trudie jump. 'What's wrong?' she whimpered. 'What did I say?'

'You said she had a baby. I never heard about any baby.'

Whispering, Trudie said, 'No, you're lying, I never mentioned a baby.'

'You just said . . .'

'There was no baby!' Trudie looked over the nurse's white shoulder, checked the whole ward, as if she was passing on state secrets, then whispered, 'She couldn't have it, see? She was just starting her career, she was only a kid herself. A baby would have ruined her life. She had this marvellous chance offered to her, but she couldn't take it because she would have started to show before they began filming. Derek Fenn said, "Get rid of it. You've got star quality," he said, "don't waste it." But we didn't have the money. I only just kept us going with what I earned in the shop, it was a real struggle for me. Derek Fenn lent us the money, he paid for the abortion and took it out of her salary over the next few months.'

'An abortion? Annie . . . had an abortion?'

'I said to her . . . "these days plenty of girls do, it's legal, it will be safe." She had it done by a proper doctor. She went in one day and was out the next, it was all very quick and simple.'

'Who was the father?' Cinders hoarsely asked.

'Nobody you'd know – some stupid boy who lodged with us for a while, nobody important.'

Trudie closed her eyes, her lips moving silently, her worn hands clenching on the bedclothes.

'Nobody, he was nobody,' she mumbled barely audibly.

The nurse watched her, realising she had drifted off again.

It was a moment or two before Trudie opened her eyes with a start, stared at Cinders wildly.

'Where am I? Who are you? You're. . .you're. . .what are you doing here?' She opened her mouth wide on a gasp of panic. 'Where am I? Where's my Annie? Stay away from me! Don't you come near me!'

'It's me . . . Cinders . . . you've been asleep and forgotten,' Cinders said, looking anxiously round the shadowy ward, in case Trudie had woken everyone else up. But nobody had stirred; the rows of bodies in narrow beds lay still in drugged sleep. Everyone in this ward got a sleeping pill; many of the old people were half-senile and if you didn't watch them like a hawk they got up and wandered off, giving hospital security a headache. It was easier to give them all a sleeping pill, including Trudie, but Cinders suspected Trudie didn't take her pill. Where was she hiding them? Maybe it was time they did another search of her bed and cabinet?

Subsiding, Trudie gave a heavy sigh. 'I . . . I thought you were someone else for a minute. I get so muddled, are they putting something in my tea? What's happening to me?' She began to cry weakly and the nurse bent over her, soothing.

'Don't cry, Trudie, there's a good girl. Look, you haven't finished your tea – and it's your favourite mug with bluebells on it.'

Trudie took it in both of her trembling hands and sipped noisily; the warm tea oozed down her throat. After a moment or two, she had calmed down enough to turn chatty again. 'My Annie bought me this – to remind me how we used to pick bluebells in Epping Forest. Bill, my second husband, drove us out there every weekend. Annie and me, we loved to pick blue-bells in the spring. There were millions of them under the trees, sheets of blue. We picked armfuls.'

'These days they tell you not to touch them,' Cinders said.

'Well, nobody told us that years ago!' she said crossly, putting down her empty mug. 'Mind you, we always took care not to pull the plants up. We broke the stems off higher up, so the root stayed in the earth. They're white, the stems at the bottom, like an onion. Wonderful smell, the earth in spring . . .'

She closed her eyes and sighed; a second later she was asleep as suddenly as if she had switched off like a light.

At noon the following Friday the crew broke for lunch. Annie had no more scenes that day and decided to eat lunch at home but as she was heading for the lift Harriet caught up with her and put a hand on her arm to detain her. 'You haven't forgotten you're doing interviews in your dressing-room?'

Annie groaned. 'Oh, no! I had. Remind me . . . who is it I'm seeing?'

'You've got a mind like a sieve!'

'I've got other things to think about at the moment,' Annie snapped, and Harriet gave her a quick, sympathetic look.

'How is your mother?'

'Much the same. Very confused, and in a lot of pain unless they dope her up to the eyeballs.'

'Sorry, Annie. It must be hard to concentrate when you're so worried.' Harriet gave her one of those comradely little pats on the shoulder. 'OK, first you're seeing a woman from The Sun. From what publicity tell me, she's working on a big spread on women playing tough roles, no problem there for you. Just give her the stuff she wants and be friendly.'

'Who is it? Do I know her?'

'Bella Oxford?'

'Never heard of her.'

'She'll be bringing a photographer.' Harriet looked her over, nodding. 'You'll be fine in the suit, that's her angle, she'll want power dressing.'

'OK. And the other interview?'

163

'A reporter from Real Life Crime International Magazine.'

'What the hell's that?'

'American originally – started up in Europe this year. They're looking for stuff about the way we research the background material; they want to know how real our storylines are, if we work with the police, if we monitor court cases. All pretty obvious, don't worry about it.'

'Surely this is one for Sean?'

'They will be talking to Sean, and me, but they want to talk to you and Mike, as well. They'll want photos, too, but not today. – Publicity are supplying stills and official photos.' Harriet gave her another encouraging pat. 'The Sun woman arrives at two; you've got a couple of hours, but don't leave the building, Annie. We don't want to have to chase after you, or make apologies to The Sun. Do you want a lunch tray in your dressing-room? Or are you going to the canteen?'

'The canteen — at least I'll get a different view,' Annie said bitterly, and Harriet grinned at her.

'Tough at the top, isn't it?'

'Oh, get stuffed!' Annie told her as she stepped into the waiting lift.

She spent an hour in the canteen talking to friends. At two o'clock she was back in her dressing-room to do the interview with the woman from The Sun; the photographer, typically, spent ages trying tricky shots using the mirrors lining the room, and then wanted to take pictures in the studio with a camera in the background. The publicity girl, who was present, quickly ruled that one out. The interview itself went quite smoothly, and then the PR girl insisted on showing the photographer and journalist out to the front desk.

She came back ten minutes later with the second reporter. Annie was just pulling a polite smile on to her face when she saw the man's face, and almost fainted. It was Johnny.

5

'Hello, Annie', he said, holding out his hand, 'Long time, no see.'

She was dazed, but she had had years of training in hiding her feelings.

'Hello, Johnny,' she said huskily, and put out her hand to meet his.

His hand was cold; that made it real, she wasn't dreaming. Her body jerked in shock. She was touching Johnny. After eight long years of dreaming about him, mourning for him, she was touching him again. It was like being reconnected to the electric main after being cut off. There was a surge of current so powerful that she couldn't breath for a second or two.

The PR girl did a double-take. 'Oh, you've met before?' Her professional smile was in place but her eyes were irritated, reproachful as she glanced at Annie. 'Annie forgot to tell me that.'

Annie could have pointed out that she hadn't been told the name of the magazine reporter she was going to see, only the name of his magazine, but she didn't, because she wasn't even listening. Nor was Johnny. They stood there, hands clasped, looking at each other without saying a word. Her ears beat with hypertension, a roaring like the sea on a stormy day. How many times in the past eight years had she dreamt of seeing him, looked for him in busy streets, from buses or trains, wondered where he was, what he was doing, and why, why, why, had he walked out on her like that?

The PR girl gave them a sharp, curious stare. 'Can I get you a drink, then? Coffee, tea?'

'Tea would be nice,' Johnny said, finally letting go of Annie's hand.

The connection broken, she snapped awake, her blue eyes opening wide, dark with shock and disbelief.

Johnny was carrying a black leather briefcase in his other hand; setting it down on the smooth plastic top of the dressing-table, he took out a tape machine and began fiddling with it, his black head bent.

The PR girl asked Annie, 'Tea for you, too? Or do you want coffee?'

'Tea, please.'

The girl went out, closing the door quietly behind her.

Annie didn't even notice her going, she was too busy watching Johnny's mirrored reflection. He looked so different. But she would have recognised him anywhere. Johnny, she thought. Johnny. He was here, in the same room with her. She couldn't believe it.

His eyes were still that dark, magnetic blue, his black lashes still as long and thick. He was not a boy any more, though. This was was a man, with a hard, striking face, rawboned and angular, very spare-fleshed, as if he ate very little.

His head lifted, he looked at her, right into her eyes.

'Where have you been?' she broke out. 'Why did you go away without a word? You might at least have told me you were going.'

His voice was harsh. 'What do you mean, without a word? I got in touch ... I told you what had happened ...'

She stared blankly at him. 'You didn't tell me anything. What are you talking about? You just ran out of the house and never came back. You left all your things upstairs in our spare room, you didn't pay that last week's rent, you simply vanished.'

'I rang to explain and . . .'

'Rang? You never rang us.' She had listened for the phone hour after hour, for what had seemed like eternity, but must have been the next week or so, but he hadn't rung.

'Yes, I did – but your mother said –'

'My mother?' interrupted Annie, stiffening, alerted by the mention of her mother. Even at the time she had known that Trudie wanted to cut her off from Johnny, but Trudie had been at the shop most of the time, she hadn't been in the house.

'Yes, I kept ringing without getting a reply, then I realised you must both be out, you at the school and your mother at the shop, so I rang after six one evening and finally got your mother, but she said you weren't there.'

'When was this?' Annie was trying to think back to that time, but it was as if there was a great stone wall in her memory; something had happened that was too painful to push through or see past. It made it hard to remember the exact sequence of events.

Johnny looked as uncertain as she felt. 'I can't remember the date . . . I was in hospital, I'd been in a crash and I had head injuries, I was still recovering when I rang, I was heavily sedated, and very confused.'

'But I rang the police and the hospital, they said they hadn't had any report of an accident that day.'

'They wouldn't know anything about it, it didn't happen up here in London, I crashed on a motorway in the West Country, not far from Salisbury.'

Her eyes widened. 'What on earth were you doing there?'

He looked paler than ever, his eyes a darker blue. 'God knows. I never remembered afterwards – I was taken to a hospital nearby, I was unconscious for a few days, when I came to I had some sort of memory blank. It was days before I could remember anything much, but when my memory started coming back I asked for a phone and they wheeled a portable phone to my bed, and I rang you, but your mother said you had gone away, she wouldn't say where, she said you never wanted to see me again, and to leave you alone.'

That was the moment when Annie believed him. She clutched at a chair, sat down. Oh, God, so that was it? All this time she had been blaming Johnny for leaving when it had been her mother who sent him away.

'I rang every day for weeks, but she just hung up every time she heard my voice,' Johnny said in a slow, heavy voice, staring at her. 'I kept hoping you would answer the phone, but you never did. Why, Annie? Why didn't you ever answer the phone? Where were you?'

'I was ill; I had . . . a sort of nervous breakdown . . .' She wanted to tell him about the baby, but she couldn't, she couldn't get the words out. She had never talked about it to anyone, it was all bottled up inside her, buried deep inside, an agony she was afraid to release because of what might spill out of her, emotions she had not felt able to face at the time and couldn't even now. Locking it all away had seemed the only way to cope with what she felt.

'Nervous breakdown?' He stared at her, his irises dilated, glistening with feeling. 'Was that over what happened with your drama school tutor? What was his name? The bastard who . . .'

'Roger Keats.' She shuddered as she said his name aloud.

'Roger Keats,' Johnny repeated, looking confused, as if he didn't remember exactly what had happened. 'That's right. But . . . you said they were going to sack him.'

'I left the school anyway, I never went back after that day. I was ill – my mother didn't lie about that. It was a bad time for me, I don't like to remember.' She had been in hospital for a few days, having the abortion, and after that she had been very depressed.

He stared at her fixedly. 'Was that because I left, then?'

She flushed. 'Oh, it was all such a muddle, I just hate remembering. I didn't know where you had gone, or why – it was a terrible time. I don't actually remember it in much detail.' She had never wanted to; she had only wanted to forget. 'I tried to find you. . .I rang the police, and the hospital, and later on. . .weeks later. . . I went to see your solicitor, but he wouldn't tell me anything. Why wouldn't he tell me you had been in an accident? Did he tell you I'd been to see him?'

'No, but I'd given him instructions not to tell anyone where I was, by then. I'd decided just to vanish, once I faced the fact that you weren't going to write back.'

Puzzled, she watched him intently. He was wearing dark blue jeans and a black shirt without a tie, open at the collar. The clothes fitted him like a glove, emphasising his long legs and small waist. He looked very fit, and yet there was a gauntness about him, as if he had been ill. His face had no colour in it which was maybe why those eyes looked so blue.

'Why didn't you want anyone to know where you were? Where have you been all this time, Johnny?'

He looked away, frowning. 'In prison.'

It was like an aftershock during a time of earthquakes; she stared at him incredulously, feeling the tremors running through her, no longer certain of the ground she stood on, afraid to move because nothing was safe or sure any more.

First she had had to come to terms with the idea of Johnny having crashed his bike, of his claim to have rung her, of her mother having lied to her in order to separate them. And now this!

He looked back at her, his mouth a white line in his pale face. 'You might as well know the truth. When I crashed I was being chased by the police for speeding. I drove off that night in such a state of mind that I didn't know what I was doing. I was doing around a hundred miles an hour, but I didn't even know it. The police stopped me, and I lost my temper, attacked one of them, hit him with a spanner, and drove off again. I crashed an hour later.'

Another deep tremor of shock shook her. 'Johnny,' she whispered. 'I can't believe it, Johnny – you of all people. I can't imagine you being violent.'

'I was almost crazy that night; half out of my mind after what you'd told me . . . I drove around in a daze, I didn't know where I was going, or what I was doing, I wanted to kill someone, and when the police stopped me I just went for one of them. He was a big chap with a bullet head; he started pushing me around, and I lost my temper. I hit him hard, I half killed him and I got ten years for it.'

171

She couldn't believe her ears. Johnny, trying to kill a policeman? She thought of him eight years ago, a skinny boy . . . Well, he wasn't skinny any more. Still slim, of course, but his shoulders were wide under that shirt, his chest deep; when he moved she saw muscles ripple against the cotton cloth. He was different in other ways; this man was not the boy she had known. She couldn't imagine her Johnny trying to kill anyone. He had been too gentle.

'Eight years in prison . . . it must have seemed like a lifetime,' she whispered.

'It did,' he flatly agreed. 'When I came out of hospital I went straight into prison. If you half kill one of them, the cops make sure you don't get bail. I had to wait months before my trial. I'm surprised you didn't read about it, there was quite a lot of press coverage.'

She shook her head dazedly. 'I rarely read newspapers, don't you remember? I still don't read them, especially the review pages. They depress me.'

And for a year or two after Johnny vanished and she had the abortion she had been so unhappy that nothing she did, nothing that happened around her, had made any impression. She had been in a fog of misery.

Johnny smiled quickly. 'I remember. I remember everything.'

They looked at each other and she could barely breath.

Huskily he said, 'I pleaded guilty, although my lawyer thought I was mad. I got ten years, but I only did eight. I came out a few weeks ago.'

'So all this time, all these years, you've been in prison?'

He nodded as if he wasn't really listening. His eyes

were staring at the wall behind her, their centres black holes into which his thoughts had vanished. What was he seeing? What terrible things had happened to him in prison? No wonder he was so pale and gaunt, as if he had been living at the bottom of a deep, dark hole. She felt her heart move with pity.

Suddenly he broke out, voice hoarse, 'And your mother never told you I'd rung? She never even told you? And the letters – I wrote to you from prison for a few months . . . and never had a reply.'

'Letters?' Annie was shaking. So there had been letters too, letters she never got. Letters her mother must have destroyed – oh, how could she? How could she do such a cruel thing?

'Why?' Johnny muttered. 'Why? Why did she do that to me, to us? I thought she liked me, I never did her any harm, I was fond of her.'

'When you rang, did you tell her you were in hospital?'

He nodded. 'Of course I did.'

'Did you tell her about the crash, about the policeman you had hit? About having to go to prison?'

'No, I just said I was in hospital. But when I wrote, later, it was from prison.'

Annie groaned aloud. 'That explains it, then.' Her mother's ambition had driven her to separate them. She hadn't approved of Annie getting involved with Johnny, anyway – he couldn't help Annie, couldn't push her towards success. When she discovered that Annie was pregnant by him she had been furious – and then Johnny wrote to her from prison. Trudie must have opened the letter. Annie could imagine her feelings when she read Johnny's news.

Trudie had always been obsessed with respectability;

her working-class background had taught her you had to work hard to survive. It was bred in her bones, the grim understanding of how easy it could be to slip, to slide down into poverty and hopelessness.

Discovering that Johnny was in trouble with the police, she would have been ruthlessly determined to part them for ever. He wasn't dragging Annie and Trudie down with him.

Johnny looked hard into her face, as if hunting for something in her eyes.

'She didn't want you involved with me any more if I was going to prison for years? Well, I can't blame her for that. I couldn't have offered you anything; I was guilty, I couldn't deny the charges, I knew I was going down for a long time. Maybe I shouldn't have tried to contact you, maybe she was right.' He held her eyes. 'But . . . if you had got my letters would you have written back, Annie?'

She nodded, unable to speak.

He looked as if he didn't believe her. 'Sure? Would you – knowing that I was going to be in prison for years?'

'Yes.' Nothing could have come between them if he hadn't simply vanished from her life. She had needed him, it had hurt her badly to lose him. It hurt her now, to realise how it had happened, to know that her own mother had deliberately separated them. And the baby, she thought, anguish turning in her like a knife. She made me kill my baby.

She pushed the thought aside. She always did. She had never been able to bear the memory. Those few weeks of her life had been hell. She had blanked them out in self-protection.

The door opened and the PR girl came in with a

tray; she looked from one to the other quickly. 'Interview going well? I'm sorry, but I'll have to hurry you, Mr Tyrone. Miss Lang is needed back on the set for a re-take in half an hour.'

'Sure,' Johnny said, switching on his tape machine. 'Now, where were we, Miss Lang? Oh, yes, tell me, how much research did you personally do before you began work on the series?'

Sean watched Marty Keats on the edge of the set; her mouth full of pins, she was adjusting the fit of a policewoman's jacket.

'It's a size too big!' protested the actress inside the jacket.

'It won't show when I've finished; stand still, for God's sake.' Marty was pinning rapidly as she spoke without moving her lips.

'Come on, come on,' shouted the studio manager. 'Harriet's waiting for her!'

Marty stood up. 'That's the best I can do.'

The actress looked into a mirror leaning against the wall, groaned, and ran.

'It looked fine to me,' Sean said, smiling at Marty Keats.

She glanced round at him, her eyes brightening at the sight of an attractive man. 'Thanks. You're the scriptwriter, aren't you?'

'That's right. Sean. Who are you, apart from being very clever with your hands?'

'Marty. Marty Keats.'

'Marty, nice name.' Sean took off his blue denim jacket and gestured to the right sleeve of his shirt. 'I don't suppose you could do anything about this rip in my sleeve?'

'I don't know if my union rules allow me to do work unless I'm paid for it!'

'Happy to buy you a couple of drinks,' he offered, giving her a slow smile.

She fluttered her thick false lashes at him. 'Now you're talking! I'll see what I can do.'

'You're an angel. I was in too much of a hurry, coming into the studio, and caught my sleeve on a door-handle.' Sean had spent some time arranging the 'accident'; he hoped it looked natural.

'You'll have to take it off, honey. I can't sew it while you're wearing it.'

Sean began undoing his buttons, slid the shirt off. Marty eyed his broad shoulders and muscled chest, her tongue-tip running around her lower lip.

She put out a hand and squeezed his arm muscles. 'I bet you work out regularly.'

'In every sense of the word,' Sean said, and she giggled.

'Naughty boy.' Her hand lingered on his bare arm, stroking him.

Her hair was the most extraordinary colour; a mass of wild orange curls, flauntingly unreal. Was it a wig? Or dyed? And how old was she? Close to fifty, he suspected. And dressing like fifteen.

She sat down and began work on his sleeve; it only took her a short while, her needle moving deftly and quickly.

'Brilliant,' Sean congratulated, shrugging back into his shirt.

As he started doing up the buttons again, she pushed his hand away and did it for him, her scarlet-nailed fingers moving slowly down his chest. Sean had to fight the impulse to shudder. He disliked her touching

176

him. Her nails were so long and so pointed, more like the talons of a predatory bird; he had a sudden image of them tearing at him, rending him, and the hairs rose on the back of his neck

'You dating Harriet?' she asked him softly.

He shook his head.

'Everyone's betting you are.'

'Then everyone is wrong.'

'Our shining, shimmering star, then?'

Sean looked blankly down at her. 'What?'

She gave him a cynical smile. 'Sweet little old Annie, darling – the star of the show, are you giving it to her?'

'No,' he said, disliking her so intensely he wanted to hit her, but trying hard not to show it.

Her fingers lingered suggestively around his belt, clipping into it, slithering down inside his jeans.

Sean tried to look as if he liked it. His smile was hurting his face and he felt cold sweat on his forehead.

'If there's anything else I can ever do for you, just ask,' she purred.

He felt sick, but said, 'We did agree to have those drinks, remember?'

'I'm working until six.'

'The pub across the road docs a great steak and we could split a bottle of red wine.'

'Big spender. OK, then – six o'clock in the pub.'

Annie said goodbye at the end of the corridor – Johnny was going to the right, to take the lift down to the exit, and she was going down the stairs to the studio.

'Thank you for a very good interview. I'll let you see a copy before it goes to the printers,' Johnny said.

'Send it to me,' the PR girl said quickly.

He nodded but his eyes stayed on Annie.

She said huskily, 'I'll give you my private number, Johnny. I'm ex-directory, so it isn't in the phone book.'

The PR girl frowned disapproval.

Johnny said, 'Is it still the same?' And said the number.

Annie gave a choky little laugh. 'My God, your memory is phenomenal. Yes, that's still it, but there's the London prefix number now, of course. 0171 comes in front of the rest.'

He nodded. 'I'll remember.'

Would he ring her? Annie stared at him, trying to decide. Did she really want him to? A whole lifetime divided them. She was not the wide-eyed girl she had been; he was not that skinny, eager, gentle boy.

The PR girl shifted pointedly. 'Sorry, but they're waiting for you on the set, Annie.'

She nodded, sighed. 'Yes, OK, I'm coming. Bye, Johnny.'

He put out a hand, their fingers touched, then she tore herself away.

Annie and Derek had to do a re-take of a brief scene they had shot that morning.

'Sorry, not your fault. We've had to chop the next two scenes, they didn't work out, so yours has to be re-shot,' explained Harriet as they hung about waiting for the cameraman to set up the same angle he had used before, for the lighting team to fix the level of lighting.

'Can't you just jumpcut?' grumbled Derek.

They usually shot three times as much film as they actually used, and when Harriet saw the unprocessed film she would simply jump-cut to make the story run well. It was unusual to re-shoot: far too costly, especially if you were working on location, but this scene had been shot on the studio set.

Harriet gave him a dry look. 'If I could, I would, thank you, Derek. I do know my job.' She handed them each a sheet of script. 'Just mull this over, then we'll do a quick run-through before we shoot.'

She darted away and Derek glared after her.

'I was on my way home when she caught me. I'm dead on my feet. This job is a mug's game, I get paid buttons and I'm worked like a slave.'

Annie was reading her lines, not listening to him. Sean hadn't altered much; she read the words again, frowning with concentration.

'I'm getting sacks of fan mail, now, you know,' Derek muttered. 'Time I had a rise. Annie, will you speak to Harriet for me? Tell her you think I should have a rise. I get almost as much fan mail as Mike Bloody Waterford.'

'I heard that! And it's a lie, you don't,' Mike said behind them. 'Stop kidding yourself. I get more mail than anyone.'

Annie looked round at him and he gave her a slow, mocking smile, one of his practised smiles, meant to make women's hearts beat faster. It did absolutely nothing for her.

'Including you, darling,' he told her. 'I get twice as much fan mail as you do.'

Annie didn't bother to answer. It was probably true; women all over the country went crazy over him, fell hook, line and sinker for the auburn hair and languorous dark eyes, the totally phoney charm of that smile.

'I bet you earn twice as much, too!' Derek complained, his face sullen.

'I'm worth every penny,' Mike said in self-satisfaction, sauntering away.

'I'm not being paid what I'm worth,' said Derek. 'Will you talk to Harriet for me, Annie?'

'Talk to her yourself. But it isn't her decision, you know that. She has to convince accounts about every single penny she spends.' Annie hunched her shoulders. 'Look, can we learn these lines? We haven't got all day.'

He looked quickly around to make sure nobody could hear them, then lowered his voice to a hissing whisper, grabbing her arm to make her look at him. 'Annie, don't force me to sell my story to the papers – because they'd pay a fortune! They've never managed to dig up any scandal about you; they'll jump at what I know. I've never breathed a word before, I don't want to – but if my back is up against the wall, I might have to.'

Angrily she pulled free of him. 'Don't you threaten me, you bastard!'

'It isn't a threat, it's a warning!' Derek snarled.

Annie became aware of people around them looking round, curious eyes, whispers.

'Just shut up, will you?' she muttered.

He lowered his voice, but wouldn't give up. 'I'm desperate, Annie. Have you forgotten how that feels? You were pretty desperate to raise money for that abortion and I came through with the money, didn't I? I didn't let you down. If it wasn't for me you wouldn't be where you are today.'

She thought of her dead baby, of the years of pain and guilt, and tears burnt behind her eyes. Was he asking her for gratitude for all that? She looked at him bitterly.

'You make me sick! Leave me alone, will you?' She walked away towards Harriet, who gave her a frown of concern.

'What's going on? Were you and Derek having a row?'

'He was on about money again, and got nasty when I refused to lend him any, or ask you to give him a rise.'

'Gambling again?' Harriet grimaced. 'It's getting worse, is it? What are we going to do about him? He is popular, can't argue with that, but if the press pick up on his drinking and gambling that could change.'

Hesitantly Annie asked, 'Could you wangle him a rise, Harriet?'

'I'll think about it. Has he got something on you, Annie?' Harriet's eyes were shrewd and very sharp. 'Could he become a problem? Because if so I'm sure Billy could deal with him. You're vital to the series. We don't want a has-been like Derek making waves.'

Annie hesitated. She couldn't face talking about the baby. The anguish welled up inside her just thinking about it; she turned her head away and closed her eyes, trying to calm herself.

Then she looked back at Harriet. 'If I need help dealing with Derek, I'll come to you,' she promised.

Harriet eyed her, shrugged. 'OK, do that.' She raised her voice and yelled. 'Derek, we're waiting for you.'

Derek sauntered towards them looking sullen.

'OK, on your marks,' Harriet said. She walked off to join the cameraman and the lighting team, who were still moving bits of equipment about to improve the lighting on the set. They were rarely satisfied; if you left them to themselves they would be there for hours, fiddling with equipment.

Derek handed Annie a small white cardboard box. 'Here, this is for you.'

She took it doubtfully. 'What is it?' The box had her name printed on it, but there was no postmark; it had not come through the post.

'Open it and see.'

'Is it from you?'

Before he could answer Harriet clapped her hands. 'Ready, Annie? We're all ready for you. Come on, we're running out of time, let's get going.'

Annie put the box into her handbag and moved to the chalk mark on which she had to stand.

When they were finished with the scene she walked over to Harriet and said, 'You free this evening?' And when Harriet nodded, said, 'Will you come to dinner at my place? I want to talk to you.'

She had to talk to somebody.

Sean was in the bar of the Green Man pub dead on six that evening. Marty was ten minutes late. The dark oak-panelled bar was crowded, but he saw her at once when she came through the swing doors, wearing a black leather coat tightly belted at the waist, stilt-like shiny black high heels, her make-up heavy, her mouth the same predatory red as her long fingernails.

She looked around the bar, Sean waved and she came over, swaying sensuously, watched by half the men in the bar. One or two wolf-whistled. She gave them a smouldering sideways look, a half-smile of encouragement.

I've ordered steak and chips, but I thought we'd have a drink first,' Sean said as she sat down opposite him. Sean pushed a glass of whisky towards her. 'Whisky OK, or would you rather have something else?'

'Whisky's just what I need,' she said, taking half of it down in one swallow. She put the glass back on the table and unbelted her coat; under it she was wearing a low-cut flame red dress; he could see her freckled pale breasts right down to the nipple. Watching Sean she said, 'How far from here is your flat?'

'Half a mile.'

She leaned over the table and her dress sank even lower; he could almost see her navel. 'After our steaks we could go on there, then.'

Sean's gorge rose at the thought, but he smiled. 'Won't your husband be waiting for you?'

She swallowed the rest of her whisky before she answered. 'The sod ran out on me years ago.'

'Sorry, did I touch on a sore point? Or were you glad to see the back of him?'

She looked down into her empty glass. 'Can I have another whisky, or is it rationed?'

He waved to the barman, mouthing, 'two more whiskies, Fred!'

'I don't usually drink that much,' Marty said. 'It's just the men in my life that drive me to drink.' She took the glass from the barman, smiling flirtatiously at him. 'But I love you, Fred, you know that, don't you?'

'Sure I do,' he said indifferently, going back to his bar.

Marty drank, her eyes half-closed. Sean was still on his first glass; he sipped a little, waiting.

'Have you got kids, Marty?'

'Oh, yeah, he left me with the kids . . . and not a

penny in maintenance, either. At least I got the house, in the divorce settlement.'

'He didn't contest the divorce?'

'We couldn't find him to tell him about it. The bastard was in Australia at the time – now he's back in England, but if he thinks he's getting any money out of me, he's wrong.'

'He's asked you for money?'

'Men always end up asking you for everything they can get. Well, he won't get anything from me. The house is mine and I'm hanging on to it.'

'Is he trying to get the house from you? Have you seen him, Marty?'

Marty frowned, staring across the table. 'You ask a lot of questions.'

'I'm just interested,' he said.

Her eyes narrowed. 'Oh, yeah? You were a cop before you got into scriptwriting, weren't you? Once a cop always a cop.' She put a finger to her nose, flattening the nostrils, made a snuffling noise. 'And once a pig always a pig.'

'Oh, thanks,' Sean said, grinning, trying to keep the atmosphere light, but she merely glowered at him.

'I might have known you were up to something, inviting me out. Why do I always get taken for a ride? I keep thinking I've learnt my lesson where men are concerned, but I keep getting suckered.' Angrily she drained her glass and got to her feet. 'I'm going. You can eat the bloody steaks yourself.'

'Did you know that he was still bothering Annie Lang?' Sean asked as she turned to go.

Marty stood still, her face blank. 'I don't know what you're talking about.'

Sean didn't believe her. 'Tell him to leave Annie alone, or he'll find himself in prison this time.'

'Is that what all this is about? You just wanted to pump me about Roger? You dirty bastard. And I thought it was me you were interested in! Serves me right for being a woman. Women are always the ones who get the fuzzy end of life's lollipop, aren't we?'

'Just tell him, Marty,' Sean insisted.

'Tell him yourself. And I hope he splits your head open with a meat cleaver.' Marty's face was convulsed in sudden fury. She pushed through the crowded bar, the swing doors parting and closing behind her.

The curtains were drawn. The light of a gas fire gave a red glow to the darkness, dimly lit up the pictures of Annie lining the walls.

Lying on his back, the man on the bed stared at them, a tiny muscle ticking beside his mouth. They were all Annie, yet a whole gallery of different women stared back at him.

Annie in a simple cotton dress looking about fifteen, with wide, innocent blue eyes; Annie cold and faintly masculine in her dark grey policewoman's suit; Annie kneeling on a bed, leaning forward, seductive in a lacy slip which showed her small breasts and a lot of her smooth, pale skin, her lips parted in a soft gasp of invitation, her eyes shimmering sensually; Annie in jeans and a black leather jacket looking tough and competent.

Which was the real woman? Or was she all of them? Or none of them?

She acted a part all the time, on the screen and off. The public thought they knew her, but they were wrong. Nobody really knew her, except him. He knew her more intimately than anyone in the world.

She couldn't hide from him; he was inside her head. He had thought about her all these years until he was under her skin, a red corpuscle in her blood, so much a part of her that no surgeon's knife could cut him out.

She knew; he had made sure she never forgot him – he was sure she looked over her shoulder all the time in case he was behind her, she listened for his voice every time she picked up a phone, she was waiting with terror for him, especially since she woke up to find that rose on her pillow, the Valentine's card beside her bed.

He wished he could have seen her face. Ever since that morning she must be on the rack, wondering what he would do next, when he would come for her.

The joke was that he was always there, she simply hadn't recognised him. She wasn't the only one who could act a part, deceive people. He could do it too; could walk the streets and not be recognised. It was amazing how little people used their eyes, how much they missed.

He looked at the picture of Annie half-naked and breathed thickly, God, she was beautiful; he thought of all the things he wanted to do to her, would do to her, soon, very soon. But she had betrayed him; she had made him suffer. She had to suffer too. She had to be punished for what she had done to him, and then he would finally have her.

Trudie was asleep when Annie got to the hospital. 'She's fine,' the ward sister said. 'It's the drugs she has to keep the pain down, they make her sleep a lot, and that's good for her, at the moment. She's doing well, don't worry.'

Annie stood by the bed looking at the frail, work-worn hands, the gaunt face. Her mother looked small, like a child, in the bed; she had shrunk overnight. Annie sat down beside the bed and held those tired hands for a long time, stroking the backs of them with her thumbs.

She left the hospital at six thirty, took a taxi and arrived home just as Harriet drove up in Sean's black Porsche.

Annie was taken aback, irritated at seeing them both – lately they seemed to be trying to take her over, run her life. But she hid her reaction, unlocked the front door and invited them both in. 'I was going to make omelette fines herbes, with salad,' she said. 'I expect I could stretch it for three.'

'I wasn't muscling in on your evening,' Sean said. 'I just drove Harriet here – but I did want a word with you.'

'Well, come in and have a drink, anyway,' Annie said, leading the way into the house. She stood in the hall, with its scent of beeswax polish, the deep-toned sound of the nineteenth-century grandfather clock which her mother had inherited from her own father, and listened anxiously to the silence upstairs. Sean watched her, frowning.

'I'll just check upstairs, shall I?' He must have picked up on her nervousness.

He ran upstairs, and Harriet gave her a sharp, curious look.

'What's going on, Annie? Oh, come on, I'm not stupid. It's obvious something is up. You and Sean have secrets, you're rowing all the time with Derek – if any of this can affect the series I ought to be warned.'

Annie sighed. 'I was going to tell you this evening – that's why I asked you over.'

Sean came back, taking the stairs two at a time. 'All clear.'

Annie led the way into the sitting-room, and poured them both a drink.

'How's your mother?' Sean asked, sitting down on a blue brocade couch and looking around the high-ceilinged room while Annie told him about her visit to the hospital. The décor was much as it had been all Annie's life; Trudie hated changes, so the room had a curiously old-fashioned feel to it. The blue-striped wallpaper had been renewed in a similar pattern a few years back and the Axminster carpet had been on this floor as long as Annie could remember. On the long between-the-wars sideboard against one wall stood two dark blue Majolica vases with pale blue irises sculpted on their sides. They had been bought by Annie's father years ago. Annie had always loved them; their deep colour had pleased her even as a child and since her father's death they had meant even more to her. Every time she saw them she was reminded of him, of how safe he had made her feel when she was tiny, how he had often carried her on his back downstairs to breakfast, how he had let her help him fill the Majolica vases with spring flowers, yellow daffodils and tulips.

'What a cosy room. It's got that lovely lived-in feeling,' Harriet said approvingly. 'I like these old Edwardian houses, there's so much space, with these big windows and high ceilings.'

As Annie smiled at her, Sean shifted impatiently. He was never interested in small talk. 'Look, Annie,' he said, 'I talked to Marty Keats. It's obvious she knows something. She says her husband is back in England, and I got the impression he was trying to get money out of her. I think she knows he's threatening you. Annie, keep Harriet here tonight – tell her everything you told me. I'd feel a lot happier if you weren't here alone.'

'I can't spend the rest of my life hiding or surrounding myself with people!'

'You won't have to. Just a few days. I'm going to arrange for someone to watch Marty Keats.'

'You aren't telling the police! Sean, I don't want the police brought in to this!'

'No, no, this is a private detective. He used to work with me at Blackfriars; now he's gone private, and he's very discreet. He's a good friend of mine. I'd trust him with my life.'

She chewed her lower lip uncertainly. 'But even if you do find Roger Keats, what can you do about him?'

'Put the fear of God into him.'

Annie half wished she hadn't confided in Sean. Her nerves were jumping like ants on a hot plate. How would Roger Keats react if Sean confronted him? She remembered his vicious fury after she reported him to the governors at the school. She'd been afraid he might actually kill her. She was still afraid of that – she had the feeling he was working up to it. He was like a cat playing with a cornered mouse. When he had got enough fun out of tormenting her, he would kill her.

That decided her. She couldn't live in this state of fear and uncertainty. She had to find out where Roger Keats was and what he was planning.

'Alright, ask your friend to track him down, Sean,' she said.

'Wise decision. It's always better to face your demons.'

Plaintively, Harriet said, 'How about filling me in on all this?'

Annie looked at her, then at Sean, her blue eyes pleading. 'Would you tell her, Sean? I'll go and start cooking. Stay for dinner, won't you? There are plenty of eggs. You do like omelette?'

'Love them. Thanks, I'd love to stay.'

She went out and began getting the salad together first, making a fresh low-calorie dressing with a dribble of walnut oil and white wine vinegar mixed with a touch of mustard. She tossed a crisp salad in it and set it aside while she reached for the china hen in which she kept her eggs.

Her arm brushed her handbag and it fell on the floor. A small white box tumbled out; she blinked in surprise, then remembered Derek giving it to her.

She had forgotten it until that moment. Curiously she opened the box and stared in shock.

Inside on a bed of tissue paper nestled a baby's bootee with a splash of red across the foot. Annie touched it with one finger and then looked at her fingertip. It was faintly sticky. Blood, Annie thought, her ears ringing with shock. It's blood. There was a card in the box too, one word printed on it in capital letters.

REMEMBER.

6

In the sitting-room, Sean and Harriet were talking in low-voices, keeping a wary ear open for Annie coming back.

'I'm seriously worried about her, Sean. She's looking ill. I'm not imagining it, am I? Strained and edgy, and as if she's on the verge of tears half the time. It's something to do with Derek, isn't it?'

'I know she asked me to tell you, but I think she should do it, I think she needs to talk.' He broke off, getting up hurriedly as they both heard a crash from the kitchen. 'What the hell was that?'

He ran out with Harriet hard on his heels as he burst into the kitchen.

Annie lay on the floor on her face, one arm flung out, the other crumpled under her.

Sean threw a look around the room, as if checking that there was nobody else there, nothing else out of place, but apart from Annie and a fallen chair there was nothing odd, so he went down on his knees beside her and turned her head without turning her body.

Her eyes were shut, but her lids were flickering, her lashes moving against her cheek.

Brushing the hair back from her face, Sean studied her, a hand on her throat, feeling for a pulse.

'She's not dead.' It wasn't so much a statement as a question, and Harriet had gone pale with shock.

'No, but her heartbeat is very slow. She's fainted, I think. Get me some water, Harriet. I'll try to bring her round.'

Harriet ran the kitchen cold tap, found a glass in a cupboard, filled it and brought it Sean, who had gently turned Annie round on to her back.

It was as he did so that he first saw the bootee; it lay under her body, where it had dropped from her hand.

'Christ!' grunted Sean and at the same time Harriet saw the bootee with the stain of blood soaking into it and took a startled breath.

'How weird – what's that doing there? A baby's bootee? Don't tell me she's pregnant, I couldn't be that unlucky. Halfway through the series and with all the scripts written and Annie in every one of them!'

She watched Sean lift Annie, an arm around her shoulders, supporting her, while he held the glass of water to her lips.

'Is that wine she's spilt on the bootee?'

Sean didn't answer; he was too intent on Annie, who had begun to splutter as the water trickled down her throat.

Opening her eyes, she looked up, right at him, her face white and blank.

'How do you feel, Annie? Can you sit up?'

'Should we call a doctor?' Harriet asked.

'No,' Annie said hurriedly.

'No,' agreed Sean. He was staring at the white cardboard box which he had just noticed under the table, where it had fallen.

'I'll be fine now, I'm . . .' Annie broke off as she saw the bootee on the floor.

Sean saw the shudder of revulsion run through her, the way her skin seemed to lose even more colour, turn the white of ice and snow, bloodless and cold.

Sliding an arm under her legs, he got to his feet holding her and walked quickly into the sitting-room, laid her full length on a deeply sprung white couch and put several cushions behind her head.

Closing her eyes again, Annie lay still, trying to control the shivers running through her.

Sean sat down on the couch beside her and picked up her restless, chilly little hands.

'Where did it come from, Annie?'

The quiet question made her stiffen. For a moment he thought she wasn't going to answer him; he could tell she didn't want to talk about it, but at last she whispered, 'Derek gave it to me at the studio today.'

'Derek?' The name jerked out of Harriet; Sean frowned round at her, putting a finger on his lips to silence her.

'What does it mean?' Sean held Annie's hands, rubbing them, trying to put some warmth back into them.

'I . . . I can't tell you . . .'

'He's blackmailing you, isn't he?'

She didn't answer.

'Who had a baby, Annie? You?'

She groaned, bit her lower lip; he saw a spot of bright red blood seep through the colourless flesh.

'There was a baby, and a death – or else why the blood? What's he threatening? To talk to the press? When was this, Annie? Recently?'

'I was at drama school, I was eighteen,' Annie fiercely said, pulling her hands away from him.

'And you got pregnant? Don't tell me Derek was the father?' Sean looked at her incredulously.

Annie's face answered for her; the shiver of repulsion was unmistakable. 'No!'

'Where does Derek come into it, then?' persisted Sean, and after a long pause she told him, her voice low and bleak.

'My boyfriend vanished, I had no money, and Derek came along at just that moment to offer me a part on TV. My mother and Derek talked me into an abortion, and because we had no money Derek paid for it. I've paid him back over and over again in the last few years.' She took a long, ragged breath. 'And, God, I've bitterly regretted it ever since. I shouldn't have listened to them, I didn't want to kill my baby – but I'd been through a bad shock just before that, I was very low – and then my boyfriend walked out on me, and I was too unhappy to care what happened, I just sleepwalked into it.' She looked up at him, her blue eyes wide and wet with tears that began then to slip down her face. 'I wish to God I could undo what I did, sometimes I have dreams about being back there, having the baby, I dream it has been born and they put it in my arms and then I see it's dead and I wake up crying.'

He brought out a clean white handkerchief and dried her face gently. 'And how long has Derek Fenn been blackmailing you over it?'

'Since the start of the series.' She gave him a cynical little grimace. 'Since I began to have money he could so-called borrow and not pay back.'

'The bastard,' muttered Harriet. 'The dirty little bastard. Well, that's it, I'm sacking him.'

'No,' Annie burst out and at the same moment Sean spoke, his voice riding over the top of Annie's.

'What do you imagine he'll do then? The minute he's fired, he'll be on to the press with his story, and they'll eat it with a knife and fork.'

Harriet stared back at him, frowning. 'So, what do I do about him?'

'Leave him to me, I'll deal with him. Once he knows I'm on to him he'll probably back off and leave

Annie alone. He's weak, and weak men are often bullies, but the first sign of anyone standing up to them and they run.' He stood up. 'Now, what about those omelettes? Annie, you stay here and rest. Harriet and I will deal with dinner.'

She protested, swinging her legs down from the couch, but he pushed her back.

'We won't take five minutes. Just shut your eyes, we'll call you when the food is ready.'

In the kitchen he found a roll of cling film and cut off a large piece, laid it on the table, picked up the blood-stained bootee and laid it on to the larger piece, wrapped it into a small parcel, while Harriet was finding an omelette pan, melting a little butter in it, keeping a curious eye on him as she worked.

'You won't get fingerprints off that, will you?'

'Unlikely, but we'll have a shot. What I do want to know is if that's real blood or fake.'

Harriet shuddered. 'I expect it's fake. You know, I'm not one of Derek's admirers, but I'd never have guessed he had such a morbid streak, or such a nasty one, either.'

'He's an actor, isn't he?' Sean put the wrapped bootee into his jacket pocket.

Harriet laughed, getting a warmed plate ready before she began cooking the omelettes. 'Can I quote you, Mr Halifax?'

A few minutes later Annie joined them in the kitchen. Harriet's omelette was light and golden, the salad was perfect. Sean left after a cup of coffee, but Annie and Harriet sat up talking for a couple of hours before going to bed.

Annie told her everything, starting from her audition at drama school and what Roger Keats had done to her that day. 'All that first term I was waiting for him to start on me again,' she whispered, shivering.

'Why didn't you tell someone? How could you be so stupid? You should have told your mother.'

'I was too scared. I didn't know why exactly, then, I hadn't worked it out, but later I realised that I knew that if I told anyone about Mr Keats I'd have to leave the school. I couldn't have stayed there afterwards, and I couldn't do that to my mother. She was desperate for me to be a success, it was all she dreamt about.'

'But you did, eventually?'

Annie closed her eyes. 'I had to, he told me to come to his room after school, and I knew what would happen if I went. I couldn't do it. Not only because I would have hated it, but because by then I'd met Johnny.'

'Johnny?' asked Harriet, eyes widening.

Her voice dreamy, Annie said, 'He was our lodger here – we fell in love that spring.'

'Ah!' said Harriet half to herself. 'The father of the baby?'

Annie's face changed. She gave a short, painful sigh. 'Yes.'

Harriet said, 'You know, I often wondered if there'd ever been a man in your life. You never mentioned one and you were always so obsessed with work, I never saw you taking anyone seriously, I wondered if you were just plain frigid. Or cold, anyway.'

Annie blushed. 'Well, we never know much about ourselves, do we? But I certainly wasn't cold with Johnny; I was crazy about him. I remember right at the beginning I used to sneak into his room when he was out just to lie on his bed and read romantic poetry, imagining how wonderful it would be if he was

196

there, too. And then one day he came back and caught me.'

Harriet laughed. 'And did he join you on the bed?'

Annie laughed, too, shaking her head. 'No, it was months before we actually made love. We were both very young, Harriet. We were wildly romantic, both of us.' There was a little silence, then she went on, 'That was why I'd have died rather than let Roger Keats touch me again. Not once I'd fallen in love with Johnny. That changed my whole life. So I had to deal with Roger Keats, do something to stop him.'

Harriet watched the determined set of her face, the fierceness in the blue eyes. Annie was a strange mixture of vulnerability and strength, that was what made her such a powerful actress. She could be ruthless and single-minded in her pursuit of what she felt necessary for a scene, and yet there was this underlying gentleness which contradicted that.

'What exactly did you do?' Harriet slowly asked.

'I went to the school governors and because they needed proof I set him up, I went to his room as he'd ordered, but I left the door a little ajar, and the governors heard everything we said.'

Harriet involuntarily wrinkled her nose and Annie flushed, looking unhappy.

'I know. It wasn't very pleasant. But it was either him or me – I had no choice. They sacked him, and the next year I got a Valentine's card from him with a very scary message in it – and he's been sending them every year ever since. That was bad enough, then this year he actually got in here, broke into my home during the night.'

Harriet listened intently, frowning as Annie told her

about the rose on her pillow, the card on the bedside table.

'You mean that that guy in Petticoat Lane, who snatched your bag. . .that could have been Roger Keats?' Watching Annie nod, shuddering, Harriet put an arm round her and hugged her. 'You have had a bad time, haven't you? No wonder you've been looking strained lately. Have you ever thought of going into analysis? You need to talk this out, Annie. You're in denial, you have never really faced up to what happened to you, you've shut it all away and that's no good. It's festering inside you. What you need to do is see a really good therapist. Let me get you a name and a number to ring? I know I brilliant guy, discreet and reassuring.'

'Maybe, let me think about it,' Annie said reluctantly. She didn't want to talk about her life to some stranger.

Harriet considered her drily, with understanding. 'I know. It's difficult, but you'll be glad you took the risk in the end, Annie. You need to let all this out, get to the heart of your own feelings. Anyone who had been through what you have would have problems, especially if they had never talked about it.'

'Maybe, later,' Annie hedged.

Harriet gave her another dry look, then yawned. 'Sorry, I'm whacked. Bed, I think, don't you?'

Annie showed her into a quiet bedroom at the back overlooking the garden. 'Lovely room,' Harriet said, pleased by the faded, muted colours.

'This was the room Johnny used.' Annie stood by the bed, touching the quilt under which Johnny had slept, her fingers caressing.

Harriet watched her curiously and, becoming aware

of her gaze, Annie pulled herself together. 'Well, sleep well. Goodnight, Harriet.'

The door closed behind her and Harriet got undressed, thinking about Annie and what she had learnt about her tonight. She wouldn't have believed it if she hadn't heard it from Annie herself. People were so unpredictable – you thought you knew them and then, Wham! something like that hit you out of the blue.

She was asleep within about ten minutes of climbing into bed, exhausted by the events of the day, but Annie lay awake, unable to sleep, agonising over the baby, wishing to God she had never given in to her mother's insistence. Trudie shouldn't have pressured her into it. She shouldn't have listened. Trudie was stronger than she was, that was the trouble. She always had been; all her life she had done what her mother wanted her to do, and she sometimes resented it, even when she was grateful for Trudie's support and belief in her. She knew her mother loved her, and she loved Trudie. But how could Trudie have been so cruel as to send Johnny away when he was in such terrible trouble?

She groaned then put a hand over her mouth in case Harriet heard her. Oh, Johnny, she thought – how could she tell him about the baby . . . his baby . . . no, their baby? Oh, God, he'd never forgive her. She knew Johnny would have wanted that child. She would have wanted it, too. She wished she hadn't listened to her mother. If only . . . she hated those words. If only. If only.

She had half hoped he would ring her tonight. That was why she had given him her number.

Why hadn't he rung her? Had he met someone else now? Was he living with someone?

No, he said he'd just got out of prison. He wouldn't have had time to meet anyone else. Why hadn't he rung? She had thought he would, had been sure he would want to see her again.

Her mind was like a white mouse on a wheel in a tiny cage. Round and round it went, in frantic circles. Her mother. Johnny. The baby. Derek. The bootee with that splash of blood, oh, God, and she had touched it, got the blood on her skin. How could Derek have done that?

She felt like screaming, but that would bring Harriet out, watching her with that quiet curiosity – she couldn't bear that.

She had to get up, she had to do something. Go for a walk. Get some fresh air, some exercise. Tire her body out and stop her mind.

Annie slid out of the bed, shivered in the bitter night air, dressing quickly.

Derek Fenn was in the bar across the street from the studio. He had been on a pub crawl and ended up there, minus a tie, his face flushed and his hair shiny with sweat.

'Let me call a taxi for you, Mr Fenn,' the landlord said politely, when he yelled for another whisky. 'Closing time, I'm afraid.'

'Another bloody whisky!' Derek snarled.

'Sorry, Mr Fenn, no can do. Why don't you be a sensible chap, go home and sleep it off?'

Derek said something crude.

The barman walked away to keep his temper.

Derek banged on the small round bar table with his empty glass and roared after him. 'Get me another effing drink!'

The bar was crowded, people stared; he looked round at all the faces and sneered. 'What're you all staring at?'

A woman halted next to the table and Derek sat, staring at the long, slim legs, the short skirt, the well-filled sweater.

'Hallo, darling, looking for me?' His eyes rose and he saw the face; took in blue eyes, a pink-lipsticked mouth, short, soft, light hair.

'Annie?' He was confused, frowned, trying to see her clearly. Was it Annie? What on earth would Annie be doing here? 'Is it . . . is that you, Annie?' He couldn't think straight, couldn't even see straight, come to that; maybe, after all, he had drunk too much. Oh, hell, what did it matter? You're dead soon enough, and life was pretty depressing. Why not choose the way you go? He made a gesture across his face as if brushing cobwebs or tears away. 'Well, well,' he thickly muttered. 'Nice of you to join me. Are you my Fairy Godmother tonight? Sit down, sweetie, let me buy you a drink.'

The barman turned round. 'Not in here, you don't.' He stared at the woman, frowning at something about her that tugged at his memory. Where had he seen her before? But then they often got famous faces in here, he'd lost count of the number of stars who had drunk in his bar, and she was standing in profile, he couldn't get a clear view of her. 'Look, lady, if you know him, take him away. He's had a skinful and he isn't getting any more drinks in here tonight. Sorry, but I draw the line at serving a man who can barely see.'

He didn't hear what she said to Derek Fenn, but a minute later the two of them had gone.

*

When he left Annie's house, Sean drove straight to Derek Fenn's flat, but there was no answer to his insistent ringing on the doorbell. He stood outside on the pavement, staring up, but the windows were dark.

Sean thought of sitting outside in his car, but Derek might be out all night, so he went home and rang Tom Moor, once, long ago, his partner in the City of London police force and now working as a private detective on the same patch, but more profitably since he had begun acting for merchant banks and insurance companies on very different work to the purely criminal activities he had investigated as a policeman.

Tom's wife Cherie answered sleepily. 'You're kidding, Sean! It's late, man; don't you sleep at nights any more? Anyone would think you were still a copper.'

'Sorry, love.' He looked at his watch and made a private face. 'If I had a wife like you I might be in bed at ten o'clock, but I'm a miserable bachelor with nothing to keep me warm at night but a hot-water bottle. You should feel sorry for me, not shout at me.'

'Oh, you poor little dear,' she crooned with mock pity, then snappily added, 'Come off it, you don't get the sympathy vote from me, Sean. A lot of ladies would queue up to fill your bed, so cut the tears. Just don't keep Tom long, OK? We have better things to do at night than chat to you.'

'Lucky Tom,' Sean teased, but it wasn't Cherie who answered, it was Tom's puzzled voice.

'Lucky, why? Is that sarcasm? A bit late at night for that, Sean. You know me, I put my brain in a glass at bedtime. What do you want? You just ruined our bedtime cocoa.'

'That's a new name for it. But sorry about that,

Tom, I won't keep you – I just wanted to know how you were getting on with that enquiry?'

'Haven't set eyes on him yet, but we're turning over every stone. I've done all the usual: checking phone books across London, credit agencies, electoral rolls. His name hasn't shown up for years. If his ex-wife knows where he is, she isn't seeing him and she's not grieving. She's out all the time, she certainly believes in putting it about. She has more men than a dog has fleas; I've spotted her with three in a row. In fact, she's out tonight. I've got a guy on her tail. I'll tell you what I turn up. Sooner or later she may lead us to him, but don't keep your hopes up.'

'Just a tip, Tom – have you tried repertory theatres? He's an actor; he might have gone back to that. Try the various theatre agents, too; he might be on someone's books. Well, thanks, Tom, I'll let you go back to Cherie now – give her a kiss for me.'

'Give it to her yourself when you see her,' Tom said, chuckling. 'Get yourself a good woman too, and then maybe you'll sleep in your own bed at night, like a Christian. Come round to dinner soon, man; we haven't done that for an age. Cherie worries about you; says you don't eat enough.'

'If she promises to make her sweet-potato pie I'll be there!' promised Sean, hanging up.

Derek stumbled across the littered sitting-room in his flat and opened a drinks cabinet, got out a half-empty bottle of whisky, looked around for glasses.

'Siddown, darlin,' he grunted, lurching into the tiny kitchenette.

He came back with two smeared glasses and set them down on his coffee table with a crash.

'There y're. Say when.' He poured, swaying; sat down on the couch and then focused on his companion. 'Oh, oh, in a hurry, aren't we?' He licked his lips, watching as one long leg was crossed over another, then the scarlet-nailed hands slowly began unpeeling delicate black tights.

'Can't wait, eh?' Derek breathed thickly. He was aroused, excited, although he had a sinking feeling that he wasn't going to be able to perform; he never could when he was really drunk, but what the hell, he thought, he'd die trying. 'Striptease, eh?' he muttered. 'Striptease, lovely, I'll play.' He had already thrown off his jacket, now he undid his shirt and took it off, aware that she had stopped undressing and was watching him. He unzipped his trousers. 'This what you want, baby?' He wriggled out of them and kicked them away across the room. 'Off, off, ye lendings . . .' His briefs followed them; he was naked, and he leered at her. 'Com'on, baby, let's do it.' He tried to get up but swayed, fell back. 'Dammit.' He began to laugh, sprawled on the couch. 'Stupid. Can't . . . can't seem to . . . get up.' He held out his arms. 'Don . . . worry . . . I'll get it up OK, come here, baby, let's do it here, why not?' He sat up and then blinked because the room seemed to be empty, she had gone.

For a second he wondered if he had imagined her. Something about it was dreamlike, a crazy, erotic dream. He'd had those before when he had been drinking, or snorting coke. Harems of women dancing naked in front of him, and him able to do it to all of them.

'Where've yer gone, baby?' he mumbled gloomily. He heard sounds behind him and tilted his head to look backwards. 'Oooh, there y'are. Wha . . . wha'yer doing there?'

She bent over him; he stupidly stared up at her. 'Wha. . .wharra y'doing?'

His eyes bulged.

He made thick, choking sounds; tried to speak, tried to scream, grabbing for her hands, trying to loosen the black snake coiling around his neck.

His legs writhed, flew upward, kicking; the glasses went, whisky splashing everywhere, on the table, on the carpet, on the couch. The bottle went, too; lay on the floor, pumping out whisky, which sank into the carpet, a brown stain spreading.

The long ward was still dark although outside the sky was filling with pale spring light. The maze of endless corridors and wards smelt of disinfectant and stale human flesh, but there was a wild scent in the air from the bathrooms adjacent to the ward; they were like a flowershop at night, crowded with vases of flowers put there overnight and brought back in the morning; daffodils and hyacinth, pure virginal white narcissus. The ward sister had a mania about flowers using up the oxygen during the night while patients slept.

Trudie was often awake at night; she slept during the day, doped up to the eyeballs. They had caught on to her pill-hiding and were giving her injections; she couldn't avoid taking them, couldn't pretend she had swallowed and then spit the pill out when nobody was looking, or hide drugs in her toilet bag where Cinders had found them before now.

A white-capped figure slowly trod along the aisle between the beds and paused beside Trudie; watched her pale, worn face, the parted lips breathing rustily, a little hair on her upper lip breathing in and out.

Trudie's face seemed to be falling in on her bones,

her flesh melting like candle wax, running and sinking into nothing. Even her hair had grown so thin it was as if it was being pulled back inside her scalp, hair by hair. She would be bald if it went on much longer.

There was so little of her left. Death would come as a kind release.

She stirred as if the intent gaze had penetrated her sleep and opened her eyes.

Fear lit them immediately. 'Who are you?' She shrank back against the pillows. 'What do you want?' Her sunken eyes looked from side to side around the silent ward. 'Where am I? Where am I? What am I doing here? I don't like this place, I want to go home.'

The nurse was carrying a white plastic kidney dish; Trudie looked at it and saw a hypodermic glisten in the half-light.

'No, I'm not having that!' she burst out. 'I hate injections, I won't have it, get away from me.' She would have scrambled out of bed and fled, but she couldn't move, her broken hip was agonising if she shifted an inch.

The nurse ignored her, rapidly threw back the bed-clothes, pushed up the white hospital nightdress, baring Trudie's thigh; the needle went in and the old woman gave a cry of pain.

'That hurt!'

Without replying, the nurse walked off down the ward, rubber soles squeaking on the floor; Trudie watched the white uniform vanish, swearing under her breath.

Seconds later she clutched at her chest, gasping, her lips blue and her eyes rolling in her head.

Annie walked and walked, through the sleeping, secret

streets of London, under street-lamps making yellow circles in the dark, and trees still bare and black, except where you saw a silver coin of a moon spinning through the sky above, passing in and out of the clouds. Few cars passed her and there was almost nobody else on foot in the streets tonight. She tried not to think but her brain was running like an over-heated engine. Johnny had come back. She still didn't know how she felt about that. She had spent years wondering what had happened to Johnny, grieving for him, missing him, and now that he had returned she couldn't make up her mind about her feelings towards him.

He had changed so much. It wasn't Johnny who had come back. Not surprising when you thought about where he had been. She still couldn't believe it. It would never have occurred to her that he might be in prison all that time. Johnny! Attacking a policeman? Nearly killing the man? She still found it hard to believe.

In another way, though, he hadn't changed at all; she could trace the sensitive, emotional boy she had loved in the man's hard features, in those dark blue eyes. Johnny had been driven nearly mad by what she told him that night; he'd hit that policeman in a fit of rage and he had suffered a terrible punishment.

She paused, exhausted and shivering in the cold night wind. Only then becoming aware how cold she was, she ducked into an empty bus shelter and sank gratefully down on a metal seat for a few minutes.

She didn't feel up to walking all the way back home, but while she was trying to decide whether or not to phone for a taxi she saw an early-morning bus lumbering towards her along the road.

It was almost empty except for a sprinkling of workmen on their way to start their day, and nightworkers going home after a long shift. Annie had a few pound coins in her jacket pocket. She paid the fare to a stop only a short walk from her home and within twenty minutes she was safely back indoors.

As she shut the door Harriet appeared from the kitchen, wild-eyed, her face drawn with anxiety.

She stared, breaking out hoarsely, 'Oh, my God, Annie, where on earth have you been? I was just going to ring the police, I've already rung Sean . . .'

'You shouldn't have!'

'Well, he wasn't at home, anyway. I only got his answerphone, I left a message.'

'Oh, Harriet! Why did you do that? He'll come racing round here thinking God knows what.'

'Well, you scared me out of my wits! There was a cat fight out in the garden, they were hissing and shrieking at each other and they woke me up, I couldn't get back to sleep, so I got up to make myself some cocoa, then as I went downstairs I noticed your bedroom door wide open and no sign of you. I ransacked the house looking for you, and realised you had actually gone out. I couldn't believe it. I didn't know what to think – someone could have got in and kidnapped you, forced you to go with him. . . I didn't know, did I? You half-scared me to death. Where have you been at this hour?'

'Walking,' Annie said on a sigh. 'I'm sorry, Harriet, I just couldn't sleep, I walked myself tired.'

'You must be crazy, going out alone in the middle of the night – anything could have happened to you!'

'Well, it didn't, I'm OK, and now I'm going to get some sleep.'

'It's past midnight, your car will be here soon, and you'll be fit for nothing. Honestly, Annie, I could kill you.'

The phone began to ring. Annie groaned.

'That will be Sean returning your call! Well, you can talk to him. Explain it was all a storm in a teacup, I'm fine and he can go back to bed.'

Harriet lifted the phone. 'Sean, I'm sorry,' she began, and then stopped, listening. 'Oh, yes, she's here, hang on.' She stopped again, listening, her face changing. 'I see. Yes, maybe. Right, I'll break it to her. Thank you for ringing. Goodbye.'

Annie was frozen on the bottom stair, her face turned towards the telephone.

'What?' she whispered, a premonition shivering through her.

'That was the hospital,' Harriet slowly told her, watching her with concern.

Annie had known it. 'My mother. My mother's dead, isn't she?' She was white to her hairline.

'No, no,' Harriet reassured her hurriedly. 'But she had some sort of crisis a little while ago – they aren't sure yet what happened, or they aren't admitting it, I got the distinct feeling there was something the sister wasn't saying. It seems. . .' She paused, biting her lower lip as if unsure how to put it. 'Well, Annie, your mother's heart stopped.'

Annie whispered, 'Stopped. . .but you said she isn't dead?'

Harriet put an arm round her, soothed, 'Now, don't get upset, Annie, it isn't as bad as it sounds, they started it again – and the sister said it has steadied a good deal, your mother's going to pull through. She's under sedation again, but if you want to visit her you can and the ward sister said she would be in touch immediately if there was any change.'

Annie sank down on the bottom stair and covered her face with both her hands, groaning. 'My whole life is falling to pieces. . .it's just one thing after another. I'm scared stiff, Harriet. What is happening to me?'

7

Annie slept deeply for six hours, her body worn out and her disturbed mind quietened by some sleeping pills Harriet had made her take. She woke up when she heard Harriet in the bathroom, showering. Annie rolled over to look at her clock and groaned.

Seven! She should have been up an hour ago. She slid out of bed and went into her own en-suite bathroom, one of the few changes they had made to the house over the past few years. She had insisted on it so that she should not disturb her mother when she got up at crack of dawn.

She got downstairs as Harriet was making coffee. 'What are you doing up?' demanded Harriet and Annie grinned at her.

'Going to work.'

'Oh, no, you're not!'

Annie opened her mouth to argue but a loud ring on the doorbell made her jump.

'Sean! He's giving me a lift!' Harriet said, and went to let him in. Seeing Annie, he shook his head at her impatiently.

'Go back to bed. I've rewritten today's scenes to cut you out. I want you to stay quietly at home. Don't brood over Derek. You'll never have to worry about Derek again.'

Annie gave him an agitated look. 'What have you done? You don't know him – he can be vindictive, really nasty. He's full of resentment because he was a star, now he's just a bit player and . . .'

'That's not your fault,' Harriet said furiously, immediately up in arms in defence of her, as she always was with any of the team who worked for her. Any maternal instincts Harriet possessed came out in the way she took care of the people she worked with, and sometimes Annie had resented the mothering bossiness. Perhaps because she had a powerful mother at home, or simply because she had a deep instinct of her own – the instinct to be free to make her own decisions, fight her own wars.

Harriet's eyes blazed. 'In fact, if it wasn't for you he wouldn't be working at all. Don't you worry about Derek, you just stay in bed and get plenty of rest. When does your cleaner get here? She can take care of you.'

Not answering that, Annie asked Sean, 'But what did you mean – I'll never have to worry about Derek again?'

Those level, cool eyes of his met her stare without blinking. Did all policemen have those observing, distancing eyes? Annie wondered. Sean seemed to stand off from life, watching it, all the time. She knew he had few real friends among the actors in the team, although they seemed to like him well enough. Maybe that was because he was a writer, used to working alone, but she had learnt from working in the series that policemen tended not to have friends outside their work; it could lead to problems. A policeman needed to be prepared to put up with unpopularity, to be something of a loner.

'I'm writing Derek out of the script. I'm going to see Billy Grenaby for lunch this week – I'll talk to him then and get his agreement.'

Harriet stiffened. 'I don't recall you discussing it with me.'

'I was going to do that today,' Sean quickly said, realising he had stepped on her toes. Harriet was fiercely possessive of anything to do with the series. Although Sean wrote the scripts, Harriet regarded the series as her property, not his. If they fell out she could always get another writer to carry on; her position in the company was stronger than his, her eyes reminded him.

'Well, good, don't forget to do that,' she sarcastically said.

Annie was conscious of the little battle between them and with her usual dislike of scenes, hurriedly said, to distract them both, 'But I want to visit my mother today, I can't stay at home all day.'

She had rung the hospital a few minutes ago, from her bedroom, and been told that Trudie was much better, but she had picked up, as Harriet had done last night, something odd in the ward sister's manner; things were not being said, questions not being answered entirely frankly. Annie was afraid the hospital were hiding something about her mother's condition; she wanted to see for herself.

Harriet frowned uncertainly. 'Take a taxi there and back, but don't stay too long.'

There she goes again – ordering me around, Annie thought resentfully. I get pretty tired of it.

But she hid the reaction because she knew in her heart that Harriet was trying to protect her, so she smiled, nodded like an obedient child. 'OK.' She was a good actress; she could always hide behind the mask of whatever character she was playing. She fooled Harriet now. Harriet smiled approval at her.

'Good girl.'

Good girl, thought Annie, her teeth grinding together. Good girl? How old does she think I am? I've spent most of my life being manipulated and ordered around by my mother, now it's Harriet doing it, and, however good their intentions, I wish to God they would stop it!

She felt Sean watching her, his expression wry, as if he had picked up on her secret feelings. She lowered her eyelashes and tried to look blank.

Looking at her watch, Harriet groaned. 'Got to rush! See you later. Come on, Sean, we must go now.'

Annie didn't go back to bed; she ate a boiled egg and toast for breakfast, drank orange juice and then coffee, sitting at the red and white gingham covered table by the window in the kitchen overlooking the long back garden with the bird table right outside, on which a few brown sparrows industriously pecked at the crumbs of her toast which she had sprinkled there.

She heard Mrs Singh, who lived in the house on the right, singing tunelessly to her radio as she got her two sons off to school. Trudie rarely talked to any of their neighbours except Mr Harris, who had lived across the street for twenty-five years. Trudie had always believed in keeping herself to herself. When they still had the shop that hadn't mattered; Trudie talked to people all day long in the shop. Since she stopped working, though, she must often have been lonely, yet she still did not encourage any of the neighbours to call.

Annie got up, ran the tap over the dishes, slid them into the dishwasher for Tracy to deal with later, and was about to order a taxi when the phone began to ring.

Almost tripping herself up in her haste, she ran to answer. 'Hello?

'Annie?' The voice was husky and uncertain, but she knew it instantly, her heart skidding.

'Johnny?' She had been waiting for him to ring; she had thought he might ring last night, had been listening for the phone all the time, yet now that he had she was overtaken by shock and surprise, as if she had never quite believed he really had come back to her. 'Is it really you?'

He was silent for a second, then said, 'Yes, it's me.'

Her heart lifted in happiness. 'I thought you might ring last night, Johnny.'

'I wanted to, but I wasn't sure you would want to . . .' He broke off.

'Want to what?' she whispered.

'Get involved.'

'I wouldn't have given you my number if I hadn't wanted to see you, Johnny!'

His voice deepened. 'Annie . . . aren't you working today? I mean . . . I thought you began very early in the morning. I rang on the off-chance, thought I'd leave a message on your answerphone if you weren't at home.'

'I'm taking a day off, I was just going to visit my mother in hospital.'

'I expect you're very busy, but if you had time I'd like to see you, Annie – we didn't have a chance to talk properly yesterday.'

'I haven't got any plans for the rest of the day,' she said quickly. 'I'm just going to take a taxi to the hospital and back, then I'll be free.'

'I could collect you from the hospital – what time will you leave there, do you think?'

'Around ten-thirty, I expect. I never stay long. Poor darling, she often doesn't know me. And it tires her, too much talking.'

Johnny was silent. She felt his anger and sighed. He was still brooding over the discovery that her mother had kept them apart all this time – and Annie knew how he felt, only too well. She had always been able to sense what Johnny was feeling. Right from the beginning, they had shown their secret selves to each other, the passion hidden inside them.

'I'll wait for you in the car park, at ten-thirty, then,' Johnny said, and rang off.

When he rang off, she put a call through to a taxi firm and was waiting for the cab to arrive when her cleaner unlocked the front door and paused, looking surprised to see her.

'Thought you were working today. Nothing wrong, is there?'

'No, I'm just taking a day off – I'm going to the hospital to see my mother.'

'Give her my best wishes,' Tracy said, studying Annie in her white jeans, white shirt and dark blue sweater. She hadn't put on much make-up, just a light film of foundation and a pale pink lipstick. Annie wore so much make-up when she was filming that she preferred to leave it off whenever she could. 'Are you sure you're well enough to go out? You're very pale.'

'I'm naturally pale,' Annie said drily. 'I'm a washed-out blonde, that's what a critic wrote in one of the tabloids, anyway. He said I was an anaemic, washed-out blonde with all the sex appeal of a piece of English cheese.'

'Why are they always so vicious?'

Annie gave her a wry look. 'It's what they get paid for. If they're too complimentary they get fired. Oh, here's my taxi! See you, Tracy.'

When she got to the hospital, she found her mother

still drowsy, but Trudie's hand felt towards her across the counterpane and Annie covered it with her own, bent to kiss her mother. 'How do you feel today?'

'I'm fine. Take me home, Annie. I want to go home, I don't like it here.' The fingers under Annie's coiled round, clutched, like ivy strangling a tree, the short nails dug into her flesh, making her start with a gasp. 'Take me home,' Trudie wailed. 'They're trying to kill me here, they tried last night, they injected me with something that made me throw up, and I had pains in my chest, I nearly died, ask them, ask them, they know it's true. I nearly died last night, and it was the injection that did it.'

Annie sat in the sister's office and watched the long ward through the glass window. She could see her mother's bed, the curtains pulled half-round it as the nurses attended to Trudie.

'She's convinced someone tried to kill her last night.'

Today, the sister in charge was someone Annie hadn't seen before, a tall, graceful young woman with long, silky brown hair plaited and then wreathed on top of her head in a coronet on which her white cap sat like a crown.

Her brown eyes thoughtfully surveyed Annie, as if she was trying to make up her mind what to say in reply.

At last she said in a quiet, level voice, 'Someone nearly did kill her.'

'What?' Annie sat up in the chair, her eyes wide open in shock. 'You're kidding!' When she had told the other woman that her mother believed someone had tried to kill her Annie had not suspected for an instant that it might be true. She had assumed that Trudie was dramatising, again, half inventing, half elaborating what had really happened to her.

'We don't know if it was an accident or a deliberate mistake, but someone gave her an injection of digitalin.'

Annie's brows met. 'I've heard of that – isn't it used for heart problems?'

'It is, yes, it's extracted from foxglove leaves, which, as you probably know, are highly poisonous. Like most drugs, it all depends on the dosage – given in a very small amount it can be useful as a heart stimulant, but if enough is given it can cause, as it did with your mother, vomiting and a disturbance in the heart rhythm. It was fortunate that the woman in the next bed saw your mother throwing up and rang for help. We were able to deal with it rapidly, and she hadn't had a fatal dose. But it could have resulted in death if it hadn't been dealt with quickly.'

Worried and angry, Annie said, 'My mother said a nurse gave her the injection.'

'Yes, I know – or someone wearing a nurse's uniform. But she's so confused we can't trust her description.'

'But obviously, it has to be someone who works in the hospital. Who else could walk into a ward and inject a patient, not to mention have access to a poisonous drug, and know how much to administer?

'We're making enquiries, of course. All the nurses on duty on this floor have been seen, none of them admit to being in here when the injection must have been given. There was an emergency on the ward next door; a fire started in one of the treatment rooms – a patient, probably. It's a male geriatric ward, and the men are always starting fires, it happens all the time. The two nurses on this ward ran to help in there, leaving this ward unattended, just for for a few minutes. During that time someone walked in here, injected your mother, and walked out again, but nobody saw who it was.'

Angrily Annie broke out, 'You have called the police, I suppose?'

'Of course. They're seeing everyone who was on the roster last night, but so far it's all a bit of a mystery. It may be that someone made a genuine mistake, injected the wrong patient – there are patients on the ward who are having digitalin. That could be the explanation.'

'Well, surely it must be easy to check that out!'

'Not really. Having made such a terrible mistake, the nurse might be too scared to admit what she had done.'

'Is any digitalin missing?'

'That's the odd thing – no, none at all. It was the first thing we checked. All our digitalin is accounted for. In fact, that's why I'm inclined to think it must have been a mistake; someone who should have had an injection last night didn't get it, your mother did.'

'If it was one of her regular nurses, surely my mother would have recognised her – but she seems confused about that, she couldn't tell me who had done it.'

'That's the trouble – in her mental condition we don't want to press her for answers.'

'No, of course – but what worries me is that it could happen again, and next time it could be fatal!'

'It won't happen again. We're on our guard.'

When Annie walked out of the main entrance, she

found Johnny standing on the steps, staring out at the traffic edging past the open gates of the hospital. He was unaware of her; she could watch him unobserved.

Staring at the width of his shoulders and the long, lean back under his dark blue denim jacket, Annie felt her ears buzzing with hypertension.

She still couldn't believe he was back in her life. It made the years disappear. She felt eighteen again – all the years of working and living, growing into the person she was now – all that vanished every time she looked at him and she became the girl she had been, wide-eyed, innocent, head over heels in love, seeing the world through a rainbow of colours.

And yet . . . was this really Johnny? Oh, it looked like him, she'd have recognised him anywhere, in an instant. But although the features and the colouring stayed the same, this wasn't the Johnny she remembered. This man disturbed her; he was a stranger in many ways she couldn't exactly define. At first she had just thought the changes physical, but it was deeper than that – how could he not have changed under the bitter pressures of life in prison?

She sighed, and Johnny swung round at once. His face intent, he looked into her eyes. 'Hello, Annie.' His voice was low, husky.

'Hi,' she said shyly, and for a second it was the old Johnny again, his dark blue eyes shining, his smile gentle, almost pleading.

'I was thinking about my grandmother's house – do you remember?' he asked her, and she caught her breath.

How could he even ask? Her mind instantly flooded with memories of them there together and her colour glowed hot, her lashes flickered self-conciously.

'I'm going to have to sell it,' he said, face [?]
held on to it all these years, I couldn't bear to lo[?]
was my last link with . . . with happier times, but n[?]
I'm having to face reality. I can't afford to live there,
it's too far out of town, and I need money to live on.
I'm only working freelance as a writer – I have to take
part-time jobs on the side to survive, and it's ridiculous
to keep the house. I'll sell it and buy myself a small
flat. The rest of the money will help me survive until I
get somewhere with my writing.'

'Oh, Johnny, that's terrible!' she said, her own face
distressed. 'I'm so sorry.'

He watched her eagerly. 'Would you like to see it
again? I thought I might drive out there this morning
and take a look at it before I get it valued. Would you
like to come?'

She didn't even hesitate.

'Where the hell is Derek?' Harriet raged, looking at
her watch. It was nearly nine-thirty. Sean had done
his rewrite and left to catch up on his sleep. They
should have started work long ago. 'Don't tell me he's
doing a Mike Waterford? I can't have two drunks
turning up late whenever they feel like it. I have to put
up with Mike because of the ratings, but I'm damned
if I'll put up with it from Derek bloody Fenn.' She
gave her assistant a glare. 'Ring him, and keep on
ringing until you get an answer. When you do get him,
tell him to get over here right away or I'll strangle him
with my bare hands. And in the meantime I'll set up
for Scene 7. I'm not wasting a location shoot hanging
around waiting for Derek Fenn. The actors in Scene 7
are all here. We might as well get on with that. Where's
Benny and the cars?'

They were filming in St Paul's Piazza, the modern square surrounded with office blocks and shops built just behind the seventeenth-century cathedral. On this chilly spring morning the square had turned into a wind tunnel; actors in police uniforms huddled together under arches, drinking coffee out of paper cups.

Harriet's assistant gestured down some steps. 'Parked down there, on the pavement.'

'OK. Before you start ringing Derek, get Benny up here, then ring Sean and ask him to get over here fast. He'll have to rewrite his rewrite, I'm afraid.'

The other girl nodded, lifting her mobile phone to her mouth. 'Benny? Harriet wants you in the square. Yes, now.'

The stunt driving would be the most complex part of the scene and would take the longest to shoot. The cars would have to drive up steps into the square and out the other side; it would take hours to set up so Harriet decided to begin with that, and, for once Mike Waterford was on time and not suffering from hangover. He actually knew his lines, too. Not that he had many.

'A minor miracle,' said Harriet thankfully to Sean when he arrived an hour later. 'I've taken the liberty of shifting to him the lines you'd given to Annie in the first version of that scene. It was the only way I could go ahead with shooting the opening pages of the scene, and, as you see, the light's terrible, and traffic is getting worse all the time. God, location work is such hell. Why do we do it? It's so warm and cosy on a studio set.'

'But it doesn't have the impact a scene shot in a real location does,' Sean said drily. 'How are Benny and his stunt drivers doing?'

'They've spent hours lining everything up, just for two minutes screen time.'

'It will be worth it! What rewriting do you want me to do, then?'

'Scene 6 – no Annie, no Derek.' She explained and Sean frowned.

'It isn't like Derek. You say you've tried ringing his flat?'

'Constantly. No reply.'

'Maybe he spent the night somewhere else?' Sean's eyes were narrowed thoughtfully. 'With Marty Keats, probably – he's seeing her, isn't he? Get your girl to ring her. Try wardrobe first, and if she isn't at work try her home number. And don't forget you and I are having lunch with BG.'

'Oh, my God, I had forgotten,' groaned Harriet. Billy Grenaby had ordered them to lunch out of the blue, having picked up on rumours, no doubt, that there were personal problems among the actors on the series. He interested himself in everything, even down to the tiniest morsel of gossip. 'I'm so crazy, with all this hassle. It's a wonder I remember my own name!' She looked at her watch. 'It's nearly eleven o'clock. I've just got an hour and a half before I have to hand over to Flora, then. OK, can you do that rewrite quickly, Sean, so that I can approve it before we have to leave? I'll get on with Benny and the boys.'

It didn't take Sean twenty minutes to rewrite the scene. Harriet glanced through it, nodded.

'That's fine. Still no sign of Derek, though, and Marty Keats isn't at work today, nor is there an answer from her home number.' Her eyes were worried.

Sean eyed her shrewdly. 'Come on, Harriet – what's bothering you?'

223

She made a face. 'Annie is home alone. What if Derek turns up there, trying to get money out of her?'

Sean's face tightened. 'I should have thought of that.' He took his mobile phone out of his pocket. 'We'll soon find out.' He dialled Annie's number. 'Hello? This is Sean Halifax. Can I speak to Annie, please? What? What do you mean, not there? Where the hell is she?' He listened, then said tersely, 'Well, when she gets back tell her to ring either me or Harriet. We'll be on this number.' He gave the number of his mobile phone. 'And tell her it's urgent.'

As he rang off, Harriet asked anxiously, 'Annie wasn't at home? She did say she was going to the hospital to see her mother.'

'Maybe she's still there, then.' Sean dialled again. 'I'll get the hospital's number from Directory Enquiries.'

He got the number and rang the hospital. After talking to the ward sister he rang off and looked at Harriet, frowning. 'She saw her mother, and left there over an hour ago. What the hell can she be doing?'

'Perhaps she stopped off on the way home to do some shopping?'

'I'll kill her,' said Sean, his voice rough. 'She's supposed to be resting, not wandering around shops.'

Mike Waterford was eavesdropping. 'Find Annie, and you'll probably find Fenn,' he drawled mockingly. 'They go back a long way, don't they, Harriet? That's why she got him that part; it was a pay-off, to make sure he held his tongue. They've been an item, secretly, for years. I'm told she even had his baby.'

Sean and Harriet stiffened, exchanged startled, shaken looks. How on earth had he got hold of that story?

Mike drawled on, 'I always knew she was a bit in the kinky line; if I so much as looked at her, she nearly threw a fit.'

'She's got good taste, that's all,' Sean said through his teeth.

Mike gave him a sarcastic smile. 'Charming. No, the reason she didn't fancy me was because she knew I'd want a normal relationship with her. She's the type that only fancies older men. The Electra complex, that's what they call it, isn't it? Always looking for a substitute Daddy.' He flicked a mocking look at Sean again. 'Tough, Halifax. You're not quite old enough for her. You haven't got a prayer.'

'Watch your mouth, Waterford,' Sean said savagely. 'There's a law about spreading scandal, especially when what you're spreading is a lie. Annie never had an affair with Derek and she never had his baby. If Annie sues you for spreading foul lies about her, it could cost you a lot more than money. Billy would sack you for damaging the series, for a start, and your fans might not be so keen on a hero who goes around spreading spiteful lies about Annie Lang.'

Mike didn't back down, he gave a defiant, cynical grin. 'Oh, but it isn't a lie – I got it from a very good source! Fenn himself!'

'Derek told you?' Harriet was appalled. 'But Mike, it isn't true, believe me – I know for certain that Derek was lying.'

'He actually told you, himself?' Sean slowly asked, frowning, and Mike hesitated, then shrugged.

'Well, no, actually it was Marty Keats in wardrobe who told me, but she's been sleeping with Fenn, and she swears he told her.'

'Well, one of them lied,' Sean bit out. 'So don't go

around repeating it, unless you want to get out of the series.'

. 'Don't you threaten me, Halifax,' Mike Waterford said. 'I'm not afraid of you!'

Sean turned on him aggressively, dark red with temper, his hands clenched into fists, and Mike looked startled, swung away, and walked off, hurriedly.

Harriet groaned. 'It must be all round the studio by now. I'm going to have to tell Billy, you know. If I don't and he finds out he'll kill me.'

As they drove through the forest, Annie felt a strange stirring inside herself, as if she was waking from a long winter dream to find spring beginning. The day was chilly but bright, sunlight pierced the forest glades, gleamed among the dark trees, lit the vistas like search-lights, and when they parked outside the old house and walked up the flagged path she saw snowdrops among the withered grass like flakes of snow.

Johnny unlocked the front door, which creaked as it swung open. Annie's heart was beating hard under her ribcage, as if trying to crash through it.

She walked into the house and heard him close the door behind them. They were alone in the house again and she was trembling.

'You're cold,' he said, concerned. 'I'll make a fire in the grate.'

'No, really . . .'

'It won't take five minutes. It's laid, ready. I just have to put a match to it.'

He knelt down in front of the cold hearth and she had a vivid flash of déjà vu. He had knelt down like that, eight years ago, in front of that hearth, on a cold dark day in winter, and lit this fire for her, and they had lain down in front of it and made love with firelight playing over their naked bodies.

A deep sadness welled up inside her at the memory. The lost happiness shone like the sun piercing the forest. It had gone, it could never return; she would never be eighteen again, or as wildly, inexpressibly in love.

Johnny used the old bellows hanging up by the fire to blow life into the wood, which began to crackle, a tongue of flame licking hot and red up the black chimney.

He stood up. 'Stay in front of the fire and I'll make us some tea.' He smiled at her and unshed tears burned behind her eyes, then he went out and she sat down on the faded old hearth rug and stared into the fire, seeing pictures in the flames. She automatically began feeding the fire with the wood kept in the brass scuttle on the hearth.

She remembered the night when a mouse had crept out from its hole while they were making love and had sat there watching them with bright, round eyes.

How many hours had they spent here, talking, dreaming, planning their lives together, making love?

She got up, finding the memories too painful, and began prowling along the bookshelves looking at the books; they smelt of damp and when she reached down a copy of Palgrave's Golden Treasury the leather was spotted with green mould and the pages breathed a graveyard air.

She flicked the pages and stopped at a poem by William Blake.

'"O rose, thou art sick . . ."' It had been one of her recital pieces at drama school. She knew it by heart, did not need to read the words on the mould-spotted page. She had tried to forget it since; it reminded her too much of Roger Keats. '"His dark secret love does thy life destroy,"' she said aloud, shuddering; but Roger Keats had never loved her, had only wanted the sadistic pleasure of humiliating her, hurting her, watching her suffer.

Johnny came back, carrying a tray of tea things that rattled as he put it down on the table. Quickly closing the book, she slid it back into place on the shelf and turned, feeling her whole body quicken into life just because he was in the same room.

Johnny gravely said, 'You don't still think of him, do you? After all these years? Forget him, Annie.'

She was taken aback – could he still read her mind, even after their years apart? It stunned her.

'I wish I could forget him,' she whispered. 'But I can't, because he hasn't gone away, Johnny. He's still around, sending me scary, threatening Valentine's cards ever since.'

He stared at her, his dark blue eyes wide with shock. 'Scary, threatening cards? What are you talking about?'

She wished she hadn't mentioned it; she had wrecked the atmosphere. Suddenly the house felt different, or was it just her who had changed?

'Oh . . . it's a long story,' she muttered, and sat down in one of the fireside chairs, crouched on the edge, holding her cold hands out to the fire, which was well away by then, the log on top crackling with resin, flames all along it, giving out a sweet apple scent.

She saw that the old Minton tiles framing the fire had cracked even more since they were last here, but their beauty was undiminished.

'I've got all the time in the world to listen, Annie.'

Johnny poured her tea, put sugar in it, brought it to her, smiling at her.

She took the cup between her palms and held it, eyes half closed, grateful for the warmth of the hot liquid, while she told him about the cards, about the burglary on St Valentine's Day this year, about the rose on her pillow, the Valentine's card with its chilling message.

'I rang the police, but they wouldn't take me seriously because nothing had been taken, and there was no sign of forced entry.'

'How can you be sure it was Keats who broke in, who sent you these Valentines?' Johnny asked slowly. 'You must have plenty of admirers.'

'I recognised the printing on the card; I got the first one the year after I got Roger Keats the sack. There were a couple of dozen Valentine's cards that year, but I knew that was from him – I don't know why, I just felt this weird shiver down my spine. The others were from fans, and they're often over the top, a bit soppy, but this was different.'

Johnny watched her, frowning, and she met his eyes, and felt her throat close up at the fixity of his stare.

How did he feel about her now? He couldn't feel the same, not after all this time. Could he?

Her heart beat thickly, her head swam, she looked away, into the fire.

It was a minute before she could go on. 'I rang the police. They just laughed at me, said they were sure I would remember who had a key, but I know nobody had one, except my cleaner and she would never let anyone else use hers. But Sean is going to track Roger Keats down and –'

'Sean?' Johnny sharply interrupted, and she gave him a startled look.

'Yes, Sean Halifax . . . the scriptwriter on our series. He was a policeman.'

Johnny's face tightened, his pallor intensifying. She picked up anger inside him and blinked, then guessed what was wrong. After what had happened to him, Johnny probably didn't want any contact with the police, and who could be surprised at that?

'Anyway,' she said uneasily, 'he's investigating it for me. He's going to track Roger Keats down and put the fear of God into him.' She gave a quivery little smile. 'And believe me, Sean could do it. He's a very tough customer. He must have been a good copper. And he's a damned good writer.'

'You like him?' Johnny's voice was low and expressionless, but Annie picked up something else in his face.

'Sean's OK,' she said, suddenly flushing. Was he jealous? Did he suspect she and Sean were more than just colleagues? She drank her tea and stood up, put the cup on the table. 'I suppose I'd better get back now. It's been nice to see the house again. I'm sorry you will have to sell it.'

Johnny was in her way. He looked down at her, his eyes dark; she saw the flames reflected in them, dancing on the glazed iris like the flames of hell. Annie stared into them, breathless.

He touched her cheek with the fingertips of one hand. 'Annie . . . Annie . . .'

She was hypnotised, transfixed, listening to that voice, that husky, familiar, beloved voice, aware of the track of those caressing fingers. Her body had hungered for the remembered touch for so long.

Johnny groaned. 'I can't believe we're here together, here, in this house, in this room. Has time stopped? Did time ever move at all? Did I dream everything that's happened since the last time we were here together? Maybe we've been here, in this room, all that time – and everything else was the dream, and this was real.'

She turned her face up, yearning; their mouths met. She ran her arms round his neck and her body moved closer, closer. Desire took over and she was helpless to fight it, didn't even want to; she wanted only the satisfaction of this terrible need, which had been frustrated for so long. She knew Johnny felt exactly the same. Her body knew everything about Johnny. He might have been away for eight years, but now they were together again their blood spoke, their flesh melted together.

They didn't talk any more.

It had the measured movements of a ritual, a dance for two; they slowly sank down on to the rug, in front of the fire, as they had the first time they made love here, and undressed each other slowly, touching, kissing, exploring.

As she felt his hard flesh enter her, she cried out in as much pain as pleasure, and he paused, looking down at her.

'Did I hurt you, darling?' he asked as he had asked that first time, his voice surprised, shaky.

'No, it's just so . . . Oh, Johnny, Johnny, I need you, so much.'

'There must have been other men since . . .'

'No,' she admitted huskily, 'I couldn't, never, I didn't want anyone else but you.'

He looked down into her eyes as if he couldn't believe what she had said.

'Nobody at all?'

She shook her head. 'I couldn't forget you, Johnny.'

He kissed her, groaning. 'Annie, Annie.' Slowly he began to move inside her while their mouths clung; she moved with him, her knees clasping him, her arms holding him tightly so that they were one body moving to one driving rhythm which quickened and deepened to a climax so shattering that Annie actually lost consciousness for a second or two, and came back to awareness to hear herself making wild, animal sounds as her body slowly shuddered to rest.

As she slackened, a sadness came down over her, and she gave a sob, began to cry, her face buried on his shoulder.

'What is it? What's wrong?' he asked, trying to look at her, but she burrowed into him, refusing to let him see her face.

'There's something I must tell you, Johnny, don't be angry with me, please don't be angry, I was so unhappy because you'd gone away and left me, I couldn't fight them.'

His hand gently stroked her tumbled hair, he held her closer, their bodies still entwined. 'Sshh. Don't cry. I'd never be angry with you, Annie, I love you too much.'

She moistened her lips and plunged. 'Johnny, when you went away, I was ... I was ... going to have a baby.'

She felt his body tense, heard the intake of his breath, and hurried on, her words tumbling out feverishly, desperate to confess to him and get it over with, because she couldn't bear to lie to him, especially after making love like that. Once they had known everything about each other, she wanted to be that way again with him, open and innocent and utterly truthful. 'But you vanished and I was scared,' she said with a smothered sob. 'And my mother was so angry with me, and you didn't come back, and Derek Fenn wanted me in his TV series . . . and . . . they made me do it, Johnny. They made me . . . get rid of my baby.'

She heard him swearing, his face against her hair, his swift breathing stirring the pale strands on her temples.

She was afraid to look at him. 'I'm sorry, Johnny, I should have been stronger, I should have fought them, but I was alone, and scared,' she whispered, trembling. 'If I'd known you would be back one day I wouldn't have listened, but I thought you had left me for good. They argued and argued with me, and I was so tired and miserable I finally said, "Oh, alright, yes," and then they rushed me off to this clinic before I could change my mind. I was in and out in two days, and that was when I had a nervous breakdown. I just went to pieces for weeks after that. I stayed in bed and cried and cried.'

Johnny didn't move or say a word, but she felt his pain, and his anger, in the tension of the warm body lying against her, in the stiffening of his shoulder and arm, the muscles tight and hard with a desire to strike someone.

Billy Grenaby had the ratings in front of him. 'Still climbing. Well, a few points up. That's fine, even a couple of points is good if it's going in the right direction.' He leaned back, his spatulate hands on the leather-topped desk which was the centre of the huge room on the top floor of the Midland TV production company building down by the river. From the huge windows on two sides of the room you got amazing views: the grey, crowded waterway of the Thames, the city roofscape, the towers and church spires. When the sun was bright, Venetian blinds filtered the light, but today they were rolled up, showing the wintry mother-of-pearl sky.

Billy's eyes skewered Harriet. 'Now, what's this I hear . . . you've got problems?'

Harriet looked diplomatically blank. She wasn't answering until she knew precisely what he was talking about.

'Actor problems,' Billy expanded, his eye commanding her.

She muttered, 'Well, you know, Mike's drinking . . . late half the time, quarrels with Annie, doesn't know his words, can't concentrate.'

Billy looked down at the long sheets of computer print-out in front of him and shrugged his shoulders impatiently. 'I'll have him to lunch, talk to him, sort him out. He's an arrogant SOB, but never forget, he's a star, no getting away from it. He's got the charisma, Harriet. He and Annie both; they're the show's biggest pull.' He glanced at Sean. "I think we should heat up their scenes even more. The ratings soar every time they have one of those spats on screen. Good stuff. But you still aren't going far enough. Sex and violence, gets 'em every time. I think it's time they actually did it on screen, don't you?'

'Annie doesn't like the idea,' Sean said wryly.

Billy gave that beatific smile which had made one TV critic call him the Evil Cherub, a description Billy cherished, and which had spawned a series of cartoons in the popular press, the originals of which Billy had paid through the nose to get, and which hung on one of the panelled walls.

'Annie will do what she's told. She's just an actress. Don't ask her, tell her.'

Sean persisted. 'I don't think it's a good idea, either, not yet.'

'Well, I do,' Billy cut across him. 'Built up at the right pace, it could mean a big rise in the ratings again. Take it slowly but make sure they all know it's coming. We want them tuning in every night in case they miss the big moment. Right? Let me see the scripts for the next month; I want them on my desk by the end of the week.'

Sean looked at Harriet, who gave him a wry smile.

'Right,' Billy said, satisfied that he would be obeyed. 'Now, what's this whisper I hear about our Annie and Derek Fenn? Surely to God it isn't true? Wouldn't do her image any good at all. Man of his age . . . and a failure . . . and what's this about a kid? Has she got a kid tucked away somewhere, or adopted?'

'No. There's no child, and she never had any affair with Derek.' How did he hear these rumours so quickly? Harriet pondered furiously. Who was his spy? One of the actors? A member of the crew? There was no point in smoking the spy out – Billy would only replace him or her.

'No smoke without fire.' Billy often spoke in little gnomic phrases, aphorisms and proverbs which served instead of actual thinking. He had a handy portable piece of wisdom for most situations.

'Unless you use a smoke machine,' said Harriet, and he laughed, showing very white, false teeth.

'Never thought of that. Good for you, Harry.'

She wished he wouldn't call her Harry, he only did

it when he was irritated with her, because he knew it annoyed her. The trouble was, she and Billy knew each other intimately by now. She wasn't unaware of the fact that Billy would like their relationship to be even more intimate. He wasn't putting any pressure on her to go to bed with him, but his eyes had a possessive gleam in them when he looked at her. In some ways, she was tempted; not simply because if she became Billy's mistress it would get her anything she wanted, while it lasted, all the clout and influence she hungered for, not to mention the freedom to make the programmes she really wanted to make but knew were something of a risk. No, quite apart from that, although he wasn't good-looking, Billy had something you couldn't ignore. Like a Roman Emperor, he had the power of life or death – and that made him intensely sexy.

It shouldn't, Harriet thought, and some women might not respond to it, but she was ambitious, she knew she wanted power, herself; she found it exciting, and it played around Billy's head like lightning, making him magnetic.

'Well, I hope Annie isn't going to unleash a scandal on us,' he was saying to Sean. 'Not her image. She's on the side of the angels. Mike could weather any amount of scandal. He's a wild boy and they like it, but they won't like it if Annie turns out not to be as pure as driven snow.' He looked at Harriet and his eyes glittered. 'So I hope you've got the lid screwed down on whatever is behind all this.'

I hope so, too, she thought, but only smiled reassuringly at him. 'We'll take care of it, BG.'

'You'd better. I can always get a new director if you let me down,' he told her silkily.

She wasn't scared by the threat, she was always conscious that if she needed to she had an ace she could play and scoop the pool.

'There's no need to threaten Harriet!' Sean said, and Billy looked at him, at once, his lip curling.

'And a new writer, too. Actually, I was thinking the other day that it was time you moved on, came up with a new series. We need a change of direction from you, Halifax, or are you just a one-idea man? That will be the acid test. Can you come up with a new idea?' His tone was scathing, dismissive, meant to get under Sean's skin and make him feel small.

Harriet glared at him – what did he think he was doing, taking her writer away from her? Any new series Sean thought up, she wanted first approval. She'd discovered him, he was her property. Billy wasn't handing him over to anyone else.

'Funny you should say that,' Sean drawled. 'Actually, I've got an idea I've been polishing for some time, but it isn't all worked out yet.'

'Well, get it ready, get it ready,' Billy Grenaby said, a little cross because he hadn't scared either of them. Billy loved to play at being a Billygoat Gruff, to watch people wince and turn pale when he growled at them.

He glanced at his watch, his face sulky. 'Sorry, got to kick you out – another appointment, I'm afraid. Keep in touch. Bear in mind what I've said.' Only when they were on their way out did he call after them, 'Oh, and dump Fenn, will you? At once. Rewrite all the scripts to cut him out.'

Marty Keats rang Sean at the studio half an hour later while he and Harriet were dissecting their interview with Billy and deciding that their honeymoon with him was over and difficult days might well lie ahead. The fact that their climb up the ratings had slowed, even if the show was still climbing, was probably what lay behind Billy's sudden hostility. You were only as good as your last ratings, as Harriet said just as the phone rang.

'Oh, hello, Marty,' Sean said. 'You got my messages, then? Where have you been?'

'What's it to you? Today was my day off. I've been out since early this morning, visiting my sister in Reading, just got back. What's all this about Derek? I haven't seen him since yesterday.'

'He didn't come to work, and he isn't answering his phone – we thought he might be with you.'

'No, he isn't. It's odd, though. It isn't like Derek, not turning up for work. Maybe he's ill? I'll go round to his flat. He has a woman in twice a week to clean for him, and she has a key. She lives across the road. If Derek doesn't answer the door I'll get her to come over and open the door.'

Sean made up his mind on the spur of the moment. 'I'll meet you there.'

Marty arrived first. She collected the key of Derek's flat from his cleaning woman, who was in bed with flu and said she hadn't been over for several days. Maybe Mr Fenn had the flu too? He might have caught it from her.

'That's probably it,' Marty agreed. Knowing Derek, if he had the flu he would dose himself heavily with whisky, his favourite medicine, go to bed and stay there in a stupor, ignoring ringing phones and knocks on the front door.

When Marty went over to Derek's flat, she met Sean on the pavement. 'I got the key,' she told him. 'But you'd better wait outside until Derek has said you can come in – he won't like it if I let you into his home without permission.'

Sean shrugged and followed her to the front door. She unlocked it and walked inside, calling, 'Derek? You home?' There was no answer. 'Smells musty in here, as if nobody's been here for days,' Marty said, opening doors and looking into rooms.

Sean's nostrils quivered. He knew that smell. His gorge rose. He saw Marty push open the sitting-room door and freeze on the threshold. Her hand went up to her mouth as if she was about to be sick, and she made a choked, retching sound.

'Come out of here,' Sean said, running.

He put an arm round her and half pushed, half carried her out of the flat.

'He . . . he . . . he's . . .' she spluttered, skin a whitey-green and eyes dazed with shock.

'I know, go outside, into the fresh air, sit down and just keep quiet,' Sean said. 'I'll ring the police.' He pulled the front door shut and pocketed the key. 'We mustn't touch anything in there. Off you go, Marty.'

As she staggered out, Sean began to use his mobile phone.

8

The murderer sat outside the block of flats, watching the coming and going of the police, watching Sean Halifax talking to them. Halifax had known Derek Fenn – how had he felt seeing him like that, strangled, the black tights still tied around his neck, his face contorted in his last agony, laid out stark naked on the couch? Naked, that is, except for the satsuma in his mouth, injected with a couple of mind-bending drugs, and, of course, wearing the frilly black silk knickers dotted with red satin bows which had been a sudden last-minute inspiration.

The man deserved to die looking like the clown he was.

No blood this time. Too much trouble, cleaning up afterwards, if there was blood. You only had to miss a little spot of it to be in trouble. Safer not to shed blood. There were lots of ways to kill which were clean and safe. But it had been fun to dress the body up a little, arrange the scene as if for a TV soap – Fenn was an actor, after all. And it would all confuse the police, keep them guessing.

The murderer's mouth twisted – had Sean Halifax liked what he saw? Didn't look as if he had. But he hadn't liked Derek Fenn much, had he? Everyone knew the two men disliked each other. Even the press.

Did the police know that? Oh, but they wouldn't suspect Sean . . . not at first, anyway. He was one of them, or had been, and they all stuck together. And, anyway, it would soon come out that the last person to be seen with Derek was a woman.

The murderer glanced at Derek's windows. Photographers were up there now. The flashes of their cameras came like summer lightning in the room. The curtains had been opened, you could see the flashes clearly.

Well, that was one picture the papers wouldn't be printing.

Bet they'd love to, though. It would sell a lot of papers if they did. But they'd never get away with it, not even today.

The murderer smiled, then stopped, eyes irritated. Derek was safely dead, but the old lady in hospital was still alive. She'd somehow survived what should have been a lethal injection. She must be tougher than she looked.

Couldn't let it go, though. No, she couldn't be left alive. His body surged with excitement and he checked it, held it down. Don't get excited, don't give yourself away. Look cool.

But she had to go. Give it a day or two and then . . . another try. And this time she must be killed outright, no trying to dress it up as an accident. Strangling, like Fenn? Too noisy; might attract attention. A knife? Blood. No blood. He hadn't liked the blood the first time, he had had nightmares about it afterwards, the splashes of blood over the walls, the floor. He'd been afraid to sleep alone, he had crept into bed with her and he'd felt her body warm and soft wrapped round him. He hadn't needed to kill again for a long, long time. He had had all he wanted and nobody tried to take it away or hurt her.

It wasn't fair. He never wanted to kill anyone. It was just that he had to; he was forced to.

A pillow over the face might be the best answer for the old woman, clean and quiet. Yes. That was a good idea.

But he wouldn't be finished even then because now he knew Sean Halifax had to go. He was too nosy. Once a policeman always a policeman. He was asking too many questions.

The murderer stretched like a cat, yawning; it had been a long night. Killing made time pass quickly but it left you sleepy – such intense, consuming emotion was draining, and there had been two last night, two in one night.

Funny, that; there had been years between the first murder and the second. Years and years. You could easily have forgotten it ever happened. It had seemed like something in a dream, a fantasy, something rather shocking but secretly pleasant to remember. Killing had brought him so much happiness. He had often thought it might be good to kill again – and then one day he was alone, and to get happiness back it had been necessary to kill again. Just as he always thought. That time had been deliberate, planned; that was when the first queer tremor of pleasure had showed up and he'd known he liked doing it. Admitted to himself. It was the sense of power it gave him.

Power of life and death; one minute blood was pumping through their veins, their hearts were beating and they gave you that look that said they were better than you, you were dirt under their feet and they were going to beat you to a pulp – and the next they were still and silent and turning cold. And you had done it. You had the controls – you flicked the switch that turned them off. Only God could do that. God – and you.

Several people came out from the flats; they weren't police, surely? No, one of them was wearing fur slippers and huddled in an old dressing-gown. They must be other tenants of the block of flats. They were talking to the police – had any of them seen anything? For a second there was a quiver of fear, then the murderer relaxed.

Didn't matter if they had. Annie Lang's face and soft blonde hair was so well known. If anyone had seen the pair who went into Derek Fenn's flat last night, they must have recognised her.

She wasn't getting away scot-free this time; she had to be punished. The police would put her through the mill.

Yes, the mills of God – and me, he thought, chuckling – grind slowly but they grind exceeding small. Oh, yes, Annie. Pain must be repaid with pain. An eye for an eye and pain for pain.

He frowned, staring fixedly at Halifax and the police.

He couldn't kill Annie, though, because, if he did, what would happen then? He had too much invested in her. He needed her alive. First the death, and then the happiness, that was the way it went, that was the pattern. The fantasy could only come true when she was his forever.

Sean rang Annie again, but there was still no reply. Then he rang Harriet, but her assistant couldn't find her anywhere.

It was half an hour before Harriet rang back on his mobile phone. When he told her what had happened to Derek, she made noises like someone who had been punched in the stomach.

'Dead? Strangled? Are you sure it was Derek?'

Sean flatly told her what he had seen in one brief glance from the doorway of the room: the sprawled, naked body, the bulging eyes, the blood-engorged features.

'No question, it was Derek.'

'Oh, Christ,' Harriet said, sounding sick. 'Poor Derek. He was always so scared of getting hurt, he wouldn't do any of the stunts himself, even the least dangerous. I hope to God he died quickly, anyway.'

'Strangling isn't much fun, but it won't have taken him long to die,' Sean said, and she made gulping sounds again.

Sean interrupted her, 'Harriet, any sign of Annie? I rang her, no reply. Her cleaner must have gone home and nobody is answering. Could you go round there? I'm worried about her. Where the hell can she be? I'd go myself, but I have to stay here. Finding a body automatically makes you a suspect. They've asked me to hang around for a bit in case they think of questions they have to ask me.'

'A suspect?' Harriet sounded taken aback. 'You aren't serious? But why should they suspect you?'

'They suspect everybody – I would, myself, in their shoes.'

She was silent for a minute, then said, 'Sean, who on earth could have wanted to kill poor Derek?'

'Somebody with a sick sense of humour,' Sean said, grimacing at the memory of the way the body looked. 'Look, don't think about it. Just go and look for Annie.'

'Of course I will. I wonder what she can be doing?'

'Ring me at once when you catch up with her, won't you?' Putting his mobile phone back in his pocket,

Sean shivered in the chill spring wind. He had told Harriet not to think about who might have killed Fenn, but he couldn't stop thinking about it himself. His mind seethed with unanswered questions. Why would anyone want to kill Derek Fenn?

'How long had he been dead?' he asked the forensic pathologist just leaving after doing a preliminary inspection of the body.

Dr Kent gave him a dry look. A small, bald man with piercing blue eyes, he had an air of sniffing every time before he spoke, his fine nostrils drawing together in an offended way.

'You don't really expect an answer at this early stage? I can't even give you a guess.'

'But last night sometime?' pressed Sean.

'If you say so.' Dr Kent left and the detective inspector who was dealing with the case came over to Sean, grinning.

'Didn't get any joy from our man, then? Well, you wouldn't. He takes his time, may be a day or two before we get an answer, and *we* are the police, remember. You aren't. Not any more. You're here to give answers, not ask questions.'

'Oh, come off it. I can't turn my brain off, I can't help trying to work out who could have done it, can I?'

'If you've got any ideas on that score, let me in on them,' the other man grated, staring at him hard.

'Well, for a start, the lipstick on the mouth, the sexy knickers . . . had he had sex before he died? I suppose he hadn't fooled us all for years – he wasn't gay, by any chance? I mean, that's what it looks like to me, a gay killing. Does it look like that to you?'

He knew from the other man's expression that the idea had already occurred to him, but shrugged.

'Have you ever heard he was gay?' He watched Sean shake his head, and said, 'Well, until I've got all the evidence I'm not making any assumptions. If all you've got is guesswork, Halifax, why don't you go home? We know where to find you if we need you.'

'What about her?' Sean gestured to where Marty Keats was sitting with her head in her hands, doubled up as if she was still feeling sick.

The inspector shrugged. Sean had known him slightly; they weren't friends but Jack Chorley wasn't so much hostile as resentful, envious, a little touch of the green eye over Sean's success and suspected earning capacity, perhaps. Sean saw it in all their faces, the policemen who knew he had once been one of them but was now famous, and, by their standards, rich.

'We still need to talk to her, she's hardly told us anything yet, and if they were sleeping together she must be a suspect, you know that.'

'So you do see it as a sex killing?'

Chorley ignored the question. 'We'll take her down to the station in a minute and see what we can get out of her. She must know more than she's admitting. At the moment, we're checking her alibi for last night and this morning.'

'If I were you I'd look for her ex-husband, too.'

Chorley's eyes narrowed, hard and bright. 'Oh?'

'She was sleeping with Fenn, and her ex, Roger Keats, was a nasty piece of work. They're divorced, but he's the type to turn vicious if he found out she was planning to marry again.'

'Was she going to marry Fenn?'

'No idea. I'm still just speculating. It would be worth checking it out. Oh, and if you find Keats, could you let me know? I'd like a word with him myself.'

'You've got a nerve. I'm not handing police evidence over to you. Go home, Halifax, and stay out of my hair.'

'If you need me, this is my number,' Sean said, handing him a printed card. 'I've got a mobile phone. I'll get your call wherever I am.'

Chorley eyed him sardonically. 'Snap,' he said, producing his own phone from his pocket. 'These days you don't have to be a bigtime TV scriptwriter to have a mobile phone. Even us poverty-stricken coppers get issued one!'

'Don't be so bloody touchy!' Sean grated. 'Just let me know if anything interesting turns up, won't you?'

'Will I hell,' said Chorley. 'Leave the policework to the professionals, Halifax; you concentrate on writing far-fetched stories for TV.'

Sean didn't bother to retort; he turned and walked over to Marty, explained that he was leaving but she would be wanted to help the police with their enquiries. She gave him a distraught look.

'They don't suspect me, do they? I didn't do it. I was at home with my children.'

'If they can give you an alibi you'll be OK, won't you?'

She wailed, 'I want to go home to my kids!' Sean watched her thoughtfully; she didn't look to him like a killer.

Derek was hardly a heavyweight, but he was a man, and wiry enough; could a woman have overpowered him? It didn't seem likely.

But if they had been having sex she might have taken him off guard. Pretty kinky sex, from the look of it. There had been something comic and revolting

247

about the satsuma in the gaping, red-lipsticked mouth.

It had made Derek Fenn an object of cheap mockery. What sort of mind could have thought of that?

And the drugs in the satsuma . . . that was something Sean had never come across before – he hadn't credited it when Dr Kent told him about the drugs which had been injected into the fruit.

'Are you sure?'

'Fairly sure. I've seen it before – they increase the sex drive. Give more of a kick to the orgasm when it comes.' He had given one of his little sniffs. 'Amazing what the human mind can come up with. What's wrong with straightforward sex, I'd like to know?'

'Works for me, every time,' agreed Sean. 'You're the professional, Doc, you tell me – why the need to dress up something so natural and powerful with drugs and kinky stuff?'

'Maybe the victim couldn't do it otherwise? Well, he was getting on a bit; maybe he'd been having a problem in that direction. If his libido was on the blink, he might have needed help to get an erection, let alone orgasm.'

'Maybe,' Sean had said, thinking . . . but a satsuma in his mouth? It was far too comic. No, Sean couldn't believe it. It must have been put there after Derek was dead. Must have been, surely, or it would have rolled out in his death throes. Strangling was a violent business unless the victim was unconscious already, and Derek clearly hadn't been. He had struggled, made quite a mess, kicking stuff off the coffee-table, having an orgasm, urinating at the same time, his bodily functions totally out of control in his last agony.

Poor bastard, thought Sean, mouth wry. An undignified way to die, and Fenn had been a man obsessed with his image, with the way he looked. He always dressed well – even when he was wearing casual gear it was usually expensive, designer stuff.

'Maybe I'd better get a lawyer,' Marty said, breaking in on his thoughts, and Sean looked at her and, as he took in what she had said, nodded.

'Might be a good idea, at that. Do you know one?'

'Guy, who did my divorce, he'll come, or send someone else to sit in on the interview.' Marty looked up at Sean, her orange hair dishevelled, her eyes smeared with tears and mascara. 'They don't really think I did it, do they, Sean?'

'I don't know what they think.'

She didn't believe him, her eyes wild. 'Oh, come on – you're one of them, they talk to you, you were a policeman.'

He gave her a dry smile. 'Once. No more. And when you're out, you are out, as far as the force is concerned, believe me. Oh, I still have friends there, but the guy in charge here isn't one of them. Chorley probably suspects me more than he suspects you, but then Chorley suspects everyone.'

'So long as he doesn't suspect me,' Marty said with a smothered sob.

'He may suspect your ex-husband,' Sean softly said, watching her intently.

'Roger?' She blinked at him, rubbed a hand over her wet, black-ringed eyes. 'Oh, my God . . . I hadn't thought of that.'

'Was he capable of murder?'

'Roger was a sadistic bastard, he was capable of anything; he once stubbed a cigarette out on my arm because I laughed at him at the wrong moment.'

*

Sean drove straight to Annie's flat and found Harriet sitting outside in her car. She got out to meet him, her sheepskin coat wrapped round her, shivering in the cold wind, her face pale and her eyes anxious.

'She still isn't back. Sean, what on earth is going on? Derek murdered, Annie vanished God knows where. I'm worried. I've got a bad feeling about all this.'

'So have I. Join the club. Marty is petrified they'll suspect her.'

'Well, she was seeing Derek, wasn't she?'

'But was she the only one? He was out every night at clubs around town, drinking and gambling – there must have been other women in his life besides Marty. Maybe men, too.'

Harriet stared. 'Men? Derek wasn't ambi, was he?'

'Could be. The way he was killed could easily be.' Sean broke off as a taxi drew up on the other side of the road. 'Hang on, I think this is Annie . . . yes, it is.'

He strode across the road with Harriet on his heels. The taxi drove off just as they got there and Annie turned to face them, flushed and contrite.

'Oh, hello – were you waiting for me?'

'And worrying ourselves sick!' Harriet indignantly told her.

Sean's narrowed eyes were searching Annie's face. She looked different. Something had happened to her, something so powerful it showed even at a casual glance. Her colour was high, her eyes fever-bright. Sean felt the clutch of jealousy, and was shaken by it. He had never felt like that before about anyone. He had always been a loner, a man who walked by himself and didn't need anybody else. What was the matter with him? Was she beginning to matter that much?

'Where have you been?' he broke out hoarsely and she turned to look at him, the glance betraying her mood even more. Annie was walking on the wind, high as a kite. She had been making love, his first instinctive awareness of it backed by the evidence of his searching eyes – her pink mouth faintly swollen, a small love-bite on her throat, under her ear. He could almost smell sex on her, and his stomach clenched. He felt almost as sick as he had when he saw Derek Fenn's body.

'I was with someone,' she admitted, defiance in her face.

Harriet was instantly distracted, her brows going up. 'A man? Annie! Who? Is this someone new? Or do we know him?'

Annie laughed, excitement glittering over her. Both Harriet and Sean were taken aback by the change in her. They had never seen her look like this.

'I've known him for years, but we'd lost touch – I met him again yesterday, he came to interview me. He works for the real-life crime magazine, remember that interview? And this morning he rang me and we met up at the hospital, after I'd seen my mother.'

'Who is this guy?' demanded Sean curtly.

She gave him another defiant look. 'I just told you. A journalist, a reporter, someone I knew years ago.'

Sean drew a sharp breath. 'This is him, isn't it? The old flame who got you pregnant?'

Her eyes widened in surprise; she had forgotten that she had ever told him about that.

When she didn't deny it, Sean said curtly, 'I told you to rest today. You shouldn't have gone out!'

'Oh, stop ordering me around!'

Sean and Harriet did a double-take, their eyes meeting in surprise. Annie had never snapped back at them like that before.

'We're not ordering you around,' Harriet protested. 'We're worried about you, Annie.' She put her arm round her and Annie shook her off.

'Well, just leave me alone, will you?' Annie walked away towards her front door and they followed her.

As she opened the door Sean bit out, 'Fenn is dead, murdered.'

Annie turned, going white with shock. 'Derek? Dead? Murdered?'

Harriet gave Sean an incredulous, furious look. 'What a way to tell her! What's the matter with you?'

Sean shrugged grimly; he hadn't meant to break it like that but his temper had got out of hand. He'd wanted to hit her for looking the way she did, for the sensuality you could see throbbing in her body, in her eyes and mouth.

He couldn't believe what he was seeing. Who was this man who could make her look like that? Was he the reason why there had been no man in her life before? Had she just been waiting for her old lover to return? All these years?

What annoyed him most was that he'd stupidly thought she must be waiting for the right man, had never met him and wasn't prepared to compromise with anyone else.

He'd even begun to think it might be him, the right man for Annie – hope it might, anyway. He should have known better; dreams were just that, dreams. They didn't come true. His whole life had told him that. You couldn't work in the police force for years without realising what a bloody awful world this was, and how unlikely you were ever to get what you dreamt about.

But he had had one dream come true – he had become a writer, a professional, highly paid writer at that, something he had never dared hope for at one time, and he had let himself begin to hope another dream might come true. From the minute he met Annie he'd been stunned by her delicate beauty, by the sudden radiance of her smiles, by her soft, clear voice. Even her coolness towards him had pleased him. Sean didn't like women to be too eager, to flirt or come on to him before he showed a sign of being interested. If there was any chasing to be done, Sean wanted to do it, but he liked to take his time. He hated making mistakes about anything, especially about women. So he'd been slowly working his way round to asking Annie out. How was he to guess she was going to meet this old flame again?

Harriet put an arm round Annie and took her into the house. Sean followed angrily and found them in the living-room, Annie half sitting, half lying on a couch, shivering, while Harriet piled cushions behind her head.

Annie looked at Sean, her eyes huge with distress. 'What happened to Derek?'

'He was strangled.'

She drew breath audibly. 'God.' She shivered.

Sean did not fill her in on the more lurid details. No doubt when the press got on to the story she would read all about it. He grimaced at the realisation that this was all going to hit the headlines. The press would have a field day. For once Billy Grenaby wasn't going to welcome the publicity. Billy! he thought. They'd have to tell him and at once before he heard it from someone else. Billy would want to get the studio publicity machine into operation with a damage-containment programme.

'Billy!' he mouthed to Harriet above Annie's head and Harriet shut her eyes, gave a smothered groan.

'I'd better ring him now. He mustn't hear about it from the press first. If he did, and then found out we knew and hadn't told him, he'd fire us both.'

How was she going to tell Billy and avoid an outburst of rage? She was going to need all her powers of tact and persuasion to stop him going spare.

Grimacing, Harriet hurried out. Annie hardly noticed her go. She seemed too dazed to notice anything.

Sean looked down at her and took a grip on his temper. It was pointless being furious with her; she had no idea how he felt. He hoped she didn't guess, anyway. He hated to think of her knowing, being kind, because Annie would be kind; he had seen her with her mother, with Harriet, or Jason, her driver, with others in the cast when they were hurt or upset. She was one of those people who noticed if someone was having a bad time and he didn't want her feeling sorry for him. His pride couldn't stand it.

Trying to sound calm and patient, he asked, 'Are you OK? You'd better have a drink, some brandy.'

She shook her head, said shakily, 'Who did it, Sean? Do the police know?'

'We only just found the body.'

'We? You mean, you did?' She looked startled, stared at him as if seeing him for the first time. 'Where? Where did it happen?'

Sean told her tersely and she listened in shocked silence.

'I'll make us all some coffee,' offered Harriet from

the door. As Sean looked round at her she added, 'I talked to Billy, he's coping.'

Billy, as she expected, had exploded at first into violent emotions: shock, then horror, then rage. Billy was given to such eruptions; for a shrewd, hard-headed businessman, he was deeply emotional. Harriet couldn't help wondering what sort of lover he would be – he wasn't good-looking but he had all that emotional power dammed up inside. What would it be like to be the one to break that dam?

She knew his marriage was on the rocks; he and his wife had separated and he had allowed her custody of their children. The gossip around the company was that Billy's wife was dull; everyone who had ever met her said she was good to look at, a tall, elegant creature with blonde hair which was always perfect, an enamelled face, long red nails and polite smile. But she was jawbreakingly tedious to talk to – all you got from her was small talk, automatic questions about how you were, was your work going well, what did you think about the latest news?

No wonder Billy spent every waking hour at work and very little time at home.

It had taken her nearly ten minutes to soothe him down, but she had finally got him into the right sort of mind to take practical steps to deal with the fall-out from Derek's death.

Sean smiled at her. 'Good girl.'

Harriet gave him a dry look. Men could be patronising jerks! And they didn't even seem to realise it. But she liked Sean a lot, so she grinned forgivingly, and vanished to make the tea; when she was upset it always calmed her down to have something useful to do. She and Billy had that in common.

She had a lot of thinking to do. If Annie had taken up with someone else now, would Sean be looking for comfort elsewhere?

Harriet always liked to keep her options open. 'Wait and see' was her motto.

When she had gone, Sean insisted on finding Annie a drink in the sideboard where her mother had always kept sherry. While he was pouring some of that into a glass, he glanced along the framed photographs of Annie which stood on the sideboard; Annie as a baby, wearing a frilly dress, with dimpled knees, her blue eyes already dominating her baby face; Annie aged about five or six in a swimsuit at the seaside, Annie in school uniform; Annie with a middle-aged man's arm around her, leaning confidingly on him. Her father? wondered Sean, turning to take the glass of sherry to her.

Annie's lower lip was trembling, her small white teeth gnawing at it as she accepted the glass. She didn't drink the sherry, just held the glass, staring up at him, her blue eyes glazed with unshed tears.

'Oh, God, I feel so bad . . . Sean, it was my fault, I did it.'

Sean looked at her in startled shock, a coldness invaded his limbs. 'What? What the hell are you saying?'

'He told me he owed money to a nasty crowd who were threatening to kill him, and I didn't believe him, I wouldn't lend him any more money. If I had, he'd be alive now!'

Sean gave a long-drawn-out sigh of relief. Oh, that was all! Women were such inveterate victims – how typical of Annie to try to take the blame for something Fenn had brought on himself!

But it gave a new perspective to the murder. He thought aloud, 'That never occurred to me, that it could have been a professional murder. Or to the police, I expect. They'll have to be told about this. I suppose he didn't mention a name? Did he say who he owed the money to?'

She shook her head. 'Only that it was a gambling debt.'

Sean whistled. 'That can be a very nasty crowd. Maybe Marty Keats will know exactly who he owed the money to.' But Sean had handled crimes involved with gambling before, and they rarely killed someone who owed them money – that would merely make sure they never got it! No, their idea of a warning was to break your arm or a leg and warn you to pay up or next time it would be worse. Sean thought of the murder scene and doubted if Derek's death had been a professional hit. There had been something nastily personal about the way the body had been arranged. Someone had hated Derek Fenn, had taken time and trouble to make him look ridiculous in death. Professionals didn't play games. They made their hit and left quickly, they didn't hang around dressing the body up.

The first press car arrived while they were drinking the coffee Harriet had made. It was Harriet who heard the screech of tyres on wet tarmac and got up and went to the window.

'Oh, no!' she groaned, staring out. 'That didn't take them long!'

Annie either didn't hear anything, or didn't care what was going on – she sat staring into the red-glowing bars of the electric fire like someone gazing into hell.

Sean gave her a concerned look, then joined Harriet at the window and scowled at the reporter and photographer running up the path. 'Hell.' Giving Harriet a furious look, he said, 'I thought Billy was supposed to be coping with them?'

The front door bell rang loudly, and a man yelled through the letter box. 'Hello? Annie? This is Jamie Bellew – remember me? I've interviewed you often enough. You know me, Annie, Can we talk? You'll have to talk to someone and you know you can trust me to put your side of the story. You want everyone to know the truth, don't you, darling?'

The photographer came to the lamplit window and tried peering through the Venetian blind over it. Before he could make out who was in the room, Sean quickly jerked the cord which closed the blind completely.

'They won't go away,' Harriet muttered to him. 'And there will be more of them any minute.'

Sean turned to look at Annie's pale face, her dilated eyes. 'Is there a back way out of here?'

She wasn't listening.

'Annie!' he snapped and her head came round. She looked blankly at him.

'What?'

'Is there a way out of here through the back garden?'

She shook her head, but he went to look out of the high window at the back of the long sitting room which ran through the whole ground floor of the Edwardian house. It was obvious to Sean that this had once been two rooms, but at some stage in the past the wall between the rooms had been removed. Long ago, judging by the décor, which was old-fashioned, in Sean's eyes.

He stared down at the dusk-filled garden. Lawn- and shrub-filled, with a couple of apple trees, it was sur-rouned by a ten-foot-high brick wall without a gate in it. They would never get over that.

'OK,' Sean said. 'Then we'll have to go through the front. Brace yourself. We must go now, before there's a whole crowd of them. Put your coat back on and we'll go.'

Annie was in no state to move fast enough to satisfy him, but she was limply obedient. Harriet got her coat back on her, they turned out the fire and the lights, and then, with Sean on one side and Harriet on the other, Annie was rushed out of her front door and down the path, with a barrage of questions fired at her by Jamie Bellew, while his photographer's flashbulbs exploded, blinding her.

They had almost reached the car when several other reporters drove up and began harrying them.

Annie felt like someone in a nightmare; hands reached to grab her, pull at her, faces loomed towards her, eyes stared, raised voices deafened her. She heard but couldn't even think about what she was asked.

'How do you feel about Derek Fenn's murder? Is it true that he was naked when they found him?'

'Were you with him last night, Annie? Were you there when he was killed? Do you know who killed him?'

'There is a rumour that he was a closet gay . . . could it be true, Annie?'

'You weren't on the set today, were you? And neither was Derek – were the two of you together? There's a rumour that you were having an affair with him. Is it true?'

'You've known Derek for years, haven't you, Annie? How intimate were you? Is there any truth in these whispers . . . that you had his child when you were still at school?'

She moved through it all like a sleepwalker, looking at none of the reporters, answering none of their questions.

Sean pushed her into the back of his car, Harriet climbed in with her, and Sean ran round to get behind the wheel, bodily throwing out a photographer who was already half into the car at the front, aiming his lense straight into Annie's white face with those deep, dark holes for eyes.

Sean slammed the door and locked the car, started the engine. On all sides the press bayed, hammering on windows, shouting more questions, taking more pictures.

Annie was too dazed even to hide her face. She just sat there in total shock. Harriet looked anxiously at her. What effect was all this going to have on her? The whole series depended on Annie; they couldn't afford to have her off for any length of time or the series would grind to a halt.

Only as they drove round the corner of the road with the press running like lemmings to their cars to follow, did she think to ask Sean, 'Where are we going to take her?'

'My place,' said Sean. 'If we take her to your flat they'll soon find her again – they all know where you live. They don't know where I live yet, I only moved there a couple of weeks ago and, even better, it's an isolated spot, for London. I don't have many neighbours.'

Harriet was curious. He'd never mentioned having a

new flat; she had thought him very happy with his old place. 'Where on earth have you moved to?'

'Wait and see!'

He drove round another corner, turned down a narrow alley and out into a side-road, then took another sharp left turn. By then they had lost the posse of cars on their tail.

It was ten minutes before Harriet realised they were heading into London's dockland, along the ancient route once known as Ratcliffe Highway, skimming the north bank of the River Thames above the warren of warehouses and tenement buildings where the poorest denizens of London's sewer streets had lived for generations, usually the newest immigrants, arriving penniless and desperate for somewhere to live. Each new wave of arrivals took the place of those who had moved on and out into better areas.

Since the Second World War, though, the London docks themselves had withered and died; no ships moored in the port, warehouses were abandoned, empty and decaying. The latest immigrants came by air, but still found their way here, to the slums of London.

But developers had moved in over the past few years. The area was changing. Sean's new flat was on the very top floor of an old warehouse right on the river edge – workmen were still busy converting the rest of it into offices and shops but Sean had managed to acquire the penthouse flat for a song because he knew the developer, he told Harriet.

'When I was still in the force, I caught his daughter selling drugs. She was more sinned against than sinning, a rather lonely, sad little girl whose mother had died when she was fourteen. Her Dad was always too busy to have time for her. He stuck her in an expensive private school and forgot about her. She met a smooth-talking bastard who seduced her and then used her to sell his drugs at parties.'

Annie stirred, suddenly tuning in to what he was saying, and winced. 'Poor kid . . . men can be vile, can't they?'

She was thinking of Roger Keats and the way he had ruined her life, and Sean knew it, looking at her in his driving mirror and seeing the misery in her face.

'Some men can be,' he grimly agreed. 'Don't tar us all with the same brush, Annie.'

A smile flickered over her mouth and her eyes turned dreamy. Sean was learning to recognise her expressions – she's thinking of *him* now, he thought, his teeth meeting. She always looks like that when she thinks of him.

'What happened to this little girl?' Harriet asked, more interested in the story he was telling.

Sean shrugged. 'I managed to persuade her to testify against her lover. When the case came to court she was put on probation. I'd made a deal with her and her father. She agreed to go to a clinic and get help, be weaned off her drugs. Of course, threats were made by the rat who'd been running her. He might be in prison but he had friends outside and she'd be sorry, that kind of thing – but I made it clear to him that if she was ever so much as touched I'd make it my business to see he didn't live to boast about it.' Sean smiled drily. 'He took one look at my expression, and he believed me.'

Annie watched his face reflected in the mirror above his head, and could believe it, too. There was something fiercely ruthless in Sean's make-up; he was a man who might be capable of anything.

Harriet said excitedly, 'You've never used that story in the series – it would make a great episode.'

He shook his head. 'I promised her Dad I wouldn't ever talk about her part in the case. He was really shaken by realising that if he had taken more notice of her she would never have got into that mess. He made sure she knew he loved her, after that. She's working with him, now; she's an accountant, and a damn good one, I gather. And that's why I got first refusal on the penthouse flat in this new development. They bought the old warehouse and began reconstructing it, and offered me a chance to buy a flat there before work even began.'

'I can't think why you accepted,' Harriet said, staring around at the bleak landscape of the riverside streets.

'Wait till you see the view from my terrace,' said Sean, slowing as he made his way along a narrow, winding road between high blank grey brick walls; behind them Harriet caught glimpses of the river, glinting black and ominous under the wharf lights. There was no other traffic around, no people, no sounds, except the rattling of mast wires in a marina some way up river, the chug of a barge passing slowly along the river.

Sean drove up an alley and parked behind one of the high warehouse buildings. Harriet helped Annie out of the car. She was shivering and looking blankly around.

'Where are we?'

Sean unlocked a high door and ushered them in, switched on lights which showed them a dusty corridor, an old metal lift like something out of a thirties film.

'Been here for years,' Sean explained, pulling the iron fretwork doors back.

The lift rose jerkily; Annie was afraid, cold sweat dewed her forehead.

'I want to go home,' she whispered, trembling.

Harriet put an arm round her. 'Don't be scared, honey. We'll look after you, me and Sean.' Her voice sounded more confident than she felt. Sean must be crazy, living in a place like this. It was so cold and grim, like a prison.

Harriet looked sideways at him, suddenly scared.

What if Sean was the crazy bastard who had murdered Derek? What if she and Annie had just walked into a trap?

9

Sean had some sleeping pills in his bathroom cabinet. He gave a couple of them to Annie with a glass of milk and Harriet put her to bed.

Rejoining Sean in the thirty foot sitting-room which overlooked the River Thames, Harriet sat down with a long sigh, looking at him.

'She's half asleep already. Those pills must be pretty strong stuff. I hope you know what you're doing, giving them to her.'

'That was the dosage for me, and she's had too many shocks over the past couple of days. I'm worried about what it could all be doing to her head.'

'She's fragile, isn't she?' Harriet heavily agreed. 'Both mentally and physically. I thought, just now, she was pretty close to collapse.'

'Yes. And a lot more is going on in her life than we know about, I think.' Sean was thinking about this old lover who had reappeared out of the blue. 'I want to know a lot more about this guy she's been with – she seemed pretty cagey about him to me, didn't she to you?'

Harriet gave him a dry glance. 'Sure you aren't just jealous?'

Sean flushed darkly. 'Why should I be? I've never had anything going with Annie.'

That doesn't mean you don't want to! thought Harriet. But most men hate to admit their feelings, and judging by all the policemen she had met since she started making this series, it was practically a crime in the police force. Their training taught them not to get too involved, not to let themselves care about the people they had to deal with – because if your emotions came into play you wouldn't be cool-headed enough in dealing with a crime, and you would get torn apart each time.

Aloud she just said, 'What with the guy who's been sending her Valentine's cards for years, and the abortion when she was barely out of school, it's a wonder she's not more mixed up than she is. In fact, having a man in her life doesn't seem to me to be anything to worry about – more like a cure for all her problems. She looked to me as if she was over the moon.'

She considered Sean's frown with a touch of secret amusement – look at him glowering, and he says he doesn't care!

'I just think it's odd, him turning up out of the blue just now,' Sean bit out.

'Well, why don't you ask her about him?'

'I'll do better than that. I'll check the guy out,' Sean said with threat in his tone.

He was taking it very personally, thought Harriet. 'Good idea. We don't want Annie hanging around with someone we know nothing about, especially after what's happened to Derek. We don't need any more bad publicity. Oh, by the way – Billy wanted us to go and see him tonight, at his house. He wants to know exactly what's going on.'

Sean shook his head. 'I'm not leaving Annie alone here. We might have been followed. I don't think we were, I kept watch for anyone who might be behind us, but I'm certainly not leaving Annie here without someone to keep an eye on her. Look what happened when we left her at her own house. She went out and vanished for most of the day.'

Harriet was frowning. 'Yes, that was weird. Do we tell the police?'

He looked sharply at her. 'Tell them what?'

She met his eyes levelly. 'That she's been vanishing a lot lately. She went out for hours the night Derek was murdered, remember?'

From his face she could see he hadn't forgotten that, but that he had hoped she had. 'If they ask, you'll have to tell the police, of course, but don't for God's sake volunteer the information. After all, you can't really suspect Annie? Of killing Fenn? Strangling him? Do you honestly see her committing murder?'

Harriet grimaced, shaking her head. 'No, of course not. I just thought you'd advise me to tell the police everything. Whether I believe Annie could be guilty or not.'

Sean hesitated and Harriet gave him another of her dry, cynical glances.

'If it was anyone else, you would, wouldn't you? But not when it's Annie. You're in love with her, aren't you, Sean?' She watched him closely, waiting for the betraying look in the eyes she had seen just now.

He reddened, eyes turning angry. 'What are you talking about? You women, that's all you ever have in your heads. Love! Look, I just don't think Annie's capable of strangling Derek Fenn, but if she comes under suspicion it could be disastrous for the series. That's what I'm worried about.'

'You and me both,' Harriet agreed soberly, frowning. 'The press are going to be everywhere, from now on, like bees around a honeypot. They seem to be on to the idea that something was going on between

Annie and Derek, which means somebody has told them so.'

'Yes, but who, I wonder?' said Sean curtly. 'Got to be one of us. Not you?' He read her annoyed face. 'No, of course not – I didn't think so. Who else knows? Who else talks to the press a lot?'

She looked blank.

'Mike?' suggested Sean and her eyes widened.

'Mike might,' she accepted.

'Well, his head has got to be straightened out. If he destroys Annie, he destroys the series. That has to be made clear to him. If he had two brain cells in that head of his he'd know that! In the meantime, we must think of some way of keeping the press away from Annie, and that will mean minimising the interest the police take in her. If I genuinely thought for a second that Annie was involved, of course I'd have to tell them everything I know, but I don't believe it, and I don't trust them not to draw the wrong conclusions. And even worse, I never knew a police station that wasn't as leaky as a sieve. There's always someone lower down who makes money on the side by selling information to the press. You know it's the same around the studio, and in the TV company. Knowledge is money in our business, and in theirs.'

'You're right. I'll tell them as little as I have to.' Harriet was frowning. Then she said, 'If Mike Waterford is leaking to the press, Billy will soon plug him up, don't worry.'

Sean's mobile phone rang; he took it out, pulled out the aerial. 'Hello? Oh, hi, Chorley, what can I do for you?'

'We have to talk to Annie Lang, Halifax. Where have you taken her?'

'What makes you think I've taken her anywhere?' Sean hedged.

'Oh, come off it, Halifax. A crowd of tabloid reporters saw you driving off with her. They lost you and you never showed up at your flat. They didn't know your address, of course, but we did. When we found out that Annie Lang wasn't at home, and had left with you, we went round to see you, but we were told you had moved out a couple of weeks ago, nobody knew your new address.'

Thank God for that! thought Sean, his mouth relaxing. He looked at his watch and calculated how long they had been on the phone – would Chorley be trying to trace the call while they talked? Better get off the line as soon as possible.

'So what is it, Halifax?' Chorley snapped. 'We must talk to her. She's a vital witness.'

'She's under sedation. She can't talk to anybody.'

'Don't pull that one on me.' Chorley's voice snarled. 'Or I'll arrest you for wasting police time and interfering with witnesses.'

'I'm telling you the truth. Annie is in shock. She can't talk to you yet. See her tomorrow morning. For God's sake, man, it's late. Go home and get some sleep yourself.'

'Give me that address, Halifax.'

'Tomorrow, at ten o'clock. I promise I'll give it to you then.'

Sean switched off his phone while Chorley was gabbling with rage, and looked at Harriet broodingly. 'Tell Billy to get her the best lawyer he knows.'

Harriet looked disturbed. 'Is she really going to need that?'

'I hope to God not.' But he sounded uneasy.

Harriet rang for a taxi and left a few minutes later. Sean stood at the window to watch her drive away; he wanted to be quite sure there were no other vehicles around. But the long, dark street was quite empty.

Sean made himself a stiff drink and was about to drink it when he heard a sound from the bedroom where Annie was sleeping.

He hurried in there, but she hadn't moved, she was still lying curled up in a foetal position under the dark blue duvet he had covered her with a while ago. He could see her hands half under her pillowed cheek, the feathery strands of pale hair hiding her eyes. She looked like a child.

The faint sounds he'd heard were coming from her. He bent to listen, tentatively brushed some of the hair away to show him her face.

Her eyes were closed, but there were tears stealing out from under the bruised-looking lids.

She was crying in her sleep. Her lips moved; he just heard the name.

'Johnny . . .' she sobbed. 'Oh, Johnny.'

Sean straightened and walked out, his face stiff and cold.

Who the hell was the guy? Well, it wouldn't be hard to find out. Hadn't she said he worked for a crime magazine? It should be simple to run a check on him.

In her dream Annie was lost in the forest, running between the trees. But it wasn't spring in her dream. It was high summer. Under the trees the green ferns whispered and swayed as she ran through them, she felt the caress of their smooth cool fronds against her bare skin.

Bare. She looked down at herself and gave a gasp of shock. She was naked.

The light filtering down through the canopy of leaves high above had a greenish tinge with sudden piercing rays of gold in it that dappled her skin and made her look like a forest animal, clothed to match her surroundings, as the deer she had once seen in a wild-life park, their smooth coats dappled to be invisible among the shadows of an English wood.

And, like the deer, she was hunted.

She heard the panting, the running of feet behind her, coming closer. Closer. Panic rose inside her. She ran on, looking over her shoulder, and with another shock recognised Johnny.

She stopped still and he caught up with her. He was laughing, then they were on the ground among the ferns, and she opened her legs, groaning with need, and shut her eyes as he sank into her like rain soaking into the earth, natural, life-giving, necessary.

When she opened them again they were in his grandmother's house, on the hearth rug, lying sated and sweating in front of the fire, still trembling after making love. Although she didn't look round, she knew the forest trees were crowding in around the window to watch them, but it wasn't frightening, or even strange – she felt they were friendly.

Johnny looked sadly at her. 'Why did you do it, Annie?'

'I'm sorry, Johnny,' she sobbed, guilt overwhelming her. 'I didn't want to kill your baby. They made me.'

'You didn't have to give in to them. You could have refused.'

'I was scared of them. I was much younger then, Johnny.'

'When I was much younger than you my father used to beat my mother up all the time. I used to listen to her sobbing afterwards, and hate him. She was smaller than you. Her hair was like yours, fair and very fine, like feathers. She had big blue eyes like yours. She was helpless. My father was a big man, and enjoyed hurting people. But I stopped him. I made sure he never touched her again.'

'But you're strong, Johnny. I'm not. I'm weak.'

'I know that now. A pity, Annie.' There were tears in his eyes. He looked at her with such sadness. 'Oh, such a pity. You're like my mother; she was weak and helpless. But I took care of her, and I'll look after you, too, don't worry.'

Annie woke up abruptly, in the dark, and lay there trembling. Some of her dream still echoed in her head. She tried to remember all of it, but couldn't be sure she was remembering what she had dreamt, or what Johnny had actually said to her, in the house in front of the fire, after they made love.

But then everything that had ever happened between them seemed dreamlike. She could almost believe she had imagined it all, or that their love had been just a dream.

Maybe she was still dreaming?

Maybe she had never woken up. Was she still asleep, but dreaming that she was awake? She couldn't even remember what had happened before she went to sleep, what had happened last night.

At that instant Derek's face swooped at her out of the dark and she gave a smothered cry, her hand at her mouth.

Derek. Derek was dead. Had been killed, murdered

– how could she think about making love with Johnny, how could she think about dreams, about happiness, when something so terrible had happened?

She had often been angry with Derek, often resented the way he preyed on her, blackmailed her . . . but she had had a sort of soft spot for him, too. There was something pathetic about him, almost lovable.

Poor man, he had not been the wise, down-to-earth figure he had played in The Force. It was extraordinary, really, the way he had managed to make that imaginary character come to life, made people believe it to be him, but then she had often been bewildered by the confusion in viewers' minds between the figure on the TV screen and the human being they met in the street.

When you went on long enough you could become confused with the character you played. You could begin to wonder who you really were. Your own identity began to crumble at times; apart from the changing emotions you acted out you had no dimension. You were just a flat image on a flat screen.

That was what had happened to Derek, too. He had been treated by the public and the press as a big name because of his part in the series, but Derek had actually been a man obsessed with failure, a star that had fallen, Lucifer-like, from a great height, after playing the major Shakespearian roles in his youth. He had drunk himself out of that world; you couldn't drink heavily and go on stage every night to act a demanding role; you began to forget your words, you fell over the furniture, you missed your cues. Derek had gone on drinking, in the end, to forget how far he had fallen. He had been a very flawed human being, but he had had his virtues as well as his failings. He had been charming, when he chose, he had been far more supportive and helpful to other actors than Mike Waterford ever was, and he was often kind, even if he tended to sudden spitting spite.

Now even his death would be written into the script. She knew how it would be – Sean would be ordered to write Derek a dramatic death. Shot on duty. Or killed in a bomb attack, or in a crashed car. Derek wouldn't be allowed the dignity of private death. He had died in reality – now he would have to have a fictional, dressed-up death.

And meanwhile the police were going to turn over every stone in his life until they found out all his secrets.

There must have been secrets, she thought, frowning. Derek must have been killed for a reason. Who could have killed him? A stranger? Had someone broken into his flat to burgle it? Or had it been someone he knew?

Oh, God. Fear made her spine icy. What if it was someone they all knew?

She closed her eyes and kept very still like an animal in a jungle which wasn't even sure what was terrifying it. She was too scared even to let herself think about who might have killed Derek.

Billy Grenaby refilled his glass, offered another drink to Harriet, watching the soft curve of her breast as she reached for it. She had changed before joining him for dinner, and was wearing a soft, clinging pink dress which kept giving him glimpses of the half-moon of her breasts. Billy couldn't stop looking at them. They were fuller than he'd imagined, and had smooth, pale skin that made his mouth go dry, made him think of touching them, letting his fingers slide down over them, to those hidden nipples.

He was used to seeing her in jeans and sweaters, low-heeled shoes or boots. He liked her that way; it amused him, that boyish look, the straight, level way she looked back at him. Harriet was someone he increasingly trusted and that wasn't a sensation he had often had. But he liked her this way, too; it excited him to see her mouth full and warm with pink lipstick, her eyes dusted with something glittery, pearl earrings in her ears.

It made it hard to keep his mind on what they were talking about, though, and he needed his wits about him over this business of Derek Fenn's murder.

He looked away, muttering, 'If Halifax thinks she may need a good lawyer it probably means he knows she's in this up to her neck, somehow. How explosive is this going to be, Harriet? Is it going to blow the series sky-high, or are we just in for a few days or weeks of rough weather?'

She shrugged. 'God knows. My priority is to keep the show on the road. Luckily, we're shooting in the studio all the next week. No more locations for eight days, then we're filming at the Stock Exchange and Billingsgate.'

Billy chuckled. 'Money and a fishy smell, eh? You know, I like the way Halifax thinks. So long as he doesn't go too far. A little political satire gives the series a kick. Not too much, mind you. We don't want to scare our audience away, they hate intellectuals.' He turned serious again. 'What about Annie? Is she needed on set?'

'Of course. She's in every script. We'll have to rewrite to take Derek out, put someone else in . . . the other sergeant will have to take over, Bedingfield, the guy Harry Nash is playing.'

'Nash?' Billy looked blank, then his face cleared. 'Oh, I've got him; tall, thin, going bald? Hasn't got the same charisma Fenn had; even though he was on the skids and a hopeless drunk Fenn could still dominate a scene without trying. Nash hasn't got that.'

'Well, we don't need anyone as charismatic as Derek as long as we still have Annie and Mike. The question is, while Sean is rewriting, should he take Annie out for the moment?'

'No. Absolutely not. Are you crazy? We use her while we have her.'

Harriet frowned, shivered. 'Don't talk as if she might be guilty of something! I'm sure she isn't. I know Annie pretty well and I can't believe she's involved in Derek's murder.'

'What do any of us know about each other?' Billy asked cynically. 'What do I know about you, or you about me?'

Harriet gave him faint, amused glance. 'Oh, I think I know what makes you tick, Billy.' She was talking about money, and was surprised to see him blush.

'That's what you think,' he growled, imagining that she had seen him looking down her dress, then hurried on, 'Anyway, working will keep Annie's mind off her problems.' Billy paused, grimaced. 'I still can't see it . . . her and Fenn . . . She has that untouched look, that's what the viewers love about her, her obvious goodness. Fenn was known for putting it about, even when he was a star. Annie was different.'

'Stop talking about her in the past tense!' muttered Harriet, scowling, and Billy gave her another quick, sharp look.

'Don't snap at me, Harry!'

'And don't call me Harry!'

'If you don't want me to give you a boy's name, don't go around looking like a boy!'

She suddenly lowered her eyelids and looked at him through her lashes. Billy watched in something approaching shock.

'Do I look like a boy tonight?' she murmured, and his breathing quickened.

God, she's flirting with me! he thought, I don't believe it.

'No,' he said, and wondered if he might finally be getting somewhere with her. He had never been sure how she felt about him. He was so much older than her, and God knew he was no oil-painting – he'd never dared risk an outright approach in case she turned him down. He hated rejection of any kind. Success was all Billy Grenaby was interested in.

Her lashes lifted and she gave him a teasing little smile. 'Then don't call me Harry. And stop talking about Annie in the past tense.'

'I'm not, it's just that all she ever seemed to care about was work. The PR people never had to take care of any little scandals for her. She rarely even went out to dinner with anyone, let alone screwed them. It doesn't seem to add up, to me. Fenn and Annie. No. Have you asked her? What does she say?'

Harriet shook her head. 'Denies it completely.'

'Well, I'm inclined to believe her. Simply on character.'

Billy leaned back in his deep, leather armchair and lit a Havana cigar. The ritual of doing so took several minutes; he didn't hurry, just waited patiently until the end of the cigar glowed red. He could be patient in other directions, too. He would wait for Harriet as long as he had to, but he felt a tingle of eagerness as he felt her watching him with a faint smile.

'So we trust to luck, in other words, and go ahead with our schedule?' she said.

'Uh-huh.' Billy smiled. The air was rich with the scent of the tobacco. Harriet had to admit it was a good smell and it always indicated that Billy had thought his way through a problem and was contented that he could handle it.

She smiled at him. 'But you will brief a good lawyer for Annie?'

He nodded. 'I'll make sure our lawyers are ready for anything. Even if it isn't Annie who killed him, it might be someone else connected with the series.' He grinned teasingly. 'Could be you, sweetheart.'

Harriet gave him a sweet smile. 'If I murdered someone in the series, it wouldn't be Derek Fenn.'

He looked intrigued. 'Who, then?'

She shrugged lightly, thinking: you! You, Billy. You monster. Annie is in bad trouble and all you can think about is your series, your money-spinning, award-grabbing series. You don't give a damn about Derek's death, except as an embarrassment to you, and maybe a drop in viewing figures. As for Annie, well, if you think you need to, you'll ditch her so fast her head will spin.

And even though you're always watching me in that obvious way you would be just as ruthless with me if you decided I had to be ditched, and I'm not taking any risks with you until I am sure where I really stand.

But Billy was a good judge of character – it can't be Annie who killed Derek. Billy's right – it wouldn't be in her nature. On the other hand, who on earth would have guessed that Annie with her innocent face and those big blue eyes had got pregnant when she was just a kid and had an abortion?

Annie woke up next day before Sean. She was bewildered for a few seconds, staring round the bedroom and not remembering where she was or how she had got there. Was it a hotel?

Sitting up, she looked down at what she was wearing – a blue and white striped cotton pyjama top? Huge, too. It wasn't hers. A man's? Panic leapt inside her. Whose? Then her memory clicked into gear; she remembered everything in a terrifying rush.

Derek had been murdered. Strangled.

The warm pink of sleep ran out of her face.

Sean and Harriet had brought her here. She remembered Harriet sitting by the bed murmuring soothingly to her. Then she must have fallen asleep. Her head felt strange. Heavy. They had given her pills, she remembered. God, they must have been strong.

Her eye fell on the small gold clock on the bedside table and she sat up hurriedly. Half-past six. She had to work today. She must get up.

She looked across the room to the open door of the en-suite bathroom. Five minutes to shower, then she might feel more human. Pity she hadn't a change of clothes. She would have to put on what she was wearing last night, the clothes piled on a chair by the bed. She had been wearing them all yesterday.

Yesterday. Her eyes closed and she gave a long, rough sigh, remembering Johnny at the house, their house, their secret place. Her body ached with pleasure and memory. She had felt eighteen again; it wasn't often that you got a chance to revisit your youth. It was so incredible, it was hard to believe it was true. But it was. Johnny was back with her again, and he still loved her.

She opened her eyes with a start, remembering that he had said he would ring her last night. She hadn't been there – he must have wondered what was going on. I should have asked for his number. I should have asked him where he lived, got his address. Why am I so stupid?

She hadn't thought of it. Hadn't thought of anything but being with Johnny again at last. She had dreamt of that for so many years, obsessed with the memories of their brief time together, a happiness made impossible to forget by everything else that had happened at that time.

It had indelibly impressed itself on her mind – her fear of Roger Keats, the shame and misery of what he had done to her, the tension of dealing with him that day in his office, and then Johnny's disappearance, without explanation, and the grief of being forced into killing their baby.

Why hadn't she fought her mother harder? Why had she been so weak and spineless? She hadn't wanted to give in, yet she had.

She lifted her hands, screwed into fists, to her face, as if to beat herself, hammered them on her forehead, groaning aloud.

Well, she had paid for it, ever since. She had been haunted by her lost baby, by memories of Johnny. In a way her whole life since had been shaped by the events of those few days eight years ago. She had only been half alive; she had put everything into her work, had very few friends and no lovers. She had been too scared to dare risk love again.

When she saw Johnny again it was like being given a chance to begin her life for a second time, wipe out the past as if those eight years had never been.

Going back to the house in the forest had made it even more dreamlike, at the same time even more real. It was so right to go there, to make love again, on the rug, in front of the fire in that room. Time, had whirled backwards; she had been a girl again, their loving so intense that it was like dying.

And yet . . . and yet she felt the same throb of fear and sick excitement, the disorientation she had felt during the night, when she woke from that dream.

Frowning, she tried to remember what she had dreamt, but it had all gone. Only the emotions remained.

What is wrong with me? she wondered. What am I afraid of?

A sound made her jump. She looked tensely at the bedroom door. It slowly opened and Sean stood there, bare-legged, in a black towelling robe which ended just at his knees. He smiled at her, raking back his untidy hair with one hand in a gesture half shy, half amused. 'Oh, you're awake. Did you sleep well?'

She was shy, too. She said, 'I slept deeply, anyway. Those pills knocked me out. I feel weird this morning.'

She could see his chest between the wide lapels of the robe. He wasn't wearing anything under it. These were presumably his pyjamas she was wearing. She shifted in the bed and realised she was only wearing the top, her legs were bare. The intimacy was somehow disturbing.

There was something so very male about Sean; you could never forget his masculinity when you were with him but especially at the moment when he was almost naked and so was she. But she couldn't think of him that way, not now. If Johnny hadn't come back she might have . . . but now she never would. Her life had taken a sudden, sharp turn up another path.

'I was just going to take a shower,' she said hurriedly.

'Do you feel up to working? At least it will be in the studio, not on location. We'll be able to keep the press away from you, and it would be good for you to work, keep your mind off . . . everything.'

Sean watched as she moved in the bed as if to get up, the far-too-big pyjama top slipping sideways off one shoulder, the lapels gaping, to show him smooth, pale skin, her throat and shoulder, the soft curve of her breast. He felt a stab of desire.

He wanted her so badly it made him angry. A month ago he had been thinking that maybe soon he would make a move towards her. There had been nobody else around then.

Now she was sleeping with this man from her past, the man whose baby she had once conceived. He hated to know that. The purity was spoilt. Seeing her, the way she had been yesterday, when she first came back from making love, her mouth like a ripe plum, her eyes drowsily satisfied, sensuality coming off her skin, she had wrecked his idea of her, of the sort of woman she was. He was bitterly angry with her.

But he still wanted her. More than ever. Knowing he had no chance made him want to smash things. He had trouble not showing it.

'I'd rather work,' she said. 'I won't be five minutes – could you make some coffee while I'm showering and getting dressed?'

'Sure. And toast? Or would you like some eggs and bacon? I'm not a bad cook – my father would be shocked if he saw me in my kitchen, knocking up breakfast for a woman, but then he's old-fashioned; he believes women belong in kitchens.'

'Does he live in London?'

'Sure he does – he was a City of London inspector when he retired. He should have gone further – he was a good copper, my Dad, but he hated being behind a desk, and he couldn't learn to play the political game, so he got stuck at inspector.'

'So you were following in his footsteps when you joined the police?'

He nodded. 'It was the family trade. My grandad was a copper down at Bow fifty years ago. We're a London family, born and bred. We don't stray far from our patch.'

'How did your dad feel when you left the force?'

Sean grimaced. 'Gutted. At first. He was afraid I'd been seduced by fairy gold – that the TV scripts wouldn't succeed and then I'd be out of a job and on the dole. My dad just couldn't believe that people like us could get into that world – actors, television, playwriting. He despised it all. A lot of poofters, he said, playing make-believe, putting on make-up. Not for his son!'

Annie smiled. 'And now?'

'Oh, now, he and my mum never miss an episode, proud as punch – although they'd die rather than let me see that.'

She watched him, hearing the note of secret pride in his voice. Suddenly she realised that they had that in common – they both came from the same background, working-class, respectable, with fierce ambitions for their children.

'Where do they live?'

'Islington, the same house I grew up in. My Dad has taken up gardening in a big way and exhibits at flower shows, and sits out in the garden shed smoking his pipe and watching his seeds grow.'

'And your mum?'

'She's doing an Open University course in geology.'

Annie's eyes opened wide. 'Geology?'

'She has been working her way slowly towards taking a science degree for three years, a course at a time. As she says, there's no hurry, and she's made a lot of new friends at the weekly class she attends, and at the reference library. Mum has always been ambitious.'

Annie watched him curiously. 'For you as well as herself?'

'I suppose so.'

'Have you got any brothers and sisters?'

'A married sister.' Sean looked at his watch. 'Did you want some breakfast or not? I think I ought to get a move on.'

'No, thanks, I don't eat in the morning. Coffee would be great, and orange juice, if you've got some. It's very good of you to go to all this trouble for me, Sean. I've never had a big brother before.'

'What a compliment!' he said, going out and closing the door carefully so that he shouldn't slam it, which was what he wanted to do. How dared she try to cast him in the brother role? He did not want to be her brother.

In the kitchen he put the coffee on and squeezed a couple of oranges, then he rang Tom Moor. As usual, Cherie answered, sounding half asleep.

'God, Sean, don't you ever ring during normal office hours?' she groaned. 'I was fast asleep.'

'Sorry, I won't have time later. Is he there?'

Cherie grunted and a second later Tom's thick voice came on the line. 'Man, I don't believe you're doing this to me.'

'I'm sorry, but it's urgent.'

'It always is. And before you ask, yes, I'm on your case, but I'm not getting anywhere. Your man hasn't been seen around his old haunts, anyway, although I heard plenty of rumours. I think he may have changed his name. Actors do that a lot, I'm told. Especially if their careers are slipping. They work under another name to protect their reputation.'

'OK, keep trying, Tom, but I've got another job for you. I want you to trace another guy. This one is definitely around – he's working for an outfit called Real Life Crime International Magazine. He interviewed Annie Lang the other day – the studio publicity outfit may have his name and address. All I know is that he's called Johnny something. Find out where he lives, where he has been living for the last eight years. Find out anything you can, in fact, and as fast as possible. I need to know all about him.'

'OK. Can I go back to sleep now? I was planning on another hour or two at the very least. And no magazine offices will be open until nine at the earliest, OK?'

'Well, get back to me by tonight with whatever you do find out, Tom.'

Ringing off, Sean slipped a slice of bread into the toaster and found a jar of peanut butter. Annie walked in just as he was taking his first bite of toast. Sean waved a hand to the glass of orange juice he had poured her and she took it and sat down, glancing at the clock.

'My driver will turn up for me as usual. I should have got in touch with the company last night.'

'That's okay, Harriet's PA will have dealt with that. You know how efficient Harriet is!'

'Poor Jason, I must buy him a box of really expensive chocolates,' Annie thought aloud, and Sean frowned.

'Who the hell is Jason?'

'My driver.'

'You are going to buy chocolates for your driver just because you had to cancel? You're kidding!' Sean stared at her as if she was crazy.

'He'll have lost his biggest fare of the day,' Annie said. 'And he can't afford to.' She started to laugh as she saw Sean's face. 'His mother is a fan, and his girlfriend, Angela, loves really expensive chocolates. But Jason can't often afford to buy them for her because he's saving up to marry her, although his mother says if he does she won't come to the wedding, but she will. She's a wonderful mother.' Annie pulled a face at Sean. 'And stop looking at me as if I'm a sandwich short of a picnic. I know what you're thinking!'

'No, you don't. I was thinking that I had the stupid idea I knew you pretty well, but I'm beginning to realise I hardly know you at all,' Sean said flatly.

Mike Waterford rang Harriet at seven o'clock; she was already at the studio, waiting for Annie and Sean to arrive. When she was told Mike was on the line, she picked up the phone with an irritated expression.

'Don't tell me! You just woke up, you're going to be late again!'

'Wrong, sweetheart! I'm up, but I'm going to be

286

late because I'm on Breakfast with Britain this morning. Thought you might like to catch me on the show.'

'Was this cleared with PR? You know you have to tell them if you do any publicity?'

'I'm telling you now, aren't I?'

'You won't talk about Derek, will you? Billy won't like it if you do, Mike! If they ask, change the subject.'

'Oh, of course,' he said, and there was something slyly amused in his voice that raised hairs on the back of her head. 'Don't forget to watch. Oh – and how about today's papers, eh? Dear me.'

'What the hell are you talking about?' she began angrily, but he had hung up.

Harriet buzzed for her assistant. 'Are today's papers in the office yet?'

'No, they should be arriving any minute, though.'

'Well, bring them in the minute they get here.'

Harriet picked up her zapper and switched on the television in the corner of her office. After changing channels to find the right one, she left the sound turned down and went on with her work on the shooting script she was annotating. Every few minutes she glanced up at the TV screen.

The intercom on her desk buzzed. 'Annie and Sean have got here,' her secretary briskly told her. 'Sean's on his way up here. Annie is going to make-up.'

'Thanks.' Harriet took a look at the TV screen again but there was as yet no sign of Mike. She was in a hurry to finish her work on the day's script so she got back to that; she had the sort of mind that could work on several problems at once without getting confused or losing concentration.

A tap on the door. 'Come in,' she called and Sean walked in, freshly shaved, his hair brushed down, looking alert and awake. He took up a perch on the side of her desk, his jeans-clad leg swinging.

'Hi. Annie's in make-up.'

'Great.' Harriet felt a leap of awareness at his proximity; he was not a man you could ignore when he was in the same room, but close up he was dynamite. She felt her mouth go dry. A pity he didn't feel the same way. It took two. She knew from his absorbed expression that he barely realised she was a woman. At least Billy noticed that. Impatiently, she asked, 'Everything OK with Annie? Did she sleep?'

Sean didn't pick up any vibes from Harriet; he was too busy thinking about Annie. 'Yes, she's a little shaky this morning, but I think she's OK. The police will want to talk to her later. I suggest we ask them to make it at midday, then we can get a morning's work done.'

'Good thinking.' Harriet relaxed, gave him an approving smile; work was what mattered most to her too. If Sean didn't fancy her, well, too bad. She turned back to her script but a moment later out of the corner of her eye caught sight of Mike's face on the TV screen and reached for her zapper, turned up the sound.

Sean looked across the office, grimaced. 'What's he doing on that show?'

'Being charming, I hope to God,' Harriet said with feeling. 'And nothing else.'

'You don't think he'll say anything about Fenn, or Annie?' Sean stood up, his body tense. 'I'll kill him if he does!'

The presenter was talking about Mike with gushing enthusiasm. 'Star of "The Force" . . . one of the top names in television . . . Mike Waterford. Here today to talk to us about his shock over the violent and tragic death of his colleague on the series, Derek Fenn.'

Mike looked sincere and shocked.

'One of his three expressions,' said Sean.

'Don't be unfair to Mike. He can act.' But Harriet was grinning.

'He can't act. He just exercises his sex appeal on television!'

Mike suddenly disappeared from the screen – apparently there was another item first, one with a man with a hat full of baby chicks which kept escaping and running all over the table in front of the two presenters. Harriet turned down the sound again as her secretary rushed in with a pile of the day's newspapers. Her expression told Harriet that the news was bad.

Snatching up the top tabloid, Harriet looked at the front page and groaned.

'Oh, my God!'

'What do they say?' Sean took another paper and began to read, making furious noises. He threw the paper on the floor and grabbed another. He read that, muttering angry words, screwed it up and hurled it across the room.

'They're all the same,' Harriet said unhappily; she had read several too. 'You don't even need to read between the lines – they're practically accusing Annie outright of being this woman who was seen with Derek in a pub. The way they've written the story, you'd have to be stupid not to get what they're saying.'

Mike's face was back centre-screen. Harriet hurriedly turned the sound up and his voice came into the room.

'Favourite with the viewers . . . a wonderful actor

with a long and honoured career behind him . . . Derek will be very much missed.'

'The rumours must be very worrying for everyone in the series,' said the presenter. 'What *was* the relationship between Derek Fenn and your co-star, Annie Lang?'

'It's true they were close, very close.' Mike paused, his eyes half veiled, his mouth curling at the edges in a cynical smile that made Sean swear.

'The bastard!'

'Mike has always been a master of innuendo,' Harriet grimly said.

Mike went on, 'Derek gave Annie her first break, her first part on TV; they were always seen around together after that.' He gave that smile again into camera and Sean made apoplectic noises.

'I'll kill him.'

The presenter asked, 'Annie has always refused to talk about her private life, hasn't she? When we had her on the programme a few months back she would only talk about her part in The Force. And there has never been any gossip about her until now.'

'I've never heard of any other man in her life,' agreed Mike, then paused, added, 'Apart from Derek.'

'Were they living together?'

Mike hesitated as if about to say yes, then softly murmured, 'You'll have to ask her that. But I'm sure the rumour that she had had Derek's baby is a lie.'

Sean swore violently.

Harriet groaned. 'Oh, no. How could he do that?'

The TV presenters were firing excited questions; Mike parried them all with a half-smile.

'I just said it was only a rumour, and I'm sure it isn't true. No, I've never seen her with a child, but then she has kept her private life very secret until now.'

From then on he said nothing new, and the interview was over a moment later; Harriet switched off the set.

She walked over to the window and stared out, face blank. At last, she said, 'If Annie is involved, you know, the series is finished.'

'For Christ's sake, Harriet, how can you even say that? That bastard got to you too, did he? I'm ashamed of you! The viewers may be stupid enough to listen to Waterford, but you know Annie. Think about her.' Sean strode over to the wall on which hung stills from various series Harriet had worked on – he flung out a hand to point to a big photo of Annie: a pale oval face, huge eyes, delicate bones. 'Look at her! Just look at her face. Can you see her strangling Derek?'

10

Harriet was desperate over the time they were losing on the schedule. The past couple of weeks had been hectic with endless rewrites and rejigging of the schedule; the scripts had been shot to pieces, they had dropped one episode altogether and substituted another, as Sean explained to Chorley that morning.

'We need Miss Lang on set for a few hours. Can't you give us that time to shoot at least a couple of scenes?'

Chorley looked sullen but finally agreed when Billy and his top lawyer showed up to back Sean. 'If I can talk to her during your lunch break, then?'

'After she has eaten – it is essential for her to have lunch first, she'll be tired,' Sean said, looking at the lawyer for support. The lawyer nodded, murmured something in agreement.

'Very well,' Chorley said through his teeth. 'One o'clock?'

Triumphantly, Sean went off to the set, where Annie was just beginning work. She looked tired and pale but composed. How much more of this can she take, though? wondered Sean.

Annie was sleepwalking through her scene; she knew the lines, she remembered the moves they had rehearsed, and she performed like an automaton, but her mind was absorbed in a confusion of memories and thoughts; she couldn't stop thinking about the way Derek had died . . . she had never known anyone who died so violently before.

These scripts they acted every week were full of violence, fights and beatings-up, deaths and rapes, but they were rehearsed and timed like a ballet – you watched them being acted out, you never believed they were real. You knew it was just a story, with actors who would get up and shower off the blood and mud, and go home to their wives, their kids, their lovers, their cats.

This was real. Derek was dead. He would not get up and go home. She would never see him again. The shock still numbed her. He had annoyed her, irritated her, amused her, she had been grateful to him, she had liked him.

Derek had aroused all the usual complex, changeable reactions human beings did. And now he was dead, but here she was, as usual, acting, pretending, playing a part.

Why did she live in this crazy way, in this phoney world of make-believe, inhabited by people like Mike Waterford . . . what did she mean, people? He wasn't people. He was a rat. A snake. Worse. She couldn't think of a word low enough to describe him.

When they broke for lunch at noon, the police refused to allow either Sean or Harriet to be present during the interview with Annie which, at Billy's insistence, took place in the boardroom on his floor of the administration building. But they couldn't refuse to allow the company's lawyer to sit in on the interview, keeping a watching brief for Billy Grenaby.

Annie was nervous before she went into the room, unsure what to expect, but the questions at first didn't seem to have any real edge to them. The two policemen spoke in quiet, polite voices and didn't seem hostile.

'Where were you two nights ago, Miss Lang? From eight o'clock onwards?'

'At home. At my house.'

'What time did you get there?'

'I don't remember. You could ask the friends who were with me, I had two of them to supper . . . Mr Halifax, the scriptwriter on the series, and the producer, Harriet York.'

'They were there all evening?'

'Yes. Harriet stayed all night.'

A long, searching stare from Inspector Chorley. 'Why?'

Annie looked blankly back at him. 'Why what?'

'Why did she stay the night?'

Annie didn't want to talk about why she had been so upset that particular night, there was no need for them to know about Roger Keats and the past, but she said flatly, 'My home had been burgled and I felt rather nervous being alone at night.'

The two men sat up then. 'Burgled? When was this? Did you report it to the police?'

'Yes, I rang at once when I woke up and found that someone had broken in.' She briefly explained about the Valentine's card and the rose in her bedroom. 'But nothing had been taken, there was no sign of damage. So the police decided it wasn't worth visiting me.'

'They what?' Inspector Chorley's eyebrows seemed to shoot up into his hair. 'Decided it wasn't worth visiting you?'

'They seemed to think it was a practical joke by someone I knew, someone who had a key. They told me to ring again if I found anything missing.'

'And did you?'

She shook her head.

'Have you found out who broke into your home?'

'No, but I had the locks changed so it won't happen again. I told Sean Halifax about it, and he thought it would be a good idea for Harriet to stay with me for a night or two.'

'So you didn't go out again once you got home?'

She hesitated, half meant to lie, then couldn't somehow. She would have felt too guilty about it if she had. 'Well, I did go for a walk later.'

She felt the tension in the room jump up. Inspector Chorley leant forward, watching her intently. 'Where did you go?'

'Oh, just walked . . . I don't remember. I ended up down by the river; I was tired, so I got a bus back.'

'Were you alone? Did your friend go with you?'

She shook her head. 'Harriet was asleep.'

The inspector's voice was incredulous, coldly doubted her. 'You went out alone, at night, on foot?'

'I needed some exercise, I don't get much, while we're filming. I couldn't sleep, so I went for a walk, but I went further than I'd intended and I tired myself out.'

'But I thought you were nervous, after this supposed burglary?'

The company lawyer leaned forward. 'Lots of people go for a walk before bedtime – I often do myself.'

'My mind was working so fast I felt like a mouse in a wheel, going round and round. I needed to walk,' said Annie, and the two policemen exchanged looks.

'Did you go anywhere near the TV studio?'

'Nowhere near it. I ended up on the Embankment below Charing Cross; a good half a mile away from the studio. I got the bus from there.'

'What number bus?'

She told them and watched them write the number down.

'And what time was that when you caught this bus?'

'I'm not sure, I wasn't watching the time – but it must have been close to eleven.'

'You're sure about that?' Inspector Chorley asked sharply, and she nodded.

'Certain – I told you, Sean had left, and Harriet and I had gone up to bed. It was well after ten o'clock when I went out, 'and Harriet will tell you what time I got back. She was up when I came in – she'd discovered that I had gone out and was upset about it. Also the bus conductor stared at me all the way – he recognised me, I think, although he didn't say anything. He was a Sikh, wearing a turban.'

The lawyer leaned back with a satisfied air. 'I think that more or less clears my client, don't you, Inspector?'

Inspector Chorley looked irritated. He ignored the interruption. 'You knew Mr Fenn very well for years, didn't you, Miss Lang?'

Annie stared at him dumbly for a few seconds, remembering the first time she'd ever seen Derek, the night she played Ophelia at her drama school, remembering the next time she'd seen him, at her home, when he'd came to offer her her first part. It was all so long ago, yet the memory was as clear as crystal. Derek had had an important influence on her life and she was appalled by the way he'd died.

Tired of waiting for an answer, the inspector pressed her. 'You knew him very well.'

And Annie nodded.

'Were you lovers?'

She flushed, frowned, shaking her head angrily. 'No, we were not!'

'We've heard a rumour that you had his baby – is that true?'

'NO!' she said explosively, her voice shaking.

'Did you see him that night, Miss Lang?' the inspector threw at her.

The lawyer answered for her. 'She has already told you – she did not leave the house until gone ten o'clock, that means she could not be involved in the death of Mr Fenn.'

Annie added huskily, 'I did not see Derek that night.'

'You may not have met him in the pub, but you might have visited him at home.'

'No, I didn't.'

'I've been told that Mr Fenn was jealous because you were seeing Mr Halifax – is that true? Did he turn violent? Attack you? If you killed him in self-defence your best chance is to be frank with us.'

'I didn't see him that night! There was nothing between me and Derek!' Annie was close to the edge, her voice shaking with hysteria. 'It's lies, all of it – who told you this stuff about me and Derek? It's all lies.'

'Inspector, I don't like the tone of this interview,' the lawyer said angrily. 'Miss Lang is leaving.'

A phone began to buzz inside the inspector's jacket. Irritably, he reached into an inner pocket. 'One moment,' he said to the lawyer, pulled up the aerial of his phone and spoke into it. 'Yes? Chorley here.'

He listened, his face changing, then said, 'I'm coming back at once. Keep her there.' Getting to his feet, he told Annie, 'Thank you, Miss Lang. I'll let you get back to work now, we must be on our way, but we may need to talk to you again later.'

Mike Waterford didn't show up until after lunch; he had been besieged by the press after the TV appearance and had had a great time parrying questions and posing for the cameras. He was smilingly indifferent to the angry complaints of Harriet and Sean as soon as they set eyes on him.

'What did I do? Told the truth, that's all. What did you want me to do? Lie?' He gave them a reproachful glance. 'Is that what you wanted me to do?'

Sean wanted to throttle him and his murderous impulse showed in his voice. 'Every other word you say is a lie, you bastard! Annie didn't have an affair with Derek, and she didn't have his baby.'

'That's what I said,' Mike assured him soulfully, opening his eyes wide in innocence. 'I told them . . . it's a lie, I said . . . all the rumours about her and Derek are a lie. That's what I said. Get a playback of the tape and see!'

'But you deliberately meant them to think the opposite!'

Mike gazed at him, blinking. 'Oh, come on – you're too tortuous for me. I'm just a simple actor, I'm not into playing these elaborate games.'

'I'll kill him,' Sean told Harriet. 'I'll throttle the life out of the bastard.'

'Like Derek?' Mike softly reminded. 'You didn't like him, either, did you, Halifax?'

Sean's eyes glowed with rage. 'Watch yourself, Waterford!'

Harriet looked at him uncertainly. Oh, of course she didn't believe for a second that Sean was capable of murder, but sometimes he alarmed her – there was always that dark capacity for violence buried somewhere inside him. But haven't all men got that? she thought wryly. However civilised they might seem on the surface, there was some part of them that flared into dangerous fury if their ego was threatened. And Sean was a bit of a control freak. He showed that where his writing was concerned; he had an obsession with patterning that she had noticed again and again. Maybe most viewers would miss it, because all they took on board was the storyline each episode. But because she had to interpret his work she saw it as clearly as you saw the dome of St Paul's floodlight by night.

Sean had a way of looking at life, at the world, that was very individual. He liked to be in control, too, and resented anyone who tried to argue with him – or even, at times, suggest alternatives. But she liked him. A lot. She wished she didn't. Because it was as clear as crystal that he was in love with Annie.

The two men were glaring at each other like rutting stags, locked antler to antler.

Harriet looked at them with sudden amusement.

'Shall we get some work done? That is what we're here for, remember? And nothing matters in the last resort except getting this series on to the screen each week.'

Sean looked round at her, a red spark in his eyes. 'Is that really what you believe?'

She didn't answer, just looked at Mike and said, 'I hope you know your lines and moves, Waterford, or I'll flay you alive and hang your skin out to dry.'

He walked away and Sean shook his head at her.

'You let him off the hook! You should have let me kill the bastard.'

'Not if it ruins my series, you don't!' Harriet met his angry stare with cool composure.

'It's my series, too, you know!'

'Then don't let your personal feelings about Annie make you forget how important it is!'

'At least I have personal feelings!' Sean threw at her and walked away, leaving her hurt and angry. She felt like going after him and telling him just how personal her feelings for him had been at one time, but what was the point? Long ago she had faced the fact that Sean wasn't interested in her. She was fast realising that Annie mattered to him more than he cared to admit, and the last thing she wanted to do now was let Sean guess how much she had liked him when they first met.

Later that afternoon, Sean discovered that Marty Keats was not back at work; she had rung the head of wardrobe to tell her that she was at the police station and would be there for some time, and when Sean went looking for Marty he got the news.

He went back to Harriet at once to tell her. 'Apparently she kept insisting that she wasn't under suspicion, she was only helping the police with their inquiries. She said her ex-husband had rung her yesterday . . .'

Harriet's eyes widened. 'So he is around, after all?'

'Not only around,' Sean said grimly. 'He said on the phone that he had killed Derek.'

Harriet gasped. 'He admitted it?'

'Boasted, according to Marty. And he warned her that he'd kill her if she started an affair with anybody else.'

'So he killed Derek out of jealousy?' Harriet gave a quivering sigh. 'What a relief – Annie was never involved at all!'

Sean did not look convinced of that. 'Roger Keats has an obsession with Annie, a dangerous obsession. If he is capable of killing Derek, God knows what he may do next. He certainly put the fear of God into Marty. She rang the police at once, and they asked her to help them track Roger down; they ransacked her house, looking for photos of Roger. She'd thought she'd thrown them all away, but they came on one or two she'd overlooked, although they were mostly taken years ago, when he was very young. According to her boss, Marty sounded scared stiff when she rang. And from what Annie's told us about Roger Keats, Marty's right to be worried. The man's obviously crazy. Not just because he killed – but the way he did it, the way he dressed the scene. Thinking about it, I should have guessed he was in the theatre. And when you've just killed someone and go to those lengths, well . . .'

'He isn't normal,' Harriet said shakily, and Sean gave a hard, unamused laugh.

'You can say that again! Anyway, Marty has sent her kids to stay with her sister, just in case Roger goes to their house looking for her, and she's asked for a few days off work, to join them.'

'But presumably he knows where her sister lives?'

'It seems she's moved since Roger disappeared. He won't know her new address – she left London and went north. Marty and her kids should be safe there.'

Harriet chewed her lip anxiously. 'Do we tell Annie? What if he comes after her next?'

Sean frowned. 'Oh, we have to tell her. She has to be warned. She mustn't be left alone for a second.'

The final scene of the day was shot just before four-thirty and Annie was only in it briefly. She went back to her dressing-room after she had finished to change back into her own clothes and take off the make-up which she found too heavy off set.

Harriet put her head round the door just as Annie was about to leave. 'I want to go home to get some clothes,' Annie told her, and Harriet nodded.

'Wait for me, we'll go together. I just have a few phone calls to make. Sean has already left. He'll see us back at his place.'

She vanished and Annie put on her coat, checked in her handbag that she had her key, sipped a little of the iced water which was always put in her dressing-room freshly each day.

Ten minutes passed very slowly. Annie impatiently looked at her watch every few minutes until the phone rang, making her jump.

'Hello?'

Jason's voice asked hopefully, 'I'm sitting outside, Miss Lang – do you want me tonight, or not?'

She made up her mind in a flash. 'I'm just on my way out, Jason. Sorry to keep you waiting so long.'

'No problem,' he said, his voice brightening.

Annie smiled and hung up. She scribbled a note to Harriet. 'Gone home alone. I'll take a taxi to Sean's, see you later.'

Harriet rang her dressing-room five minutes later, but didn't get a reply. She sent her assistant along to look for Annie while she made another transatlantic phone call. Harriet had just been invited to go to Los Angeles for three months on a swap with an American TV producer who wanted experience of working in London.

Billy had set it up on one of his frequent visits to the States and Harriet was torn between being excited about it and being worried about leaving someone else in charge of The Force. Billy had arranged for the swap to begin as soon as they finished shooting the present series, but Harriet wouldn't be back in time to start working with Sean on the new scripts for the next series. She would have to leave that to whoever Billy put into her job during her absence.

When she had finished her call, she didn't get up to go, she sat staring out of the window, chewing her pencil, scowling. Was Billy using the idea of three months in Los Angeles learning about American TV as a trap for her? What if his real objective was to detach her from The Force for good?

He had this crazy theory that it was bad news for a producer or writer to spend too long on one programme. Billy liked them to move on; he had kept trying to persuade Sean to move, and had hinted that Harriet should start a new series and let someone else take over The Force. She might come back to find she was off the series, and her temporary replacement had become permanent.

If that is what he's up to, I'll hand in my notice and get another job!

Her mind was in confusion; she was angry and hurt and puzzled all at once. I thought he really liked me. Was I imagining it? Why is he sending me away? Three months looked like a lifetime to her, and she couldn't be certain if it was the series, her friends, or Billy himself she was going to miss.

Her assistant came back and said, 'She's gone.'

Harriet did a double-take. 'What? Gone where?'

Her assistant handed her the note she had found in Annie's dressing-room.

Harriet read it and swore. She dialled Sean's number, but only got his answerphone, brisk and impersonal.

'Annie went off home without me, Sean,' she said hurriedly. 'I'm still at the studio. Should I follow her to her place, or come to your flat and wait for her there? If you haven't rung back in fifteen minutes I'll come to your place. Annie may well be there by then.'

On her way home Annie called at the hospital to see her mother. She found Trudie still lethargic, saying very little, but looking better than she had. The police were no longer by her bedside, and she was back on the general ward. Annie held her hand and smiled at her, kissed her cheeks, which looked in this dry, over-heated atmosphere like a petal from a dying rose, faded and crinkled, and had the same soft, powdery scent.

'I want to come home,' Trudie whispered.

'I wish you could. I miss you. I've had Harriet for company, but it isn't the same.'

'Why can't I come home, then? You don't want me, that's it, isn't it? You've stuck me in here and you're leaving me here.' Trudie pulled her hand away and turned her head on the pillow, closed her eyes. 'Go away, leave me alone.'

'Of course I want you home, Mum, I'd take you home now if they'd let me! But you're ill, very ill.'

Trudie ignored her.

'Oh, Mum,' Annie said hopelessly, on the point of tears. Her mother had always been so strong, always there for her – and now, just when she needed her most, Annie felt her mother had abandoned her.

She bent to kiss Trudie and got shoved away violently. Her mother looked at her with hatred. 'You leave me alone! Go on, get out! You're not my Annie ... I don't know you, who are you? It's you, isn't it? You, you're trying to kill me!'

The noise brought a nurse hurrying over. 'What's all this?' She smiled at Trudie. 'Now, don't be naughty, Gran. Don't get into one of your little tantrums.' She looked at Annie and said soothingly, 'Better go, now. She'll be quiet once you've gone.'

Annie bit her lip and walked away, fighting with tears. In the corridor she walked into a little bevy of student nurses who immediately surrounded her asking for autographs and firing questions at her about The Force.

'Have you ever shot any scenes in here, in the hospital itself?'

She shook her head. 'We did shoot a scene outside, but they wouldn't give us permission to shoot in the actual hospital.'

'If you ever did, we could be extras!' a Chinese girl giggled, her hand politely in front of her mouth.

'Less noise, please!' the ward sister said, coming out to frown at them. 'We have some very sick old people in this ward – we don't want to upset them, do we?'

Annie made her excuses and left. None of the students had asked her why she was there.

Twenty minutes later, as Jason drew up outside her home, Annie saw Johnny's car parked just in front of them. Her heart at once seemed to implode as if a giant hand was squeezing it; she could scarcely breathe and yet she was intensely happy.

Giving Jason a radiant smile, she handed him a £50

note. 'I'm sorry you missed your fare yesterday, Jason. My fault. Buy Angela something pretty with this.'

He didn't argue; the note vanished into his jacket as if sucked in by a vacuum cleaner. His grin broadened his face. 'You're an angel, Miss Lang. This'll make our night. We're going to a rave, out at Milton Keynes – starting at eleven o'clock; huge, utterly huge, should be magic, especially if I've got some cash to spend. Dancing in that sort of crush makes you real thirsty; they sell around a million popsicles.'

'What?' asked Annie, baffled.

He laughed. 'Frozen drinks on a stick; really refreshing. You get hot enough to explode after a while – the bouncers walk around all night squirting the dancers with cold water. The floor's like a lake by the early hours.'

'Sounds too exhausting for me! Especially if it goes on most of the night!' said Annie.

'I bet you'd love it!' Jason hesitated, then said, 'My mum was real upset about Mr Fenn, she was a fan – and she said to tell you those things the papers printed about you, well, everyone knows they're liars, nobody is going to believe stuff like that about you.'

His mother had said to him explosively that she'd like to go down town and burn those newspaper offices to the ground, printing lies about Annie Lang. A person only had to look at her lovely face with those big, innocent eyes, to know it couldn't be true. Some actresses might go in for that carry-on, she said, but not Annie. She was much too nice.

Annie smiled at him. 'Thank your mum for me – I only wish everyone was like her, but there is always someone who'll believe the worst.'

'Ain't that the truth?' agreed Jason.

'But give your mum my love, and enjoy your rave.'

Annie got out and heard Jason drive off smoothly as she unlocked her front door. She switched off the burglar alarm she had set the last time she left the house, and switched on the hall lights.

Without turning round she heard the firm tread of his feet and closed her eyes, waiting, her pulses wild. The door closed and Johnny's arms came round her possessively; she leaned back on him for a second then turned with uplifted face, her mouth parting.

They kissed as if for the first time, and also as if for the last time, with need and hunger and desperation.

I must be a masochist; I never thought I was, thought Annie, eyes closed, arms round his neck, almost strangling him they held him so tightly. Loving Johnny was a sort of self-torture, it hurt so much and yet even the pain of it pierced her with happiness.

'I can't lose you,' Johnny muttered into her open mouth. 'I would die if I lost you again.'

'Me, too,' she said. 'Oh, Johnny, I love you so much it's killing me. I almost wish I was dead because this would be the right time to die, while I'm so happy. I've never really been happy since you vanished like that. I'm scared, Johnny. What if we're never this happy again in our lives? It would be better to be dead.'

He drew his head back to look down at her and she saw he had turned pale.

Then he began kissing her again, even more feverishly.

Sean had been taking a shower when the phone rang and hadn't heard it, but when he was dressed again he noticed a light on his answerphone and switched on the playback.

Harriet's voice made him stiffen.

'God, can't anyone do a simple job?' he muttered, and rang her back at the studio.

'How long ago did she leave?' he bit out, and Harriet stammered, hearing the rage in his voice.

'I don't know——'

He exploded. 'Christ, Harriet, how could you leave her alone, even for a second? I warned you!'

'I asked her to wait for me. She knew where I was, just in my office, I had to make a couple of very important phone calls – Annie shouldn't have left without me.'

'Well, she hasn't got here yet. I'll ring her at home,' Sean muttered, and hung up with a crash that made Harriet go deaf for a second.

She was so angry that she decided to go home herself instead of rushing over to Sean's flat. Why should she let him bawl at her like that? Who did he think he was?

But when she was in her car she changed her mind. After all, Annie was Roger Keats's chief target – if he was somewhere out there in the city, Annie was in danger every second of the day and night.

Sean drove to Annie's house so fast that he was lucky not to crash into another car. It was getting dark now, traffic leaving London in the tidal wave that flowed in and out of the capital every morning and evening. Several other drivers hooted viciously as he wove in and out at high speed, but he ignored them, cutting corners, taking short cuts, his tyres screeching.

She lived in one of the inner suburbs on the north

side of London, within walking distance both of Regent's Park and the big mainline railway stations on that side of London.

The wide, tree-lined streets had been mostly built in one of the great waves of property development that came every decade or so during the nineteenth century.

You could guess by the style of housing in a road just when it had been built. Every generation spawned a new style. Annie's house came from the Edwardian period when large families and a confident middle class demanded space, and even a smaller terrace house had a long garden in front of it, a black and white tiled pathway edged with scalloped red tiles, and a hedge to shield it from the outside world. The row of plane trees planted along the pavement gave the road a sleepy, country air, even now, when the branches were bare.

Sean parked, jumped out of his Porsche and ran to the golden oak front door. There was no answer to his ringing and knocking. He went to the front windows to peer through the blinds, but could see nothing whatever inside.

A man across the street working in his garden looked over and called to Sean, 'If you're the press, she's not there. Left ten minutes ago.'

Sean hurried over there. 'Was she alone? In a taxi, or . . .?'

'Are you the police? Or the press?'

Sean eyed him narrowly. 'What difference would it make which I was?'

'The press pay for information – the police don't. My name's Phil Grover, by the way. What's yours?'

Sean's teeth met. He was inclined to throttle the

man, who was a short, skinny, ferret-faced creature, could be in his thirties, might be younger. He was wearing jeans and a sweater, trainers – teenage gear, but he was no teenager.

'Never mind my name, Mr Grover, I prefer to be anonymous.' Sean pulled out a twenty-pound note and proffered it.

The other man snorted. 'Think again, Mr Anonymous.'

Grimly Sean found another couple of notes. He had no time to haggle over money with the bastard. Every second counted; he was terrified for Annie.

Pocketing the notes, the other told him. 'She left with some guy, in a rather ramshackle old car; not her style at all, I'd have said. She usually comes and goes in a chauffeur-driven limousine – one brought her home this evening, black guy driving it. It's usually him, I've noticed him before. But there was this other car parked in the street, I noticed that, too, because I was suspicious, after all the police activity in the street lately. I was thinking of ringing the police and getting them to come along to take a look at this guy. I mean, he might have been the guy who murdered Derek Fenn. You hear about these crazy fans, don't you? Look at the guy who shot John Lennon. What do they call them? Stalkers? Well, he looked as if he could be one of them – there was just something about him. He just sat in his car, watching her house. Might have been a reporter, I thought, and I did wonder if I ought to go over and talk to him, but on the other hand. . .he made me a bit nervous, actually.'

Good for him, thought Sean, disliking Phil Grover so much he wanted to smash him in the face with a fist.

He forced himself to keep calm, though; he needed the man's information.

'Just as I was thinking of ringing the police, though, Miss Lang arrived in her car, and went into the house. The chauffeur drove off and the guy in the old car got out and went into the house too. Miss Lang was expecting him, I'd say, because she left the front door open for him and I saw her waiting in the hall.'

'Waiting for him?' Sean broke out hoarsely. 'Sure about that?'

Phil Grover gave him a sly grin. 'Thought you'd be interested in that. Yes, she definitely waited for him to join her. He shut the front door as he went in, and then about ten minutes later they both came out. He was carrying a suitcase. He hadn't had it when he went in. They got in his car and drove off.'

'I don't suppose you got the number?'

Phil Grover grinned again. 'If I did, it would cost you another forty quid.'

Sean's hands screwed into fists by his sides; the other man looked down at them with a flicker of nerves, backed a little, then said, 'Well, do you want the number or don't you?'

Sean sat in his car and rang Tom Moor before he drove off; Tom was out and Cherie took the call.

'He's working on your case,' she assured him.

'Can you get one of his assistants to check a licence number for me with the police computer?' Sean read it out. 'And ring me back as soon as you get the name and address of the driver.'

'Sean, is this case dangerous for my Tom?' Cherie asked, anxiety in her voice.

'I doubt it, unless he's very stupid,' Sean curtly said.

'You know my Tom can be very stupid,' she groaned. 'If anything happens to him I'll never forgive you, Sean.'

'I'd never forgive myself! Tom's one of my best friends, you know that.'

'Yes, I know that.' Her voice softened. 'I still wish he was in some other business. It was bad enough when he was a copper and I never knew when – or if – he was coming home again, but at least there he was backed up by mates. Now he's out there on his own.'

'That was his choice, Cherie! But don't underestimate Tom's sense of self-preservation. Stop worrying, Tom's a big boy. Look, will you also tell him that Roger Keats has surfaced at last? He rang his ex-wife last night, it seems, and boasted of having killed Derek Fenn. Ask Tom to try all his friends still in the force to see if they've come up with any more than that. If they track Keats down, for instance.'

'Tom says Chorley told him to bug off last time he bumped into him down at the nick.'

'Charming. Chorley's such a nice guy. Well, when Tom does ring you, ask him to give me a ring, would you? Bye, Cherie, love to the kids.'

Sean rang off and stood at the window, his fists pushed into his denim jacket pockets. While he was talking to Cherie, he had kept his thoughts at bay, but now they came back like a tidal wave, swamping him.

Where in God's name was Annie? Sweat started out on his forehead and in the palms of his hands.

He didn't want to know what she was doing. He could guess. Unfortunately. That was what was grinding in the pit of his stomach like a surgeon's knife, the images of what he suspected she was doing – jealousy was the cruellest emotion you could ever feel, but he could live with that. If he had to. He had learnt long ago to accept what he could not alter.

A policeman learnt to discipline his imagination – to deal just with facts and evidence and never let himself think about the pain and suffering he sees. The world was a pretty nasty place in some corners of it. Sean had thought himself totally cauterised against emotions.

He hadn't reckoned with his own. For one particular woman. Annie had got under his skin, into his bloodstream – day by day she had come to mean more to him than he had ever thought any woman could.

He liked women, but had only twice come close to a serious relationship – one when he was in his late teens, with a girl from his school who went off to university and dropped him within weeks when he became a police cadet. She wrote explaining that she wasn't dating a policeman, thanks! He gathered he was no longer good enough for her. Policemen were the wrong income group. The last he heard she had married a stockbroker and was living in Pinner. He hadn't cried over her, he'd been too furious. Later he'd started dating a secretary who worked in the same police station; they'd seen each other for several years until she went to a police union conference, got drunk and spent the night in a wild orgy with a number of other delegates. It hadn't taken twenty-four hours for the news to reach Sean; the whole station was buzzing about it before she even reappeared at work. That had been the end of that relationship – not so much because he was jealous, or angry, as because he could no longer trust her. He no longer liked her, either. He felt a fool for having been so wrong about her.

It had left him cynical, disillusioned, inclined never

to take women on face value, and what he had learnt about Annie over the past days had reinforced his cynicism, but he didn't care about any of the secrets from her past that he had uncovered. He could forgive her anything. . .so long as she was safe, but his mind was possessed with dread, afraid that the next time he saw her she would be lying on a mortuary slab.

Annie and Johnny stopped on the way to the forest to buy a take-away meal, Greek kebabs and pitta bread and rice which she re-heated in the kitchen oven for a couple of minutes while Johnny was lighting the fire in the shabby drawing-room. They drew the curtains to shut out the forest and lit candles to give the room a shimmering glamour it did not have by the harsher reality of electric light.

Since Johnny had got out of prison he had visited the house a number of times, he told her, to take the covers off the furniture, have the electricity switched back on, heat up the house with electric fires and log fires to get rid of the faint dampness and smell of mould which years of emptiness had build up. His lawyers had had a woman come in once a month to clean the place and had paid any bills for rates and water. There had been just enough money from his grandmother's insurance policy to pay for that.

They ate from one large plate, using the slit pitta bread to hold their food; Annie had mixed salad with the meat before she filled the hot pittas. The food seemed ambrosial; she had never tasted anything so good.

Johnny put Tchaikovsky's Piano Concerto Number I on the old gramophone; the romantic music and the candles and the firelight took them to a dimension where only they existed and there was no world outside.

She had forgotten Sean and Harriet completely; it never occurred to her to ring and explain where she had gone. When she was with Johnny nothing else mattered.

After they had eaten they drank coffee and Johnny lay with his head in her lap while she stroked his thick black hair and watched him. This time they did not feel a deep urge to make love at first, although they couldn't stop touching each other, as if needing the reassurance of touch to believe that they were really together again. He gazed into the flames, listening to the music, and she simply looked at him, drinking him in through her eyes. Every so often he would catch her wrist and pull her hand down to his mouth, kiss her palm.

'Oh, Annie, God knows how many times I've dreamt of being back here with you when I was in prison. At night when we were locked up in our cells I'd lie on my bunk and stare at this tiny square in the wall that was my only view of the sky; sometimes you could see a star or two, or even the moon, although the prison wall was ringed with electric lights that reflected back from the clouds and made it hard to see anything else. I'd blank it all out, imagine this room, and you. It kept me sane. They let me have headphones and a personal cassette player. I had a tape of this music, and played it all the time because we'd liked to listen to it together, remember?'

'I remember.' Lying there, he looked so much like the boy she had known. She had waited for him all these years. Only now did she realise that she had turned her back on any other possible happiness because she secretly believed that one day he would come back to her.

And he had. No wonder it was easy to tell herself that nothing had changed between them, their love was exactly the same. At first it had seemed true.

But she was starting to doubt it. How could they both be the same?

No matter how you tried, you could not stay unchanged for years. Even for a short time, come to that. Life wouldn't let you.

She was not the shy eighteen-year-old who had known Johnny eight years ago. He was not that gentle, eager boy. She wasn't sure what changes time had made in her – but she could see some of the differences in Johnny, the visible ones, anyway. She smoothed out with her fingertips some of the lines etched into his brow and he closed his eyes, sighing.

'That's nice.'

'You didn't have any lines there, eight years ago,' she thought aloud.

He laughed. 'Maybe you just don't remember them.'

'I remember everything,' she said, and he smiled again.

'Do you, Annie? So do I. But I've had some help, of course. I've had pictures of you to remind me. Over the years I cut out hundreds of pictures of you from magazines and newspapers – and when I was arrested there was an old photo of you in my jacket pocket, taken here, in the garden, feeding the birds – do you remember that day?'

She nodded, and he gave a ragged sigh.

'I had that next to my bed, all the time I was in prison, alongside a photo of my mother.'

'You loved her very much, didn't you? I used to feel quite jealous, the way you always talked about her.'

'She was wonderful. I wish you'd known her, I know she'd have loved you.' His eyes glowed and she smiled down at him.

'I'm sure I'd have loved her, too.'

'She was always delicate. The years with him didn't help – my father, I mean. He used to beat her up all the time. He couldn't hold down a job, we never had any money – so he drank to forget what a stupid, useless failure he was. I hated him.'

His body was tense and strained, his face dark with angry blood. 'If he hadn't died I know he'd have ended up killing her.'

Annie was horrified. 'Oh, Johnny!'

He picked up her disbelief and said fiercely, 'Yes, he would! I'm sure of it. But once he was gone, everything was so different – we were so happy together. I was shattered when she died while I was still at school.' He sighed. 'At least she never had to know I was sent to prison.'

Hesitantly, she asked him, 'Was it really awful being there?'

His eyes were wild. 'It was a nightmare. Being shut in one tiny room year after year. I nearly went mad. Almost every night since I got out I dream I'm back there and I wake up sweating. I've got claustrophobia now; it started in prison. I felt the walls were starting to close in on me, I couldn't breathe, thought I'd suffocate. I don't know how I got through those eight years. I had no one to talk to – the other prisoners didn't like me because I wasn't one of them; I was educated, I'd been to college, I read a lot. We had nothing in common. And I was a target for some of the warders because I'd half killed a copper.'

Annie shivered. 'Don't talk about killing! Oh, Johnny, isn't it terrible about poor Derek? I can't believe it – he was the last person I would have expected to get murdered. Did you see Mike Waterford's interviews in this morning's newspapers? I was so angry!'

'So was I. I'm amazed the TV company let him talk about you that way. It must have done the series a lot of damage.'

She groaned. 'That's what I said. I hope to God the police don't believe what he's suggesting – it wasn't true, any of it, but people are always ready to believe the worst. Oh, Johnny . . . who can have killed Derek? Some of the press seem to think he was gay and picked up somebody dangerous, but I keep thinking . . . what . . . what if it was Roger Keats? He was the type to resent his wife having another man. I wouldn't put murder past him. But if it was him . . . I can't help thinking . . . he might come after me.'

Johnny sat up and took her face between his hands, kissed her softly, looking into her eyes. 'Don't look so scared, darling. You're safe while you're with me.'

Mike Waterford got a call that evening. The voice was low and husky, a man's voice. He didn't recognise it. 'I saw you on breakfast TV this morning. Talking about Annie Lang.'

Mike was about to hang up. He had been getting hostile calls all day from her fans; he was sick of listening to them going on and on about her and what a wonderful person she was and how much they hated him for talking like that about her. Some people didn't want to know the truth.

'I know something about her that nobody else knows,' the voice whispered, and Mike froze, listening. 'Something that would ruin her, if it got out.'

Mike's eyes widened. He tried not to sound too eager. 'What?'

'Not over the phone. And I want something in exchange.'

Mike smiled cynically. 'Oh, blackmail, is it? If she doesn't pay up you'll go to the press with what you know? You'd better talk to her, not me – or to the company's lawyers.'

Again he was about to hang up, but the man quickly said, 'No, you don't understand. I don't want to talk to any lawyers. Look, I'm just around the corner from your place – I can prove what I'm saying.'

'Who is this? How do you know where I live? Where did you get my phone number? Do you work for the company – is that it? Do I know you? Is that why you've rung me instead of contacting the company or Annie herself?'

'Yes, I know you, and I think you'll be very interested in what I'm going to show you. You hate her, don't you? If I go to the press they'll probably swindle me. I'm not a famous actor; they won't dare pay you in peanuts, though. I think we can make a deal, don't you?'

Mike hesitated only a second or two. It wasn't so much the money, although that could be useful; it was more the sheer enjoyment of dragging Annie Lang even deeper into the mud. She had sneered at him once too often.

11

Tom Moor rang Sean on his mobile phone at eight o'clock. 'Where the hell are you? I'm at your place.'

'I'm sitting outside Annie's house, waiting for her – she's vanished again. Have you found Keats yet?'

'I've found out too much to talk over the phone – I'll come there. Wait for me.'

He hung up and Sean yawned, stretching and looking at his watch. It would take Tom a good twenty minutes to drive here. Sean needed to stretch his legs, he was cramped and he needed to go to the lavatory. He got out, locked his car and walked up the road to a pub he had noticed on the corner. A sign swung over head, creaking in the wind – a very shabby-looking lion, the red paint largely gone.

Opposite on the other side of the road which made a T-junction with Annie's road stood a few shops; a butcher's, a greengrocer's, a newsagent's. They were all shut now. There was nobody much about in this suburban street. People were home from work and watching TV or eating supper. A memory stirred in Sean's mind – hadn't Annie mentioned that her mother once ran a shop just round the corner from their house? Maybe it was one of these? None of the shop fronts carried the name Lang. No doubt it had been changed when her mother sold out.

Sean walked into the pub; it wasn't busy, just a few regulars playing darts and listening to a juke box. They looked round at Sean hopefully. 'D'you play? Want a game?'

He shook his head. 'Sorry, not stopping.' He bought a couple of cans of ice-cold beer to take back with him, used the lavatory, then walked down the road again. In case Annie was back he rang her doorbell; the house was still dark, no sign of her.

Five minutes later, Tom Moor's car drew up and he got out and came to sit in Sean's Porsche. He looked tired. There were flecks of red in the whites of his eyes and a telltale muscle jerking beside his mouth, noticed Sean with contrition.

Tom talked as fast as ever, though, and didn't complain. Much. 'God, I'm dead on my feet. Why can't you bring me nice quiet cases I can follow up on the telephone sitting in my own chair in my own office?'

Sean offered him one of the cans of beer, still dewy from the pub fridge. Tom drank it as if it was milk, his eyes closed.

'Man, that was good. You can read my mind.' He scrunched the can and dropped it on the floor. 'OK. Still no news of Roger Keats. Chorley's people are on his trail since his wife told them he'd confessed to killing Derek.'

'Who's your line into Chorley's office now?'

Tom laid a finger along his nose. 'Ask no questions, hear no lies. Anyway, so far they haven't found this guy Keats. Meanwhile I've checked out Johnny Tyrone for you. Now he was easy. The magazine were very open about his background. In fact, they're proud of him. They boasted about where they'd got him from. He's just done eight years for attempted murder.'

'What?' Sean hadn't expected that. His jaw dropped.

Tom Moor grinned at his visible surprise. 'Yeah.

He stole a car, was stopped by a police constable, and bashed his head in, left him for dead. He got away, but later the same night he was arrested after a car chase and charged with attempted murder in the furtherance of a crime – the poor bastard he hit didn't die, but his brains never worked so good since. Tyrone was found guilty, got ten years, should have got out on parole after about six – he was a model prisoner, it seems, no trouble at all – until there was another incident. He had a fight with a prisoner and injured him pretty badly. No explanation, neither of the men would talk, but it set his parole back, which is why he did eight years. Seems he was a journalist before he went to prison and while he was there he edited the prison magazine – that's how he met the editor of this crime magazine, he wrote articles for them about life in prison and some on big-time criminals, the editor liked his stuff and he was offered a job when he got out.'

Ignoring all the career details, Sean said, 'So he's violent and dangerous.'

He couldn't help a quiver of satisfaction; his instincts about the man had been spot on. Once a cop, always a cop, he thought. I knew. I just knew.

And Annie was with this man somewhere. Did she have any idea about all this? Surely she wouldn't be seeing the guy if she did?

'He has a rather sad family history, too,' Tom said.

'Par for the course with types like that,' said Sean, not wanting to be forced to have any sympathy for the man at all. 'I'm a great believer in genetics. I don't hold with all that stuff about it being society's fault.'

'Fifty-fifty,' argued Tom. 'Genetics and environment, they're both important. Even a basically good kid can turn bad if he gets kicked around all his life – I've seen it, time and again. They get mad because they aren't getting nowhere however hard they try, and it's damned unfair, and then they start on drugs and next thing their whole lives are a mess.'

'We'll talk this out another time,' Sean impatiently said. 'What did you find out about Tyrone's family background?'

Tom gave him a look, but shrugged. 'He's from Essex, the London fringe, born in Chingford, lived on the edge of Epping Forest most of his life – I got his date of birth from the magazine, he had to fill in the usual income-tax and national-insurance forms. I checked up in the Records Office, drove over to Chingford, managed to find someone who'd lived next door to his parents years ago and remembered him – an old girl with false teeth that didn't quite fit, she whistled on every other word. But her memory was as clear as a bell. She told me which school he'd gone to, I called in there, pretending to be checking references – several teachers remembered him; they liked him, gave him a rave report, in fact. They told me something else, too – I checked it out in the back issues of the local newspaper, and they were right. He's an only child and his parents both died while he was young. His mother when he was in his teens, his father when he was about six – and listen to this, it seems his father fell downstairs in their house and was killed outright. He was drunk at the time; the inquest brought it in as an accident.'

In the shadowy car, Sean turned his head to stare at him, narrow-eyed. 'But you don't think it was?'

'I wouldn't go that far. Just a hunch.'

'I trust your hunches, Tom, always have.'

Tom grinned. 'Thanks. OK, then, from the report in the local paper both the boy and his mother were upstairs at the time – they claimed to have been together in the boy's bedroom when they heard him fall. He'd been drinking for hours, and the forensic report given to the coroner confirmed that. But the widow admitted that her husband had been knocking her about before he fell – the police evidence was that when they saw her that night she was covered in bruises, had a split lip and a black eye. And a neighbour heard her screaming, but apparently that was normal for this pair. They were always fighting.'

'I think I get your drift,' Sean said slowly. 'You mean – did he fall, or was he pushed? And how old was Tyrone then?'

'Six.'

Sean grimaced. 'Yes. A bit young to start out on a career as a murderer, but if he was there and saw it happen it must have set up a trauma, reinforced any hereditary tendency to violence. I suppose the mother didn't come to a violent end too?'

'No, she died of natural causes, and I'm told the boy worshipped the ground she walked on. He was devastated when she died, these neighbours told me, and listen to this – they said he was a quiet, dreamy, gentle boy, wouldn't say boo to a goose.'

'But half kills policemen,' muttered Sean and Tom nodded.

'Weird, isn't it? Anyway, he had to go and live with his grandmother, in Epping Forest. She was his mother's mother, and had hated his father, had tried to stop her daughter marrying him. A shrewd old woman, obviously, if the guy used to beat up the daughter. I got out of the magazine editor that Tyrone

324

is crazy about the house he used to live in with his grandmother, a big, detached place . . . the editor called it a folly, but I don't know what that means, except it sounds like a white elephant to me. Tyrone inherited it when the old lady died eight years ago.'

'Eight years ago?' repeated Sean sharply. 'Again? Everything in this story seems to lead straight back to whatever happened eight years ago.'

Tom looked blank. 'It does? What haven't you told me?'

'Oh, never mind – carry on, I was just babbling.'

'Uh-huh?' Tom said drily, but went on. 'He kept the house on while he was in prison because he got some insurance money left to him by his grandmother, but that's all eaten up now and he's having to sell the house because he can't afford it.'

Sean stiffened. 'Did this editor give you the address?'

Tom Moor turned to look at him, picking up on his tone. 'He didn't know it. I asked him. He gave me Tyrone's current address – it's just a bedsit.'

Sean stifled a groan. 'Well, give that to me, Tom.'

Tom handed over a folder. 'Here you are – photostats of the birth certificate, the death certificate of the father, and the coroner's report, his home address, income-tax number, national-insurance number . . . I practically got his vaccination certificates!'

'Thanks,' Sean said, punching his arm lightly. 'I owe you one. Great work. You go on home to bed now, and tell Cherie I'm sorry.'

'Won't make no difference, man. Cherie hates you. And wait till you see my bill – you won't owe me nothing when you've paid that!' Tom chuckled and got out of the Porsche, leaned on the roof and said,

'Hey, think I'll get me one of these after you've paid my bill.'

When Tom had gone, Sean drove to the address Tom had given him. It was a huge, rambling late-Victorian house in the back streets of Hackney which had been converted into single-room flatlets. The one Johnny Tyrone occupied was dark and nobody answered when he rang the bell although a few faces showed at windows and stared down at him in a hostile way.

He yelled up at them but none of them opened a window; they vanished again when he waved and shouted up again.

Sean drove back to Annie's house; that was still dark, too, and nobody answered the bell there, either.

They're together, he thought. But where? His stomach burned with acid. He settled down in his car again, to brood and wait.

Annie got back home at ten o'clock. Johnny had wanted her to spend the night with him, but she had yet to learn her lines for the next day and she had to be up at six, she told him.

'I'd love to stay all night, but I know from bitter experience that if I don't sleep I'm good for nothing next day.'

Holding her close he asked, 'When, then? Do you realise we've never spent a night together? We've only ever snatched a few hours and then had to hurry off, even when we were living under the same roof, in case your mother caught us.'

'At the weekend? Saturday night, Johnny – I don't have to get up on Sunday, I have the day off. We could sleep here that night, or you could come to my house.'

'Here,' he said. 'This is our place, it always was.'

She had known he would say that – it was how she felt, too. This was their place, their secret hiding place. Nobody else ever came there and almost no traffic ever went past. Only the trees knew where they were.

'Give me your phone number, Johnny, in case I need to talk to you. I always have to wait for you to ring me.'

'I don't have a phone of my own.' He wrote down the number of his magazine. 'They'll pass the message on to me; I call in every day. And this is my address. It's just one room, though, a bedsit – until I sell this house I won't have the money to get myself a place of my own. This is just a room in a run down old place divided into a dozen bedsits. I haven't been there long and I can't wait to get away.'

Huskily, she said, 'You could come and live with me, Johnny – why not? I have plenty of room.'

He shook his head, his face obstinate. 'I won't live in your house, Annie, it has to be a place we share. As soon as I've sold this house we'll find a place where we can be together.'

An idea hit her and her eyes lit up. 'I could buy this house, Johnny!' She wondered why she hadn't thought of it before. 'I could buy fifty per cent of it – that way, you would have some money, and we would each own half the house!'

He flushed with excitement. 'That never occurred to me! I've had it valued at a hundred and fifty thousand – could you raise seventy-five thousand to buy half of it? But it does need a lot of work, Annie. I know it's fun camping out here now, but if we were to live in it we'd have to have the roof seen to, and a number of windows need to be replaced, not to mention that every single room needs to be redecorated. We wouldn't be able to move in for months.'

'It would be fun, though, seeing it come back to life!' Her eyes were like candle-flames at the very thought of it. 'We would have a wonderful time doing it, Johnny.'

He dropped her off at her home half an hour later; they were still talking eagerly about what they would do to the house once the legal problems had been sorted out. She kissed him goodnight reluctantly and got out, hurrying across the pavement to her house.

It was only as Johnny's car accelerated away that Sean woke up. He had fallen asleep, his head on the wheel of his car, his mind almost at burn-out after weeks of stress. Blinking and red-eyed, he sat up, yawning, stretched his weary body, and looked around, dazed, until he remembered where he was and saw that the front door of Annie's house was now open. Annie had let herself in, and was going through the usual routine of switching off the burglar alarm and putting on the light.

As she turned to close the front door, someone hurled himself at it, forcing it open again. She stumbled backwards with a cry of alarm, then saw it was only Sean.

'What on earth do you think you're doing?' she breathlessly accused.

'What am I doing? That's the question I've been waiting to ask you! You were supposed to go to my place with Harriet – but you ran out on her.'

She bit her lip. 'I'm sorry, Sean. I didn't mean to vanish – Harriet went off to her office and I got bored waiting. When my driver turned up, I decided to go on ahead.'

'You'd no right to do that! It isn't the first time, is it? You keep vanishing without a word. Do you realise how worrying it is? You know how much rides on you – if anything happened to you, it could be the end of the whole series.'

She made a weary gesture and he snapped at her angrily.

'Oh, you may not care about that, but what about the rest of us? Me and Harriet and the rest of the cast, and the camera crew, and everyone on the team? All those jobs would go whistling down the wind, just because you got bored waiting for Harriet!'

'Oh, all right, I'm sorry, I won't do it again – I just thought, while I was waiting I might as well visit my mother.'

His face was unrelenting. 'I know you saw her, I rang the hospital – you only stayed ten minutes. Where have you been since?'

She looked away. 'I was with Johnny.' She walked away into the house and Sean shut the door and followed her.

'I've been checking up on him.'

She looked round at him, stiffening, and his eyes bored into her.

'Did you know he'd been in prison for eight years for attempted murder?'

He saw from her unsurprised face that she had known. 'How dare you pry into my affairs!' was all she said.

He laughed angrily. 'How many affairs are you juggling at the moment?'

She almost slapped his face. Through clenched teeth

she muttered, 'That's pretty cheap, isn't it, Sean? Cheap and nasty. Why don't you just mind your own business.'

Sean curtly said, 'You are my business. The whole series depends on you. I need to be sure you aren't in danger – and with this guy I'd say you were asking for trouble. Do you know what he did? He attacked a policeman who stopped his car. No reason at all – hit him so hard he was off work for a year. I take that very personally, Annie. It could have been me.'

She looked at him with slight shock, never having seen it in that light before. She should never forget that Sean had been a policeman.

'He's paid for it, Sean. After all, eight years in prison is a long, long time. And it wasn't like him; Johnny isn't the violent type.'

'Not violent? Beats a policeman's head in and you say he isn't the violent type?' Sean almost laughed but was too angry. 'As an ex-copper, let me tell you I can't agree.'

She gave a shuddering sigh. 'No, I know . . .' she admitted. 'It was terrible, he knows that, but . . . oh, Sean, that was the night I told him about Roger Keats; he ran out in a state of terrible shock. That's why he attacked the policeman. He'd never do it again.'

'Oh? Did he tell you about the next guy he attacked?'

Her face was shaken. 'What?'

'Another prisoner. He nearly killed him, too. That's why he did eight years, and didn't get parole earlier. Annie, don't kid yourself – the man is dangerous. He's violent and unpredictable. If you go on seeing him you're asking for trouble. So much rides on you, Annie. You've no right to take risks with your life.'

She couldn't think straight, she was too confused and disturbed by what he'd just told her – Johnny had never said anything about attacking anyone else. Automatically, though, she stammered, 'Johnny would never hurt me! You don't know him!'

Sean's eyes were hard. 'I know this – even if he never slips up again, and there's no guarantee of that – he could still destroy your career, if the press find out about his past. The publicity would be disastrous. It would ruin your image. You can't get mixed up with a violent criminal, Annie, and not expect the public to react.'

She put her hands over her ears. 'Stop it!' she yelled. 'You aren't making me give him up again. My mother made me give him up, made me kill my baby . . . I'll never let anyone do that to me again. From now on, I make my own decisions, and I won't listen to a word you say. I love Johnny. Nothing can alter that. Nothing, do you hear?'

He stared at her in grim silence.

'Go away, Sean,' she wearily said. 'I'm tired. I'm going to bed.'

'I'm not leaving you here alone. Not with Roger Keats prowling around. Until the police catch him you mustn't be left alone, especially at night. I'll sleep on the couch down here.'

Annie opened her mouth to argue, then thought better of it. She was angry with Sean but she had to admit she was nervous about being alone in the house since Derek's death. The mere idea of Roger Keats somewhere out there made the hairs stand up on the back of her neck.

'Oh, do as you like,' she said with a tired sigh, and Sean's eyes flashed.

'You should be careful how you phrase remarks like that – some men might take it as an invitation.'

Startled, she flushed, then laughed a little uncertainly. 'It was nothing of the kind, so don't even think about it!' She had felt, lately, that they were becoming friends; she had learnt so much more about him during the hours they'd spent together. Realising they came from the same background, the same sort of family, with the same attitudes to life, had made a bond between them. She hoped Sean wasn't taking too personal an interest in her; she would hate to hurt him and she didn't want their friendship to change, either, but she would have to slap him down if he started flirting with her, and she knew enough about Sean to realise how he would react if she rejected him. His pride would be hurt, and he would probably avoid her altogether, which she would regret now.

Sean saw the changing expressions crossing her face and could read them pretty well.

Offhandedly, he said, 'Oh, don't worry, you're in no danger from me — it was just a joke!'

Annie wasn't sure she believed him, but she hoped to God he was telling the truth. 'I'll get you some pillows and a quilt,' she said, turning away to go upstairs.

Sean followed. She turned to look at him. 'I'll bring them down. You stay here, make yourself a drink, if you like.'

'I think I ought to check the rooms upstairs – just in case.'

Annie didn't argue. She went to the linen cupboard above the central-heating boiler upstairs, found spare pillows and a thick patchwork quilt her mother had made many years ago from old clothes cut up in squares and diamonds, and brought them out to the landing. Sean was quickly going through the bedrooms to make sure they were all empty and the windows locked.

He came back to her, nodding. 'Everything's fine. If you hear a sound during the night, though, yell like crazy, and I'll come running.'

She handed him the bedding. 'Thanks, Sean,' she said gratefully, and he smiled at her a little wryly.

'My pleasure.' Something in the way he said it made a shiver run down her back, but then he asked, 'I'm going to make myself some hot chocolate – do you want some?'

She shook her head, her throat dry.

'Goodnight, Sean.'

He nodded, turned away and went downstairs saying, 'Goodnight,' over his shoulder. Annie went quickly into her bedroom and locked the door. She knew she wouldn't sleep, not with her mind buzzing with everything Sean had just said, the way he had looked at her just now. Oh, please don't start looking at me like that! she thought, confused and upset. Why was life so complicated? For years she hadn't met anyone she liked that much, now, suddenly, Johnny was back and then Sean . . .

Oh, no! she thought, thumping her pillow. She'd have to take a sleeping pill, and she hated doing that, partly because they made her feel as if her head had been stuffed with cotton wool the following day; and partly because she knew they could be addictive if you got used to taking them every night. She kept them for emergencies.

She took a pill, put out the light, and finally drifted off to sleep, but a sleep troubled by dreams she couldn't remember when her alarm went off next morning.

She showered in luke-warm water, to wake herself up, and dressed quickly in dark green ski pants and a beige shirt topped by an olive-green sweater which had a fleeting resemblance to army combat gear. With her short, blonde hair slicked back and faintly damp, she looked even more like a boy when she saw herself in a mirror, and her mouth twitched ironically. Maybe she had subliminally picked this outfit? No man was going to be turned on if she looked like this!

In fact, Sean was just as pale and red-eyed from lack of sleep as she was; neither of them could face anything but coffee and orange juice.

Before they left for the studio Sean asked her, 'Where's that gun you were presented with?'

She gave him a startled look. 'Upstairs in a drawer.'

'Get it and carry it in your handbag,' he ordered in a tone that made her chin come up.

'I don't want to carry a gun around with me!'

His teeth met; his voice grated between them, 'Don't keep arguing. For God's sake, Annie, take this situation serious. There's a crazy guy out there – you should have some protection. Get the gun. I'll put the bullets in for you.'

When Annie got out of make-up that morning, she heard Harriet complaining loudly that Mike was late again, but that was nothing unusual, Annie took no notice, and although Harriet was irritated she didn't actually need Mike yet, he wasn't in the first scene they were to shoot, so she carried on working while her assistant rang him.

Work went well that morning. There were only a

few stoppages and nobody forgot their words, or made a wrong move, although Annie had dark shadows under her eyes and was faintly lethargic.

She and Sean had driven in to work together hours ago, barely speaking. She avoided his eye when she saw him around on the set that morning.

They broke at ten, with scene 1 in the can, and had coffee while the set was changed; the next scene was to be shot in the police canteen, which involved the scene-shifters moving a lot of chairs and tables, while the cameras and lighting were switched over to that side of the vast, barnlike studio, with its cavernous, echoing roof, festooned with lighting tracks and cables. A dozen extras in police uniform came on set to sit at some of the tables and provide background noise for the scene; Harriet's assistant went over to talk to them, remind them what to do and when to move.

Annie slumped in her chair, massaging the back of her neck with one hand while she held her paper cup of coffee in the other and took an occasional sip. When you were working under the hot lights you didn't notice, but once the lights switched off and you stopped moving you soon began to feel cold.

There was no heating; every time the double doors were opened the wind blew in around them, which was why all the women studio technicians wore woolly leggings under their jeans and several layers of warm clothing on top. What the men wore was anybody's guess, but they tried to keep moving a lot, and flapped their arms and stamped their feet on very cold days.

Harriet, in her duffle coat, wearing a woolly hat with earmuffs, which made her look like a gnome, perched on a chair beside her, zipping through her words and movements for the next scene.

'You turn then; close-up; we want a worried look as you realise your back-up hasn't arrived – OK? Then Mike comes in . . . where the hell is he? Can't he ever get here on time?' Harriet broke off as a couple of policemen in uniform walked over towards them. She gave them a startled look. 'Now what?'

'Miss Lang?' one of them said to Annie. 'Inspector Chorley has sent us to fetch you – he wants to talk to you again.'

Harriet groaned. 'Oh, no! Things were going too well. I might have known it was too good to last. Look, can't this wait? I've got a programme to make and I can't make it if my star keeps being dragged away to answer police questions. This can't be urgent.'

The constable's expression was totally wooden. 'Sorry, miss, but we were told to bring Miss Lang back with us.'

'Why? What's happened? Have you caught the murderer?'

The policemen exchanged glances, but before they could answer Billy Grenaby came hurrying towards them, barely avoiding tripping over the snaking cables littering the floor, startling Harriet out of her wits because he rarely appeared on the floor of the studio while they were filming.

For once he was pale, agitated, none of his usual bounce in evidence. He burst out at once before he got to them, 'Harriet, my God, this is terrible . . . I can't believe it . . . first Derek, now Mike! The series is finished – it can't go on after this.'

Everyone within earshot froze, listening, staring, the cameramen and sound technicians, the studio manager in his headphones, the other actors, faces startled.

'Mike? What are you talking about?' Harriet said,

eyes wide and shocked. 'You don't mean . . . Mike's . . .' She turned to stare at the police, her face questioning, incredulous, horrified. 'Mike's not . . .'

A buzz ran round the studio, a gasp of shock and disbelief. Harriet's assistant dropped the clapperboard and the sound rang like a shot, making everyone jump and stare.

Annie looked at the policemen, too; they were watching her in a way that made her blood run cold. Oh, my God, it's true, she thought; Mike's been killed too. She could read it in their quiet, watchful faces, the careful eyes which told her as little as possible, never wavering as they stared at her. She couldn't believe it was happening; it was like a nightmare, first Derek, now Mike. Had he been killed the same way as Derek? She swallowed a wave of sickness. How horrible . . . horrible. Then she thought: surely to God the police don't think I did it? They can't believe that. They can't.

But who did? Roger Keats? Why would he kill Mike Waterford? Mike wasn't seeing Marty. What on earth would be the motive in killing Mike? But there had to be some connection. It couldn't be coincidence, not when both actors were stars in this series. First Derek, now Mike? What is going on? What is going on?

People were whispering to each other all round the studio, and they were staring at her, now, with changing expressions. The police had come to get *her* – she could see that everyone was wondering why, asking themselves if she was suspected, what she had done. The only ones who weren't staring at her like that were Harriet and Billy Grenaby; they were looking at each other, their eyes silently talking. The two of them often did that, they seemed able to talk without words.

But what were they saying to each other now? she wondered. Surely they didn't believe she was involved in these murders?

'*Has* there been another murder?' Harriet asked the policemen.

'I'm sorry, but we can't answer questions, miss,' one said gruffly. 'Better come along at once, Miss Lang. The inspector's waiting.'

But Billy answered Harriet, his voice rough. 'Mike's been killed. The same as Derek — exactly the same. Strangled.'

Harriet groaned and he nodded.

'God, when is this going to end?' he asked her rhetorically. 'What the hell is happening here? The PR people are going crazy trying to talk on every phone in their office. Of course, the press know all about it.' He almost seemed to wring his hands, his face distracted. 'I'm beginning to think we'll have to come off air. Shut the whole production down.'

'Over my dead body,' Harriet said, then began to laugh hysterically. Everyone looked at her, shocked and startled. 'S-sorry,' she gulped, getting herself under control. 'We use these phrases without thinking, don't we?' Tears suddenly came into her eyes. 'I can't believe it. Mike. Dead.'

She had been close to being in love with him briefly; it had left a tenderness. He was a bastard, of course; but he had had charm and his body was fantastic. They had never been to bed, but Harriet was a highly sexed woman and very aware of Mike that way.

'I'll miss him,' she realised, then, in bewilderment, 'Who would kill Mike?' she whispered.

Nobody answered her.

It was a short drive from the riverside studios to the police station, a modern building with a view of the river from its top floors, the windows all dark glass to cut down the glare of the sun in summer, the roof bristling with scanning devices and electronic equipment.

Annie was taken in through a police car park enclosed with twenty-foot-high wire fences; the gates opened and shut electronically. She just had time to see a horde of reporters clustering outside the station entrance who turned and saw the car, came running, shouting, blinding her with flashlights as they took blind shots. The police car shot through into the yard and drove right up to the back of the building.

Annie was rushed out of the car and into the station while behind her cameras went on flashing and the reporters yelled and fought to get at her. She had been exposed to press interest for years, but it didn't prepare her for this. She was trembling, and it didn't help to meet more stares inside the building; there were policemen everywhere, behind the reception desk on the ground floor of the station, hurrying along corridors, turning to look at her curiously, waiting for lifts, a battery of eyes that were an ordeal to face.

'This way, Miss Lang,' said the policeman guiding her, and took her into the end lift, up to an interview room on the second floor.

Annie was kept there answering questions for several hours. Billy had made sure their lawyer joined her to sit in on the interviews, but she didn't try to evade any of the repeated questions about her whereabouts the night before, her relationship with Mike, how they had got on, how she had felt about his recent comments to the press about her, if she had seen his interview on breakfast TV.

'Were you angry with him?'

The lawyer stirred, frowning, but Annie answered. 'Yes,' she said frankly, meeting the inspector's eyes. 'But not enough to kill him! And I doubt if I could, anyway. Mike was very fit, I'd never have been able to overpower him.' She held up her small, slender hands. 'Do these hands look strong enough to strangle a man?' A shudder ran through her at the thought.

Inspector Chorley shrugged. 'He was drugged before he was killed – the stuff had been put into a glass of whisky, we found traces of it in the sediment in the bottom of the glass. He was unconscious when he died, and you wouldn't need strong hands – he was strangled with a woman's tights, in exactly the same way Derek Fenn was. Anyone could have killed him. Tell me, did he know this ex-tutor of yours, Roger Keats, the man who claimed to have killed Derek Fenn?'

She shook her head, face uncertain. 'I doubt it. I suppose he might have done. A lot of actors either studied at the school or visited it later, when they were professionals. The school liked to get well-known names along to give workshops or judge competitions.'

'Did Mike Waterford ever come to the school when you were there?'

'No, I don't think so. I never met him, if he did.'

'But he might have done?'

'The theatre is a small world. Everyone knows everyone else, actors and directors are obsessed with work, it's all they talk about. Mike obviously knew people who'd been to the school, apart from me, I mean. He may have known Roger Keats.'

'But you don't recall Mr Waterford ever mentioning his name?'

She shook her head.

'Apart from having a quarrel with him after he talked about you so freely on television the other day, how did you normally get on with Mr Waterford? Did you like him?'

She was tired of being wary and careful; she just told the truth, although she could see from the lawyer's face that he was appalled by her frankness as he listened.

'He was unprofessional, selfish, wanted to hug the limelight. He enjoyed making little digs at you, he could be spiteful and his ego was monstrous. He had all the worst faults of actors, magnified a hundred times. No, I did not like him.'

The inspector half-smiled, she sensed he hadn't liked Mike much on television, and he was secretly amused by what she had said. But he said, 'It can't be a coincidence, you know – that first one member of the cast is killed, and then another. And both men were important in the series, weren't they? Have you got any ideas on that? Why would this murderer want to kill Mike Waterford?'

Her eyes were wide, troubled, baffled. 'I don't know – I can't work it out at all.' She looked at the inspector, searching his face. 'Do you think it was Roger Keats who killed Mike? But why should he?'

He shrugged. 'At the moment all I have is a lot of evidence to sift before I can make guesses. OK, Miss Lang, that will be all for now. If you think of anything else, ring me, won't you? Any little detail, anything you remember . . . it could be very important. Oh, and you'd better give me your boyfriend's address, and

341

where he works? We'll need you to sign your statement too. Constable Higgs will print it out at once – just wait two minutes, please.'

A policewoman had sat in the corner taking down her words on an almost silent word processor; Annie heard the hum of it beginning to print as she looked through her bag to find Johnny's address.

She was given the statement to read, and then sign. As she handed it back, the inspector said, 'And please be careful, Miss Lang, won't you? Two of the stars of your series are dead. We don't want to be looking into your murder next.'

Did he think that hadn't occurred to her? If Roger Keats *was* killing people, she would be on the list. That thought had been at the back of her mind ever since she heard Mike was dead. But why would he kill Mike? Derek, yes, Roger had a motive for that – he might have vanished from Marty's life for years but he was crazy enough to resent her taking up with another man.

'You won't want to run the press gauntlet,' said the inspector. 'So we'll take you out the back way again – apparently there's a car waiting for you there. We'll be in touch if we need to talk to you again.'

Annie assumed the studio had sent Jason to get her, but when she walked out of the back of the police station the first thing she spotted was Sean's black Porsche. He leaned over to open the passenger door. Annie hesitated, then got in.

'What are you doing here?'

'I came to give a statement too – confirming the time you left the studio yesterday, your visit to the hospital, what time you got back to your home, the fact that you met Johnny Tyrone there, and left again with him, and what time you returned later that night.'

Her head almost exploded. 'God, I'm so sick of all this prying and snooping and having to answer questions!'

'I know, it's tough, but a second murder has really put Chorley under pressure to find the killer, and fast. They'll give the case to someone else if he doesn't get someone soon, and Chorley's whole career could be blasted.' Sean grimaced. 'Not that I'd care about that, I can't stand the man, but I understand the sort of stick he's getting from above.'

Annie leaned back in her seat while they drove out of the car park with the press heaving around them and trying to take pictures through the car windows even as Sean accelerated.

Several of them actually tried to stop the car by lying across the bonnet and Sean had to swerve to throw them off while he shot away.

He was muttering angrily under his breath about them. 'Vermin, scum of the earth . . . I'd like to drive right over the whole pack of them.'

Annie giggled, almost hysterical suddenly. 'And you an ex-policeman, too! I'm shocked.'

He turned to grin at her. 'Policemen are human beings!'

'I'm not so sure about Inspector Chorley!' Annie noticed him turn the car northwards, into the stream of traffic which would pass through the London Borough of South Park eventually, and realised he was going to drive her home. 'I want to visit my mother, Sean, before I go home. You can leave me at the hospital. I'll get a taxi home later.'

Sean didn't argue; he turned off a few streets later, and headed for the hospital instead.

'Do you ever miss being in the police force?' Annie asked, trying to avoid talking about Mike and the murder, or even thinking about it.

'Not in the slightest. No, I was mad keen on it, in the beginning. It was the family job, after all, and I'd badly wanted to be a copper. It can be an absorbing job, but it can be deadly dull, too; there's too much paperwork, too much plain footwork, knocking on doors, asking the same questions over and over again, observation for hours in the freezing cold street, sitting in cars waiting, endlessly waiting. In a way it's a bit like filming; you spend an awful lot of time waiting for something to happen, and filling in your time with boring stuff that leaves a lot of your mind with nothing to do. On the other hand you meet a lot of people, hear some very odd stories, a lot of pain and grief – it is a very human job.'

She thought about what he had said and nodded. 'Is that why you started to write – or did you always want to write?'

'I always liked reading, especially detective stories – I started thinking I'd like to write one when I was in cadet school, then I thought of writing for TV. I tried out a couple of scripts, but didn't dare send them to anyone until I met Harriet at a writing weekend, I showed her what I'd done, she liked them and that was how The Force started.'

He pulled into the hospital car park and Annie smiled at him a little shyly, her blue eyes darker than usual. 'I'm a fan, you know, Sean – you're a terrific writer. I love working with you.'

A flush crept along his cheekbones. 'Thanks. Same here. I'm a fan of yours, and you're a joy to write for; you always make my words sound as if you just thought of them. At times even I wonder if you have.'

'I'm not that clever. I'm just an actress, that's all. Thanks for the lift. Bye.' Annie dived out of the Porsche, flurried by the exchange of mutual admiration, and rushed into the hospital. Sean waited until she was out of sight, then he drove to the hospital and parked where he could see the main entrance. He knew Annie wouldn't stay long; she always found it painful to see her mother the way she was now. But from now on he wasn't allowing her to go anywhere without someone watching her. First Derek, then Mike. . .if he didn't do something to stop it, the next victim might be Annie, and Sean wasn't letting that happen.

That afternoon there was a long meeting to decide the future of The Force in Billy Grenaby's office. Half a dozen people sat around his desk, with very long faces.

Only when the directors had debated for several hours did they call Harriet up to that floor. She had got straight back to work again after Annie's departure, shooting bits of scenes which didn't require either Annie or Mike. For Harriet work was always the best medicine.

She was drawn and pale when she came into Billy's office. He was alone now, seated behind his desk. Looking like someone facing a firing squad, she met his eyes.

'For the moment we've decided not to make a decision,' he said drily, and she breathed again. 'Carry on with the schedule. If Annie is cleared, if the police catch the killer, we may be able to salvage the series. We'll play a waiting game for now.'

Harriet sat down facing him. 'Billy . . . about this swap you've arranged? Do I have to accept?'

'No, but I thought it would be useful for you to be over there while I'm there.' His eyes drifted down to his desk and he looked self-conscious; as always when he wasn't easy in his skin he ran a finger under his collar, straightened his tie, like a nervous schoolboy.

'You're going over to the States too? Why?' Harriet's mind worked overtime on what he had said, the implications of Billy wanting her near him while he was in the States. She still hadn't made up her mind how she felt about him, but a little quiver of excitement ran over her, raising goose-bumps on her skin.

'One of their networks is interested in doing a deal with us to produce stuff specially tailored for American markets; they would come up with half the funding, I'd have to find the rest. I need to spend some time over there, exploring the current trends, assessing the atmosphere, before I decide.'

'Sounds fascinating. Are you thinking of asking me to produce anything, if it comes off? Is that why you want me over there?'

Billy moved things on his desk, staring at his hands, then looked up at her.

'I want you there because I'd miss you if I was away for three months.'

Harriet breathed carefully.

'Think it over,' Billy said, voice husky. 'Why don't we have dinner tonight, and talk?'

Harriet had made up her mind. 'I'd love to,' she said, and watched his eyes glint, his mouth relax.

'I'll pick you up at seven-thirty, then.'

'I'll be waiting,' she said, and went back down to the studio floor briskly. The technicians and actors were taking a long tea break, talking their heads off, their faces worried. 'OK, people, back to work,' she said, clapping her hands, and they saw from her face that they were not out of a job. Yet.

As they rushed to get back to their places, Harriet looked at her watch. Three hours since Annie and Sean left. Her lighthearted mood dissolved. What were the police asking Annie that took so long?

She swallowed. If they lost Annie too that really would be the end of the series. It couldn't go on without her.

Surely to God the police don't suspect her? She thought of Annie's big eyes and delicate face – how could anyone think that was the face of a murderer? Then she remembered the rumour that a woman just like Annie had been seen with Derek the night he died. What if Annie had been seen with Mike last night?

She pushed the idea away, grimacing angrily. What was she thinking about? The idea was crazy. Annie, commit murder? Strangle people? She wasn't capable of it.

But who was doing this? They're destroying my series, she thought, trembling with anger and fear. It could have run for years yet. Now there's every chance it will come off at the end of this season.

Harriet set her teeth. Not if I can help it! Her hands clenched at her sides. I'll use every weapon I can get, but I'm not just letting them kill my series.

Trudie was in a strangely talkative mood; she was back in the past again, a happier past, remembering Annie as a little girl, talking about her dead husband as if he was alive.

Annie let her talk, holding her hand and watching her wistfully. Her mother had always been so strong, so certain. Now she was shrunken in the bed, she barely made a bump under the bedclothes; how child-like she looked in the white cotton nightdress, and her hair had been brushed back off her face, silver, glistening.

Suddenly Trudie was silent. Talked out, she lay back against the pillow, eyes closed.

'I suppose I'd better go, now,' Annie said, and her mother's fingers clutched at her.

'Annie . . . don't leave me here, someone wants to kill me. He came back last night, but Sister came in, and he went away.'

Annie stared down at her. 'He? It wasn't one of the nurses, then?'

Trudie looked confused. 'It was a nurse. Yes. A male nurse. Cinders. I call him Cinders because he's only here at night. It was him who gave me that injection. I remembered, yesterday, but Sister took no notice, she told me to go to sleep, I was imagining things again.'

Annie talked to the ward sister who was very polite at first but became stiff and irritated when she heard what Trudie had said.

'Yes, she did make some vague accusations against one of my night nurses, but she's mistaken. He wasn't on night duty the night she was given the injection of digitalin. He was not in the hospital that night. It's true he was here last night, but only briefly – he came in to say goodbye to the night staff, he has decided to leave us. He wasn't working. He went in to say goodbye to the patients, too, which was when your mother got so upset. She started screaming, I'm afraid.'

'Have you told the police about this?'

'Told them what, Miss Lang? That your mother

had made unsubstantiated accusations about one of my nurses? Do you realise how contradictory her accounts of this incident are? She can't actually remember exactly what happened. It's a typical pattern. We get these accusations all the time. Old people forget and then when they're cross about something else they think up wild accusations. Look, my own opinion is that your mother was given digitalin by mistake – it should have been given to another patient that night. It has to be that. No digitalin is missing. There were several patients on the drug but they are all just as unreliable as your mother and they didn't remember whether or not they had had their medication. I am not going to have another pointless upheaval by having the police back here.'

Annie could not believe the woman's indifference. 'And what if it happens again? What if my mother dies next time?'

'I have improved security on this ward. It won't happen again.' The woman's assurance was impregnable.

Annie stared at her, trembling with anger. 'If it does, and if anything . . . happens . . . to my mother, I'll blame you!'

Sean watched from his car as Annie left in another taxi, which he followed back to her house. As he'd feared, there were a couple of press cars waiting outside, but they were half asleep after a long wait, took too long to get out and sprint after her, and just missed catching her before she got indoors. They rang the doorbell and stood about on the path shouting until a woman next door threw a bucket of ice-cold water over them.

They scattered like tomcats and she yelled after them, 'If you don't clear off I'll set my dog on you!' The dog snarled beside her in the upstairs window, a heavy Alsatian who looked as if he ate postmen and journalists for breakfast.

The press retreated to their cars again and, after waiting another few hours and deciding Annie wasn't coming out again that night, drove off together.

Sean rang Tom Moor on his mobile phone. 'I want someone watching her twenty-four hours a day – can you arrange that?'

'Nothing easier, but it will cost you, Sean. Twenty-four-hour surveillance comes expensive.'

'Look, two men are dead, and her mother was almost killed – I don't care what it cost. I want her protected night and day.'

'I'm surprised Chorley didn't give her police protection – I'd have thought it was warranted, with two members of the cast murdered.'

'He thought of it, but he can't spare the men, and it would be open-ended. Who knows when this killer will hit again? Twenty-four-hour surveillance comes expensive, as you just told me. Chorley knows I'm keeping an eye on her.'

'You like this girl, don't you, Sean?' Tom said softly.

Sean didn't answer. 'I'll stay here until your man arrives,' was all he said.

'It will be me,' Tom said. 'Why should I pay someone else when I can earn the money myself?'

'Cherie is going to love me!'

Next day Harriet watched Annie carefully while they were shooting three short scenes. She's at the end of her tether, Harriet thought. I think we should stop using her for a couple of weeks. Send her away. A health farm, where she can get some peace and quiet? Or abroad to get some real sunshine? She needs a complete break.

Over lunch, she said as much to Annie, who smiled and shook her head. 'I can't go away. I have to be near my mother. And I have a contract, a job to do. I'll take a holiday when we finish filming the series.'

Sean hadn't shown up that morning; if Harriet needed any rewrites she could always call him, and so far it hadn't been necessary.

'I wonder if Sean's with the police this morning?' Harriet thought aloud. 'They keep interviewing members of the cast. They even had a couple of secretaries there. I was stunned to hear that Melanie Brown had had an affair with Mike – did you know about that?'

'No, but I'm not surprised. She's pretty, and silly enough to fall for him. Mike liked his women stupid.'

'Annie! Don't be so nasty about him, poor man. You really didn't like him, did you?'

'No, and I'm not pretending I did. Hypocrisy is stupid. I'm sorry he died like that, of course I am – but I did not like him much.' Annie looked at her watch. 'I've only got another scene to do. Can I leave when I've done that? I want to visit my mother. The most convenient time is when I'm on my way home, the earlier the better.'

'Sure,' agreed Harriet.

When she had finished her filming for the day, Annie went to change back into her own clothes and take off the heavier make-up she used on camera. Normally she hardly wore any make-up at all. She preferred the natural look.

While she was brushing her hair, Sean put his head round the door. She stiffened.

'What do you want now?'

'I need to talk to your boyfriend, Annie. The police have been looking for him at his lodgings but he hasn't been there all day. Do you know where he is?'

'You're not the police,' Annie said. 'Or are you? I thought you'd left the force.'

'Where is he, Annie?'

'I've no idea. Leave me alone, will you?' She pushed past him and Sean tried to hold her arm.

'I'll take you home.'

She glared at him. 'No, you won't. Stay away from me, and my home!'

Sean couldn't leave the studio just then; he had been summoned to rewrite a scene which wasn't working. He hurried back to the office, worked for half an hour, handed the scene to Harriet and got a nod of approval, then he was free to go.

He reached Annie's house, parked and walked up the path to the front door, then put his thumb on the bell and kept it there. Let her ignore that!

The murderer sat in Annie's house, listening to the imperious summons of the bell.

Through the slits in the blinds covering the sitting-room window, Sean was clearly visible. Once it became obvious that he wasn't giving up or going away, the murderer walked slowly towards the front door, working out how to kill him.

Sean was going to be difficult. He had been a cop. He was big and powerful. And he would be on his guard now. But he had to die and now was as good a time as any.

12

Annie rang for a taxi before she left the hospital. 'I'm afraid all our cabs are out. There'll be a ten-minute delay,' said the receptionist booking the call.

'I'll wait,' Annie said in resignation. It would be too much hassle to ring round the other firms. Hanging up, she got herself a cup of coffee from the machine in the hospital reception area, pretending to be unaware of the stares she was getting, and sat down near the door where she could watch for the cab.

There was a large television set into the wall above the rows of chairs where patients sat waiting for appointments.

Annie sipped her coffee, staring at the TV to avoid catching the eye of anyone around her. She ignored the whispers.

'Annie Lang . . . there, over there . . . No, it isn't. Is it? Smaller than you expect . . . pale, isn't she? What's she doing here? She looks so . . . ordinary . . . don't think much of her clothes . . .'

The news began. The first few items were international news; a war zone zoomed into shot, a face talked at them, there was a sound of gunfire, refugees limped along a wide road lined with burnt-out cars and tanks.

What a world we live in! thought Annie grimly. Why do we kill each other with such enthusiasm?

She finished her coffee, scrunched up the paper cup and hurled it into a nearby bin, looked out of the glass doors, watching for her taxi, but there was no sign of it yet.

At that instant she heard the newsreader say, 'A body was discovered today in an isolated house in Epping Forest . . .'

Annie instinctively looked round, wondering if she knew the place, and then her heart almost stopped as she saw a shot of Johnny's house, blackened and ruined, the arch of the Gothic windows empty of glass.

'Fire broke out somewhere upstairs during the night,' the newsreader said. 'The fire service believe it may have started in electrical wiring. The house was unoccupied at the time, although it looked as if tramps had been camping out downstairs.'

Had a tramp broken in and somehow accidentally set fire to the house? Oh, poor Johnny – he wouldn't be able to sell his home now. It was a shell. Of course, there would be the insurance – if he had any!

Then she remembered the drawing-room the way they had left it yesterday; candles burnt down, in candlesticks and on saucers, the fire almost out in the fire place, cushions and a rug on the floor where they had made love.

Was that what had made the police think a tramp had been there? How easy it was to make something beautiful sound ugly!

Oh, but then whose body . . . Johnny? Oh, God, it wasn't Johnny they had found dead in the house?

Then the newsreader said, 'It was while the fire brigade were clearing debris that they found a skeleton under the floorboards in a cupboard under the stairs.'

Annie was trying so hard to hear what he was saying that she almost screamed at a nurse who came to call one of the waiting patients, her voice booming over the sound of the television, drowning the next couple of sentences.

Annie ran towards the set and stood as close as she could, straining to hear. It was an old house; there might not be a crime involved, the skeleton could have been left there by a medical student, by a doctor. There could be a dozen explanations.

She just heard the newsreader's next sentence. 'The body has been identified as that of Roger Keats, a teacher from a London drama school, who disappeared eight years ago.'

Annie's taxi deposited her home half an hour later. She paid the driver and was walking towards her house when she noticed Sean's black Porsche parked just up the road.

She had been trying to ring him from the hospital, but he hadn't been at work or at home. Annie hadn't been able to get Harriet, either. She desperately needed to talk to someone. Her heart lifted as she recognised Sean's car and she hurried over there, but when she bent to look inside the car was empty. Straightening, she looked up and down the street, but there was no sign of him.

Her heart sank again. There was a man sitting in a small blue van parked across the street, but he was black, wearing workmen's blue denims, and wasn't looking at her, but gazing fixedly at a house opposite hers which had a For Sale sign up in the garden.

Frowning, Annie walked back towards her home. Dusk was falling and there was a scent of spring on the air. It had been much warmer today; there were a few early daffodils out in a terracotta urn in her garden, their fragrance lingered now that the sun was going down, but Annie was cold to the marrow of her bones.

Where was Sean? For days he had been following her around, and now when she really needed him he wasn't here.

She was still in shock, still trying to decide what to do. After all, the police knew about her connection with Roger – they would come looking for her if they wanted to talk to her, and obviously they would, sooner or later. Should she ring them? She wanted to know if it really was Roger – yet at the same time she was afraid of the answer.

If it was Roger, how had he died? Had it been an accident? Had he committed suicide?

Don't be stupid! How could he bury himself under floorboards? she thought.

Who would have wanted to kill Roger?

Marty, for one, she thought, opening the front door, and then she paused involuntarily to look back over her shoulder, as if expecting Sean to rush her, as he had last time she came home, but there was still no sign of him.

But why on earth would Marty bury him in Johnny's house? She had never been there, she knew nothing about the place.

You know it wasn't Marty! a voice in her head said grimly, and she shivered. Yes, she knew it wasn't Marty who had killed Roger.

Across the street the black man in the parked blue van was watching her. Their eyes met and then he looked away. She frowned. There was something odd . . . intent . . . about the way he watched her.

Oh, stop imagining things! she told herself. He only looked at you. Every stranger you see isn't a killer.

All the same, she began to close the front door hurriedly. Until she heard a movement in her kitchen.

She froze, listening.

There it was again, the sound of a footstep.

There was somebody in the house. Her heart began to beat painfully under her ribs, her breathing dragged.

Then it dawned on her that it must be Sean – why else was his car parked outside, empty? Yet how would he have got in here?

Oh, well, that would be easy enough for him. He had been in and out of the house for days; nothing simpler than to make a copy of her key when she wasn't looking, that would be no problem for him, and how many times had he watched her punching in the code of her alarm? Damn him, he had a hell of a nerve.

Rage flared inside her. How dared he break into her home? She'd a good mind to call the police and charge him with burglary.

But at the same time she felt a dew of relief break out on her forehead. Thank God he was here, anyway; she could tell him what was bothering her, the crazy thoughts she had been having ever since she heard the TV news.

There was a faint rattle from the kitchen – he was putting on a kettle! she worked out. Making himself tea, no doubt. Good God, anyone would think he lived here! He seemed to think he could walk in and out of her life as if he owned her.

But her anger was only skin-deep; she was far too pleased to find him waiting for her to really care how he had got in! But she would make him jump! Careful not to make a sound, she closed the front door and tiptoed towards the kitchen, then paused as she passed the open sitting-room door; she could see a pair of legs in black jeans.

She knew at once that they were Sean's legs, unmistakably Sean's, and her heart constricted as though squeezed by a giant hand.

He was lying on the floor, not moving. She took a shaky step nearer and saw his hand flung out, palm upward in a gesture of helpless weakness. In the kitchen, someone was whistling.

The hair stood up on the back of Annie's neck. Who was in the kitchen? And what had happened to Sean?

She knew the answer to that, but she didn't want to face it yet. It would hurt too much. The whole universe seemed to have slowed to a crawl; she was barely breathing, let alone thinking.

She could have turned and run back to the front door and out into the road, but she hesitated, watching Sean's hand, the long, strong fingers strangely still.

Was he dead? She couldn't get out without knowing. She bit down on a cry of agony. Oh, God, don't let Sean be dead!

On tiptoes, she ran into the room, trying to make as little noise as possible, and knelt down beside his body, looking at his face in a spasm of dread. Sean was very pale, his eyes closed. He was unconscious, but breathing, she saw, with a rise of the heart. Putting her fingertips on the side of his neck, she felt the deep pulsing of his blood. Thank God; he was alive.

On the floor beside Sean lay a small bronze statuette of a horse she had once been given by a famous theatre director. Tracy kept it highly polished.

Now the base was smeared with blood.

She felt sick. Dark blood matted Sean's hair on the back of his head. She touched it tentatively, trying to part the hair so that she could see the site of the wound; the blood was no longer seeping out, it had stiffened in the thick strands of hair, but the red came off on her fingertips, making her shudder.

There was a movement across the other side of the room; Annie looked up in terror, her blue eyes dilated, glazed, enormous.

Johnny stood in the doorway to the kitchen, staring at her.

Her entire stomach seemed to sink down through her. Oh, no, she thought, tears beginning to burn behind her eyes. Not Johnny. Oh, God, no, not him.

Yet hadn't she known, the minute she heard that Roger Keats was dead, had been dead for eight years? If Roger was dead, who had been sending her Valentines all that time? It had to be the man who killed Roger – and that meant he must have killed Derek, too.

'I didn't hear you come in,' he said, sounding so normal that she got confused again, because how could he sound like that if he was a killer? 'I just made myself some tea – I'm amazingly thirsty,' he said, smiling. 'Do you want some?'

She couldn't pretend everything was normal. She couldn't. 'Johnny . . . what happened?' she whispered. 'Sean's hurt, what happened?'

He gave Sean's prone body an indifferent glance. 'He asked for it. He was making a nuisance of himself, asking too many questions, following you about. But don't worry, darling, he won't make any more trouble for either of us.'

Her breathing hurt. She had never before felt such grief, even when they made her kill her baby, Johnny's baby.

'Oh, Johnny,' she said brokenly. 'Johnny, darling.'

'It's OK, Annie,' he comforted her. 'I'll deal with

it. I'll take him away when it's dark. He had his keys on him, I can take him home and leave him there. I know where he lives – I'd already reconnoitred the place. I knew I'd have to kill him sooner or later. He's the only tenant in that block so far, isn't he? And the builders working on it knock off around five. It might be days before anyone found him.'

A sob broke out of her and she put a hand up to her mouth to stifle the sound.

Johnny stared at her fingers, his face changing. 'You've got blood on your hand,' he said with a frown of distaste.

Annie looked at her hand and shivered. Sean's blood. What was that phrase people used? His blood is on your head. Sean's blood was on her hand. Was it all her fault, all of this? Wouldn't anyone have died if it hadn't been for her? Guilt welled up through her very skin.

In that matter-of-fact voice Johnny told her, 'You'd better go and wash. Blood is always a problem, it's so hard to clear up, but he wouldn't drink his whisky, I suppose he guessed I'd put something in it. I had to hit him.'

She was fighting not to go mad, break down, cry her heart out. 'Why, Johnny, why?' she managed to ask and he stared at her as if it was her who was mad.

'I just told you, he was a threat to you, to us. He was too nosy. Once a copper, always a copper. I found out all about them when I was six years old and they talked to me for hours, trying to get me to tell them what really happened to my father. They guessed we were lying to them and because I was just a little kid they thought they'd get it out of me if they leaned on me long enough.' His mouth curled in contempt, his

360

eyes that deep, dark, angry blue. 'They tried everything – they gave me sweets and comics and patted me on the head, they made veiled threats about my mother, said I'd be taken away from her if I didn't tell them everything, they tried to trip me up, tried to trick me into saying something, but they were stupid. They didn't guess the truth at all. They thought my mother did it.' He smiled at her in blazing triumph. 'You see? They're stupid, all policemen are stupid.' His eyes slid to Sean. 'He was stupid, too, walking in here – he thought he was a match for me, he thought he was bigger and stronger, and cleverer, too.' His mouth twisted in triumph. 'He was wrong.'

The room swam in front of her eyes; Annie staggered to an armchair and sat down.

Johnny was mad. He had to be. Completely out of his mind. Why hadn't she seen it before? Had she been so blinded by love?

Johnny quickly came over, knelt down beside her, looking up into her face with anxious eyes.

'You look as if you're going to faint – are you OK, darling? It's shock. I'll get you that tea, tea's good for shock. Shall I put some brandy in it?'

She shook her head dumbly.

'Just tea? Well, I'll put in some extra sugar, then.' He gave Sean another look, hesitated. 'If the sight of him is upsetting you, I'd better just finish dealing with him, first.'

'No!' she burst out, and Johnny's face altered, hardened.

'Why not? What's he to you?'

She saw jealousy in his eyes and quickly said, 'It isn't that, it's just that I . . . Not here, Johnny, don't do . . . anything . . . to him in front of me, please.'

His face cleared and he gave her a radiant smile. 'Don't worry, darling, I wasn't going to kill him here. That would make it hard to move him later. You have to take rigor mortis into account. I'll just gag him and tie his hands and feet for now.'

Out of his pocket he pulled a length of twine, knelt down and tied Sean's feet together, then his hands, the twine pulled so tight that she could see it would be cutting into Sean's flesh. Trussed up like a chicken for the pot, Sean stirred, his mouth parting in a low moan of pain, and Annie saw his lids flicker.

Johnny gagged him a second later with a white silk scarf Annie recognised as one of hers. He must have got it from a drawer in her bedroom. He had been exploring her house. Or had he explored it long ago? That was when it occurred to her how very wrong she had been all along. If Roger Keats had been dead for years, long enough for his body to reduce to a skeleton, which probably meant he had died eight years ago, then it hadn't been him who broke into her house and left that rose and the Valentine.

She whispered, 'Was it you who sent me those Valentines, Johnny?'

He looked round at her, those beautiful dark blue eyes brilliant, smiling. 'Of course. I couldn't believe it when you told me you thought that bastard Keats had sent them. I was sending you my love, Annie. I thought you would know that. It was a shock when I realised you'd never known.'

'I'm sorry. I was so worried about you, I wish I had known – oh, God, Johnny, why didn't you let me know where you were all those years? Why didn't you sign your name in the Valentines?'

'You aren't supposed to sign Valentines, Annie.' His

tone was gently teasing. He smiled at her quite naturally and she swallowed hard. 'And it was just as well I didn't sign them, and always printed the messages, or your mother would never have let you see them. I used to get them posted from outside the prison by a prison officer who was a decent sort.'

'That must be why my mother let them through, because she never identified them as coming from a prison – and by the time the first one arrived I was getting lots of fan mail, including Valentine's cards.' She went on working the whole thing out aloud, frowning. 'So it was you who broke in here that night and left the rose on my pillow?'

His eyes glowed passionately. 'You looked so lovely in your bed, I was dying to stay and make love to you, but I was afraid if I woke you up you'd be scared stiff and start screaming. And, anyway, I'd planned to see you again for the first time as a reporter – I needed to know how you felt about me, if you still cared.'

She swayed, white as paper and so cold she couldn't stop trembling. He looked at her anxiously. 'You aren't going to faint, are you? Hang on, I'll get that tea and the brandy.'

Johnny hurried out and she put her hands over her face. What was she going to do?

A hoarse, muffled sound made her jump. Her hand dropped and she looked in shock across the room at Sean. His eyes were open; he was twisting on the floor, trying to free himself. He jerked his head at her, the signal obvious. He wanted her to untie him. She half rose but then heard Johnny coming back. She sank down again, giving Sean a warning look. Sean had heard Johnny, too. He shut his eyes and lay still again.

Johnny came over to her with the cup of tea and held it to her lips. She drank it eagerly, needing the brandy as much as the heat of the tea. She didn't normally take sugar in her tea, but her body fiercely needed it now. Johnny put an arm round her and she fought not to show her horror and fear. Deliberately she leaned on him and closed her eyes, felt him softly stroke her hair.

'Darling Annie, I'd do anything for you, you know,' he murmured. 'I love you as much as I loved my mother. You're very like her. She was delicate and easily hurt, too. I used to get so angry when I heard my father hurting her. That last time I crouched on the landing, crying, feeling so useless because I was too small to hit him the way he was hitting her. She was screaming and begging him to stop, crying, saying, "Please stop . . . don't . . ."'

Annie listened, aching with pity and horror.

Johnny's face was white and fierce with feeling. 'Then he came out of their bedroom and saw me. He glared at me and said, "What are you looking at you, you little bastard?" He hit me across the face and then he started to go downstairs. I went up behind him and I kicked the back of his legs. He looked round at me.' Johnny's voice was strange, hoarse. 'He looked so surprised . . . scared . . . but he couldn't save himself. He toppled forward, grabbing for the banisters, and fell all the way down, crashing from one wall to the other, screaming. The noise seemed to go on for ever. Then he lay at the bottom, staring up at me, but he never moved again. My mother came out sobbing. She knew at once that I'd done it. She said to me, "Oh, Johnny, what have you done?" She kept crying, she was so scared, and there was blood everywhere. I was scared, but it was easy to lie to the police. After all, I was only six – how could I have killed my father?'

He grinned at her with something close to triumph. She couldn't take it all in; it was too disturbing, especially after realising he must have killed Roger Keats. Oh, God, who else had he killed? She whispered, 'Johnny, have you seen the news?'

He frowned impatient over the change of subject. 'The news? No, why?'

'Your house . . . the house . . . burnt down last night.'

She felt his shock, the stiffening of his body. 'Burnt down?'

'I'm so sorry, Johnny. They think the fire started because the wiring was so old.'

'Was it badly damaged?' His voice was thick with disbelief.

'I'm afraid so. It's a ruin, Johnny. It was insured, though, wasn't it?'

'I don't know, I never thought . . . my lawyer might have kept up the insurance, if there was one. I haven't.' A silence, then he broke out hoarsely, 'I never have any good luck. Everything goes wrong, all my life everything has gone wrong. There was only ever you – I suppose I had to pay for getting you, my one wonderful piece of luck.'

He smiled at her with that radiance that always turned her heart over, but she had to tell him the rest.

'Johnny, there's something else,' she whispered. 'They . . . they found a body – under the floorboards in the cupboard under the stairs.'

He was very still.

She hurried on, 'They identified it, Johnny. There was a letter in the lining of the jacket.'

Bitterly, he said, 'And it survived the fire! You see –

luck again. No matter how well you plan, you still get caught out by sheer bad luck. When I killed him I was taking his body to the house to bury it when that copper stopped me. I had the body in the boot of my car. I couldn't let the nosy bastard find it, could I? I had no choice. I had to knock the copper out – I hit him harder than I meant to, that's all. Then I drove to the house, but the business with the cop had made me jumpy. I was afraid the guy would remember my number plate, so I had to hurry. I remembered the loose floorboards in the cupboard, so I shoved the body in there and drove away again. I had to lose that car. I'd stolen it, it might have been reported by then, so I headed down west, and sure enough the police picked me up a couple of hours later, and chased me until I crashed.'

She fought not to cry, said in a voice salted with misery, 'You killed Roger because of what he'd done to me, Johnny, didn't you? So this is all my fault. If you'd never met me none of it would have happened. You wouldn't have killed him, or gone to prison. It was all because of me.'

He put a finger under her chin and lifted her head, kissed her on the mouth warmly, softly, then smiled at her.

'Don't blame yourself, darling. He was a dirty, rotten bastard. He deserved to die. When I went to see him he was alone, at home. I rang up first, asking for his wife, and he told me she was at the prize-giving at their two daughters' school. So I knew he would be alone. I worked out my plan there and then. It was all very carefully thought through.' He sounded so rational and down to earth, as if he was discussing a business project rather than a murder.

'I didn't intend to kill him in his own house, of course, that wasn't part of my plan. I told him I knew what he'd done to you, and I wanted him to come and apologise to you, and he laughed. He was vile, said you'd enjoyed it, you'd wanted it but you'd been angry because he had other girls, so you shopped him to the governors at the school. I lost my temper, I hit him. Too hard, again. It's always a mistake to lose control. You start making mistakes. I started beating his head in with a poker, I went mad and couldn't stop – there was blood everywhere, it took me ages to clear it up.'

She felt his hands on her, the hands that had killed Roger Keats and Derek and Mike . . . and were stroking her so tenderly. She had to fight not to scream. She had to keep calm. He must not guess how she really felt.

'I didn't want the body found too soon,' he said conversationally. 'I had to hide it, cover my tracks. I'd stolen a car. I backed it into his drive, wrapped him in a plastic sheet, and put him in the boot. It all went smoothly after that – my plan worked well. I should have known it was too good to be true. Sure enough, when I was only ten minutes from the forest I got stopped by this copper. If I hadn't I'd have gone back later and buried the body in the forest – that's what I meant to do. But I never got the chance. I can't think why I forgot to do it once I got out of prison.'

The matter-of-fact voice was making her nerves jump with horror.

Johnny seemed unaware of her reaction. He clicked his tongue like someone who felt he had made a silly but forgivable mistake. 'That's what I should have done. I had every chance to bury him in the forest without anyone seeing me, but I'd forgotten he was there, you see.'

Forgotten! she thought dazedly. How could you forget that you had killed someone and buried them under the floorboards of your house?

He looked down at her, his finger stroking her cheek. 'Once I got out, all I thought about was you, of course.'

He didn't look mad, those dark blue eyes were wide and clear, but she would never be able to look at him again without remembering that they had made love in that house – and all the time Roger Keats had been buried under the floorboards. Horror darkened her sight.

'I hate violence, but I couldn't let Keats get away with what he'd done to you, Annie. When I was in a prison up north I shared a cell with a sex offender. The first day they moved him in with me he looked at the pictures of you on the wall and made some gross remarks about why I had them there. I wasn't having that, so I went for him. I half killed him before they got me off him. I was put in solitary for weeks, and it set my parole back.'

'All because of me,' she thought aloud, her hands clenched. 'I suppose it was you who killed Derek, too?'

'He was blackmailing you, and he was the one who paid for you to have the abortion – if it hadn't been for him you would never have had it. That's why I left the parcel with the bootee in it on his dressing table.'

She started. 'He said Marty Keats had given it to him!'

'Maybe she did – but I left it in the dressing room that had his name on it when I visited the studios.'

'But Marty got a phone call from Roger!'

He laughed. 'If you whisper through a handkerchief it's impossible to tell whose voice it is. You gave me the idea when you kept saying Roger was still around. I thought, well, why not throw all the blame on him? I only said a few words, very quickly, so that she didn't have much chance to identify the voice, anyway.'

'But the police said a woman was with Derek the night he died.'

A grin appeared on his face, making her sense of horror deeper. He looked so boyish, pleased with himself.

'Something else I learnt in prison – we had a dramatic society. Of course some of us had to play women. Make-up, a wig, clothes . . . simple. I can even walk like a woman, in high heels.'

'You were the woman?' She was incredulous. 'And Derek didn't notice you were really a man?'

'He was too drunk. He was past noticing anything.' Johnny's mouth twisted. 'I made up to look like you – he was so interested in that that he didn't think about anything else. I wanted to tell him why he had to die, but he was too drunk to listen. It was a death for a death. He murdered our baby.' His eyes flashed. 'And you let him, Annie.'

She shut her eyes, swallowing, terrified. 'I'm sorry, Johnny, oh, God, I'm so sorry.' But even with her eyes shut she could still see the pain in his face, and the anger. Fear dragged at her; he might love her, but she sensed he half wanted to kill her, too, that he was torn between his love and his rage over the death of their baby, and what he saw as her betrayal of him.

Is he going to kill me, too? she thought, trembling.

He bent and kissed her. 'No, don't look like that,

darling. I was angry with you for a little while, but I can't bear to see you unhappy. Don't worry, I've forgiven you. You didn't want to kill our baby, you loved me and you wanted my baby, you told me that. I know who was to blame. They talked you into it, they lied to you, Fenn and your mother.'

Her eyes opened again in shock. 'Johnny . . . my mother . . .' Somehow that was the biggest shock. She loved her mother, and she knew Trudie loved her too. Whatever Trudie had done had been for her. 'Did you try to kill her too?'

He looked quickly at her, a shade of anxiety in his face. 'I'm sorry, darling, I had to, you know. She hated me.'

'But . . . she said . . . a nurse . . .'

'Oh, I'd been working there part-time on night duty ever since I got out of prison. I told you I worked in the hospital prison, didn't I? I'd taken some of the nursing exams while I was there.'

'So you are a qualified nurse?' She was taken aback and Johnny laughed.

'Of course not, but I knew enough to get by in practice, because I'd done the job for a couple of years, and it's easy to get forged papers. I learnt a lot in prison, including how to get forged official documents. I borrowed a set from a nurse I'd met in prison and had them forged by someone else, a guy who'd shared my cell for a year. Clever guy; he can forge anything, money, documents, even paintings. Annie, I needed the extra money. The magazine I was working for didn't pay me enough to live on. It was a coincidence that your mother turned up on the ward.'

'Was it you she saw the day she wandered out and went to that park? Did you try to kill her that day?'

'No, not that day. I saw her walk off down the road in her dressing-gown. I was worried about her, would you believe that? I liked her then, I thought she had liked me. I followed her and she turned on me. It was only later that I found out what she'd done, how she'd made sure you never got my messages and letters. She told me about the baby when she was on the ward, and I nearly killed her then, but once I'd talked to you and realised just what she had done to me . . .' He put his cheek down, on Annie's hair, murmured, 'She hated me, darling. And she hurt you, just as Fenn had hurt you, and Roger Keats. I would never let anyone hurt you and get away with it, Annie. I'll always look after you. When we've got rid of Halifax we'll go away together.'

She couldn't take it all in; how many people had he killed? His father, Roger, Derek.

'Mike?' she thought aloud.

'Waterford?' He nodded. 'I saw him on breakfast television, sneering about you, making those vile suggestions about you and Fenn. And you'd told me how much you hated him, so I knew you would want him to pay. I'll always protect you from men like that – men like Fenn, and Waterford, and Halifax here, men who try to abuse you and hurt you, the way my father hurt my mother.'

What was she going to do? He was mad. And she still loved him. But he had to be stopped. If she didn't stop him he would kill Sean. And she couldn't let him do that. He mustn't kill again.

Johnny frowned, sighing. 'A pity about the house . . . I meant us to live there forever; we would have been so happy, wouldn't we?'

He looked at her and she managed a quivering smile, nodding. 'Yes, Johnny, we'd have been happy.'

His eyes burned. 'And we still will, I promise. I'll find us somewhere else – somewhere better. We'll be together, Annie, just the two of us, and I'll take care of you and make you happy.' He bent and his mouth searched hungrily, caught hers, held it. Annie surrendered, fighting the shudder that ran through her entire body. She knew she would feel the touch of his mouth for the rest of her life.

When he lifted his head she asked him, 'Could I have some more tea, Johnny? I need another drink.'

He got up, took her cup. 'More brandy, too?' he asked, smiling down at her as if she was a child, teasing her.

She nodded, watching him with an aching heart. 'I love you, Johnny,' she said, and his eyes blazed with answering love.

'Darling. I know you do. Of course I know. You wouldn't betray me, the way your mother did, you wouldn't lie to me.' He glanced at Sean. 'Don't go near him, darling. Just pretend he isn't there. I'll get him away soon.'

He walked out and as soon as he had gone Sean opened his eyes, jerked his head peremptorily, lifting his arms to ask her to untie his hands.

She didn't get up. She ignored him, the way Johnny had told her to, and Sean made stifled, angry sounds, his body struggling violently.

Annie opened her handbag and got out the gun Sean had made her put there. He saw it, his eyes widening, and he was suddenly still.

Annie held it the way she had been taught, her finger on the safety catch, watching the door to the kitchen.

Johnny walked through it a second later. He halted

mid-step, seeing the gun. 'Where did you get that from?' His eyes rose to stare at her face – he looked startled but not afraid. 'Guns aren't a good idea, too much blood . . . I told you, we mustn't have any blood, it's so hard to clear up, it takes too long to make sure you've got rid of every trace. Better give the gun to me.'

He held out his hand, coming towards her. She was shaking. She'd never been so cold in her life, she could quite literally hear her teeth chattering. But she clicked the safety catch off and Johnny heard it, went very pale.

'Annie, for God's sake . . . what are you doing? Stop pointing it at me. Don't play silly games, guns are dangerous.'

'I can't let you kill anyone else, Johnny. You can't go on killing people.'

His eyes went oddly blank as if he didn't want to hear what she was saying.

'But I did it for you, Annie – I couldn't let anyone hurt you and get away with it. I stopped my father hurting my mother, and I've stopped Keats and Fenn and Waterford too – they had to be dealt with. I was only taking care of you, darling. Tomorrow we'll go away together, we can cross over to France on the ferry and wander across Europe like gypsies. Do you remember how we used to talk about doing that, in front of the fire?'

'I'm sorry,' she whispered, and her finger tightened on the trigger. 'There won't be any tomorrow for us, Johnny.'

She saw his face change, the realisation coming into those dark blue eyes. 'Annie . . . Don't, Annie!' he cried out, springing forward.

She had been trained by a first-rate marksman. She killed him with her first shot, but she couldn't stop firing. Her finger was frozen on the trigger; the crash of the shots echoed inside her head, and she knew she would hear them for the rest of her life.

Johnny was flung backwards violently, his body arching, his arms thrown back. The cup smashed, tea soaking into the carpet.

Annie stopped firing and dropped the gun, almost falling out of the chair, to run shakily, stumbling, to where Johnny had fallen.

She didn't hear Tom Moor shouting, or hear the window implode as he smashed it with a spanner, she didn't see him reach in and open the latch then leap through into the room over the showered broken glass littering the floor.

He stood there, briefly taking in what had happened, trod carefully over to where the gun lay on the floor, wrapped a handkerchief round his hand and reached for the gun.

Annie knelt down beside Johnny, sobbing hoarsely; she cradled his head in her arms and rocked him like a baby, kissing his face over and over again, telling him, 'I'm sorry, I'm sorry, I had to, I couldn't let you kill anyone else, you had to be stopped, I didn't want to do it, God knows I didn't want to do it.'

Sean made angry, jerky movements at Tom, muffled sounds from under the scarf. Tom wrapped the gun entirely in the handkerchief and pushed it into his jacket pocket, then knelt beside Sean and untied him.

'Man, I thought you'd had it when I heard that gun go off,' he said, grimacing.

'I thought I'd had it, too,' said Sean, getting up

374

stiffly, rubbing his wrists where the twine had bitten deeply, leaving a red bracelet.

Tom walked over the tea-stained carpet to stare down at Annie, who was oblivious of him, still holding Johnny, rocking him against her like a sleeping child.

Tom had been going to make quite sure that Johnny was dead, but, observing the red stain spreading across Johnny's shirt, he knew there was no need to check the pulse; no one could live with a hole like that in him.

It was clear to both Tom and Sean that Annie didn't even remember they were there. All she could see was Johnny.

'Bullseye,' Tom said softly over his shoulder to Sean. 'She shot him? Some shooting.'

'Police trained,' Sean said. 'She's good.'

He was staring at her and Johnny, frowning. Tom discreetly turned his back, went over to the phone. 'I'd better ring Chorley. He isn't going to be too pleased about this.'

Sean walked nearer to Annie and she looked up, her face wet with tears, her eyes dark with grief.

'I had to stop him, it couldn't go on – I couldn't let him go on killing, I couldn't let him kill you, but I couldn't let them put him back in prison, he would never have got out again, he would have spent the rest of his life in a cell, and he had hated being in prison, he said it drove you mad . . . I couldn't let that happen to him. You understand, don't you, Sean?'

'I understand,' he gently said. 'Let him go now, Annie. It's over, let him go.'

She looked at Johnny, drew a long, harsh breath, and laid his head carefully down on the carpet again.

Sean lifted her to her feet, put his arms around her and held her shaking body until the police arrived.

CHARLOTTE LAMB

DEEP AND SILENT WATERS

Laura would never have gone to Venice if she had known she would meet Sebastian Ferrese there: for the past three years, she has fought her attraction to the enigmatic film director and has no wish to lay herself open to temptation yet again.

But her nomination for an award at the Film Festival proves too much of an enticement – and when Laura sees Sebastian, she finds herself swept up in his overwhelming magnetism once more. It is a dangerous infatuation. For death seems to follow Sebastian around – and Laura begins to suspect that he is no innocent bystander . . .

'The romantic city of Venice and the glamorous and illusory world of film-making are the subjects of bestselling author Charlotte Lamb's latest novel, *Deep and Silent Waters* . . . lose yourself in this irresistible mystery' *Woman's Realm*

HODDER AND STOUGHTON PAPERBACKS

CHARLOTTE LAMB

WALKING IN DARKNESS

Two worlds separated them. But the dark eyes that watched over each were the same . . .

Beautiful heiress Catherine Gowrie had spent her life protected by one of America's wealthiest families and married to one of Britain's most successful men. Now her all-powerful father was close to his greatest ambition – nomination as Presidential candidate. Nothing must be allowed to stand in Don Gowrie's way.

Sophie Narodni shared only Catherine's beauty. Her father killed before she was born, the young journalist from Prague had worked her way out of poverty to travel the world. But with her she carried a secret: a secret that could destroy everything Don Gowrie had dreamed of. If he didn't silence her first . . .

PRAISE FOR CHARLOTTE LAMB:

[Her novels] are rip-roaringly, mind-boggingly . . . heart-poundingly successful'
Radio Times

'One of the secrets of [her] phenomenal success is her magnificent moody heroes'
News of the World

'The secret of her success is that both reader and writer get their fix, identifying totally with the heroine'
Daily Express

HODDER AND STOUGHTON PAPERBACKS

A selection of bestsellers from
Hodder and Stoughton

Deep and Silent Waters	Charlotte Lamb	0 340 71283 X	£5.99	☐
Walking in Darkness	Charlotte Lamb	0 340 72866 3	£5.99	☐
Charlotte's Friends	Sarah Kennedy	0 340 68934 X	£5.99	☐
Sisters Under the Skin	Willa Marsh	0 340 70798 4	£6.99	☐
That Was Then	Sarah Harrison	0 340 70731 3	£6.99	☐
In the Heart of the Garden	Helene Wiggin	0 340 69571 4	£6.99	☐
Marriage Games	Amanda Brookfield	0 340 67152 1	£6.99	☐

All Hodder & Stoughton books are available at your local bookshop or newsagent, or can be ordered direct from the publisher. Just tick the titles you want and fill in the form below. Prices and availability subject to change without notice.

Hodder & Stoughton Books, Cash Sales Department, Bookpoint, 39 Milton Park, Abingdon, OXON, OX14 4TD, UK. E-mail address: order@bookpoint.co.uk. If you have a credit card you may order by telephone – (01235) 400414.

Please enclose a cheque or postal order made payable to Bookpoint Ltd to the value of the cover price and allow the following for postage and packing:
UK & BFPO – £1.00 for the first book, 50p for the second book, and 30p for each additional book ordered up to a maximum charge of £3.00.
OVERSEAS & EIRE – £2.00 for the first book, £1.00 for the second book, and 50p for each additional book.

Name _____

Address _____

_____

_____

If you would prefer to pay by credit card, please complete:
Please debit my Visa/Access/Diner's Card/American Express (delete as applicable) card no:

Signature _____

Expiry Date _____

If you would NOT like to receive further information on our products please tick the box. ☐